An avid reader since childhood, **Beverly Barton** wrote her first book at the age of nine. She wrote short stories, poetry, plays and novels throughout high school and college, and is now a *New York Times* bestselling author, having written over sixty books since she was first published in 1990. Beverly lives in Alabama with her husband.

D1391005

BEVERLY BARTON

DYING FOR YOU

MIRA

Published in Great Britain 2010
MIRA Books, Eton House, 18-24 Paradise Road,
Richmond, Surrey, TW9 1SR

© Beverly Beaver 2008

ISBN 978 0 7783 0426 5

56-1010

Printed in the UK
by CPI Mackays, Chatham, ME5 8TD

This book is dedicated to my readers, especially those who have followed THE PROTECTORS series over the years. Thank you. I appreciate each of you so very much.

PROLOGUE

ARTURO TORRES-RIOS killed his first man when he was fourteen, his first woman when he was seventeen and his first child when he was twenty. Some would call him a murderer. He disagreed. He was an executioner. In his thirty-two years, he had acquired many useful skills that he used for profit and occasionally for pleasure. As an assassin, he had few equals. He preferred jobs where he had little or no personal contact with the victim, but on occasion and for the right price, he used his talents as a torturer or a kidnapper or a thief.

He disliked Americans, especially the owners and employees of wealthy companies here in South America like the ones who were making deals with Ameca's government to go into partnership with his country's oil tycoons. Ameca was oil-rich, but the people lived in poverty, as Arturo had lived as a boy. His dislike for Americans was well-known and although he had been hired by more than one American to do their dirty work, Arturo never had direct contact with the bastards. Josue Soto, a lawyer and long-time friend, brokered all of Arturo's deals, working as a middleman. Josue was well worth the ten percent Arturo paid him. His childhood friend could be trusted.

They never met at Josue's office or his home, nor did they meet at Arturo's home. Instead, whenever a new business deal was in the works, they met at St. Salvatora, the old mission church in Puerto Colima, the fishing village where they had both been born.

"If you accept this assignment, you will be paid a quarter of a million dollars, then another quarter million after Phase One and the final million and a half at Phase Two when the assignment is completed," Josue told him.

"Two million dollars makes this a tempting offer."

"You don't even have to get your hands dirty. All you have to do is oversee the job and make sure nothing goes wrong. I am certain you can put together the right team for an assignment such as this."

"Is the person hiring me for this job an American or someone from Ameca?" Arturo asked.

Josue sighed heavily. "Why do you ask when you know it is better for you and for our client if that information is not shared, to protect both your identity and the client's?"

Arturo smiled. Josue was right. It did not matter to him who wanted to employ him. His skills were for hire on the open market. "Forget I asked."

"You have less than a month to prepare. Everything must be in place by the fifteenth of September. It will be up to you to choose the exact time and place, but the opportunity to act is brief, a few days at most."

"That is not a problem." He eyed the thin folder in Josue's hand. "This contains all the information and instructions?"

Josue nodded.

Arturo took the folder, opened it, scanned the three pages several times, and then returned the folder to his friend. Arturo had taught himself to memorize data quickly, to keep information in his head. It was safer for him that way. No paper trail.

"Then I can make contact today and say that we have accepted the assignment?"

"Yes. Tell them to wire the money to our account immediately. Once that is done, I will formulate a fool-proof plan and assemble the perfect team."

"No one is to be killed," Josue reminded him. "Not until the order is given."

Arturo and Josue rose from the wooden bench and shook hands. Josue left first, exiting through the front doors. Arturo slipped out the back door, put on his sunglasses and, after checking the debris-strewn alley, walked briskly to his parked car two blocks away.

CHAPTER ONE

DAISY HOLBROOK PRIDED herself on doing her job as Dundee's office manager with expertise and finesse. She kept up-to-date on dozens of cases and, at present, twenty full-time agents, numerous contract agents and six members of the office staff. The Dundee Private Security and Investigation Agency handled assignments within the United States and internationally and was known worldwide as one of the premiere agencies of its kind. Sam Dundee, the owner, visited their sixth-floor office complex in downtown Atlanta annually and was only a phone call away in emergencies. But CEO Sawyer McNamara oversaw the agency, hired and fired personnel, assigned cases and ruled Dundee's with an iron fist. His word was law. Many agents became friends and fraternized while between jobs. Not Sawyer. He maintained a professional distance between himself and the employees. Even if all the agents didn't like Sawyer, to a person, they respected him. The office staff, except for Daisy, trembled in fear whenever the big boss came anywhere near them and all the female staffers had secret crushes on him. Daisy understood why. Sawyer was not only intimidating, thus causing apprehension, but he also dressed like a *GQ* model, was tall, dark and handsome, and oozed sex appeal. Daisy had to admit that when she'd come to work here, straight out of college, and met him for the first time, she'd had a bit of crush on him herself.

She'd gotten over it.

As she turned on lights, checked to make sure the cleaning crew had left each private office in perfect condition, and put on two pots of coffee in the staff lounge, Daisy briefly recalled her first day on the job eight years ago. She had been nervous and unsure of herself, but determined to do her best. Within two years, the office manager had retired, leaving the position open. Daisy had been surprised, to say the least, when the then new CEO, Sawyer McNamara, had promoted her to the coveted position.

"You're intelligent, efficient and levelheaded," Sawyer had told her. "And you don't tremble in your high heels or swoon like a love-struck teenager when I speak to you."

After eight years in Dundee's employ, Daisy had gained the nickname Ms. Efficiency, of which she was extremely proud. She considered most of the agents to be her friends, some even close friends, and one in particular had stolen her heart several years ago. Everyone at Dundee's, except the man himself, knew that Daisy was in love with the rugged former SAS officer, Geoff Monday. Not only was he a womanizer, a confirmed bachelor and fifteen years her senior, but Geoff also treated her like a kid sister. Not once had he ever looked at her as if she were anything other than a buddy. Unrequited love was a bitch!

Marching down the hall toward her workstation in the center of the main office, Daisy checked her wrist-watch. 8:10 a.m. She arrived promptly at eight each morning, an hour before the other members of the staff. As a general rule, unless there was some type of emergency, the boss arrived anywhere between nine and ten. The agents who were not on assignment came and went from headquarters at various times. Just as she approached her desk, the distinct sound of the elevator stopping and the doors opening alerted her that someone was coming into work early. It would be either the boss himself or one of the agents. The office staffers usually rushed in at the last minute.

Daisy looked down the short hallway and watched while Lucie Evans exploded from the elevator, her long, curly red hair bouncing on her shoulders as she stomped her sandal-clad size-nines up the carpeted corridor.

Uh-oh. Daisy knew that look. Spiting mad, fire shooting from her dark eyes, cheeks flushed and determination in her stride. Lucy was pissed. Royally pissed, and there was only one person who could make her that angry.

"Is he in yet?" Lucie demanded when she neared Daisy's workstation.

"No, I'm afraid not."

"Call him and tell him to get down here as fast as his half-million-dollar Mercedes will go."

"Is there some type of emergency?" Daisy knew better than to disturb Sawyer at home without a very good reason.

"Oh, yes, there's an emergency." Lucie snarled. "I'm the emergency. Tell that son of a bitch that unless he wants all those pretty paintings and sculptures in his office destroyed, he'd better be here in twenty minutes."

"Lucie, you aren't threatening to—"

"Damn right, I am." Her lips curved into a wicked smile, one that told Daisy she meant business.

"If you start tearing up Mr. McNamara's office, I'll have to call security."

"Call Sawyer instead," Lucie said, as she moved past the workstation and headed farther down the hall. "I promise not to touch a thing for the next twenty minutes."

"Where are you going?"

"To get a cup of coffee first, and then I'll be waiting in the big man's office."

Daisy followed Lucie into the staff lounge. "Whatever it is, do you want to talk about it? Tell me what's wrong and I'll—"

Lucie turned on her. "You'll what? Try to calm me down? Play interference between me and Sawyer? Sorry, sweetie, not this time. It's gone beyond anything anyone can say or do."

"All right. I'll call Mr. McNamara and let him know you're here and that you're upset."

"Tell him he's got twenty minutes."

Daisy paused in the doorway. "You promise that you won't do anything destructive for the next twenty minutes."

Using her index finger, Lucie marked her chest with an X and said, "Cross my heart."

As she made her way back to her desk, Daisy heaved a worried sigh. This was far from the first time Lucie Evans had been upset with Sawyer. Except for one incident when she had actually broken Sawyer's Water-ford crystal paperweight, she had never been destruc-tive. Whatever had happened to push her to the edge had to be worse than anything that had occurred in the past. In the eight years she had worked at Dundee's, she had watched the war between Lucie and Sawyer with as much interest and morbid fascination as the rest of the staff and all the agents. No one understood why, although the animosity between the two could easily set off World War III, Sawyer hadn't fired Lucie or why Lucie hadn't quit. Daisy didn't know for sure, of course, but she suspected that since both of them were as stubborn as mules, neither would back down, or give an inch. Sawyer was waiting for Lucie to resign; and Lucie was waiting for Sawyer to fire her. Stalemate.

When she returned to her desk, Daisy called Sawyer's private home number. He answered on the third ring.

"Good morning, Daisy. Is there a problem?"

"Yes, sir, I'm afraid there is." She dreaded telling him. Usually just the mention of Lucie's name could alter his mood from positive to negative.

"Well?" he asked impatiently.

"Lucie Evans is here." Daisy waited for his reaction.

"Ms. Evans is supposed to be on assignment. Did she give you any explanation for why she walked out on a client?"

"No, sir, she didn't mention the client, but she demanded that I contact you and ask you—" Daisy cleared her throat "—actually tell you that if you're not here at headquarters in twenty minutes, she is going to wreck your office."

"Call security and have her— No, wait. Tell her I'll be there. And if she's touched even so much as a paper clip in my office, I'll have her butt hauled off to jail."

"Yes, sir, I'll inform Ms. Evans right away."

Daisy found Lucie in Sawyer's office, sitting behind his desk in his plush leather chair. When Daisy walked in, Lucie swiveled around and smiled at her.

"Well?"

"Mr. McNamara will be here in twenty minutes."

Lucie lifted the glass paperweight from Sawyer's desk, a replacement for the one she had broken a couple of years ago. Daisy hurried into the room, reached out, took the paperweight from Lucie's hand and set it back on the desk.

"Promise me that you'll be a good girl." Daisy looked right at Lucie.

Lucie glanced at her wristwatch, tapped the face and said, "I'll be as good as gold for the next twenty minutes."

SAWYER POURED the contents of his cup into the sink, rinsed out the sink and placed the cup in the dishwasher. His coffeemaker would shut off automatically, so he left the half-full pot on the warmer. Mrs. Terrance, his housekeeper, would arrive at ten and tidy the kitchen.

He went to his bedroom, put on his jacket, picked up his briefcase and headed straight for the garage. Usually, it took him thirty minutes to drive from his home to the downtown office building that housed Dundee's. This morning, he had to find a way to cut that time by ten minutes, if possible. He had known Lucie

Evans long enough to know that the lady didn't bluff. And he also knew Daisy Holbrook well enough to know she would not call security until the last possible moment, which meant that Lucie could wreck his office before the guards arrived to stop her.

After getting into his Mercedes-Benz SLR McLaren, one of his most prized possessions, Sawyer put his Bluetooth earpiece into place, backed out of the driveway and onto the road. Once in the middle of bumper-to-bumper traffic, he placed a call, which after six rings went to voice mail.

"You've reached Lucie Evans. I'm not available to take your call. Please leave your number and I'll get back to you as soon a possible."

"Damn!" Sawyer muttered under his breath.

She wasn't going to answer her cell phone. She wanted to make him squirm.

He called her again. Once again, she didn't answer.

After her recorded message ended, he said, "Touch one thing in my office and I'll contact the police."

Lucie was a loose cannon. If he'd been smart, he would have fired her when he took over the CEO reins from Ellen Denby six years ago. Actually he had thought she would resign once she realized she'd be taking orders from him. But in typical Lucie fashion, she had dug in her heels and stayed on at Dundee's. For six years, she had done everything humanly possible to make him fire her; and he had done everything within his power as CEO to make her quit.

Lucie wasn't cut out for the line of work she had chosen. Not now or in the past. Whatever had possessed her to think she would make a good FBI agent, he'd never understood. She'd had the intelligence, the grit and the determination, but not the temperament. Lucie had always been volatile. Even as a kid, she'd been high-strung and emotional.

There had been a time when they hadn't been enemies. When they were teenagers, he had looked out for her the same way he'd looked out for his kid brother, Brenden. But that had been a long time ago. A lifetime ago.

Sawyer placed a call to the security office in the building that housed Dundee's. When one of the officers on duty answered, Sawyer said, "This is Sawyer McNamara. Send someone upstairs to the Dundee Agency on the sixth floor. Have him go to my office and wait there with one of my agents, Lucie Evans, until I arrive."

"Yes, sir. Is there some problem we need to know about?"

"Ms. Evans has threatened to wreck my office if I don't arrive there within the next fifteen minutes. I prefer not to contact the police, but handle this internal problem myself."

"Yes, sir. I'll send someone immediately."

"Thank you."

The next call Sawyer made was to Lucie's abandoned client who had hired Dundee's for a bodyguard assignment. Taylor Lawson was a has-been TV star whose claim to fame was a role as a brash young space cadet on a futuristic drama that ran four seasons some twenty years ago. He had been invited to act as host for this year's TV Sci-fi convention in Las Vegas.

"I want a capable bodyguard," Lawson had said.

"But I want a woman. A good-looking woman that I can pass off as my girlfriend."

"I know just the agent." Sawyer had known immediately that it was the type of assignment Lucie would hate. And whenever possible, the cases she hated were the ones he chose for her.

"Yeah, who the hell is this?" the man bellowed and Sawyer realized he had no doubt disturbed Taylor Lawson's sleep.

"Mr. Lawson, this is Sawyer McNamara from Dundee's. I'm calling in reference to—"

"That crazy bitch you sent me tried to murder me," Lawson said. "I've got a good mind to sue Dundee's and you and her."

"Exactly what happened?" Sawyer asked.

"I told you, she tried to kill me."

"Why would Ms. Evans try to kill you? Her job was to protect you."

Lawson coughed a few times, and then grumbled several obscenities. "She was supposed to play the part of my girlfriend. That was understood when I hired her."

"Yes, sir, that's correct."

"Well, apparently you didn't make that part of her assignment clear because she sure as hell refused to act the part."

A nagging suspicion tightened Sawyer's gut. "Precisely what did Ms. Evans refuse to do?"

"She refused to sleep with me. I paid top dollar for her services and I expected her to be worth every cent. But when I told her to strip and get in bed, she refused, so I took matters into my own hands."

"And did what?" Sawyer swallowed hard.

"I slapped her and the crazy bitch sucker punched me. Knocked me on my ass and—"

"Mr. Lawson, Dundee's provides bodyguard services, nothing more. I thought I made that perfectly clear to you. If Ms. Evans had to defend herself, then consider yourself lucky that she didn't kill you. Believe me, the lady is more than capable."

"Hell, you'd think she would have been thrilled to have Lieutenant Jack Starr fuck her. Most women would be."

"Then there's your problem. You see, Lucie Evans is not like most women."

"I figure she's a butch, despite the way she looks. You should have warned me. You'll definitely be hearing from my lawyers. I've got a broken nose, a couple of cracked ribs and a black eye."

"Unless you want Ms. Evans to file charges against you for attempted rape, then I'd think twice about siccing your lawyer on us. Now, you have a good day, Mr. Lawson."

Son of a bitch! That over-the-hill has-been had tried to rape Lucie. No wonder she was pissed at him. He'd known Lawson was a sleaze, but he'd also known that Lucie could handle him. And she had. What he hadn't considered was that the man might actually try to rape her.

LUCIE EYED THE security guard with disdain. *Don't blame him. He's just doing his job, doing what Sawyer told him to do. Watch her and make sure she doesn't follow through with her threat to demolish the CEO's office.*

Even though she had no intention of actually

wreaking havoc on Sawyer's expensive sculptures and paintings—she had too much love and respect for good art to destroy such beauty—he had no way to know for sure what she might do. Yes, she had, during one of her classic hissy fits, broken a Waterford crystal paperweight, but the piece had not been one of a kind. A duplicate now resided on his desk in the precise spot where the original had sat. She would no more toss one of his Salvatore Fiume or Marino Marini pieces on the floor than she would take a knife to his Charles Ginner or Clare Avery paintings. One of the things she admired about Sawyer was his eclectic tastes in art, music, food and sports. He was a man who enjoyed the good things in life and appreciated them to the nth degree. He possessed a suave sophistication that disguised the primeval warrior beneath his Reuben Alexander suits.

Lucie knew how ruthless he could be. She had seen the man in action and had been the recipient of his cold, relentless retaliation for the past nine years. If she had thought time would soothe his inner demons, she had been wrong. Like Jane Austen's fictional Mr. Darcy, Sawyer's favor once lost was lost forever. Even now, despising him for the way he'd treated her—the way she had allowed him to treat her—Lucie could not deny that some small part of her still held on to a tiny shred of hope. Someday Sawyer McNamara would forgive her. But before he could forgive her, he would first have to forgive himself.

No, she wouldn't have harmed his expensive artwork, but if not for the ever watchful guard she would have dearly loved the chance to do some damage.

Maybe she could have removed the contents of his desk and scattered it all over the floor. Or better yet, she could have tossed his laptop out the window. A six-floor fall onto the solid concrete below...

"He should be here soon," Daisy Holbrook said, breaking the awkward silence. "While we're waiting, would either of you like coffee? Or maybe a Danish or muffin?"

"No, thank you, ma'am," the young, intense guard replied.

"Nothing more for me, thanks." Lucie offered Daisy a don't-worry smile.

"Then if you'll excuse me..." Daisy looked pleadingly at Lucie. "If you need to talk afterward, I'll take an early break."

"Okay. I'll stop by your desk on my way out."

Daisy tried to smile, but the effort failed. Lucie genuinely liked Daisy Holbrook and the two had formed a strong friendship over the years despite the difference in their ages. But she supposed a seven-year gap wasn't a great barrier between women over twenty-one. If they were ten and seventeen, it would matter. But at twenty-nine and thirty-six, they were contemporaries.

As the minutes ticked by, Lucie sat behind Sawyer's massive desk, occasionally tapping her foot on the floor or drumming her fingernails on the desktop. She checked her watch. It had been twenty-one minutes since Daisy had called him. Unless she missed her guess, he would arrive sometime within the next few minutes.

Brace yourself. Gird your loins, Miss Lucie. This

*day has been a long time coming. If you want to walk
out of here with your pride in tact, keep your emotions
under control. And whatever you do, don't cry. God in
heaven, do not cry.*

TWENTY-THREE MINUTES from when he'd taken Daisy's
call, Sawyer entered Dundee's sixth-floor office
complex. Daisy hopped up from her workstation chair
and rushed toward him as he made his way down the
corridor toward his office.

"She hasn't touched anything," Daisy assured him.
"The guard is keeping an eye on her."

Sawyer paused, patted Daisy on the arm and assured
her, "Everything is going to be all right. I spoke to the
client personally and understand why Lucie left her assignment without notice. I'll talk to her privately."

"She was fit to be tied when she first got here, but
now she's calm. Much too calm."

"I don't think you need to worry as long as Lucie's
not armed."

Daisy gulped. "I'm afraid she is."

Sawyer tried not to grin. "She won't shoot me, if
that's what concerns you. If she were going to shoot me,
she'd have done it before now."

"Yes, sir, I'm sure you're right."

The door to his office stood ajar, the security guard
standing at attention a few steps over the threshold.
Sawyer cleared his throat. The young man turned,
looked at him and seemed to instantly relax. He entered
his office, shook the guard's hand and effectively dismissed him.

"Thank you," Sawyer said as he glanced around the room, noting that nothing was out of place. "I'll take over from here."

Once they were alone, Sawyer closed the door and faced the woman who had been tormenting him for the past nine years.

Lucie rose from his chair to her full five-eleven height, a look of pure defiance on her face. Her long, curly hair hung in loose disarray over her shoulders and down her back. Apparently, she had forgone refreshing her makeup and had combed her hair with her fingers. Only a hint of eyeliner remained and that was smudged. The only color on her lips was a naturally healthy pink.

She walked out from behind the desk and glared at him, her two-inch wedge sandals lifting her almost to his eye level. He noted the bulge her shoulder holster made beneath her gray cotton jacket that covered her white T-shirt and skimmed the top of her faded blue jeans.

"I appreciate your giving me fair warning," Sawyer told her. "You could have come in here and ripped the place apart before Daisy could have stopped you."

"Believe me, I thought about it. On the flight from Vegas, I not only envisioned tearing your office apart, I plotted how I could kill you and get away with it."

"I understand your anger."

She lifted her brows in surprise. "Do you really?"

"I spoke to Taylor Lawson. He told me what happened. I'm sorry, Lucie. I had no idea—"

"Bullshit. Don't tell me that you didn't know the man's reputation before you assigned me as his bodyguard. You didn't give a damn what I had to put up with. You never do. As far as you're concerned, the worse my assignments are, the better. But this time, you reached an all-time low, even for you, Mr. McNamara."

He surveyed her from head to toe. "You don't look any worse for wear."

"You don't think so?" She lifted her T-shirt high enough to reveal the white lace bra beneath and the bruises on the swell of her breasts. "Pretty, aren't they?"

"Lucie—"

"Would you like to see the others—the ones on my hips and butt?"

"I'm sorry things got out of hand, but I never doubted for a minute that you could take care of yourself. You're a trained professional."

She hissed like a snake preparing to strike. "You son of a bitch. You heartless, uncaring, unforgiving son of a bitch."

She reached out and slapped him. The force of her open palm against his cheek sent him reeling backward. The lady packed quite a punch. He stared at her, oddly surprised by her physical attack.

"I've put up with your crap for nine years," she told him, her voice deceptively calm. "I've jumped through hoops for you. I've taken every assignment you've given me, no matter how unpleasant, stupid or demeaning. I've taken and taken and taken, all in the hopes that one day you'd give me a chance to explain, to listen to my side of—"

"There is nothing to explain. There's no your side or my side. We both know what happened and why. And do you honestly think you're the only one who's been put through the wringer day after day for the past nine years? Lady, you've put me through hell."

"I'm glad to know that I haven't been the only one suffering."

They stood no more than two feet apart, their gazes riveted with mutual anger and distrust.

"This is your lucky day," she told him. "I'm going to give you something you've been wanting for a long time. Let's call it a Get Out of Hell gift card."

He eyed her quizzically. "What are you saying?"

"Mr. McNamara, I quit. I'll submit a written resignation later, but consider this my official notice."

CHAPTER TWO

"CARA, SWEETHEART, ARE you listening to me?" Grayson Perkins asked.

"Huh?" She wasn't paying any attention to Gray. She was too busy watching Bain Desmond, sitting three tables over, and hating the way he was smiling at his companion. She wanted to scratch the petite brunette's eyes out.

"I said we need to finalize plans for your trip to Ameca."

"Ameca?"

"Are you feeling all right? You don't seem to be yourself this afternoon."

Forcing her gaze away from the ruggedly handsome police detective and that brunette hussy, Cara Bedell turned to her brother-in-law. Former brother-in-law actually. Grayson Perkins had been married to her older sister, Audrey.

"I'm fine, just preoccupied with business." The business of keeping tabs on Lt. Desmond. She had lunch every Friday at the Hair of the Dog pub because she knew Bain would be there and it was her only chance to see him, even if from a distance.

"If there's something wrong, something bothering you, and you want to discuss it, you know you can count on me to listen." He reached across the table and took her hand. "You must know how much I care about you."

She eased her hand from his. "It's nothing, really." She looked directly at Gray. He was much too handsome, too tanned, too buffed and polished. He had the same kind of old-time movie-star good looks that had made her grandmother's generation swoon over matinee idols. "But I suppose we should discuss my trip to Ameca."

"Good, good. You realize that if you can pull off this deal with either Senor Delgado or Senor Castillo, you'll prove once and for all that you're definitely Edward Bedell's daughter."

Cara offered him a halfhearted smile. She knew he'd meant it as a compliment, about being Edward Bedell's daughter. Her father had been a genius at the art of making money, as had generations of Bedell men before him. But the patriarchal line had ended with her father. She was the last of the Bedell line and she had been trying for the past few years, since taking over the reins at Bedell, Inc., to give back to the world instead of simply taking, as her family had been doing for the past hundred-plus years.

The pending oil deal promised a new source of oil to the United States and would no doubt make hundreds of millions for both Bedell, Inc. and whichever Amecan oil company she chose. If Cara had her way, one fourth of the profits would be reinvested in the people of Ameca. The country's population was divided into the haves and have-nots, but in unequal proportions. The haves who ruled the small South American country consisted of less than three percent of the population. There were two major oil producers in Ameca: Delgado Oil and Castillo, Inc. Both were eager to do business with Bedell, but Cara was leaning toward Delgado because of the owner's sympathy for the people of his struggling nation. Of course, Cara wouldn't have known anything about either Delgado or Castillo without the input of Lexie Murrough Bronson, who headed the international charity organization Helping Hands, which Bedell, Inc. funded. Lexie had done her homework and presented Cara with the facts several months ago.

"Your meeting with Senor Delgado is set for mid-September," Gray reminded her. "That gives you only three weeks to pull together all your facts and figures, arrange for me to take over your duties while you're away and decide whether or not you're going to meet with Senor Castillo while you're there."

"You think I should set up a meeting with Tomas Castillo, don't you?"

Gray nodded. "You could at least listen to what he has to say. After all, you owe it to the shareholders to broker the best deal possible for Bedell, Inc."

Cara heaved a resigned sigh. "I know you're right. It's just that Castillo has a reputation, if true, I can't condone. But if I meet with him, I can report to the board that I met with the heads of both oil companies. That should satisfy them."

Gray grabbed her hand, lifted it to his lips and kissed it. "I'll miss you terribly while you're away, but someone has to stay here and keep the good ship Bedell afloat."

She wiggled her hand, trying to free it from his tight grasp. He gave it a gentle squeeze as he looked longingly into her eyes.

"You know I adore you, Cara. When are you going to put me out of my misery and marry me?"

Oh, God, not again! For the past few months, Gray had begun pursuing her relentlessly, begging her to marry him. For nearly a year after Audrey died, he had asked her at least once a month. The second year, he had pulled back and reassessed the situation, proposing only three times. As time went by, his pursuit became more subtle and the proposals diminished to no more than three a year. She had hoped he had finally given up and accepted their relationship for what it was, and for what it would always be—a friendship based on family ties and a business association. But a few months ago, he had once again declared his undying love for her and since then hadn't given her a moment's peace.

Cara managed to free her hand. She looked at Gray with what she hoped was warmth and caring. After all, she was fond of Gray and oddly enough felt sorry for him. She knew he didn't love her, that although he had loved her sister in the early years of the marriage, what Gray loved most in this world was Gray. His love for the Bedell sisters was rooted in his love for the Bedell fortune. But Gray was family. Her father had loved him like a son. And at one time, when she'd been younger and very foolish, Cara had thought she was in love with him. Despite all his faults, she still had a soft spot in her heart for him and always would. And because of her father's training, Gray was a good businessman and had become an asset to Bedell, Inc.

Why couldn't Bain Desmond be lured by the Bedell billions the way most other men were? Why was it that she could probably have any man she wanted—correction, she could probably buy any man she wanted—except the one man she loved?

She glanced across the room. Bain and his date were leaving. Her gaze took in every inch of the brunette. Five-three, slender, delicate and totally feminine.

"Cara, sweetheart." Gray wanted an answer to his proposal.

How many ways can a woman say no? She supposed telling him that she wouldn't marry him if he was the last man on earth wasn't really an option. She would never hurt Gray that way.

The words *No, Gray. I'm very fond of you, but I won't marry you* were on the tip of her tongue. But before she could speak, she sensed someone approaching their table. When she looked away from Gray, she saw Bain and the brunette coming toward them. Her heart did an erratic rat-a-tat-tat just because he was so close. She could easily reach out and touch him.

"Afternoon," Bain said, his expression totally emotionless as he glanced from Cara to Gray and back to Cara. "How are you, Ms. Bedell?"

"I'm fine, Lieutenant. How are you?"

"No complaints." He cupped his companion's elbow. "Ms. Bedell, Mr. Perkins, I'd like y'all to meet my sister, Mary Ann Nelson."

His sister! Cara could barely contain her joy. She wanted to jump up and hug Mary Ann.

Gray rose to his feet and nodded curtly to Bain's sister. "It's a pleasure, Ms. Nelson."

"Thank you," Mary Ann replied.

Cara smiled warmly at the attractive brunette. "It's very nice to meet you."

Mary Ann returned Cara's smile. "Bain speaks very highly of you, Ms. Bedell. I'm happy that I finally have this chance to meet you in person."

Apparently Bain had confided in his sister. But exactly what had he told her? *There's this billionaire heiress I've got the hots for, but because I'm an old-fashioned, macho kind of guy, I could never get seriously involved with her. And God forbid that I marry her and adapt to her opulent lifestyle. I'm the kind of man who needs to be the breadwinner, to wear the pants in my family.*

"Are you staying in Chattanooga long?" Cara asked.

"Just for the weekend. Keith and I brought the children to visit their Uncle Bain and while we're here we're taking in some of the local attractions. Keith has them at the aquarium right now, giving Bain and me a chance for some brother-sister time. Tomorrow, we're going to Rock City and riding the Incline."

If she and Bain were actually a couple, she would invite his sister and her family to her home for dinner. Heck, she'd invite them to stay with her. God knew she had more than enough room at the Bedell estate.

"I've got to be back at headquarters in fifteen minutes," Bain reminded his sister.

Mary Ann smiled warmly, offering Cara an I-know-how-important-you-are-to-him farewell glance.

Bain's gaze connected with Cara's for a millisecond, just long enough for a current of electricity to pass between them. Then the moment ended and Bain and

Mary Ann were gone, heading out the door. As he sat down, Gray watched her watching Bain.

"He's the reason we have lunch here every Friday, isn't he?" Gray said, a resentful tone in his voice. "Ever since he came into our lives to investigate Audrey's disappearance and murder, your feelings for me have changed."

"I'm not going to discuss Bain Desmond with you."

"Why not? It's more than obvious that he's the reason you won't marry me." Gray shook his head in disgust. "What you see in that uncouth ruffian, I'll never know. It's apparent he doesn't return your feelings and it's rather pathetic the way you moon over him. I'd think you had more pride and dignity than to—"

"Shut up, Gray."

"I'm sorry if—"

"My feelings for Lieutenant Desmond are my business, not yours. And the reason I won't marry you is because I'm not in love with you."

"Yes, I know." Gray heaved a deep, dramatic sigh. "But we could have a marriage based on other things. Love is highly overrated. I loved Audrey and see how that turned out?"

She looked right at him. "You need to be satisfied with what you have. You're a VP at Bedell, Inc., with a high six-figure salary and an almost limitless expensive account. None of that will change if you find yourself a lovely woman to marry, someone who'll make you happy. So, please find someone else. Someone who would love to be Mrs. Grayson Perkins."

"Perhaps I'll do just that." Gray shoved back his chair and stood. "And when you finally realize that you

don't have a snowball's chance in hell with Lieutenant
Desmond, you may regret that I've moved on and found
someone else."

She sighed. "Anything is possible." *Anything except
my regretting not marrying you.*

"LUCIE HANDED IN her resignation?" Geoff Monday
shook his head in disbelief. "I didn't think anything he
did would ever make her quit."

"Believe it," Daisy told him. "She packed up all her
stuff and made three trips to her car. Then she gave me
her letter of resignation to give to Sawyer."

"Did she share any of the particulars with you?"

"Not really, only that this last case he assigned her
was the final straw. When she arrived this morning, she
was ready to kill Sawyer, but when she left she was as
cool as a cucumber. I've never seen Lucie that calm."

"Do you think the boss might need a pal about now?
He did call me personally and asked me to meet with
him."

Geoff winked at Daisy, who blushed sweetly. He
supposed he shouldn't flirt with her, especially since he
knew she fancied him. But she understood that it was
all in fun. He kept things between them friendly, but
never romantic. It wasn't that he didn't find her appealing. He did. A bit too appealing. But good God, he was
practically old enough to be her father. A pretty little
thing like Daisy needed a young, reliable fellow, not a
battle-scarred old warrior.

"I wouldn't enter the lion's den if I were you, not
until he tells me to send you in. He knows you're here."

Daisy shook her head sadly. "He's in a bad way. When I delivered Lucie's letter, he practically bit my head off. And he had a bottle of whiskey on his desk. I've never seen him take a drink this early in the day. It's not even three o'clock."

"Well his high-and-mighty sent for me," Geoff said. "He said he had a one-day assignment for me, something that required my expert skills."

Daisy lifted her brows in an inquisitive manner. "I certainly don't like the sound of that."

"Think he wants me to kill someone?"

Geoff chuckled when he saw the shocked expression on her face.

"I was joking, love. My solider-of-fortune days are long behind me."

Apparently realizing she was staring at him with a hungry look in her big brown eyes, she dragged her gaze away from his. "You'll stop by on your way out and give me details, right? I'll need to know where you're going, make your flight and hotel reservations and—"

"Monday, what's holding you up?" Sawyer shouted from where he stood outside his office door.

"See what I mean," Daisy said quietly. "He's like a bear with a thorn in his paw."

"Already missing our Lucie, no doubt." He leaned over and tickled Daisy under her chin. "See you on my way out."

Geoff whistled as he walked down the hall. From his experience, he had learned that when there was as much animosity between a man and a woman as there was between Sawyer and Lucie, it usually meant they'd had a personal relationship. A sexual relationship. It certainly didn't take a genius to pick up on the vibes between the gorgeous Amazonian redhead and Dundee's CEO. And it was a lot more than the fact that they seemed to hate each other.

By the time Geoff reached Sawyer's office, the boss had gone back inside, but had left the door open. Geoff paused, peered into the office and grunted. He watched while Sawyer downed the last drops of liquor from his glass: then he picked up the open bottle of Johnnie Walker Blue and refilled his glass with the two-hundred-dollar-a-bottle scotch.

"Monday reporting for duty, sir." Geoff clicked his heels and saluted.

Sawyer glared at him, his hazel brown eyes narrowed to mere slits. "I'd like for you to talk to a man named Taylor Lawson. He's in Las Vegas right now. You can get the information on where he's staying from Daisy." He took a hefty swig of whiskey and made a face as the liquor burned a trail down his throat.

"Yes, sir. Would you mind defining exactly what you mean by talk to him?"

"Scare the shit out of him. Leave a few bruises. But I want this done discreetly. I don't want any repercussions. Understand?"

"Yes, sir."

"When you finish talking to him, leave him a parting message."

"And that message is?" Geoff asked.

"Tell him to think twice before he tries to rape another woman."

Geoff sucked in his breath. Was that what had happened to Lucie? Had a client tried to rape her? "May I ask if this has anything to do with why Lucie resigned from Dundee's?"

Sawyer's sharp gaze nailed Geoff to the spot. "That's none of your concern." He put the glass to his lips and swigged down another large gulp of scotch.

"You're knocking back the booze a bit heavy, aren't you, sir? You don't want the office staff to see you totally pissed, do you?"

"When I want your advice, Mr. Monday, I'll ask for it."

"Yes, sir. I'll get the information I need from Daisy and take the first flight out—"

"Take the Dundee jet. Have Daisy authorize the flight. I want this taken care of tonight."

"Do you want me to report in directly to you when the mission is accomplished?"

"Yes. You have my home number. I don't care what time it is."

"Yes, sir, I have your home number and your mobile number."

With a half-full glass of whiskey in his hand, Sawyer turned his back on Geoff and walked to the wall of windows that overlooked the town center, effectively dismissing his employee.

LUCIE EVANS WAS the only person on earth who could drive him to drink. The last time he had gotten fall-on-his-face drunk, Lucie had been the cause. Sawyer stared at the bottle of Johnnie Walker on his desk, then down at the empty glass in his hand. He'd had enough, more than enough. He probably couldn't walk a straight line and he sure as hell couldn't drive himself home, but he was sober enough to feel guilty. Damn her for making him feel this way.

He had sent her off on her latest assignment, as he had many times over the years, knowing full well that she'd hate every minute of it. But if he'd had any idea that Lawson would try to rape Lucie... He wanted five minutes alone with the guy. Five minutes. But he didn't dare handle this himself. He might actually kill Lawson. No, better to allow an expert like Monday to put the fear of God into the scumbag who had attacked Lucie.

She's gone for good, now. You finally got what you've wanted ever since she followed you here to Atlanta and Ellen Denby hired her as a Dundee agent.

When he had resigned from the FBI and Sam Dundee had offered him a job, he had believed he would be starting a new life, a Lucie Evans-free life. He'd been in California on an assignment when Ellen hired Lucie, otherwise he might have been able to dissuade her or perhaps convince Sam that Lucie wasn't any more Dundee material than she'd been FBI material.

"Why are you doing this?" he had asked her. "Why can't you leave well enough alone and stay out of my life?"

"Because I love you," she'd told him. Straightforward and to the point. "And I believe that deep down under all the pain and guilt you feel, you still love me."

She'd been wrong. He didn't love her. He had never loved her.

Sawyer set the glass on his desk, flopped down in his leather chair and huffed out a deep, exasperated breath. He loosened his silk tie and undid the top button of his linen shirt.

If he knew Lucie, she didn't have a nest egg socked away for a rainy day. She lived in the moment. Always had. She was generous to her friends and a sucker for every sob story she heard. She gave away too much of her hard-earned money to charities she believed in, those for women, children and animals.

He'd see to it that she received a generous bonus from Dundee's. He could also shred her letter of resignation and have Daisy report that she was laid off, that way she could at least draw unemployment.

You can do better than that. You can give her a glowing recommendation. Or he could make a phone call and get her a new job.

"That's it." When he tried to snap his fingers, he realized he was drunker than he'd thought. He couldn't seem to make his fingers cooperate.

He picked up the interoffice phone and hit the office manager's number. When she answered on the second ring, he said, "Daisy, look up Cara Bedell's phone number for me. Her office number. She should still be there."

He waited while Daisy found the information he had requested. When she recited the number, he jotted it down quickly. After taking a steadying breath, he dialed Cara's number. Her secretary answered.

"This is Sawyer McNamara from the Dundee Agency. I'd like to speak to Ms. Bedell."

"Just a moment, sir."

A couple of minutes later, Cara came on the line. "Mr. McNamara, what can I do for you?"

"You can tell your new security chief to hire one of my former employees."

"I take it that you didn't fire this person, otherwise you'd hardly be recommending him to me."

"Her. It's Lucie Evans. You remember Ms. Evans, don't you?"

"Yes, I remember her."

"Lucie needs a job. I thought perhaps as a favor to Dundee's, you might consider hiring her."

"Fax her resume first thing in the morning. Send it directly to me and I'll hand deliver it to Deke."

"Thank you." He swallowed. "Just one more thing."

"Yes?"

"I'd prefer that Ms. Evans not know that I had anything to do with her being offered the job."

"All right. I'll have Deke fabricate a white lie to cover for you, if necessary."

"I'd appreciate that."

Sawyer hung up the receiver. There, that was done. Lucie had a job. She'd be moving two hours away, from Atlanta to Chattanooga. Two hours, twenty miles, a hundred miles or a thousand, it was all the same. It meant that, if he were lucky, he'd never have to see Lucie Evans again as long as he lived.

TOMAS CASTILLO met privately with his friend, President Emilio Ortega, to discuss Cara Bedell's upcoming visit to Ameca. He and Emilio had known each other for quite some time and he had contributed generously to his friend's campaign for reelection against the opposition leader, Naldo Salazar. Salazar was a man of the people who wanted all kinds of ridiculous government reforms. Felipe Delgado, Tomas's rival in the oil business, had campaigned for Salazar.

"Ms. Bedell is set to arrive in San Luis in three weeks," Emilio said. "I plan to host a dinner here at the palace for our American friend and hopefully your new business partner."

"I understand she has been invited to stay with Delgado and his family while she is here. Perhaps you should make a counteroffer. After all, if she refused the president's request for her to stay at the palace…" Tomas smiled. "Ms. Bedell is unmarried, I believe. It would be my great pleasure to be her devoted servant while she is in my country."

Emilio laughed. "Ah, Tomas, you wicked devil. You intend to seduce the American senorita, no? She may have great respect for Delgado and like his ideas of returning a portion of the profits from any deal they make to the people of Ameca, but I would lay odds that once you romance Ms. Bedell, she will sing whatever tune you want to hear."

"Indeed. I admit that I do have a way with the ladies. But if Ms. Bedell can't be charmed, then all is not lost. There is more than one means of persuasion, is there not?"

"Enough." Emilio held up a hand in a stop signal. "What other plans you may have, I do not want to know them."

"Of course, my old friend, the less you know, the

better. But be assured that I will not fail. I intend for Bedell, Inc. and Castillo, Inc. to become partners in a lucrative deal that will benefit both parties. I am prepared to do whatever it takes to secure that bargain."

CHAPTER THREE

LUCIE SLEPT UNTIL ten o'clock that Saturday morning. After glancing at the clock on her nightstand, she rolled over into the center of the bed and sprawled out on her stomach. Yesterday, after lugging five boxes of personal stuff from her office to her car and then from her car to her apartment, she had dropped onto her comfy old sofa, slip-covered in a stain-resistant cream fabric, and sat there for nearly an hour. Most of that time had been spent staring out the southwest windows directly across the room as the afternoon sun slowly sank lower and lower. The harder she had tried not to think about what she'd done, naturally, the more her mind had focused on the fact that she had resigned from the Dundee Private Security and Investigation Agency. The rest of the evening she had simply gone through the motions: eaten a salad for supper, taken a long soak in the bathtub, brushed her teeth, watched the late night news, and gone to bed. The only problem was, she hadn't slept more than two hours straight and not more than four and a half all night. That might be enough sleep for some people, but not for Lucie. She was an eight-hour-a-night kind of gal.

Groaning at the thought of getting out of bed this

morning and facing her first full day of unemployment, she lifted her arms, balled her hands into fists and beat furiously against the two stacked feather pillows. When she wore herself out pummeling her grandmother's old pillows, she picked up one of them, covered her face with it and screamed. She had learned at an early age what great sound buffers feather pillows made. After tossing the pillow aside, she took a deep breath and got out of bed. Standing there on the wooden floor in her bare feet, she squared her shoulders.

There, she felt better. A mini-hissy fit had done the trick. Whenever she tried to control her emotions instead of releasing them, she wound up making herself sick. If Lucie had learned anything about herself, it was that she should never try to repress her emotions. She just wasn't geared to calm internalizing. No sirree, in order to function, she needed frenzied externalizing.

Five minutes later, as she emerged from the bathroom, face washed and hair brushed, she heard her doorbell ring. Who on earth? It was ten fifteen on a Saturday morning.

She made her way out of the bedroom and through her combination living room/dining room. When she reached the front door, she peered through the view-finder, then grinned broadly and unlocked the door.

Daisy Holbrook held a drink caddy in one hand and a small white sack in the other. "I come bearing gifts. White chocolate lattes and sinfully decadent cream-filled doughnuts, two for each of us."

"Well, get in here, girl." Lucie issued the invitation with a sweep of her hand. "Put the goodies on the coffee table and we'll dig in."

Lucie smiled at her next thought. Daisy looked fresh as a daisy. But then she always did. Dundee's Ms. Efficiency had the wholesome good looks of a healthy farm girl, bred for marriage and birthing babies. Young, pretty, slightly plump, Daisy dressed in classic clothes. Sweater sets, pearls, tailored slacks. Today, away from the office, she wore jeans and a cotton sweater. But the jeans weren't low-cut, faded, or ragged-hemmed; instead they were pale blue stone-washed, neatly pressed, and accented with a small pink belt that matched her sweater. She had her long, chestnut-brown hair pulled back in a ponytail and her only makeup consisted of light blush and lip gloss.

Lucie curled up on the sofa. Daisy lifted each of the coffee cups from the carrier and placed them on hand-painted metal coasters atop the coffee table. Then she removed several large paper napkins from the sack and put two sugar-glazed doughnuts on the napkins.

"You do realize that after we consume this sinful food, our hips will expand at least half an inch and we'll have gained no less than three or four pounds," Lucie said, as Daisy sat down beside her.

"I'm willing to make the ultimate sacrifice for a friend." Daisy grinned. "After all, I couldn't think of anything else that might cheer you up this morning."

"Just seeing you cheers me up."

"But seeing me with lattes and doughnuts makes my visit even better, doesn't it?"

Lucie reached for the latte. "I can certainly use a little caffeine and sugar this morning, something to perk me up as well as wake me up."

"Rough night?" Daisy lifted her doughnut, napkin and all, from the table.

"I spent most of the night arguing with myself, part of me convinced I'd done the only thing I could possibly have done by resigning and another part of me convinced that quitting one job before I have another is a definite sign of mental instability."

"You'll get another job without any trouble."

Lucie eyed her friend speculatively. "Without a recommendation from Dundee's—"

"That's not a problem."

"Really? Hmm... Tell me, Daisy dear, just what have you done?"

"Nothing. I simply asked Sawyer about including a letter of recommendation in with your severance package and he okayed it."

"Did he?" *Don't read anything into it. He's glad to be rid of you. He's simply doing what he considers the honorable thing. You know how Sawyer is about right and wrong, all black or all white, no shades of gray.* "I should have known that since I wasn't fired, he probably thought giving me a recommendation was the right thing to do."

"He got drunk yesterday afternoon," Daisy said between sips of latte. "I had to drive him home."

"What!"

"He made a big dent in a bottle of Johnnie Walker Blue."

"So, Sawyer really got drunk? I haven't seen him drunk since— Not in nine years. Not since his brother died."

"I didn't know Sawyer had a brother, but then none

of us really know him, except maybe you." When Daisy took a large bite out of her doughnut, the cream center oozed out and stuck to her mouth. Looking right at Lucie, waiting for a response, she licked the gooey filling off her lips.

"I used to know him. Or I thought I did. But I guess everything I thought I knew about him turned out to be wrong." *Except his innate sense of right and wrong, good and bad, innocence and guilt.*

"Look, I'm not asking you to betray any confidences. You don't have to tell me anything. We've been friends for years and I've never asked, have I?"

"No, you haven't and I appreciate that. What happened between Sawyer and me…well, it's better to stay just between the two of us."

"Sure." Daisy popped the remainder of the doughnut into her mouth.

"I may ask you about him every once in a while. You won't mind, will you?"

After she swallowed, Daisy replied, "I'll give you a weekly report, if that's what you want."

Lucie forced a smile, knowing if she didn't, she would wind up crying. Damn Sawyer McNamara! "No, I don't want to hear about him that often."

"Oh, Lucie, honey…"

"It's not what you think. I'm not in love with him or anything like that."

"Of course you're not."

"I'd be a fool to still care anything about him. And I'm certainly not a fool."

"No, you're not."

"Actually, if I feel anything for him at all, it's…it's… Damn! I hate him. I swear I hate him."

"Yeah, I can tell how much you hate him."

Lucie glared at Daisy. She grabbed her doughnut off the table and ate it in three huge bites. She washed it down with the latte, then reached over and grabbed the bakery sack. "I wish you'd bought a dozen of these things." She opened the sack, stuck her hand in and brought out another doughnut.

"Some people use whiskey to drown their sorrows," Daisy said, far too all-knowing. "And then some of us prefer dulling our pain with sugar."

"He hates me," Lucie said. "He can't bear to be in the same room with me. Every time he looks at me, he has to face his own guilt. Now, he won't have to do that, not ever again." She set the latte and doughnut on the table. "Let's go shopping." She jumped up and planted her hands on her hips. "Give me thirty minutes to get ready and we'll head out to Lenox Square. My Macy's credit card is paid off, so I can buy myself a new outfit for job hunting."

"What are you waiting for? Go, go. Get ready. Shopping is the next best thing to overdosing on sugar."

LUCIE HAD SPENT all day Saturday with Daisy. The name *Sawyer McNamara* had not crossed their lips again. They had shopped until they dropped, had eaten an early dinner out and then seen a movie. Sunday, she had awakened early, dressed and gone for a long walk. Later, she had stripped her bed and remade it with fresh linens, done all her laundry, cleaned the entire apartment and called her grandmother. Nonna lived in Florida, in a retirement village.

"I'm surrounded by the sun, the sea, and lots of senility," Nonna had joked the last time they'd talked.

She adored her paternal grandmother, Molly O'Riley Evans, from whom she had inherited her height, her curly auburn hair and her Irish temper. Her nonna had raised her while both of her parents worked in the mill, her mother as a secretary and her father as a midnight-shift foreman. And when her parents had died in car wreck when she was twelve, Nonna had packed their bags six months later and moved them to her hometown of Wayside, Mississippi, where Nonna's three other children lived. It was there that Lucie had met Sawyer and his younger brother, Brenden. And she had fallen in love with Sawyer the moment she saw him. Twenty-three years ago.

Last night she had taken an over-the-counter sleeping pill, so when she woke this morning, she'd had a too-much-sleep hangover. Now, on her second cup of coffee and with her brain starting to function, she sat down in front of her laptop, which was situated on the dining table, and stared at the screen. Even though Daisy told her that she would receive one month's salary in her severance package, she knew that wouldn't last more than a couple of months. She had exactly one thousand four hundred and twenty-six dollars in her checking account and many of her monthly bills would come due on the first. Unless she had no other choice, she didn't want to dip into her retirement fund, which was the only savings she had. Lucie wasn't good at saving money. She was good at spending it and giving it away.

She needed to find a job, sooner rather than later. She hadn't worked up a resume in years—nine years to be exact.

So, what were her qualifications? High school degree, college degree, six years with the Federal Bureau of Investigation, nine years with Dundee's. She supposed she could go into law enforcement again, something local maybe. Or she could check out other private investigation and/or bodyguard firms. Maybe she could move to Florida, somewhere near Nonna. One thing she knew for sure—she was leaving Atlanta. She would do what she should have done nine years ago and put some distance between her and Sawyer.

As she finished off her coffee and was considering a third cup, her phone rang. When she stood up, she glanced at the wall clock. Nine thirty-two. She hurried to pick up the receiver, taking only enough time to glance at the caller ID.

Bedell, Inc.

Who from Bedell, Inc. would be calling her?

"Hello."

"Ms. Evans, Lucie Evans?" the baritone voice asked.

"Yes, this is she."

"Lucie, this is Deke Bronson."

"Oh, Deke, hi there. How are you doing? How are Lexie and the baby?"

"They're fine. Emma weighs twenty pounds and is almost as beautiful as her mama." Deke cleared his throat. "You probably know that I took over as head of security at Bedell, Inc., last year when Larry Nesmith retired."

"Yes, I'd heard. Congratulations."

"Thanks. Look, Lucie, the reason I'm calling is because I heard through the grapevine that you've left Dundee's and might be looking for a job."

He'd heard that through the grapevine? What grapevine? The Daisy Holbrook grapevine, maybe?

"That's right," Lucie said. "I am looking for a job."

"Would you be interested in working security for us? The pay is probably not quite what you were making at Dundee's, but we provide a nice package, including three weeks paid vacation after the first year, excellent health care, retirement benefits and bonuses."

"Yes, I might be interested."

"Good. Why don't you drive over to Chattanooga tomorrow and meet with me, say around ten-thirty."

"Yes, thank you. I'll be there. Ten-thirty sharp."

Lucie replaced the receiver, released a deep breath, spun around a couple of times and laughed out loud.

Daisy, if this was your doing, then you, sweet girl, are my guardian angel. Bedell, Inc. was a multibillion-dollar conglomerate with branches worldwide. Maybe she could get Deke to assign her to one of their foreign offices in some exotic locale. The farther she was from Sawyer McNamara, the better. For both of them.

"WHAT DID SHE SAY?" Cara Bedell asked.

"She'll be here for an interview at ten-thirty tomorrow," Deke Bronson replied.

"Good. Put her through the regular interview process, then call her Wednesday morning and tell her she got the job."

"Yes, ma'am. You're the boss."

"And hurry her through the indoctrination process. I want her assigned as one of my personal bodyguards when I go to Ameca. With Wanda on maternity leave, I'll need a seasoned female bodyguard on this trip and Ms. Evans has nine years experience with the premiere firm in the nation."

"You're right. Lucie will be an asset for our security team."

"Start Ms. Evans out at top level pay. With her background, she shouldn't be starting at the ground level."

Deke nodded. "I agree. Anything else?"

"No, that's all. Just remember that Lucie isn't to know who recommended her for the job."

"She won't hear it from me."

Smiling, Deke turned around and exited Cara's private office. As soon as he closed the door behind him, she picked up the phone and dialed Sawyer McNamara's cell number.

"It's done," she said. "Ms. Evans is coming in tomorrow for an interview and she'll start work on Wednesday."

"Thanks," Sawyer said. "I owe you one. By the way, my name wasn't mentioned, was it?"

"No."

"Good. I'd like to keep it that way."

"Sounds to me like you're losing a good employee. I'm surprised you didn't try to persuade her to stay."

"Lucie needs a change."

"Well, she'll get a big change soon. I'm taking her to Ameca with me in three weeks to act as one of my personal bodyguards."

Having learned in the past that Sawyer wasn't a man who indulged in idle chitchat, she didn't prolong their conversation. Still holding the receiver in her hand, Cara considered making another phone call. Since seeing Bain this past Friday, she hadn't been able to get him off her mind. Why she put herself through the torment of going to the Hair of the Dog pub every Friday just to get a glimpse of him, she didn't know.

Liar. You do know.

She couldn't bear the thought of never seeing him. Better a few stolen glimpses from across the room than nothing at all. How pathetic was that? About as pathetic as finding reasons to call him occasionally, just to hear his voice.

Cara replaced the receiver, walked across the room and stood in front of the windows that overlooked downtown Chattanooga. She was standing in her plush office suite inside the Bedell Building, headquarters for Bedell, Inc. How many people would kill to be in her shoes? She had wealth, power and an unequaled social position. She had everything that money could buy. Unfortunately, the one thing she wanted more than anything else in the whole wide world was not for sale.

ARTURO TORRES-RIOS paid the men in cash, a down payment, one-fourth of what they would earn if they did their jobs well. He had hand-picked these men, as he did whenever he needed a team. Each of them had worked for him before and although he knew better than to blindly trust any of them, they understood one another. In his business, betrayal was punishable by death. Usually a slow, painful death. These men knew his reputation, had seen him in action, and were familiar with how he dealt with anyone who wasn't loyal.

"We will go over the plan again and again until every man knows his job perfectly. There is no margin for error."

He glanced around the room. Four men. He could have used six. But the more people involved, the more chances for mistakes. The odds were better with only four. Manuel would be the driver. Hector and Pepe would take possession of the package. Rico would safeguard the hideaway. And then the four would alternate twelve-hour shifts, two working together. They would report in to him at the end of each shift.

"Travel the route in a different car and at a different time each day. We may not know until the last minute exactly when to strike. I'll make arrangements tomorrow for the hideaway and I'll see to it that the place is well stocked. I don't know how long it will take to accomplish the mission. Maybe only a few days, but more than likely, a week or more. I don't want any of you making trips into town and drawing attention to yourselves."

"This package, it is very valuable, yes?" Rico asked.

"Very valuable," Arturo agreed.

"Must it be returned in perfect condition?"

The other men laughed. Arturo sliced his sharp gaze from one man to the other, effectively cutting off their laughter and silencing them. "Your assignment is to take possession of the package, guard it and return it to its rightful owner when I give the order. Is that understood?"

"Yes, yes," they all said in unison.

"Good. You may look, but do not touch," Arturo told them.

"What happens if anything goes wrong?" Hector asked. "Do we dispose of the package?"

"No. I will take charge of the package and dispose of it myself."

These men did not know her name nor had he shown them a photograph of her. That would come later, when it was absolutely necessary. The less they knew beforehand the less chance of anyone accidentally leaking any information. To a trusted friend. To a lover. To a family member.

Arturo wanted this assignment to go off without a flaw. If it did, a month from now, he would be a very wealthy man.

CHAPTER FOUR

ONE OF THE three Bedell private jets, this one kept in a hangar in Chattanooga for the exclusive use of Cara Bedell, landed in San Luis, Ameca, a little over two weeks after Lucie hired on with Bedell, Inc. Deke Bronson, who had also once been a Dundee agent, had rushed Lucie through the orientation process and prepared her for her duties as Ms. Bedell's bodyguard. Whenever she traveled, a female agent traveled with the Bedell CEO.

"Cara wants you to accompany her and Jason Little to Ameca as her personal bodyguard," Deke had explained. "Wanda Marcum, who usually travels with Cara, is on maternity leave. At present we don't have another female guard with your credentials."

Ameca was a small, oil-rich country on the eastern coast of South America. Settled by the Spanish, who had intermarried with the natives, the country had seen an influx of various nationalities during the past sixty years. Although Spanish was the official language, more than half the population spoke fluent English. From her crash course in the country and its economic, political and social structure, Lucie had learned that the vast majority of Amecans lived in abject poverty. Governed by an elected president, the country boasted of its democratic principles; yet every president for the past half century had emerged from the Amecan army to run for the highest office in the land.

As they disembarked, Lucie breathed in the warm, tropical air. The San Luis airport ran parallel to the coastline and the Atlantic Ocean could be seen from the tower. Thankfully, the flight had proven to be uneventful in any negative sense. Lucie had flown on the Dundee jet numerous times and had been duly impressed during her first flight. But as luxurious as the Dundee jet was, it paled in comparison to Cara's private plane. Other than the Bedell jet being larger, one of the obvious differences was the fact that on the Dundee jet, the occupants prepared their own meals, whereas on the Bedell jet, a chef prepared four-course meals.

Tugging on the lapels, Lucie pulled her beige blazer together as she emerged from the plane, making sure her shoulder holster wasn't visible. Cara followed her, with Jason Little directly behind her. Diplomatic arrangements had been made to allow the CEO of Bedell, Inc. and her bodyguards to forego the usual entrance procedures at the airport. Instead, a representative of President Ortega was there to expedite matters and officially welcome Senorita Bedell to Ameca.

A bodyguard should always be as unobtrusive as possible, keeping a low profile. By doing this, it allowed the principal—in this case, Cara Bedell—and those with whom she came into contact to feel comfortable. Although Lucie loved clothes—bright colors, frills, dangling earrings and heels that lifted her to a towering six-feet-plus—whenever she was on duty, she dressed accordingly. Today she wore brown dress slacks, a sleeveless, pale yellow tank and a beige cotton blazer, sensible brown flats, and no jewelry except tiny gold studs in her ears and a wristwatch. Her unruly curls were subdued in a thick, loose bun at the nape of her neck. By dressing in a nondescript manner, she didn't draw attention to herself.

She and Jason had done their homework well in advance, familiarizing themselves with the layout of the airport and the route they would take to Senor Delgado's home. They had requested and received a blueprint of their host's hacienda and surrounding estate grounds. Although they had no reason to suspect that Cara might be in danger during her visit to Ameca, a woman worth billions should always be considered a target.

Senor Vito Aguilar-Vega, a small, dark man in his late forties, welcomed Cara to his country and presented her with a bouquet of white roses and lilies. After making a glowing speech in Spanish, he translated a few words into English, telling Cara that the president was eager to meet her and wished to host a ball in her honor during her visit.

A tall, distinguished gentleman, with thick salt-and-pepper hair and a generous mustache, spoke to Senor Aguilar-Vega, who frowned disapprovingly, but stepped aside to allow the older man to approach.

"Senorita Bedell, I am your host, Felipe Delgado. Welcome to Ameca." He bowed with a quick snap of his head. "My car is waiting. I have arranged for someone to pick up your luggage later." He glanced from Cara to Jason and Lucie, who were posted on either side of her, Jason slightly behind her, Lucie a few steps ahead of her. "There are three of you, yes?"

"Yes, thank you." Cara took Senor Delgado's arm. Lucie and Jason fell into step, Jason ahead of them and Lucie behind them.

Lucie slid into the backseat alongside Cara while Jason climbed in the front with the chauffeur. Once on the road, making their way through downtown San Luis traffic, Cara introduced her two bodyguards to their host. During the twenty-minute drive from the airport to his home, Senor Delgado kept the conversation light and casual, speaking of his wife, his three children and five grandchildren, his love of sailing, his hobby of stamp collecting and his stable of fine Arabian horses.

The estate bordered the ocean on one side, with the two-story, salmon-pink stucco, red tile-roofed hacienda built on the rocks overlooking the pristine beach below. The well-manicured lawns were a luscious green, no doubt watered daily. Bougainvilleas draped the fencing, a combination of stucco and black wrought-iron. Flowering shrubbery, neatly maintained, grew in abundance, adding to the tropical-paradise aura of the estate.

When the chauffeur parked the Rolls-Royce on the circular brick drive in front of the house, a small, plump woman with a mane of black hair arranged in a soft bun atop her head came out of the house and stood on the veranda. When Senor Delgado exited the car, he reached in to assist both Cara and Lucie.

"Your guards may relax somewhat," Delgado said. "I have my own guards here at my estate and my home is quite safe for me, my family and my guests."

The small woman, dressed impeccably in a lavender linen skirt and white silk blouse, came forward and draped her arm through her husband's.

"My dear," Delgado said, "may I present Senorita Cara Bedell, Senorita Evans and Senor Little."

She smiled at each of them in turn, but her dark eyes returned to Cara when she spoke. "*Mucho gusto*, Senorita Bedell. Welcome to our home." Her English was not as smooth as her husband's, but fluent enough so that she didn't struggle with her words.

"Senorita Bedell, this is my wife, Suelita."

The mistress of the house herself showed Cara to her room, which turned out to be a beautiful suite with a balcony that faced the ocean. Jason was given a room across the hall and Lucie the room next to Cara's.

"They seem very nice, don't you think?" Cara asked Lucie when they were alone.

"Yes, quite nice."

"I'm seventy-five percent decided about choosing Delgado Oil over Castillo, Inc.," Cara said. "I hope you don't mind my thinking out loud and using you as a sounding board. Wanda's accustomed to listening and giving me her honest opinion. I hope you'll do the same."

"Yes, ma'am. If that's what you want."

"It is. And please, dispense with the 'ma'am,' and except when it seems inappropriate, call me Cara."

Lucie smiled.

Cara retuned her smile. "I've received proposals

from both Delgado and Castillo. On the surface they seem equal in benefits to Bedell, Inc., but from my reports, personally, the two owners are vastly different. Delgado grew up poor. He's one of the people. And ever since he became a multimillionaire, he has helped with various charities, and in the last election, he worked to get Naldo Salazar elected president. Salazar is a reformist. Since the election, he has kept a low profile because there are rumors his life could be in danger. On the other hand, Castillo came from wealth and privilege. He's a playboy who lights his cigars with hundred-dollar bills, as the old saying goes. He backed President Ortega and supposedly the two are very close. Ortega represents the status quo."

"If your goal is profits for Bedell, Inc., and nothing more, than I'd say all things are equal." Lucie wondered if Cara realized that by giving her permission to speak her mind, Lucie wouldn't hold back or sugarcoat anything. "But if your goal is profits for Bedell, Inc. *and* to help the people of Ameca, then you have only one choice. Isn't Senor Delgado proposing that his company and yours invest between a sixth and a fourth of the revenue from this joint deal in programs for the needy citizens of his country?"

"Yes, that's part of the deal, and it's tempting to simply sign the contracts with Senor Delgado now and deal with my board of directors later. But I think I owe it to my stockholders to at least meet with Senor Castillo and find out if he's interested in making a counteroffer that includes a similar provision to help his fellow countrymen."

"Is meeting with him your idea?" Lucie asked, somehow doubting it was.

"Actually, Gray suggested that my meeting with Castillo might appease the stockholders and the board, some who will definitely not be happy giving away such a large percentage of our profits."

"I guess it's true."

Cara looked at Lucie quizzically.

"Enough is never enough. And you can't be too rich or too thin." Lucie chuckled. "Well, at least too rich."

"I know that I make the Bedell board members sound like a bunch of greedy, heartless millionaires, but they're not. At least most are not. But in order to do my job representing Bedell, Inc., I have to appease the board of directors and the shareholders, even if I am the majority shareholder."

Lucie laughed. "Poor little rich girl." Uh-oh, she'd done it now. Let her big mouth get in her trouble again. "I'm sorry. That just slipped out."

Cara smiled. "Don't apologize. I appreciate your honestly. Besides, that's exactly what I am—a poor little rich girl. You have no idea how well that term fits me."

JOSUE SOTO entered the church shortly before sundown. There were three other people there; one old man lighting a candle and a young couple kneeling in prayer. After slipping into one of the back pews, Josue sat, closed his eyes and pretended to pray. Ten minutes later, when the young couple had left and only the old man remained—he was now seated on the front row, his white head bowed reverently as he mumbled to himself—Arturo eased in beside Josue.

"She arrived today," Josue said, his voice little more than a whisper. "She is staying with Felipe Delgado. As you know, his estate is practically impregnable. She brought two personal bodyguards with her, one man and one woman."

"I need to know when she will be outside the estate, when she will be on the road and in town."

Josue nodded. "I am working on acquiring a copy of her itinerary, but as you know, information such as that does not come cheap."

"Do not squabble over money. Pay whatever is necessary."

"Yes, of course."

"She will be in Ameca for two weeks, yes? That has not changed, has it?"

"No, not as far as I know. Her plans remain unchanged. I have heard that President Ortega plans to have a ball in her honor while she is here. And there is speculation that she may meet with Naldo Salazar, as well as Tomas Castillo."

"Good. Good. This means she will not remain in seclusion at Felipe Delgado's estate. At some point during her stay here in Ameca, she will become accessible to us. It's only a matter of choosing the right moment."

"The only way to do that is by keeping her under surveillance."

"Do not try to tell me how to do my job," Arturo said, a tinge of anger in his harsh voice. Josue knew better than to upset his friend. Where he, Josue, was a businessman, a lawyer, merely a deal broker who was smart enough to keep his own hands clean, Arturo was a killer. He enjoyed what he did. He was truly a man without a conscience.

"I would never tell you what to do, old friend. I spoke out of turn. Forgive me."

"You are forgiven." Arturo rose to his feet. "Contact me as soon as you have her itinerary and any other information of importance."

"Yes, of course."

Josue stayed for fifteen minutes after Arturo left the church. This time, when he closed his eyes, he prayed in earnest. Despite how lucrative his business association with Arturo was, there were times when he wished he could free himself of their arrangement. He feared that someday, in some way, he might offend his old friend and not be forgiven.

FOUR DAYS INTO her trip to Ameca, Cara attended a gala ball at the presidential palace, an invitation she could not refuse because she was the guest of honor. She knew that for her security team of two, a social engagement such as this one could be a nightmare; but with security already at maximum for the president and other officials, that reduced the responsibility for her bodyguards to a minimum. Keeping an eye on her, the surroundings and anyone with whom she came into contact was essential. Understanding that bodyguards needed to fit in and be inconspicuous, especially at gala events such as this one, Bedell security guards dressed according. Male Bedell guards wore a simple black tuxedo with a plain white shirt. Female agents wore black, unadorned, floor-length gowns and carried their weapon in an evening bag.

Cara had chosen a pale yellow silk sheath with a side leg slit that ended midthigh. Yellow was a color she wore often, because it complemented her red hair and hazel eyes. She wasn't overly bosomy, but her breasts were full and high, so she could wear gowns such as the one she had on tonight, cut to her waist in the back and draped in folds across her collarbone in front. She had chosen her golden topaz and diamond earrings and matching bracelet and a small bag covered in topaz crystals as her accessories. She wore flats tonight, as she often did because of her nearly six-foot height.

President Ortega was short and stout, with jet-black hair and a pencil-thin mustache. He spoke English with a heavy accent and danced as if he had two left feet. Cara had danced the first dance with the man who insisted she call him Emilio, and not Mr. President, and found him to be rather charming. She guessed his age to be somewhere around fifty, but estimated his wife, the luscious first lady, to be no more than twenty-five. When she had seen her in the receiving line, Cara had mistakenly assumed she was the president's daughter, but he had introduced her as his wife, Carmela. Later in the evening, Suelita Delgado explained that the president's first wife had been discarded, along with his two daughters, when the present Mrs. Ortega became pregnant with Emilio's son, now four years old. Cara had discovered that Suelita was a fount of San Luis gossip. The lady knew everyone and delighted in sharing dirty little secrets and scandalous rumors.

During the past two hours, Cara had met the crème de la crème of Ameca society, the wealthy and powerful. Just as she finished a second glass of excellent champagne and had downed two shrimp-and-crab canapés, Emilio approached her, but not alone. His companion was a tall, elegant gentleman in his early forties. He was rather handsome in a sleek, slick, dark and dangerous sort of way. Clean-shaven, his black hair salon-styled and his bronze skin natural and not the result of a tan, he had rich Latin Lover written all over him.

"Senorita Bedell," the president said. "May I introduce my good friend, Tomas Castillo."

Senor Castillo bowed curtly, then reached out, took her hand and kissed it before she could say "pleased to meet you."

"Senorita, I am honored," Castillo said, his accent discernable but light. "How is it possible that someone so young and beautiful can command all of Bedell, Inc.?"

She realized he'd meant his comment to be a compliment. First of all, she might be young, but she was not nor had she ever been beautiful. Passably attractive thanks to the trappings of great wealth, but short of plastic surgery on her face and body, beauty was unobtainable for a large-boned, wide-hipped, freckle-faced redhead whose greatest asset was her brains. But she was willing, up to a point, to play along with Mr. Smooth and pretend she'd bought his line of bull.

"Why, thank you, senor. You're too kind. And I am in charge of Bedell, Inc. because, as I'm sure you know, I inherited the family business."

"As did I." Tomas Castillo smiled, revealing a set of perfect sparkling white teeth.

"Would you honor me with a dance?" he asked, and without giving her a chance to respond, he slipped his arm around her and waltzed her onto the dance floor.

Apparently Senor Castillo was a man accustomed to having his way, especially with the ladies.

"Ah, the rumba. A sensuous dance, is it not? Perfect for us, yes?"

For you, maybe, Cara thought.

If his intention had been to impress her and possibly titillate her, he had achieved the first and failed at the second. His dancing was as smooth as his tongue and by the end of the hot, tempestuous rumba, Cara was thankful she had chosen to wear topaz crystal-encrusted sandals that matched her evening bag. Not the most graceful person in the world, she might not have managed to keep up with Tomas's passionate dance steps if she'd worn heels.

As far as arousing her, unless you counted being damp with perspiration, a bit out of breath and having a face flushed with warmth as titillation, then he hadn't accomplished that goal. She supposed if she hadn't already experienced being infatuated in her past with a suave, sophisticated, egomaniac by the name of Grayson Perkins, she would be more susceptible to Tomas's undeniable charm. But her taste in men these days ran to the strong, rugged, hard-working type, like a certain Chattanooga police detective.

For the remainder of the evening, the handsome oil tycoon showered attention on Cara, but not once did he mention business. If she hadn't known better she would have sworn that he was infatuated with her. But despite his expertise as a seducer, she knew that what he wanted was a deal between Castillo, Inc. and Bedell, Inc. If he thought bedding the CEO of Bedell would gain him the upper hand over Delgado Oil, he would make mad, passionate love to Cara whenever she snapped her fingers.

Four hours into the gala, Cara had had more than enough. But when she said good-night to Tomas, he begged her not to go, then begged her to allow him to escort her home.

"I have my own transportation," she told him, then glanced from Lucie to Jason. "And my own private-duty guards to escort me."

Tomas grasped her hand, kissed it and looked longingly into her eyes. "Tomorrow night, you must dine with me on my yacht. Or better yet, pack a bag and we'll take a short cruise."

Easing her hands from his possessive hold, she smiled warmly. "I'm afraid this trip to Ameca is more for business than pleasure. Instead of dinner tomorrow evening, why don't we meet for a business lunch tomorrow and you can tell me why Bedell, Inc. should sign with Castillo, Inc. instead of Delgado Oil."

"Ah, I see you are a woman who prefers to put business before pleasure." He shrugged dramatically. "So be it. Lunch tomorrow to talk business. But afterward, I hope that I can persuade you to indulge in something that will give us both far more pleasure."

Barely managing to keep her smile in place, she replied, "We'll see, senor. We'll see."

Lucie fell into step alongside her as they made a hurried exit. Cara grumbled. "Deliver me from a guy who thinks he's God's gift to women."

"Senor Castillo seemed quite smitten," Lucie said, humor in her voice.

"*Seemed* being the operative word. I swear, I believe if I'd given him the least bit of encouragement, he would have made love to me on the balcony, under the stars." Cara laughed.

Lucie laughed, too. "A prospect many women would have found irresistible."

"Not this woman."

When they reached the front entrance, Lucie halted Cara while Jason walked down the steps and requested their car, another Rolls-Royce from Senor Delgado's collection of five.

When the valet brought the car around, Lucie followed Cara down the steps, but just as they reached the driveway, a slender, bearded man in a sport coat and slacks came out of nowhere and called Cara by name. Lucie stepped in front of Cara while Jason made a mad dash toward them.

"Senorita Bedell, I must speak with you," the man said.

"Hold up," Jason called to him, his hand on his shoulder holster. "Who are you and what do you want?"

Suddenly two men, both with rifles over their shoulders, slipped out of the darkness and came up behind the other man. Jason pulled his Beretta from the holster. Lucie snapped open her evening bag and retrieved her weapon.

CHAPTER FIVE

"I AM NALDO SALAZAR, Senorita Bedell," the man told her, his voice deep and soft. "I mean you no harm. But I must speak to you. Privately."

"Then why not set up an appointment with me?" Cara asked. "You're a friend of the Delgado family. You could visit with me at Felipe and Suelita's home—"

"No, that is no advisable. At present, I am—" he searched for the correct term "—persona non grata. Since losing the presidential election, it has become necessary for me to, as you Americans say, go underground. I do not wish to create problems for my friends, those such as Felipe and Suelita, who might put themselves in danger by welcoming me into their home."

"I don't pretend to understand the complexities of Amecan politics, senor," Cara said. "But accosting me in this manner is hardly the way to gain my approval."

"I apologize, but I had little choice. If perhaps you will allow me to ride with you for a few miles and my men follow in a separate car, I can explain. You may have your guards check me for weapons, if you like, before we leave."

Lucie could tell that Cara was considering this man's

request. An uneasy feeling settled in the pit of her stomach. Before she had a chance to voice her opinion, Cara instructed Jason to frisk Salazar. Once that was done, she invited the man to join her. He ordered his guards to follow; or at least that's what Lucie thought he said. Her command of Spanish was so-so, enough to get by, but she certainly wasn't proficient in the language.

Jason remained outside the Rolls until Cara, Senor Salazar and Lucie were seated in the back, then after scanning the area, he slipped into the front with the driver, one of Delgado's trusted employees. Once outside the gated palace grounds, Salazar faced Cara in the semidark interior, the only illumination coming from the lights of San Luis as the car eased through the late-night traffic.

"I wish to plead my case in person," Salazar said, his dark eyes searching Cara's face for any expression of understanding.

Lucie eased her handgun back into her evening bag, but kept the bag open. She studied the man who had made a reputation for himself worldwide as a radical reformist, a man intent on dethroning Ameca's privileged kings of finance. He didn't look dangerous; if anything, he looked like the stereotypical mild-mannered professor with his graying hair, his outdated black-framed glasses and his seen-better-days suit that was slightly too large for his tall, lanky frame.

"I am certain that you have much information about Ameca at your fingertips and you have, no doubt, investigated both Felipe Delgado and Tomas Castillo and their oil companies," Salazar said. "I also know that you

are the chief benefactor of Helping Hands, yes?" He
nodded, but didn't pause for her reply. "You are a very
wealthy woman, but one with a big heart who wishes
to do much good with your money. My people need the
kind of help that a contract between Delgado Oil and
Bedell, Inc. will provide. If you sign a deal with Tomas
Castillo, there will be no benefits for the poor and needy
of Ameca."

"Senor, I assure you that I will make an informed
decision, one that will benefit both my company and the
people of Ameca."

"I had hoped that while you were staying with Felipe
and Suelita, they could sway you to our side. But I was
informed that you spent a great deal of this evening with
Senor Castillo. He can be a charming man, one very
popular with the ladies, and when he wants something,
he goes after it without thought of the consequences to
anyone involved. I warn you, Senorita Bedell, you
cannot trust this man."

Lucie noted the way Cara didn't respond immediately and knew she was thinking, going over everything in her mind. No doubt, she was wondering just
how Salazar had known that she had been in the
company of Tomas Castillo for a large portion of the
President's ball. And how Salazar and his men had
managed to get past the guards at the gate. Just as Lucie
surmised that Salazar had spies within the palace walls,
she knew that Cara would come to the same conclusion.

"I appreciate your concern," Cara said. "And I realize
you took a risk by coming here tonight to plead your case
and warn me against Senor Castillo. But as a business-

woman who must consider all aspects of any deal I make with an Amecan oil company, I intend to have lunch with Senor Castillo tomorrow and listen to his proposal."

"Por qué?" Salazar asked, obviously upset. "I tell you that he cares nothing for others. He is not a good man."

"I understand what you're saying. And if Tomas Castillo is not willing to include provisions in the contract that will return a portion of his profits to Ameca, then I won't—"

"To Ameca? No, senorita. Be careful. He may agree to your terms, but giving profits to Ameca through the government will help only Castillo and Ortega and their kind."

When Cara reached out and touched Salazar's hand, Lucie sucked in a deep breath. The opposition leader, the radical reformist, tensed at Cara's touch, but did not withdraw his hand.

"I promise you that any decision I make will benefit those in greatest need here in Ameca, as well as make profits for both Bedell, Inc., and either Castillo or Delgado." Cara lowered her voice to a whisper and said, "Unless Tomas is more convincing at our lunch tomorrow than he was wooing me tonight, then I can promise you that Bedell, Inc. will be signing with Delgado Oil."

Salazar sighed heavily, but he didn't smile. Nor did he thank Cara. He merely spoke to the driver in Spanish, asking him to pull over as soon as possible. The driver asked Cara for permission, which she gave. When Salazar got out of the car, he turned, leaned into the backseat and looked directly at Cara.

"I will be waiting to hear about your decision. For

all our sakes, I pray it is the right one." He walked away and got in the car that had pulled in behind the Rolls.

Cara glanced at Lucie. "Should I take what he said as nothing more than him stating his opinion or should I take it as a threat?"

"With a man like Salazar, it's difficult to know," Lucie replied. "But from what I've read about him, he's a man who backs up his words with actions."

THE RESTAURANT WHERE Cara met Tomas Castillo for lunch the next day was no doubt one of the most elegant and expensive in all of San Luis. Cara wasn't surprised. After all, Tomas would want to impress her. The tile-roofed building faced the bay, and the tropical garden patio, shaded by enormous umbrella-covered tables and towering palm trees, was bright and airy and caught the afternoon breeze off the ocean.

In typical old-world macho style, Tomas ordered for both of them. She smiled indulgently, fully aware that objecting was not worth the effort. It was obvious that this man had no idea what it took to truly impress her. He ordered cream of prawn soup, a seafood mousse, veal chops with shitake mushrooms and an excellent wine to complement their meal. In true gentlemanly fashion, he complimented her in every way possible and refrained from mentioning business until the end of their delicious meal.

As they sipped on hazelnut daiquiris, he said, "Castillo, Incorporated has much to offer, far more than Delgado Oil. You received our initial proposal, yes?"

She smiled. "Yes, but I must admit that it lacked a

great deal of what I need to see in such a monumental deal, one that will have long-range effects on both my country and yours, as well on both of our companies."

Tomas frowned, but quickly erased the negative reaction, once again smiling cordially as he reached for her hand. What was it with this guy? Did he actually think that kissing her hand would affect her ability to reason?

As soon as he planted a featherlight kiss on the top of her hand, she eased out of his grasp.

"Simply tell me what you require and it will be done," he said.

"Other than the fact that I don't care for a few of the minor particulars about percentages and just whose oil tankers would be moving the product, my chief concern is that there are no provisions to provide any financial benefits to the people of Ameca."

Tomas laughed, the sound hollow. "I promise you that regardless of what you may have been told about me, I care deeply for Ameca and want only good things for our people. If funneling some of our joint profits to Ameca is, as you would say, a deal breaker, then I will make sure my attorneys include a clause stipulating a generous percentage—say one-sixth of our profits—is to be invested in Ameca."

"Invested in what way?" Cara asked.

He eyed her curiously, as if surprised she would question him about details. Hadn't he ever dealt with a woman whose business sense was as sharply honed as any man's? Was she actually a first for him? It was all Cara could do not to laugh.

"There are government agencies that could easily

handle overseeing the funds," Tomas told her. "As my personal friend, Emilio Ortega would exert his influence to make sure the money was channeled properly."

Yes, of course, President Ortega would most definitely handle the money exactly the way Tomas told him to. He'd put it right into his own pocket! "I prefer that the profits we donate to Ameca be channeled through charity organizations such as Helping Hands, headquartered in the United States, and your country's relief association, supervised by the church."

Was that another vaguely disguised frown she saw marring Tomas's handsome face. A smile twitched the corners of her mouth, but she managed to keep her expression placid.

"Now that I fully understand your desires, I am certain we can come to an agreement that will be good for both of us," Tomas said. "I will need a few days to discuss all the particulars with my lawyers, but if you will be kind enough to grant me the necessary time, I am sure I will be able to make Bedell, Inc. an offer it cannot refuse."

Interesting. Unless she had seriously misjudged Tomas Castillo, she didn't think he would ever agree to turn over even a small percentage of his profits to his impoverished countrymen. No, he had something else in mind. The problem was Cara didn't know what his next move would be.

"Of course, feel free to present Bedell, Inc. with an offer to equal Delgado Oil's offer and I will certainly consider it," Cara told him.

"*Muchas gracias.* Now that our business for the day

is concluded, allow me to be your tour guide and show you around San Luis."

"I appreciate the offer, but I'm afraid I have other plans," Cara said, fabricating a white lie in order to escape an afternoon of pretending she enjoyed being with Tomas. "Perhaps some other time."

"May I see you to your car?" he asked.

"No, thank you. I have my people here with me." She inclined her head toward the table across from theirs where Lucie and Jason kept watch.

Tomas rose to his feet swiftly, bowed, forced a smile and said, "I shall count the hours until I see you again, senorita."

After he left the restaurant, Cara finished her delicious daiquiri, then motioned to her bodyguards. "I have the afternoon free. I'd like to go shopping in the market. I know my being in the middle of a crowd is something y'all would rather avoid, but if I don't take the opportunity now, I may not get to soak in any of the authentic atmosphere of San Luis before I leave Ameca."

"You're the boss," Jason reminded her. "But I'd suggest you try to pass yourself off as a tourist."

"I suppose that means ditching the Rolls and either walking or taking a taxi or bus, right?" Cara wanted a few hours free from business. Tomorrow would be soon enough to tell Felipe Delgado that Bedell, Inc. would be going into a lucrative partnership with his oil company. Whatever repercussions she'd have to face before leaving Ameca and then once back in Chattanooga, she didn't have to deal with them today.

"I suggest that you and Lucie change clothes," Jason

said. "Go to one of the local boutiques first and buy items that tourists would buy and wear. Lucie can stay at your side and the two of you will appear to be two American women on vacation. I'll keep a low profile, but remain close by. Lucie will be the frontline defense in case of trouble. I'll be monitoring the crowd and alert her to any sign of trouble."

"I want a floppy straw hat, some big sunglasses and flip-flops," Cara said. "What about you, Lucie?"

"No flip-flops for me, but I'll take a big straw hat and a colorful outfit."

Cara draped her arm through Lucie's. "Then let's go. And buy whatever you want at the clothing boutique. Don't even look at the price tags."

WHEN HIS CELL PHONE RANG, Arturo glanced at the caller ID. Josue did not telephone him unless the matter was urgent.

"Good day, my friend."

"The package must be obtained today," Josue said. "The client insists that this matter cannot wait."

"I will not take undue risks, but if it is possible to collect the package this afternoon, we will do so."

"Our client will wish to be informed. Once the package is in your possession, please contact me and I will inform the client."

THE PLAZA BAZAAR was two blocks south of the trendy boutique where Cara and Lucie purchased their new attire, so they walked to the open-air market that boasted a vast range of wares and supposedly the best bargains in San Luis. Cara had changed into a flowing, green cotton skirt, lemon-yellow blouse and cushioned green flip-flops. Lucie had chosen the same colors, but in reverse. She wore a yellow skirt, a green blouse and sandals in a soft yellow leather. She had removed her shoulder holster and placed it in the open-top shoulder bag she carried. As they weaved in and out of the crowd, stopping at various booths in the market, Jason kept a discreet distance, all the while staying in bodyguard mode. Anyone seeing him wouldn't suspect he was tailing the two attractive American redheads in their bright attire and large sunglasses.

"Look," Cara said. "There's a booth with nothing but hats. Maybe we can find what we're looking for there."

Lucie followed her boss, who was acting more like a friend this afternoon, someone Lucie could learn to like a great deal. They had stopped at numerous booths—pottery, guitars, mirrors, rugs and wooden masks—but this was the first booth containing hats, and already Lucie saw the one she wanted. Yellow straw with a green grosgrain ribbon tied in a loose bow around the crown of the wide-brimmed hat. When they stopped at the booth, Cara reached up and grabbed the exact hat Lucie had chosen, plopped it down on her head and turned to Lucie for approval.

"What do you think?" Cara asked.

"I think it's perfect. It matches your outfit and suits your coloring."

Cara studied Lucie for a moment, then reached up, pulled down an identical hat and placed it on Lucie's head. "There. It's perfect for you, too."

They both laughed as Cara turned to the vendor and asked the price. When he quoted the amount, not outrageously expensive, but apparently more than Cara thought they were worth, she began haggling with the vendor. Lucie grinned as she tried to keep up with the conversation taking place in a mixture of Spanish and English. Finally Cara and the vendor agreed on a price.

The afternoon passed quickly while they explored the market, and by early evening they both carried large cloth sacks filled with a variety of purchases, everything from silver bracelets to heavily embroidered white blouses.

"I'm starving," Cara said. "Didn't we pass a couple of restaurants about fifteen minutes ago, just before the pottery display?"

"El Recoveco looked like a nice place," Lucie said. "I think there was a buffet on the patio."

"Perfect, but first I need to make a stop at the ladies' room. What about you?"

"Yes, definitely," Lucie replied.

"I imagine Jason could use a short break, too."

"El Recoveco was an indoor-outdoor restaurant, with a buffet meal served on the patio, but they probably have an order-from-the-menu three-course dinner available inside."

"I vote to eat inside where it's cool."

"Sounds good to me," Lucie said.

Jason followed them as they backtracked through the market until they reached the restaurant. Using her wireless communication device, Lucie contacted Jason to explain that she and Cara were going to the restroom, so he should take this opportunity for a break.

"I'll be waiting for you outside the restrooms," Jason said.

After ordering drinks and putting their names on a short wait list, Cara and Lucie asked about the restroom and were given directions. The men's was on the left side and the women's on the right, both marked with cute primitive drawings, one of a man and the other of a woman. The poorly lit interior of the restroom was like a stucco cave, the walls painted a cinnamon-red, the two stalls a dark green, and the ceiling a mustard-yellow. There was an out-of-order sign nailed to one of the stall doors.

"You go first," Lucie said, as she removed her sunglasses and hung them on the elastic neckline of her blouse.

"No, go ahead." Cara removed her hat, fanned herself and then shoved her sunglasses up on top of her head. Then she put her heavy bags on the floor, laid her hat on top of the bags and removed her cell phone from her purse. "I should call Suelita and let her know not to expect us for dinner. I've been having so much fun that I forgot about our host and hostess."

Lucie placed her shopping bags on the floor beside Cara's, but she carried her purse with her as she shoved open the door of the in-working-order stall. "Don't leave the restroom."

"I won't," Cara said, then Lucie heard her begin a conversation with Senora Delgado, explaining where they were and what they were doing.

HECTOR AND PEPE entered the men's restroom directly behind Cara Bedell's bodyguard, the man who had done a good job of stalking his employer without being obvious about it. They each smiled and spoke to the American as they approached the urinals. After he finished and washed his hands, Pepe walked out of the restroom a couple of minutes ahead of his companion, just as they had planned. Their instructions had been clear. They had to do the job today.

Pepe lay in wait for the bodyguard. When he saw the man exiting the restroom, he went over to him, keeping his broad, toothy smile in place.

He tapped his naked wrist. "I do not have a watch. Do you know what time it is? My wife will be angry if I'm late."

Although it was obvious that the man was uncomfortable with Pepe's friendliness and probably suspected him of being up to no good, he didn't immediately reach for his concealed weapon. While Pepe tried to distract the bodyguard, Hector came out of the restroom, moved in behind the man with silent precision and before he could react, Hector drove his knife into the man's back, puncturing a kidney. Pepe grabbed the man as he slumped forward, holding his body upright. Hector assisted Pepe and together they dragged the dying man out into the alley behind the restaurant.

CHAPTER SIX

LUCIE CAME OUT of the bathroom stall and went straight to the single decorative sink to wash her hands. When she turned on the faucet, she discovered there was no warm water, so she hurried through the process. At least there was a stack of paper towels on the tiled shelf above the sink.

"I spoke to Suelita to let her know not to wait dinner for us." Cara hung the strap of her small leather bag over Lucie's shoulder. "Keep that for me, will you?" Then she disappeared into the stall.

Lucie checked her makeup in the mirror and decided that since they were going to eat soon there was no point in applying lipstick until later. Just as she readjusted her straw hat and removed her sunglasses from where she'd hooked them on her blouse, she heard the bathroom door squeak open. In her peripheral vision, she noticed a dark figure, and then suddenly realized a man had entered the ladies' room. Immediately sensing danger, she reached down for the Glock in her shoulder bag, but before she could reach it, the man wearing a fake beard and mustache lifted his foot and knocked her hand away from the purse. Pain shot through her hand

and up her arm, but she jumped back, hurriedly assessed the situation—one man, no visible weapon—and prepared to defend herself.

"Do not fight me, Senorita Bedell," the man said, in heavily accented English. "I do not wish to hurt you."

"What's going on out there?" Cara called from inside the stall.

"Stay where you are, Lucie," Lucie said to Cara, realizing that this man believed she was Cara Bedell. "Don't come out. Please, stay there. Do you hear me? Stay where you are. That's an order."

"You do not wish your bodyguard killed," he said. "That is good. You will cooperate, yes?"

The door opened again and another man, also wearing a fake beard and mustache and with a 9mm pistol pointed directly at Lucie, entered the room. He spoke rapidly to the other man in Spanish. Lucie wasn't able to make out everything he said, but she got the gist of it. They were going to kidnap Cara and kill her bodyguard. Only they thought Lucie was Cara and vice versa.

Damn, where was Jason? He was supposed to be waiting outside for them. If she hadn't been confident that he was watching their back, she wouldn't have been caught off guard this way.

"Wait," Lucie said, speaking directly to the two men. "Don't harm my bodyguard and I'll go with you without putting up a fight. Both of us will cooperate." Lucie glanced toward the stall door, which was easing open. God, she had to stop Cara. As long as these men thought she was their target and Cara stayed put, they both had a chance of coming out of this alive. "No, Lucie, please stay there and don't come out. Do as I say. I'm bargaining with these men for our lives."

"Uh…all right…Ms. Bedell," Cara said, her voice trembling.

Thank God, Cara had realized these men had mistaken Lucie for Cara.

The unarmed man grabbed Lucie, yanked Cara's shoulder bag down her arm and then tossed it on the floor. It took all her willpower not to fight him. If Cara's life wasn't on the line, she wouldn't hesitate to defend herself.

"You understand Spanish, senorita? I must remember that." He tugged on her arm. "Come with me." He glanced at the closed stall door. "Please stay there and do not try to follow us. If you disobey, it can mean death for you and Senorita Bedell."

"I—I'll stay here. I swear," Cara said.

Lucie knew that the only way to keep Cara safe was to continue the pretense and allow these men to believe that she was Cara Bedell. It was her job as Cara's bodyguard to be prepared to lay down her life, if necessary.

They hurried her out of the bathroom, down a poorly lit back hallway and out the door leading into the alley. A few feet away, shoved up against a row of stinking garbage cans, lay a man's crumpled, lifeless body. Now she knew why Jason hadn't come to their rescue. As they hurried her past the bloody corpse, she glanced back, praying that Cara could handle herself on her own and make the right decisions about what to do next. If Cara made even one mistake, Lucie was as good as dead.

CARA COUNTED to a hundred. Her hands shook. Her stomach churned, creating a bout of nausea. She had obeyed Lucie's orders, knowing her bodyguard's training served them both well. She had listened to the two men speaking in Spanish and realized that they believed Lucie was Cara and they intended to kidnap the American heiress and kill her bodyguard as they had killed the other one. That meant Jason was dead. And if she hadn't done exactly as Lucie had instructed, she, too, might be dead. Or she would be the one they had kidnapped and Lucie would be dead.

Cara eased open the stall door and peered out into the bathroom. Empty. She walked out into the room and took a deep, calming breath.

Stay here, think, reason this out and make a logical decision.

Jason was dead. Those men had killed him. She couldn't look to him for help. Oh, God, poor Jason. He had a wife and teenage son.

She was on her own. She could call the local police. Absolutely not. The San Luis police were part of the Amecan government, which was run by Ortega and his kind. She could call Felipe and Suelita. Maybe. She trusted them.

No, I can't call them. I can't risk having the truth about the abduction leak out here in San Luis. I have to buy time. I have to keep up the pretense as long as possible. Apparently the kidnappers think Lucie and I look enough alike that, at least for now, they don't know the difference. If they discover that they've abducted the wrong woman, that they took Lucie Evans instead of me,

*they'll kill her. I have to contact Deke. He'll know what
I should do to help Lucie and keep myself safe.*

She looked down at the floor beside the sink and saw
her shopping bags and Lucie's, too, side by side. They
had enjoyed their afternoon jaunt through the market.
Cara couldn't remember the last time she'd had so much
fun. She liked Lucie so much. She had to find a way to
save her.

She scanned the restroom and saw her purse lying
on the floor, as if it had been tossed aside. Cara bent
over, grabbed the purse and unzipped it. She rummaged
around inside until she found her cell phone. She
checked the information bars. Batteries fully charged.
But she couldn't stay here. Someone could come in at
any moment. Leaving the shopping bags where they
were, she opened the bathroom door. When she peeked
out into the hall, she heard the hum of voices and music
coming from the restaurant, but she didn't see anyone.
She slipped out into the hall.

Now what?

*Find a back entrance and leave quietly. Once you're
outside and in a safe spot, call Deke.*

She made her way quietly down a back hallway and
breathed a sigh of relief when she saw a door that she
thought probably led to the alley. After glancing over
her shoulder and seeing no one, she shoved open the
door and entered the putrid-smelling alleyway. Early
evening shadows fell across the dirt-and-gravel path.
The sun would set soon and it would be dark. She had
no time to waste.

Covering her nose with her hand as she approached

the trash cans, she gasped when she saw the man lying on the ground. Jason! She stifled the scream that vibrated in her throat. Oh, God. Oh, God!

There's nothing you can do for him now. Keep moving. Get away from this place. But where can I go? The church.

On their way here, she'd seen a church half a block from the Plaza Bazaar. She could find sanctuary there.

Cara removed her hat, threw it in one of the open trash cans and then ran her hand through her shoulder-length hair. Perspiration bubbled on her forehead and upper lip and rivulets of sweat glided from between her breasts to her belly button. All but running down the alley, away from Jason's body and the sickening garbage odor, she stayed in the back alleys as much as possible, but had no choice but to slip in and out of the marketplace, which amazingly was still crowded with people, mostly tourists. She could see the entrance to the plaza. Safety was nearby. The church was close.

After slipping into the alley behind a pottery shop, she sucked in deep breaths of semifresh air. With twilight fast approaching, she hit the number that put her directly through to Deke Bronson's cell phone.

He answered on the third ring. "Good evening, Ms. Bedell."

"Deke, we… I have a situation here. I need help and I need it immediately."

"Where are Jason and Lucie?"

"Gone. Jason's dead and Lucie has been kidnapped."

"Are you all right?"

"For the time being, but I won't be for long and

neither will Lucie." She hurriedly explained what had happened, not pausing until she had given Deke all the details.

"You have no idea who these men were or why they kidnapped Lucie…that is, why they kidnapped Lucie thinking she was you?"

"No idea whatsoever."

"For your safety and Lucie's, we have to keep the fact that they kidnapped the wrong woman a secret," Deke told her.

"Yes, I've already figured that out. So how do we do that?"

"Do you have somewhere you can go for a few hours, somewhere no one will notice you or bother you? A movie theater or—"

"A church," Cara said.

"A church would be perfect."

"There's one nearby. I can go there. But what then?"

"I'll get in touch with Sawyer McNamara. Dundee's has contacts all over the world. My guess is that they have someone there in San Luis. I'll try to call you back and give you the name and a description of your contact person, but I'm going to give you an ID phrase you can use and the response to expect from your contact." He recited the comment and the response. "This person will take you somewhere you'll be safe until we can get to Ameca, hopefully by early morning."

"Whoever kidnapped Lucie kidnapped her thinking they have a billionaire to bargain with," Cara said. "I'm authorizing you to do whatever is necessary to meet their demands. Gray will be in charge of Bedell, Inc.

temporarily and he and the board can authorize the release of whatever ransom is requested."

"Let's not put the cart before the horse," Deke told her. "We don't know for sure money is the reason she was abducted. Don't forget that Cara Bedell is supposed to make a multimillion-dollar deal with one of two oil companies vying for her favor."

"Oh, God, I as good as told Tomas Castillo today at lunch that I would probably sign with Delgado Oil. You don't think Castillo ordered my kidnapping, do you?"

"There's no way to know for sure. Not yet. That's why you cannot trust anyone down there and it's the reason no one, and I mean no one, even Grayson Perkins, can know that you weren't the one kidnapped."

Cara started to protest, and then in a clearly lucid moment, she realized that Deke was right. Gray might let the truth slip and if he did...

"I understand," Cara said. "I'll go to the church and wait for your call or for a person who can reply correctly to my comment."

"Repeat it for me."

"I'm not Catholic. I hope it's all right that I've come here to pray. That's what I say. And the correct response is I'm not Catholic, either, but I come here every night and pray to live to be a hundred and three, just as my grandmother did."

"Cara, be careful. For now, you've got not only your own life in your hands, but Lucie's, too."

"Do you think they'll hurt her?"

Deke cleared his throat. "That depends."

"On what?"

"On the reason they kidnapped her."

LUCIE DIDN'T STRUGGLE against the ropes that bound her hands and feet nor did she try to chew through the rag effectively gagging her. Her kidnappers were not amateurs. It was obvious that they had done this type of thing before and were taking no chances. Shoved into the trunk of an older model Ford Taurus, she had no idea in which direction the driver was headed. They would take her somewhere isolated and secluded, which meant in the basement of a building or out in the country. She estimated that they'd been on the road for nearly an hour, but she couldn't be sure of the time. An hour's drive meant that they had left San Luis. Since the ocean was to the east and the border was less than fifty miles north, that meant either south or west. The nearest village to the south was…? Think, damn it, Lucie, think. Mundaca. If they went west, there were miles of tropical forests and dozens of small villages. But what if, for some reason, they hadn't left San Luis and were simply driving around the city?

Either way, it didn't matter. She had no way to contact anyone. She was on her own. Escape might not be an option, so she had two immediate goals: stay alive and keep her abductors in the dark about her true identity. She had to count on Cara knowing what to do.

Please, God, let her call Deke. And let her stay out of sight until he sends help.

SAWYER FINISHED his workout in the basement gym, which he had designed himself. He prided himself on staying in tip-top physical condition and he had to admit that every year past thirty-five had increased the struggle. He stripped out of his jogging shorts and stepped into the steam room. He sat down, leaned back and relaxed as the warm steam enveloped him. Nothing of any importance in his life had changed in the past few weeks. He had maintained his routine—work five days a week, personal time on the weekends. For the past three weeks, he had taken a different lady out every Friday and every Saturday night, dating more often than he usually did. At forty, he went in for quality over quantity in most aspects of his life, including sex.

At his age, most men were married and either had children or were seriously planning for children. He had been engaged once, years ago, but he'd never really been in love. Hell, he wasn't even sure if he believed there was such a thing, at least not for him. Lust, yes. Love, no.

He knew what lust was, the kind of lust that drove a man to do things he would never otherwise do. The kind of lust that could make him betray—

Damn, don't go there! You can't turn back the clock and change what happened nine years ago. She's gone, out of your life for good. Let it go, all the regrets, all the guilt. Move forward. Don't look back.

Lucie Evans wasn't around any longer to remind him of what a fool he'd been. She wouldn't be marching into his office and chewing his ass out ever again. His Waterford paperweight was safe. And he was safe from temptation.

Twenty minutes later, as he emerged from the steam room, his naked body drenched and dripping with perspiration, he heard his cell phone ringing. He grabbed a towel off the bar near the door, wiped his face and hands, and hung the towel around his neck. By the time he reached the plastic holder on the treadmill he'd used earlier and retrieved his phone, it had stopped ringing. But no sooner had he checked the caller's identity than it started ringing again.

He answered, "Hello, Deke."

"Does Dundee's have any reliable contacts in San Luis, Ameca?"

Sawyer's gut tightened. "What's happened?"

"Jason Little, one of Cara's bodyguards, has been killed, Lucie has been kidnapped and Cara has gone into hiding," Deke said and then went on to explain the entire situation. "We need to get someone to Cara as quickly as possible. She needs to be kept hidden and protected until—"

"Dundee's will handle it," Sawyer said. He ignored the pounding of his heart and the sick feeling in the pit of his stomach. "Unless you're planning on going down there yourself, my agents are far better qualified to handle this type of situation than your Bedell security force."

"I'm well aware of that fact. I need Dundee's. My suggestion, if you want it, is to send in Geoff Monday to find Lucie and send another agent to get Cara out of Ameca as soon as possible. I'll arrange a safe place for her here, somewhere she can go and stay out of sight until this thing plays out."

"I'll make some phone calls immediately and find out who we've got in Ameca, maybe even in San Luis,"

Sawyer said. "Give me those phrases again so I can pass them along to the contact."

Deke repeated the code sentences.

"I'm going to call Sam. He's got contacts in Washington that I don't have. We're going to need to get Cara out of the country without a passport and keep up the pretense that she's Lucie Evans."

"It's a damn good thing that Cara and Lucie are about the same height and size and they both have red hair. Apparently the kidnappers didn't know the difference."

"Apparently not." Although the two women were both nearly six-foot-tall redheads, Sawyer couldn't see how anyone would mistake one for the other. Cara Bedell had hazel-blue eyes and was freckled, attractive but not pretty, and a good twenty pounds heavier than Lucie. Lucie had a mane of curly auburn hair. Her skin was flawless, not a freckle in sight. And she was beautiful.

"I suppose all tall redheaded American women look the same to them," Deke said. "Let's just hope for Lucie's sake that these guys don't realize their mistake."

"If they do, they'll kill Lucie." The words cut him to the quick. He might want Lucie out of his life, but he didn't want her dead.

CHAPTER SEVEN

SAWYER CONTACTED Daisy Holbrook, gave her a succinct briefing and asked her to find out if Dundee's had a contact in Ameca.

"Get back to me ASAP."

Then he called Sam Dundee and explained in more detail what had happened to Lucie and Cara Bedell. Sam assured him that he would use his government connections to arrange for Cara to leave Ameca and reenter the U.S. without a passport.

"Your plan is for one of our agents to accompany Ms. Bedell back to Chattanooga or wherever Deke arranges a safe place for her to stay until Lucie is rescued. And you're sending a couple of agents to Ameca to find Lucie. Who are you sending?" Sam asked. "I suggest Geoff Monday and—"

"Monday is my next phone call," Sawyer told him. "And I'm going with him. I intend to personally handle this operation."

"Do you think that's wise considering your past history with Lucie?"

"I'm going. Don't try to talk me out of it."

"It's been a while since you've been in the field. Don't you think—?"

"Just take care of things on this end," Sawyer said. "I'll find Lucie and bring her home."

Minutes after he got off the phone with Sam, Daisy called. "Our contact in Ameca is female. A lady named Rita Herrera. Lucky for us, she just happens to live in San Luis."

"Good. I need to reach her immediately," Sawyer said. "And I have to round up Geoff Monday and—"

"I've already called Geoff and he's getting in touch with Ty. I just told them that they were to meet you at airport in an hour. You can fill them in on what's happened en route to Ameca. The Dundee jet is being fueled and will be ready to leave in an hour and a half."

Sawyer grunted. "You're one step ahead of me, aren't you?"

"I assumed you'd want Geoff, considering his SAS background, as your partner when you go in to rescue Lucie. And Ty is available and qualified to handle getting Ms. Bedell out of Ameca."

"How did you know I'd be going myself and not sending—? Don't answer that. Forget I asked."

"You'd never send someone else to save Lucie," Daisy said quietly, almost reverently.

"I just hope we can save her. The odds aren't in our favor."

If the kidnappers even suspected that they had abducted the wrong woman, they would kill Lucie. And if she didn't use her brains and make logical decisions and not emotional ones, she didn't have a prayer.

"If anyone can save her, you can. You and Geoff."

Sawyer clenched his teeth together and closed his

eyes. He wished he believed in the power of prayer. If he did, he'd get down on his knees right here and now.

"Daisy?"

"Yes, sir?"

"If you think praying will help—"

"I've already been praying," she told him. "And I'll keep on praying until all of you return home safely."

LOW-WATTAGE wall sconces and flickering candlelight illuminated the interior of the small church where Cara had been waiting for her contact for over two hours. After entering the building, she had rummaged in her purse and found a monogrammed handkerchief that she'd opened and placed on her head, doing so out of respect for church tradition. She had chosen a pew in the middle of the sanctuary, halfway between the entrance and a side exit door, and then had sat down, removed her cell phone from her purse, set it on Vibrate and slipped it into her skirt pocket. Once her eyesight adjusted to the dim light, she had glanced around and noticed a handful of people scattered about, including a young priest. She'd bowed her head and prayed in earnest.

The tingling sensation against her hip alerted her that her phone was ringing. Keeping her head bowed, she eased the phone out of her pocket and nearly dropped it because her hands were trembling. She noted the caller ID and answered quietly.

"Yes?" she whispered.

"Her name is Rita Herrera," Sawyer said. "She should be there in the next thirty minutes."

"You're sure I can trust her?"

Sawyer hesitated. "Yes, I'm sure. Her credentials are solid gold."

"Okay." Cara wasn't sure exactly what solid gold meant, but she guessed it didn't really matter. All she needed to know was that Rita Herrera was going to help her.

"How are you doing?"

"Holding it together," she told him. "Barely."

"I'm on my way to the airport right now. Geoff Monday and Ty Garrett are flying in with me. We should be there sometime early in the morning."

Cara knew both Geoff and Ty. The last time she had hired Dundee's, they had been two of the agents she employed, along with Deke Bronson, who was now her chief of security at Bedell, Inc.

"Y'all don't know anything about Lucie, do you?" she asked. "Has anyone contacted Grayson about a ransom?"

"No word on Lucie. And I don't expect we'll hear from the kidnappers until tomorrow."

"If anything happens to her, it'll be my fault. She let them believe she was Cara Bedell. She did it to save me."

"Lucie was doing her job. She's been trained to protect the client and be willing to risk her life if it's necessary. In this case, Lucie believed it was necessary."

"You'll do everything you can to save her, won't you?"

"Everything humanly possible," Sawyer said. "Now sit tight and wait for Senora Herrera."

"I will."

Cara slipped the phone back into her skirt pocket and waited. Suddenly she noticed the young priest coming in her direction. What if he spoke to her? What if he asked her why she'd been here praying for nearly two hours? She kept her head bowed as he approached. When he paused by the pew where she sat, she glanced at him. He smiled and nodded. She returned his smile. Her heartbeat roared in her ears. He hesitated, as if expecting her to ask for his help, but when she returned to her prayers, he moved on without speaking to her.

Thank you, God.

Although not more than thirty minutes had passed when a small, plump woman in her early forties slid into the pew beside Cara, it seemed as if it had been hours since Sawyer called her.

"Hello, Senorita Evans," the black-eyed woman said in almost perfect English. "I am Rita Herrera."

"Hello, Senora," Cara said, then recited the phrase she'd been told to use to ID the contact person. "I'm not Catholic. I hope it's all right that I've come here to pray."

"I'm not Catholic, either, but I come here every night and pray to live to be a hundred and three, just as my grandmother did."

Cara felt a rush of tears burn her eyes. "I'm very glad to meet you, Senora Herrera."

The woman clasped Cara's hand. "Call me Rita. Come with me. My car is waiting outside."

"Where are we going?"

"I have rented a room for us at Hotel Rosita, less than a mile from the airport. That's where we'll wait for your friends."

"WHAT DO YOU MEAN Cara has been kidnapped?" Grayson Perkins demanded as he glowered at Deke Bronson. "What the hell were her bodyguards doing?"

Deke had phoned the Bedell, Inc. vice president and told him there was a security emergency that needed his immediate attention. Perkins had requested Deke meet him in his plush office at the company's downtown headquarters.

"Jason Little is dead," Deke said.

Perkins gasped.

"And Lucie Evans barely escaped with her life." He had no intention of sharing the truth with Grayson Perkins. The fewer people who knew, the better. Besides, Perkins was, for all his business acumen, an idiot. A charming, handsome idiot, but an idiot all the same.

"Do you have any idea who did this?" Perkins asked. "Or why?"

"No. We have to wait and hope someone makes contact. I want your permission to do whatever I deem advisable here at Bedell headquarters."

"Yes, of course."

"I've already spoken with Sawyer McNamara. He and several Dundee agents will go to Ameca and bring Lucie Evans home. I took it upon myself to authorize Dundee's to keep agents in Ameca."

"Why keep agents in Ameca?"

"For the time being, we're not involving the local San Luis authorities. Ms. Bedell's abduction could have international repercussions if it's known that Amecan citizens kidnapped her. We want our own team in place, hopefully to exchange a ransom for Ms. Bedell."

"Yes, yes, I see. Of course. You're the expert, Mr. Bronson. Cara wouldn't have hired you to replace Larry Nesmith if she didn't trust you implicitly. You certainly have my permission to do whatever you deem necessary to save Cara."

"Thank you. And you should be prepared to arrange for a large sum of money to be transferred from Bedell, Inc. to a bank in San Luis."

"Yes, I…yes, certainly." Perkins shook his head. "I can't believe this has happened. But I suppose, considering how wealthy Cara is… If anything happens to her, I'm not sure I can go on. You know what she means to me."

"Yes, sir, I do."

Deke wanted to tell this preening peacock not to waste his crocodile tears on him. From what he'd learned about Grayson Perkins the past couple of years, the man was a leech who had married one Bedell sister for her wealth and now would love to marry the other for the same reason. Deke's wife, Lexie, was one of Cara Bedell's best friends and she confided in Lexie. Perkins was the last man on earth Cara would ever consider marrying.

"If there is a ransom phone call, we'll monitor it," Deke said. "As the VP temporarily in charge of Bedell, Inc., you will have to authorize payment, but either I or one of the Dundee agents will negotiate with the kidnappers."

"As I said, I'll leave everything in your capable hands."

"Good. I suggest you go home and try to rest. If we're contacted tonight, I'll get in touch with you immediately."

"Do you think I should stay? I can sleep on the sofa here in my office."

"If you'd prefer to do that, then yes, stay."

"Oh, well…yes, I'll do that."

It was obvious that Perkins had not really wanted to stay and hadn't expected Deke to agree with his suggestion.

"If you'll excuse me, Mr. Perkins, I have work to do."

As he walked out of the luxurious office, Deke knew who he had to contact next. Although he had asked for Perkins' consent to take charge of the situation, he had already done just that. Everything was set for a ransom call. All he had to do was wait.

When he exited the elevator and headed for his office on the first floor of the Bedell Building, he nodded at the two guards on duty at the entrance. Once at his desk, he placed a call to Lt. Bain Desmond, who answered on the fourth ring.

"Yeah, Bronson, do you need a cop or are you just calling a friend?" Desmond asked.

"I need to speak to the man who loves Cara Bedell." *No use beating around the bush. Just tell it like it is.*

"What's wrong?"

"First thing you need to know is that Cara's all right, as far as I know."

"What do you mean as far as you know?"

"I just informed Grayson Perkins that Cara Bedell has been kidnapped."

"Cara's been—"

"Shut up and listen. Lucie Evans has been kidnapped," Deke said. "A case of mistaken identity. Lucie let the kidnappers believe she was Cara in order to protect Cara."

"Good God! Is Ms. Evans—?"

"We don't know. We haven't heard from the kidnappers and have no idea who they are or why they wanted to abduct Cara Bedell." Deke went on to give Bain the details of who, what, when and where.

"I'll get in touch with the chief tonight and request a leave of absence," Desmond said. "I'm going to guard Cara, got that? No Bedell security guards, no Dundee agents."

"I thought that's what you'd want."

"Damn right it is."

"If all goes as planned, Ty Garrett will bring her back to the U.S. sometime tomorrow. You'll need to make arrangements tonight and get back to me. Find someplace safe to keep her until we get Lucie back."

"I need to make one phone call," Desmond said. "To my sister. Her in-laws have a place in the mountains. Only one way in and one way out and no place for a chopper to land. She should be able to get the keys to me in a few hours. If she does, I'll want Ty and Cara to fly into the Knoxville airport and I'll be there to pick her up."

"I'll let Sawyer know."

"How's Cara, really?"

"Last I heard, she's fine. The lady handled this situation like a pro."

"That's my girl."

"Get in touch as soon as you know for sure. In the meantime, I'll be here in my office at Bedell, Inc."

"Waiting for the kidnappers to call."

"Hoping they call."

LUCIE FELT THE balmy night air drift across her face and arms as a pair of rough hands dragged her up and out of the car trunk. The man tossed her onto the ground, then reached down and untied her hands and ankles.

He grabbed her by her hair and yanked. "Get up."

She finally managed to stand on wobbly legs after several failed attempts. She glanced around, but saw nothing except a lone flickering light coming from a nearby window. Candlelight? Did that mean there was no electricity?

He punched her in the back with the gun he held. "Move."

As she started walking toward the open door to what she thought was a one-story house, she cast her gaze skyward. The half moon was partially obscured by clouds. There wasn't a star to be seen. Listening for a recognizable sound, she heard the heartbeat of the wooded area surrounding them, the nocturnal hum made by insects and animals. She realized then that her captors had taken her out of San Luis and driven west, probably into the tropical forest that covered one-eighth of the country.

Even if she had some means of communicating with the outside world, what could she tell them? *I'm being held captive in the tropical forest, somewhere an hour or two outside the capital city?* How many thousands of acres did that cover?

This is no time to feel sorry for yourself or give up

hope. It's early days yet. Just bide your time, keep a cool head and continue pretending you're Cara Bedell. If Cara has done her part, no one will know that she is the one who is safe and her bodyguard was the woman abducted.

When she entered the house, one of her bearded kidnappers waited for her inside while the other stood behind her. She paused and looked around at the small, sparsely furnished room. What she had thought was a candle when she'd looked through the window was actually a kerosene lantern sitting on a rectangular table behind an old stained sofa and a tattered easy chair. A pair of straight-backed chairs rested against the back wall.

"Take her in the bedroom and lock the door," a voice came out of the darkness. It was then that she noticed the shadowy figure standing in the corner. He kept out of sight so that the only thing she saw was his scuffed boots and the outline of his stocky body. "Leave Manuel with me. We'll take the first watch."

The man who had dragged her out of the car trunk clutched her arm and yanked her along with him as he headed toward the back of what appeared to be a small, run-down house. He opened the door on the right of the narrow, shallow hallway, and then shoved her into the room and closed the door. The distinct click of the lock told her that he had followed orders. The room was pitch-black except for miniscule shards of light seeping through what she surmised were cracks in the windows that had been boarded up, probably from the outside. Putting her hands out in front of her to use as sensors, she took several tentative steps back toward the door, then pressed her ear against the door and listened.

The distance between this room and the room where her kidnappers were muffled the sound of their voices. She couldn't make out anything they said.

She needed to get the lay of the land, so to speak. With her arms open wide, she felt her way around the walls. Her leg bumped into something that came up from the floor and reached her midthigh. Using her hands to see, she felt of the object and realized she had found the bed. After making her way around to the foot of the bed, she returned to her trek around the walls. By the time she made it back to the bed, she had discovered that the bed and a table were the only pieces of furniture in the room. She had also discovered that the door through which she entered was the only door and the two windows had indeed been boarded over from the outside.

What were the odds that she might be able to kick the boards loose and escape without her captors hearing her?

Slim to none.

Right. Even if she managed to escape, she might find herself in the middle of the forest, alone and lost. So that meant being a good little girl and not causing trouble. At least for now.

Lucie sat down on the edge of the bed. The lumpy mattress sagged beneath her weight. She slid her hand down inside her blouse, inserted two fingers and her thumb into her bra and searched for the object she had hidden there. Her fingertips encountered the small, closed switchblade. Using the weapon would be a last resort. If she sensed that they were going to kill her, she would choose her battle, hopefully against only one of them, and give him the fight of his life.

RITA HERRERA and Cara waited at the Hotel Rosita, an old but clean lodge on the outskirts of San Luis. Rita had retrieved canned colas and packs of crackers from a vending machine and offered them to Cara. She'd drunk one of the colas, but had turned down the crackers. She didn't think she could eat a bite. Her stomach was tied in so many knots she doubted it would ever recover. All she could think about was Lucie. Was she still alive? If so, how was she being treated? Had she been beaten? Raped? Tortured? What price was she paying for protecting Cara?

Being less than a mile from the airport, they could hear planes taking off and landing and could see the lights from the tower and the runway in the distance. Cara stood by the windows and stared out into the night.

She altered between pacing the floor and standing by the windows. Filled with nervous energy, she simply couldn't stay still. On the other hand, Rita sat in one of two uncomfortable-looking chairs and watched the nineteen-inch television. She had the sound turned down low, so Cara could hear only a quiet rumble of Spanish.

Rita's phone rang. Cara gasped and they both jumped even though they had been expecting the call.

Rita put the phone to her ear. "Yes?"

Cara turned away from the windows and watched Rita.

"The Hotel Rosita. Room twelve." She paused and listened. "Yes, we'll wait here." When she ended the conversation, she looked at Cara. "That was Sawyer McNamara. The Dundee jet just landed. He and his agents are meeting us here."

Cara nodded. "Is that all he said?"

"He did not mention the woman who was kidnapped, if that is what concerns you."

"I don't know much about these things, but it's been hours since she was taken. Shouldn't they have contacted someone by now to ask for ransom?"

"Not necessarily," Rita replied. "It is possible that the men responsible for the kidnapping have to report to someone else. If that is the case, it may be tomorrow before any demands are made."

"Do you think there's a chance that they won't kill her?"

"That depends on too many different things for me to be able to give you an opinion."

Cara nodded. Rita didn't want to speculate on the odds that Lucie Evans would or would not come out of this alive.

Fifteen minutes later, a soft knock on the door, followed by the sound of Sawyer McNamara's voice, alerted them that the cavalry had arrived. Rita peered through the viewfinder, then cracked the door, all the while holding her 9mm in her hand. She and Sawyer exchanged hushed words, then she lowered her weapon and opened the door.

Sawyer rushed into the room. Cara cried out and ran straight into his arms. "Thank God, you're here. You have to find Lucie." Tears seeped from her eyes and trickled down her cheeks.

Sawyer grasped her by the shoulders and shook her gently. "Listen to me, Ms. Bedell. You're leaving right now with Ty Garrett for the airport. The Dundee jet is waiting for you. Arrangements have already been made for you to simply board the plane. Do you understand?"

"Yes and no. I—I don't have Lucie's passport or—"

"That's been taken care of," Sawyer told her. "All you have to do is keep pretending you're Lucie Evans. There should be no problems either here or once y'all land in Knoxville."

"Knoxville?"

"Your bodyguard will be waiting there at the airport when you and Ty land. Ty will turn you over to him and he will take you to a safe place. Even I don't know the exact location. He's the only one of us who does. You'll stay with him until we rescue Lucie."

"You're going to try to rescue her? But how? You don't know where she is, do you?"

"Not yet. But that's not your concern right now. All I want you to think about is staying with Ty, following his directions, and getting out of Ameca and back on U.S. soil."

"What about Felipe and Suelita? They must be worried sick by now, wondering where I am."

"We took care of that," Sawyer told her. "Deke contacted them and told them that there had been a business emergency, and you had flown home immediately. He explained that it might be a week or more before you'd get a chance to speak to them personally. If there's one thing Felipe Delgado understands, it's the urgency of handling a business problem."

She grabbed Sawyer's arm. "Please, keep me posted on what's happening. Contact the agent you've assigned to guard me and give us updates."

"We'll try."

Sawyer walked her to the door where Ty Garrett and Geoff Monday waited outside in the hallway. She offered each man a wavering smile, then looked at Ty.

"I'm ready to go."

He nodded, took her arm and led her down the hall to the back stairs. She paused, glanced over her shoulder and saw Geoff Monday and Sawyer rejoin Rita Herrera in the rented room.

"Don't worry," Ty told her. "They'll find her even if Sawyer has to tear apart Ameca brick by brick, tree by tree, mountain by mountain, and person by person."

CHAPTER EIGHT

THE DUNDEE JET landed at the McGhee Tyson airport outside Knoxville, Tennessee. Cara, wearing a scarf and sunglasses, emerged from the private plane. Dundee Agent Ty Garrett escorted her straight to…Bain Desmond! Oh, God, it really was Bain. She broke free from Ty's grasp on her elbow and ran straight into Bain's arms. He hugged her to him, his strong arms wrapped possessively around her. For the first time since Lucie had been kidnapped, Cara felt safe. Truly safe.

Bain grasped her shoulders and pushed her away from him, just far enough to look into her eyes. "You're okay?" he asked, concern in his voice.

She nodded. "I am now."

"I've been instructed to turn her over to you," Ty told Bain. "Any communication should go through the Dundee office. Speak only to Daisy Holbrook and no one else. She will forward messages to you and from you. Understand?"

"Yeah, I understand." Bain grasped Cara's elbow. "I've got a rental car waiting for us." He glanced at Ty. "No luggage?"

"No," Ty replied.

"All I have is what I'm wearing," Cara said. "I don't even have a toothbrush."

"That's not a problem. I figured you'd need some stuff. I took care of it." He nudged her elbow. "The sooner we get out of here, the better. Keep the sunglasses and scarf on, even in the car."

Bain shook hands with Ty, who then turned to leave. Was he going back to Ameca? Or just home to Atlanta? She didn't know and hadn't even thought to ask.

"Please, make sure someone let's me know about Lucie," Cara called to Ty. *Her quick thinking may well have saved my life.*

Ty paused, glanced over his shoulder and nodded before he headed straight for the Dundee jet.

Bain led her past two federal officers, who did little more than glance at her before stepping aside to allow them to leave the airport without going through any checkpoints. The compact rental sedan waiting for them in the parking lot was a nondescript black midsize vehicle. Bain opened the passenger door and helped her get in, and then he rounded the hood, opened the driver's door and slid behind the wheel.

"Where are we going?" she asked.

"My sister's in-laws have a place in the mountains, in the Gatlinburg area. It's pretty secluded and you'd just about have to know exactly where you were going to find it. Her in-laws are on a six-week tour of Europe so there's no chance of them or anyone else showing up unexpectedly."

Bain eased the car out of the parking area and onto

the highway. He focused on the road ahead, not even glancing at Cara.

She settled into the slightly worn cloth seat, adjusted the scarf covering her hair, and leaned back against the cushioned headrest. "I didn't expect to see you when we landed. I thought there would be another Dundee agent waiting for me."

"You didn't honestly think I'd trust anyone else to protect you, did you?"

His hands on the wheel tightened.

"What about your job?"

"I took a leave of absence for personal reasons." He glanced at her then, cutting his eyes quickly in her direction and then looking back at the road.

"Deke called you, I guess. Right?"

"Yeah."

"Deke knows, he and Lexie." Cara stared at Bain's sharply chiseled profile, his well-defined cheekbones and chin. "They know about us, how we feel about each other."

"Yeah."

He wasn't going to discuss their relationship. He never wanted to talk about how they felt about each other. But they each knew, without saying it, exactly how the other felt. They were in love. Hopelessly in love. But Bain Desmond, damn old-fashioned man that he was, wouldn't marry a woman worth billions when he lived week-to-week on a Chattanooga police lieutenant's salary.

"I can't believe this has happened, that someone actually tried to kidnap me." Cara hugged her arms around her waist, crossing her arms and cupping her elbows. "If they hurt Lucie…if they kill her, it will be my fault."

"How do you figure that?"

"First of all, I'm the one who wanted to go to the open market in San Luis and act like a regular tourist. And secondly, Lucie let the kidnappers believe that she was Cara Bedell. She exchanged identities with me to save my life."

"While you were gallivanting around playing tourist, you had two trained bodyguards with you. Both of them did their job. That's why you're safe."

"Jason's dead and Lucie may pay with her life."

"That could have happened no matter where you were or what you were doing. Jason Little and Lucie Evans knew the risks involved in bodyguard duty. Lucie's odds of surviving are greater than yours would have been. She knows what to do and what not to do as a hostage."

"If they find out that she really isn't Cara Bedell… Oh, God, Bain, they'll kill her for sure, won't they?"

Bain huffed. "You have to stop thinking like that or you'll go nuts. What you have to concentrate on is doing your part to keep Lucie safe. That means hiding away and keeping totally out of sight until Lucie is rescued. My job is to protect you." He took a deep breath. "I'm not going to let anyone hurt you. I'll die first."

Cara swallowed the swell of emotion in her throat. She was on the verge of tears and that would never do. She wasn't the weepy type. Never had been and she sure as hell wasn't going to be one now, not when strength and courage were needed in double portions.

Over an hour later, they finally approached the cabin. When he'd said this place was secluded, he hadn't been kidding. The word *secluded* was an understatement. The narrow roads into the mountain high above downtown Gatlinburg crisscrossed and intersected again and again, many cutting off into little more than gravel pig trails like this one. The path took them deep into a wooded area where a single cabin lay hidden, surrounded by the forest and situated on the edge of a sloping cliff.

Bain pulled the car off the gravel road, onto a side yard, and killed the engine. After undoing his seat belt, he turned to Cara. "Mary Ann and Keith know that I'm here, but they don't know why or that anyone is with me. I told them it was a combination of personal and business and I'd explain later. The fewer people who know you're here, the better."

Cara tried to smile, but couldn't quite manage it.

"I came up here early this morning and brought in enough supplies to last for a month," he told her. "I picked up some toiletries for you. Shampoo, deodorant, a toothbrush, toothpaste, some feminine hygiene items and some makeup. I guessed about the right colors." His gaze caressed her face.

"God, I must look awful." She undid her seat belt and scooted over so that she could look at herself in the interior rearview mirror. Damn, it was even worse than she'd thought. No lipstick, makeup gone except for smudged eye liner, and every freckle on her face glistened like newly minted copper pennies.

When she groaned and closed her eyes, Bain slid his

arm around her shoulders. Her eyes popped open. He was close, almost nose-to-nose with her. She drew in a gasping breath.

"You look beautiful to me," he said, his voice a raspy whisper.

"Oh, Bain." Tears misted her eyes.

He cupped the back of her head, pulled her to him and kissed her. Hungrily. Thankfully. And she returned his kiss, glad to be alive, joyously, crazily happy to be here with him.

He ended the kiss, eased away from her and blew out a hot breath. "I needed that. But from here on out, I'll be on my best behavior." He opened the car door and got out.

Cara sat there for a couple of seconds, allowing her breathing to return to normal. Bain jerked open the passenger door and held out his hand. "This place is pretty rustic. You'll be roughing it. There is electricity, indoor plumbing and hot and cold running water, but that's about it. No TV, but there's a radio and an old record player and a bookcase full of books."

"Compared to what Lucie's going through, this will be paradise." She looked at him longingly. While Lucie's life hung in the balance, Cara would be here with the man she loved, safe and secure. If Lucie came out of this alive, Cara would owe her more than she'd ever be able to repay.

LUCIE HAD BEEN allowed to use the outhouse behind the ramshackle adobe cottage. The bed where she had caught a few hours of sleep during the night was lumpy and the sheets were old and tattered. But since she wasn't itching this morning, she assumed it was free of bedbugs. One of her keepers had brought her a bucket of water, a bar of soap, and a rag, and she took full advantage of all three to wash herself. She would have liked to use the water to wash out her panties, but she wasn't going to remove them, wash them and hang them up to dry where her jailers could see them. So far, they hadn't tried to touch her intimately and she wanted to keep it that way.

When she'd been outside, she had scanned the area and done her best not to be obvious about surveying the landscape. With the sun just coming up in the east, she got her bearings, but little good it would do her unless she found a way to escape. They were in the middle of the tropical forest and Lucie had no idea in which direction the nearest village lay. And even if she could make it to a village, would there be any telephone service?

She could possibly overpower one guard, but probably not two, even if she could manage to cut one guard's throat. Her best bet for the time being was to sit tight and find out if they intended to exchange her for a ransom or if, when all was said and done, they intended to kill her.

Just as she finished bathing and tossed the rag into the dingy water, the bedroom door flung open and a man she didn't recognize entered. He frowned as he placed a mug and something wrapped in cloth on the table.

He spoke to her in Spanish. "Eat now."

Lucie nodded. She'd be damned if she'd say "thank you."

He picked up the bucket of dirty water by the handle, walked out of the room and locked the door behind him.

Lucie heaved a deep sigh.

Apparently there had been a changing of the guards, which meant that the one in charge of her now was fresh and alert, less likely to succumb to lack of sleep. There were probably four of them taking shifts. Twelve-hour shifts? Her instincts told her that these men were working for someone, which meant whoever had hired them was giving the orders, but staying out of sight.

Lucie glanced at the mug on the table. What were the odds that there was coffee in the mug? She walked over, picked up the mug and looked down at the dark liquid inside. After smelling it, she surmised that it was indeed coffee. She took a sip. Bitter, black and lukewarm. But it was coffee. She eyed the other item. *Please, let whatever it is—be edible.* She unwrapped the cloth and discovered two tortillas. Her stomach rumbled. She hadn't eaten since lunch yesterday and she was hungry. She grabbed a tortilla, ate it quickly and washed it down with the coffee. Then she ate the other one more slowly and finished off the remainder of the almost-cold brew.

Well, at least she was being treated humanely. No sexual advances. A bed to sleep in. Bathroom privileges. A whore's bath. And food. It was more than some prisoners got from their captors.

They intend to keep you alive and healthy. At least for now.

She had to remain calm and not react emotionally. Surely Cara had gotten in touch with Deke Bronson. *Please, God, please.* And Deke would have contacted Dundee's immediately. No matter how much Sawyer despised her, he wouldn't let her die. He was too honorable to let that happen. He would take charge of the situation and probably send in a couple of agents to try to find her while they negotiated with her kidnappers.

Not her kidnappers. Cara Bedell's kidnappers.

She had to trust that Cara knew what had to be done and was now in Dundee custody, hidden away somewhere for safekeeping.

Lucie felt certain that she was relatively safe for the time being. Whoever had hired these men to kidnap her wanted something. Either money or perhaps even Cara's signature on a contract with one of the Amecan oil companies. Once the ransom had been paid, would they let her go free? Possibly.

No use pacing nervously around the room. That would accomplish nothing. Instead, she sat on the floor and began a series of exercises. Physical and mental exercise, along with eating every scrap of food they brought her and drinking every drop of liquid, would help keep her alert and prepared for whatever happened.

THE CALL CAME IN at Bedell, Inc. headquarters at noon the day after Cara Bedell had been abducted. Although the call had been directed to Grayson Perkins, Deke Bronson answered the vice president's phone.

"Mr. Perkins?" the voice asked, and Deke caught a hint of an accent.

"This is Deke Bronson, chief of Bedell security."

"I wish to speak to—"

"Mr. Perkins has authorized me to take all of his calls."

"I see." He paused briefly as if considering what this unforeseen development meant. "Very well. Listen carefully. Your employer's life depends on your doing exactly as you're told."

"I understand." Deke motioned to Ty Garrett, who was in charge of tracing all phone calls and switching calls from one location to another. Ty nodded.

"I want twenty-five million dollars."

"That's a great deal of money."

"It is a small amount compared to your employer's vast holdings. I will give Mr. Perkins five days to—"

"I want to speak to Ms. Bedell," Deke said. "I want proof that she is alive and unharmed."

"Mr. Perkins has five days," he repeated. "I will call you four days from now and give you the account number for where the funds are to be deposited. Once the transaction takes place, Cara Bedell will be released. Unharmed."

"There won't be any deals made until I speak personally with Ms. Bedell."

"That can be arranged."

"When?"

The dial tone hummed in Deke's ear. He cursed under his breath, and then glanced at Ty, who shook his head.

"He's probably Amecan," Deke said. "And the call probably came from somewhere in that country, but even if we knew what city or town, it's probably not the same location where Cara is being kept."

"Why did you argue with him?" Grayson Perkins rung his slender hands together, the diamond ring on his left ring finger rubbing against the ruby ring on his right. "You made demands. Why? What if they don't call back? What if they kill her? Don't you know that nothing matters—"

"Cara's life is what matters. I want proof that she's alive and well. Otherwise…" He didn't bother finishing his sentence. He could tell from the shocked expression on Pretty Boy's face that he understood. "Ty will remain here with you. When they call again, if I'm in my office instead of here in yours, he'll transfer their call directly to me. In the meantime, I suggest you do whatever you need to do to get your hands on the ransom money—twenty-five million."

Perkins's eyes widened in surprise. "Twenty-five million? You can't be serious. I'll need the board's approval to—"

"Then get it," Deke told him. "But you'll have to do it without revealing the entire truth. Tell them Cara needs it for some reason and wants it transferred as soon as possible."

"How long do I have?" Perkins asked.

"Five days."

"I'll get it, no matter what I have to do. I can't live without Cara. I love her more than life itself." Huge tears pooled in Perkins's eyes. He blinked several times, sighed and laid his hand over his heart.

Get real. This guy was full of bull. He was too much in love with himself to ever love anyone else.

Deke excused himself, eager to get away from Perkins, and even more eager to contact Sawyer McNamara.

As soon as he returned to his own office and sat down at his desk, he used his secure cell phone to call Sawyer in Ameca. His old boss answered on the second ring.

"Give me a minute," Sawyer said, then apparently put his hand over the phone as he spoke to someone else before getting back to Deke. "You have something to report?"

"I just took a call on Grayson Perkins's line. The caller was male, with an accent. My guess is he called from Ameca and he's a native. He wants twenty-five million in five days."

Sawyer let out a long, low whistle. "Then it's money they want and not an oil deal."

"Apparently," Deke said. "Unless they add the oil deal to their demands later on."

"What proof did you get that Lu— Cara Bedell is alive?"

"I demanded to speak to Ms. Bedell before any money changed banks."

"And?"

"And they agreed. We're waiting to hear back from them."

"Whoever called doesn't have her with him. They're holding her somewhere else, so even if we could find our caller…" Sawyer cleared his throat. "We're dealing with a group, probably one leader making all the decisions and he may not be the caller."

"I agree."

"If he gets in touch again, record the call. If you speak to her, she'll try her best to give you some kind of clue. It's what she's been trained to do. We'll want to listen to the tape and to go over every word she says. Again and again."

SAWYER HAD SEEN photos of Naldo Salazar in battle fatigues, looking like a weary warrior, but today his appearance was totally different. He appeared to be a struggling businessman in his off-the-rack dark suit. He stood eye-to-eye with Sawyer, making him around six-two, but he was slender, almost skinny. And with his thinning gray hair, thick beard and black-framed glasses, he didn't look like the world-famous radical reformist who had almost brought his country to the brink of civil war.

"Senor McNamara." Salazar offered his hand.

Sawyer shook hands with the man. "I appreciate your meeting with us."

"We have mutual friends." Salazar glanced at the woman who stood quietly in the corner. Rita Herrera was a Dundee contact. But she was far more. The lady was a contract agent for the CIA. Her loyalty to her country put her on the side of Senor Salazar and against President Ortega. As an agent, she had learned to walk that fine line between legal and illegal, doing whatever was necessary to accomplish her goals, be they Dundee's goals, the CIA's goals or Naldo Salazar's goals. In this case, all three goals appeared to be the same: the rescue of Cara Bedell from Amecan kidnappers.

"Rita has explained about Senorita Bedell," Salazar said. "I have people already searching for any clue as to who abducted her and where she is being held."

"We're grateful for any help you can provide," Sawyer said. "Ameca is your country and you have resources here that we need. Dundee's is willing to give you whatever you require in the way of money or assistance."

"Having money to pay for information will help. But you must leave locating the senorita to me. If you try to interfere—"

"You find her. We'll stay out of it until then. But once she's located, Dundee's will take over. Are we in agreement?"

"*Sí,* senor. We are in perfect agreement."

"We have five days until the ransom has to be paid," Sawyer said.

"I will do all I can to locate Senorita Bedell before then."

"I'll wait to hear from you, but if you haven't come up with something in a few days, we'll have no choice but to stir things up with our own investigation."

"That will not be necessary. We will find her."

FOUR HOURS LATER, Sawyer received a call from Deke Bronson.

"They called back," Deke said. "They're going to let her talk to me. Ty has things set so that not only will he record the message, but you can listen to the conversation, too. So get ready. They're bringing her to— Yes, I'm here and ready to speak to Ms. Bedell."

Sawyer clenched his jaw. Deke was speaking to the man holding Lucie hostage.

"You have sixty seconds," the heavily accented voice said.

"Put her on the line," Deke told him.

"Deke, is that you?" Lucie asked.

"Yes, Ms. Bedell, this is Deke Bronson. Are you all right?"

"I—I'm okay. No one has hurt me. If you do as they say and have Gray authorize the twenty-five million to be transferred to their bank account, they'll let me go."

"Mr. Perkins is working on that right now."

"Is Lucie all right?"

"She's fine. Dundee's has given her some vacation time."

"I guess I'm taking a vacation, of sorts, but this isn't quite the Green Mansions resort."

"No, ma'am, I guess it's not. But you can be sure that everything possible will be done to meet their demands. You'll be home by week's end."

"I'm looking forward to that. I miss having four—"

"You have spoken to your employer and know that she is alive and unharmed," the man said. "You may speak to her again when you have the money ready to transfer. And once the money has been transferred, we will release Senorita Bedell."

"I'll need more than—"

The dial tone hummed in his ear. Son of a bitch. The guy had hung up on him again. He glanced at Ty, who nodded.

"Did you hear her?" Deke asked.

"Yes, I heard her," Sawyer replied. "She sounded calm. That's good. With Lucie, you never know."

"Want Ty to play back the conversation?"

"Yes. I think she gave us a couple of clues, but I want to listen again just to make sure."

Deke motioned to Ty, who played the recorded message for Sawyer.

After he listened, he waited for the moment when Lucie had said, "It isn't quite the Green Mansions resort." Then right before the man had cut her off, she'd been saying, "I miss having four—"

"Did you get anything?" Deke asked.

"Yes, thank you. Keep me informed about what's going on there and I'll relay anything of importance back to you," Sawyer said. "Contact Daisy and have her call Bain and let him know that you've spoken to Lucie and she's okay. And if for any reason you can't get in touch with either me or Geoff, contact Rita Herrera." Sawyer gave Deke Rita's cell number. "Lucie mentioned the number four, which probably means there are four kidnappers, but that's just a guess. And she told me she's being held in a tropical forest. That narrows it down to a few thousand acres of Amecan tropical forest, but at least I can tell Salazar where not to look."

"How did you get that she's being held in the—?" Deke chuckled. "I'll be damned. Green Mansions. She wasn't referring to a resort, was she?"

"No, she wasn't."

Lucie had to have known that he would hear her message and figure out the clue she had sent him. *Green Mansions*, a novel by W. H. Hudson, had been one of Lucie's favorites as a teenager. The heroine, Rima, was a girl who lived in a South American tropical forest.

I'll find you, Lucie. I swear to God, I'll find you.

CHAPTER NINE

LUCIE BROKE IN TO a run as she neared the hill overlooking the old church and cemetery on one side and the river on the other. Brenden had told her yesterday that Sawyer was coming home for the weekend, that he had an important decision to make about his future. His father wanted him to go into the family business, but that wasn't what Sawyer wanted. However, as the elder son, Sawyer always tried his best to fulfill his father's wishes. The fact that Barnett Lee McNamara had recently been diagnosed with cancer would greatly affect Sawyer's decision.

It was terribly unfair of Mr. McNamara to use his illness as leverage to persuade Sawyer to come into the business instead of applying to the FBI for a position as a special agent.

During the four and a half years she had known the McNamara brothers, she had idolized Sawyer as everything fine and noble and admirable to be found in a man. At eighteen—or at least she'd turn eighteen in a couple of months—she was madly in love with Sawyer, but he seemed oblivious to the fact. He saw her as a friend, actually more as Brenden's friend than his. He had always been nice to her, treating her like a kid sister and never truly looking at her and seeing the young woman she had become.

Whenever Sawyer brooded or needed solitude and peace, he came to Tobin's Hill, half a mile from his ancestral home built in the middle of a five-hundred-acre estate. Lucie and her grandmother lived less than a quarter of a mile in the opposite direction, closer to downtown. She couldn't count the times that she had sat with him on the grassy knoll, watching him in silence as he gazed off into the distant horizon. How was it possible that he had never noticed the lovesick adoration in her eyes? Maybe because Brenden had a crush on her and had been asking her for a date the past couple of years, Sawyer thought of her as his younger brother's girlfriend, which she was not. She loved Brenden, as a friend, but nothing more. Her heart belonged to Sawyer. It always had and it always would.

When she neared the old church, unused now and opened only for summer tours along with other historical structures in and around town, she looked up at Tobin's Hill. Her heart skipped a beat when she saw the lone figure standing by the massive oak tree. She slowed her pace, straightened the neckline on her sundress— yellow and purple polka dots on white cotton—and glanced down at her lavender toenails peeking out of her white sandals. After threading her fingers through her long, curly hair, she took a deep, steadying breath and walked leisurely up the front side of the sloping hill.

She didn't want Sawyer to think she was stalking him, that she had come here specifically to see him, even though she had. After all, she did have some pride and she'd die if Sawyer ever pitied her.

He didn't seem to hear her as she approached, but when she was only a few feet away, he glanced over his shoulder and smiled at her.

"Hello, Lucie Locket."

Her heart did an erratic little rat-a-tat-tat. No one else had ever called her Lucie Locket. Only Sawyer. She had once told him that her mother had chosen her name from the old nursery rhyme, but preferred the L-u-c-i-e spelling to the traditional L-u-c-y.

She smiled at him and said, "Hi." *I love you. I love you. I love you. I want to rush into your arms. I want to kiss you. I want you to love me, too.*

"What are you doing out here in the middle of nowhere?" Sawyer asked.

"I come here a lot," she said. "To think about things and sometimes just to daydream."

"You look mighty pretty today, all dressed up as if you were on your way to a party."

I put on my new sundress just for you. "I am a woman, you know, and I like to wear pretty things and look nice all the time."

He surveyed her from head to toe. "You are all grown up now, aren't you? You've turned into a beautiful young woman. No wonder you're all Brenden talks about. You really should put him out of his misery and go out on a date with him."

"Brenden and I are just friends."

"That's not the way Brenden sees things." Sawyer chuckled.

"I adore Brenden. I always have, but I just don't feel that way about him."

"I'm sorry to hear that." Sawyer's smile wavered. "I think you'd be good for Brenden. He's moody and emotional and sensitive, but when he's around you, he seems happier and more carefree, the way an eighteen-year-old should be."

I'd do just about anything to make you happy, but I am not going to date your kid brother. How can I date him when I'm desperately in love with you?

She turned away from Sawyer and looked out over the valley below. Everything was springtime green, with flowering trees and wildflowers dotting the landscape. And the narrow Tayanita River rippled melodically over moss-covered rocks in the shallows at the foot of the hill.

Sawyer came up alongside her. They stood there, neither saying anything for several minutes. Lucie wished that he would reach down and take her hand. If he'd hold her hand, she'd be happy. That would be enough for now. Just to feel the touch of his hand in hers.

"My father's dying," Sawyer said.

Lucie snapped around and stared at him. "He's dying? But Brenden told me that—"

"Brenden doesn't know. Dad told him about the cancer, but he didn't tell him the prognosis. It's inoperable. Dad's got six months at most."

"Oh, Sawyer, I'm so sorry." Instinctively, without even thinking about what she was doing, Lucie reached out, clasped his hand in hers and squeezed comfortingly. She hadn't realized what she'd done until he squeezed her hand in response and gripped it tightly.

"When I graduate next month, I'm coming home and going to work for McNamara Industries. It's what Dad wants and it will make things easier for him knowing I'll help Uncle Wilson keep the family business up and running."

"You're sacrificing your dreams for your father's sake," Lucie said. "That's so like you. You always do the honorable thing, don't you?"

Still holding her hand, he looked at her. As if he were seeing her for the first time, his eyes widened, his gaze softened and he smiled again. "I'm not a saint or a knight in shining armor, so don't put me up on a pedestal, Lucie Locket. I'm just a man doing what he knows is right."

Unable to stop herself, she gazed at him adoringly. "It's too late, you know," she admitted. "I put you up on a pedestal when I was thirteen and you've been there ever since. I think you're wonderful."

Oh, God, had she really said that? Stricken with fear that he'd laugh at her or even worse that he would feel sorry for her, Lucie gasped. "I mean…I—"

"It's all right." He lifted her hand to his face and pressed it against his stubble-rough cheek. "I think I've always known how you feel, that you admire me the way Brenden does, as a much-loved big brother."

"I've never thought of you as my big brother."

His smile vanished.

Oh, crap. She'd done it now. Why hadn't she kept her big mouth shut?

"You're Brenden's girl." Sawyer looked her in the eye.

"No, I'm not. I've never been Brenden's girl."

"He thinks you are."

"He's wrong."

"Damn, Lucie, don't look at me that way."

"What way?"

"As if more than anything in this world, you want me to kiss you."

"I do," she told him. "More than anything."

He groaned deep in his throat, as if racked with an inner turmoil, and then he reached out and cupped her face with both hands. Her mouth opened on a pleading gasp as he lowered his head and kissed her, soft and gentle and sweet. His mouth took hers tentatively; and then when she responded, he deepened the kiss. Everything feminine within her came to life, exploding like buds bursting open on a flowering plant.

The kiss was all that she had dreamed of, all that she had longed for—and more.

A DOOR SLAMMED. Loud voices carried from the outer rooms to the bedroom. Lucie woke with a start. Still in a half-asleep state, it took her several minutes to realize where she was and remember what had happened to her. She rolled over on the scratchy sheet, closed her eyes and moaned. She'd been dreaming. Dreaming about a day long ago, the day Sawyer kissed her for the first time. Curling into a fetal ball on the lumpy mattress, she wished she could go back to sleep and return to that wondrous moment in time.

The kiss had been electric, sending a sexual current

through her young body. If Sawyer had asked her to lie down in the grass there on Tobin's Hill and let him make love to her, she would have done it willingly. She had been so in love with him, in a way only the young and very foolish could be in love.

But after the kiss, he'd been a perfect gentleman. Naturally. After all, he was Sawyer, the white knight, the fine and honorable man she had worshipped for years.

He had grabbed her shoulders and pushed her away gently, then looked directly at her. "I shouldn't have done that, but God help me, I wanted that kiss. You have quite an effect on me, Lucie Locket. But I can't let it happen again, not knowing the way Brenden feels about you."

The door to the bedroom creaked as it opened. Lucie turned over, shot straight up and glared at the man who entered carrying a cup of coffee and tortillas wrapped in a cloth. He had served her the same breakfast each morning.

He asked her if she needed to go to the bathroom.

"Yes, I do."

He motioned for her to stand. She got up and walked toward the door. He marched her through the living room where the other three men sat talking, apparently discussing something important during the shift change. The man she'd heard the others call Rico ushered her quickly out of the house, but not before she heard and understood part of the conversation. During her time in captivity, Lucie had overheard other snippets of conversation, enough to put two and two together and come to the conclusion that a large ransom would be paid for Senorita Bedell soon and they would all be very rich. This information implied that money was the motive behind her kidnapping and not the pending deal with Delgado Oil. Of course, it was possible that she didn't know the entire story, that a cash ransom was only part of the kidnapper's demands.

Rico stood guard while she entered the outhouse. God, what she'd give for a real bathroom and a huge bathtub. Bubble bath, deodorant, toothpaste, mouthwash, some scented lotion, shampoo and conditioner. *Oh, how we take things for granted, little things that we use every day.*

On the way back through the house, she asked Rico for her morning bucket of water and he told her that Hector would bring it to her later. Oh, great, just what she wanted, to eat her meager breakfast with unwashed hands.

"I do not kill women," the one named Manuel said in Spanish, his voice gruff and adamant.

"None of us will have to kill her," Hector said. "When the time comes, Arturo will do the job himself."

Lucie pretended she hadn't understood what she'd heard. When Rico looked at her, searching her face for a reaction, she thanked him and did her best to seem unaffected by the news that someone named Arturo was going to kill her. She grasped the doorknob, opened the door and went into the bedroom. Rico closed and locked the door.

Lucie gasped for air as the reality of her fate hit her full force. Someone had hired these men to abduct her and demand a huge ransom. A man named Arturo had been hired to kill her once the ransom was paid.

No, not kill her, Lucie Evans. He had been hired to kill Cara Bedell.

SEVENTY-FIVE HOURS after their arrival in San Luis, Sawyer and Geoff met with Naldo Salazar for the second time. Rita Herrera had driven them during the early morning hours to the village of Santa Clara, deep within the tropical forest where Salazar was waiting for them in the ruins of an old mission on the outskirts of the small town. When they emerged from Rita's eighties-model Jeep, two armed guards came forward and escorted them past the crumbling ruins into a roofless room shaded by the towering trees surrounding the building.

Salazar stepped out of the shadows, motioned for his guards to leave him and then faced Sawyer. The solemn expression on his deeply tanned face made Sawyer wonder just how bad the news was.

"The man behind Senorita Bedell's abduction is Arturo Torres-Rios," Salazar said. "The man is an assassin, a killer for hire. And he has committed other crimes, including kidnapping, for the right price."

"Then he orchestrated Cara Bedell's kidnapping for the ransom money," Sawyer said.

Salazar shook his head. "No. He was hired to do this job. Someone else is giving the orders."

"Any idea who that might be?" Geoff asked.

"No, senor. And it is possible that we may never know."

"How does identifying the man in charge of the kidnapping help us find Cara?" Sawyer wanted something more concrete to go on than just a man's name, a man who was simply a hired gun.

"Torres-Rios does his own killing," Salazar explained, "but for other jobs that require hands-on contact with the subject, he uses a team of men he knows and trusts. In this case, one of the men has a girlfriend who comes from the village of Morelos. The girlfriend likes to brag to her friends about her rich boyfriend, Pepe. It seems that he will soon be coming into quite a bit of money. He is one of four men guarding a very wealthy American woman."

"How do we find this girlfriend?" Sawyer asked.

"She has been found," Salazar said.

"And?"

"The American woman is being held in a house about three miles outside of Morelos, a house that once belonged to Pepe's girlfriend's aunt and uncle, who are now both dead. The house has been abandoned for years."

Sawyer felt a rush of adrenaline shoot through his body. Salazar had found Lucie for them two days before the ransom deadline. Whatever this Arturo Torres-Rios had planned for her, he would see to it that she stayed alive until the money had changed hands. That had been one of Deke Bronson's stipulations, that he talk to Cara Bedell again on the day the twenty-five million was transferred to a Cayman Islands bank.

"I owe you a debt of gratitude," Sawyer told Salazar.

"I met Senorita Bedell. I believe her to be a good person who will do the right thing for my country. I would not wish to see anything bad happen to a woman who can help my people."

Sawyer nodded. "My associate—" he inclined his head toward Geoff Monday "—and I will take it from here."

Salazar narrowed his gaze as he studied Sawyer's face, then he surveyed Geoff from his short blond hair to his broad shoulders to his booted feet. "The two of you are not in this alone."

"We'll make arrangements with some of Rita's friends," Sawyer said, but didn't explain any further, knowing Salazar would understand someone had pulled a few strings to involve the CIA in this mission.

Salazar offered his hand. "Then I wish you luck, Senor McNamara."

Sawyer shook hands with the man, then he and Geoff headed back to where Rita waited by the Jeep.

"Salazar found Ms. Bedell," Sawyer told her. "We're going in tonight and bringing her out. Get in touch with your U.S. contact as soon as possible. I want a rendezvous location set up where we'll meet him. Once we free Cara, we'll want to get out of Ameca immediately."

"Where is Ms. Bedell being held?" Rita asked as she got into the Jeep.

"Outside a village called Morelos." Sawyer rounded the Jeep and hopped in on the other side.

"I know the village. There is an abandoned coffee plantation about twenty miles between Morelos and the next nearest town, Zaragosa."

"How big is Zaragosa?"

"Big enough for a small airport, and as luck would

have it, the mayor and other officials are friendly to Salazar's cause. That will make it easier for us. I will see that arrangements are made for a Cessna to be on standby to take the three of you out of Ameca. You can have the Dundee jet waiting at the nearest large terminal across the border."

As soon as Geoff jumped into the backseat, Rita started the engine, shifted into Reverse and backed up the Jeep. "I'll give you exact directions to the old coffee plantation. It's an ideal place for us to rendezvous."

"I'm not sure what we'll run into or how long it will take us to reach the rendezvous point," Sawyer told her.

"That is not a problem. I will have someone in place tonight. And if it takes you until morning or even if something goes wrong and it takes you a couple of days, there will be someone waiting for you."

"How far are we from Morelos?"

"Morelos is about forty miles from Santa Clara and there are two-lane roads all the way, some curving upward into Mount Reyes. Both Zaragosa and Morelos are in the valleys between the mountains. You can expect a gravel road, possibly even a dirt road, when you leave Morelos."

"I need as much information as you can get on a guy named Arturo Torres-Rios," Sawyer told her. "Find out if he's the type who would betray his employer for the right price. I want the person who hired him."

"I will see what I can do."

"We'll need equipment." Geoff's meaty hand grasped the back of Sawyer's seat as he leaned forward and made his request.

"Whatever you need," Rita said. "Name it."

Geoff grinned. "Well, love, a couple of M16s would be nice."

LUCIE KNEW THAT if she wanted to live, she had to escape. If she'd understood her captors correctly, she had two days until the ransom deadline and that meant she had to come up with a plan and act on it sometime in the next twenty-four hours. Despite all her training, she didn't think she could manage to overpower two armed men. But what other choice did she have? Her best bet was to take on one of them when he escorted her to the outhouse, either tonight or in the morning. She might have to kill him. The thought of taking a human life bothered her. Yes, she'd spent six years as an FBI agent and the past nine as a Dundee agent, but she'd never had to kill anyone. Her training had been in self-defense, not in killing. Only once had she been forced to shoot an assailant.

If she escaped tonight, she could easily get lost in the forest, with only the moonlight to guide her. Other than her switchblade, she had no weapons and no other equipment of any kind. She had no idea where she was, but she did know, from eavesdropping on her captors' conversations, that they weren't far from a village. The only problem was she didn't know in which direction to go and she didn't dare follow the dirt road that led away from the adobe cottage.

If she escaped in the morning, she would have the advantage of daylight, but so would her kidnappers when they came after her. Both escape plans had draw-backs, not the least of which was actually being able to take her captor off guard and subdue him. She was a big woman, but all of her jailors, except one—Rico—were at least five-nine and muscular.

Lucie walked over to the boarded windows and studied them. If only she could knock the boards loose from one of the windows, she could climb out and make a run for it. But the only way to remove the boards was to add pressure, which meant beating or hammering on them. It was unlikely that she could do that without making any noise.

Where is my rescue team? She'd thought that by now several Dundee agents would have stormed this place.

What if they can't find me? If they hadn't managed to locate her in the next forty-eight hours, this guy named Arturo would kill her, believing he was killing Cara Bedell.

Come on, guys, please find me. I'll give you until tomorrow night. If she hadn't been rescued by then, she would have no choice but to try to escape on her own.

CHAPTER TEN

CARA CURSED UNDER her breath when she tried to open the package of sliced cold cuts and the damn thing wouldn't come apart properly. *So much for easy open and easy reseal.* What she needed was a pair of scissors, but there didn't seem to be a pair in the cabin's less-than-adequate kitchen. She took the butcher knife and sliced open the cellophane wrapping.

"Need some help?" Bain asked as he came in the back door.

"No, thank you. I think I can manage. After all, making a couple of sandwiches is hardly rocket science, is it?"

Bain shrugged. "Suit yourself. I just thought that since you're used to being waited on hand and foot, you—"

"That's it!" she yelled at him. "For the past three days, you've treated me as if I'm some helpless child who doesn't have sense enough to come in out of the rain. Damn it, Bain Desmond, I run a multibillion-dollar conglomerate. I think I can make my own bed, wash a few dishes and spread some mayo and mustard on two slices of bread."

His lips twitched. She knew he was on the verge of

laughing and that simply made her angrier than she already was.

"Don't you dare laugh at me."

He couldn't manage to hold it back any longer and chuckled despite his best efforts not to. "Sorry, sugar, but watching Cara Bedell roughing it is amusing. If you could see yourself from my viewpoint, you'd understand."

Heat rose up her neck and flushed her face, her scrubbed-clean, pale, freckled face. After using the foundation makeup Bain had purchased for her, she discovered that it turned her skin a lovely shade of orange-tan and made her look like a spotted pumpkin. She'd tossed the bottle of cheap liquid foundation into the trash, along with the green eye shadow. Since then, she'd used only the brown eyeliner, the peach blush and the coral lip gloss.

Bain was seeing the real Cara on a daily basis. But what difference did it make? It wasn't as if it mattered one way or the other if she looked her best. Bain Desmond, male chauvinist Neanderthal that he was, wouldn't touch her with a ten-foot pole. Oh, it wasn't that he didn't want her. She knew better. Sometimes, the looks he gave her were hot enough to liquefy metal. But he'd told her in no uncertain terms, more than once, that he would not become her lover.

"If we made love, I'd never be able to let you go," he had told her quite some time ago. "And we both know that it just wouldn't work between us. We live in two different worlds. You'd hate living in mine and I couldn't exist in yours."

Cara glowered at Bain, but she managed, just barely, to stop herself from blasting him with a zinging rebuttal on how funny she was from his point of view. Instead, she concentrated on preparing the sandwiches for their late afternoon lunch. Bain had been in charge of the meals every day, including cooking bacon and eggs for breakfast, and she had to admit that he was a pretty good cook. He had also made her bed—he was sleeping on the sofa since the cabin had only one bedroom—washed the dishes, and had done their laundry, except her underwear, which she washed out by hand, even though it was cheap cotton. From the appearance and quality of the clothes he had bought for her, she figured he'd purchased them at a discount store. But at least he'd guessed right about the sizes.

Any attempts she had made to prove to him that despite her privileged upbringing, she could be domestic if she set her mind to it, had failed miserably. So, today, while he'd gone for a walk outside, she had decided to make lunch. And by God, she intended to do just that. Sandwiches, pickles, potato chips, canned colas and a banana each for dessert.

When she had everything placed on the bar that separated the small kitchen from the living room, she cleared her throat. He ignored her, pretending interest in something outside the window.

"Lunch is ready," she told him.

He turned, smiled at her and walked over to the bar. He pulled out the wooden bar stool for her, but when he held out his had to assist her, she ignored his offer and hoisted herself up and onto the stool without his help.

"Still mad at me?" he asked, a hint of humor in his voice.

Damn it, yes, she was still angry. And he was still laughing at her.

She glared at him. "I'm not sure your guarding me instead of having a Dundee agent do it was such a good idea. All we've done for the past few days is get on each other's nerves."

"There was no way I'd let another man stay cooped up in this cabin with you for God only knows how long." Bain wasn't smiling.

Cara's pulse accelerated. "I don't see what difference it makes. It's not as if you've been going along on my dates or have supervised my sex life before now."

Bain growled. The sound came from deep in his chest and rose to his throat. "Yeah, but I don't know about your dates with other men, do I? And I can pretend that you aren't having sex with any of them."

Cara swallowed. Her heartbeat hammered inside her head. "I hate every woman you look at or talk to and the thought of your making love to another woman drives me crazy."

Clenching his jaw, he huffed loudly. "That's why we're getting on each other's nerves. I haven't been screwing anybody else and my guess is neither have you. We're both frustrated as hell."

She sighed heavily. "You—you haven't had sex with…? Oh, Bain. I haven't, either. How could I when you're the only man I want."

He closed his eyes and the expression on his face told her all she needed to know. She reached over and gently clasped her fingers around his upper arm. He groaned, as if in pain, and jerked away from her.

"I can't do this," he told her. "I'm going back outside. I won't go far. And when I come back, we're not going to talk about sex."

He stomped across the room and went out on the front porch, slamming the door behind him. Cara stared down at her food. Tears gathered in her eyes. As they trickled down her cheeks, she swatted them away, slid off the stool, walked over to the windows and stood there watching Bain as he headed down the dirt path in front of the cabin.

LUCIE LAY AWAKE in the darkness of her prison, her thoughts a jumbled mess of past, present and future. But did she have a future beyond tomorrow? If she tried to escape and failed, would they kill her? No, they couldn't, not if they wanted their boss to collect the ransom money and make them all rich. If she didn't speak to Deke Bronson the day after tomorrow to assure him she—Cara Bedell—was alive and well, he would not authorize Grayson Perkins to make the bank transfer. So she was safe for the time being.

She had two chances to live beyond the next forty-eight hours. One: she could manage to escape from her captors and somehow find help in a nearby village. Two: whoever Sawyer had sent to find her—and she knew he had sent someone—would rescue her before it was too late.

There had been a time, long ago, when Sawyer wouldn't have left the job of rescuing her to anyone else. He would have flown to Ameca himself and tracked her down. But that had been the old Sawyer, the man who hadn't hated her.

Looking back, she wondered if she had it to do all over again would she do anything different. Hindsight was indeed twenty-twenty. But considering the circumstances, how much could she actually have changed? She'd had no control over the way Brenden had felt about her any more than she'd had over the way she'd felt about Sawyer. The heart wants what the heart wants. Love was seldom logical. How different everything could have been for all three of them if she had been in love with Brenden and not Sawyer. Or if Brenden hadn't been in love with her.

Brenden Lee McNamara had been a beautiful person, inside and out, with the same smoldering good looks Sawyer had, but softer and smoother. Brenden had been a pretty boy where Sawyer had always been ruggedly handsome. Even as a teenager, Brenden had been sweet and gentle. There had been something almost angelic about him, with his curly dark hair and luminous dark eyes. She could still see him in her mind's eyes, smiling at her, joking with her, making her laugh. And she could still hear the sound of his voice, an octave higher than Sawyer's deeper baritone, and with a soothing quality that made whatever he said seem to have been spoken out of kindness.

But the last time she had heard his voice…

"Damn you! Damn you both! How could you do this to me?" Brenden's final words echoed inside her head and the image of him staring at her with a mixture of love and anger and hurt in his eyes haunted her still, after nine years.

Oh, Brenden, I'm sorry, so very sorry.

Lucie sat straight up in bed and hugged herself. She heard the distant sounds of the nighttime jungle, the warm wind sighing through the trees, and the hum of a battery-operated radio playing in the other room.

If she came out of this alive, she knew what she would do. She'd celebrate being alive by putting the past behind her. She had wasted nine years of her life trying to achieve an unachievable goal. She had bet her heart and her life on being able to earn Sawyer's forgiveness and she'd lost almost everything, including what little pride she'd had left.

Leaving Dundee's had been the first step, the first thing she'd done right in her insane relationship with Sawyer in the past nine years. If only she had been able to accept the truth sooner—that Sawyer would never forgive her because he would never forgive himself—she could have made a new life for herself years ago. If she had, she might not have been in Ameca and wouldn't have been so willing to sacrifice her life to save Cara Bedell. She could have been married by now and possibly have a couple of kids.

Okay, Lucie, who are you kidding? There is only one man on the face of this earth for you and you damn well know it. Sawyer's It. Think about how unfair it would be to another man to be unable to love him with your whole heart.

Why was she doing this to herself? What was the point? She should be concentrating all her physical and mental energy on plotting her escape. And that's just what she was going to do.

To hell with Sawyer McNamara!

DAISY ANSWERED the phone on the second ring, not bothering to check caller ID. She had already gotten one wrong number and two solicitors this evening while she'd been waiting to hear from Geoff and Sawyer. Geoff had reported in every day since they'd left Atlanta and if he didn't check in tonight, she'd worry herself sick.

"Hello," she said breathlessly.

"How is it that such a sweet young thing can have such a sexy voice?" Geoff asked teasingly.

"Just lucky I guess." He was the only person who'd ever told her she had a sexy voice. That had to mean something, didn't it? Or was she reading far too much into mere words?

"She's been located," Geoff said, his tone changing from playful to dead serious. "We're going in to get her tonight."

"Oh, thank the Lord. Please, be careful. Both of you."

"Don't worry about me, love. I'm practically bullet-proof. I survived fourteen years in the SAS and another five as a mercenary before I joined Dundee's. And if you're worried about Sawyer, I'll do my best to keep the boss man safe. If I let anything happen to him, Lucie might never forgive me."

"If anything happens to you, I'll never forgive you."

He chuckled. "That's the same as saying if I die, you'll kill me."

"Don't joke about it. Please."

"Ah, come on, my little Daisy, don't waste your worry on an old solider like me."

"You're not that old! You talk like you're eighty."

"I'll be forty-five my next birthday. That's old compared to a child like you."

"I'm hardly a child. I'm twenty-nine. I'm old enough to vote, you know. And I'm years past legal drinking age. A lot of my friends who are my age are already married and mothers."

"Then you should find yourself a young man, get married and—"

"Don't tell me what to do or what to think or how to feel," she shouted. "And if I want to worry myself sick about you, I will. Got that!"

"Yes, ma'am. I got it." He paused and the silence on the line lingered until he finally said, "Daisy?"

"Hmm…?"

"If I were ten years younger…"

Tears filled her eyes. "Don't you dare get yourself killed, Geoffrey MacDougall Monday."

"I'll see you soon, sweet Daisy."

"Geoff…"

"'Bye for now."

The dial tone hummed. "I love you," she said, her voice a soft echo in the stillness of her apartment. "Come home safe. Come home to me."

SAWYER SAT ALONE in the rusty, battered truck that Rita had commandeered for them, along with weapons, ammunition and supplies. She had followed them on their journey from Santa Clara, leaving them several miles back before they reached the outskirts of Morelos. If all went as planned, they would rendezvous with her and one of her CIA contacts later tonight at the old coffee plantation.

Although he'd taken part in several dangerous operations during his years with the FBI, he'd never played commando on a rescue mission. But Geoff had. The guy knew what he was doing and had prepared Sawyer, as best he could, for what lay ahead of them. He could have sent another Dundee agent with Geoff, someone with a military background, someone who'd been trained, as Geoff had. But the hostage wasn't just anybody. It was Lucie.

His Lucie.

No, not his. Never his. She was Brenden's Lucie.

He remembered the first time he saw her. She'd been thirteen, tall, gangly, all long arms and legs. The cut-off jeans she'd been wearing showed off her great legs. His first reaction had been purely physical, but once he'd moved his eyes upward and saw that mane of thick, curly, red hair and those chocolate-brown eyes, his heart had stopped. Of course, he hadn't realized she was just a kid because she looked older. Even though he'd been only seventeen at the time, finding out that he'd been lusting after a thirteen-year-old had made him feel like a dirty old man.

When he'd seen the way his brother looked at Lucie, he had known he wasn't the only McNamara who'd fallen for the redheaded spitfire. He figured Brenden had fallen in love with Lucie on sight and had loved her until the day he died.

I'm sorry, Brenden. God, I'm sorry. I'd give anything if I had the chance to undo the past. We both need your forgiveness, Lucie and I. We've been living in hell these past nine years.

She thinks I hate her. You know that's not true. Neither of us could ever hate Lucie, could we? But I couldn't bear looking at her, not after what happened. I've done some really shitty things to her, but I didn't want to hurt her. All I wanted was for her to go away, to leave me alone, to get out of my life. But she wouldn't leave; she hung on like a bull dog with a bone. You know how stubborn and tenacious she can be.

Geoff called out as he approached the Jeep, "Daisy sends her love. She expects me to bring all of us home without a scratch." He swung up and into the driver's side of the old vehicle and grinned broadly. "I told her I'd do my best. She's threatened to kill me if I don't make it back alive." Geoff chuckled.

Sawyer smiled. "Our Daisy's a wonder, isn't she?" He noticed the expression on Geoff's face and recognized the look for what it was. He had seen it often enough in his own mirror. "The guy that wins Daisy's heart will be one lucky son of bitch."

Geoff's smile vanished momentarily, and then he forced a laugh. "Yes, he will. I told her it was time she found herself a nice young man and got married."

"Good advice."

When Geoff started the engine, it huffed and puffed and sputtered, but the seen-better-days Jeep came to life. "When this is over, we can't count on getting back to the Jeep. It's possible one or both of us will be on foot. If there's a choice, I want you to take the Jeep and get Lucie to safety. I'll manage on my own."

"As far as we know, there are only two men at a time guarding Lucie," Sawyer said. "The odds are on our side since there are two of us and we have the element of surprise, right?"

"True enough, but it's best to be prepared for the unexpected."

"Such as?"

"All we know is that these four men take shifts," Geoff said. "It's possible the four of them are staying at the cottage and we'll be up against double our numbers."

"You've been in situations before where you and your men were outnumbered. You're the one with the experience, so you'll be the one calling the shots. Tonight, you're the boss. I'll do whatever you say to do."

"You have one objective—rescue Lucie. I'll do whatever is required to make that possible. You let me handle the guards, whether they're two or four. You go to Lucie and get her out. Don't look back. Don't give me a thought. I'll rendezvous with you as soon as I can."

Sawyer nodded. Both he and Geoff knew that a rescue operation such as this would end in casualties and that it was possible Geoff might not come out of this alive. And if things went wrong—bad wrong—he and Geoff and Lucie might all end up dead.

CHAPTER ELEVEN

LUCIE WOKE SUDDENLY from a fitful sleep, not knowing at first what had awakened her. As she became more alert, she realized that the door to the bedroom was creaking open. Lying there in the darkness, she listened as someone entered quietly. She slipped her hand down inside her blouse, inserted her thumb and index finger into her bra, and pulled out her small switchblade. With her heartbeat doing a war dance, she watched as the large shadow of a man carrying a rifle drew nearer and nearer.

Why now and not before had one of her guards decided to keep her company in the middle of the night? If he thought she wouldn't fight him, he was wrong. Dead wrong. She'd gut him like a fish. But she couldn't react too quickly and give him the upper hand. She had to wait for him to set aside his rifle and get in bed with her. When he came down over her, he would get the surprise of his life.

When he stood by the bed and hovered over her, she released the catch on the knife, opening the blade.

"Lucie?" the man's voice whispered.

Oh, God! Oh, God! She would know that voice anywhere.

She shot straight up. "Sawyer?"

"Are your hands and feet bound or are you free?"

"I'm free," she told him.

He reached down, grabbed her arm and yanked her up and onto her feet. They stood toe-to-toe, their breaths mingling as their gazes connected in the darkness, with only slivers of faint moonlight shooting through the cracks in the boarded windows.

"Are you okay?" he asked.

"Yes."

"We took care of the two guards. Geoff's waiting in the other room for us."

She clutched his forearm. "There are four guards. Y'all got only the two on duty. There are two more. Did you see a van parked outside?"

"Yes."

"The other two sleep in it."

"Then we'll have to be very quiet and not disturb them."

"Do you have a gun for me?" she asked. "I've got this—" she held up the switchblade "—but I'd rather have some firepower if we wind up having to shoot our way out of here."

Sawyer eased a weapon out of the shoulder holster and handed it to her. "I'm planning on you and me getting out of here with as little fanfare as possible. Geoff will handle things while we get away, then he'll follow us. Understand?"

"Yeah." She understood. If the two remaining guards woke up, Geoff would deal with them while she and Sawyer made a run for it. She knew the drill. Rescuing the hostage was the number-one priority.

Holding the pistol in one hand, she flipped the switchblade in her other hand closed and dropped it back down inside her bra.

"Stay behind me and don't do anything stupid," he told her.

She wanted to tell him that she had managed not to do anything stupid while she'd been held captive these past few days and she thought she could continue using her brains for at least a few more hours. But now was not the time to argue with Sawyer. The man was rescuing her for God's sake! The least she could do was cooperate with him. And be grateful.

"I'll be a good girl and follow orders," she said.

"That'll be a first," he mumbled under his breath.

She followed him across the dark room and over to the half-open door. When he peered into the other room, she looked over his shoulder. Geoff Monday stood guard at the front door. When he saw them emerge from the bedroom, he motioned with his rifle, silently instructing them to come to him. As they passed through the living room of the adobe cottage, she glanced right and saw the guard named Pepe lying in a pool of blood that had drained from his slit throat. She swallowed hard. He had been a criminal, one of her kidnappers, and wouldn't have hesitated killing her. She couldn't waste her sympathy on him.

As they neared the front door, Sawyer maneuvered her around the second lifeless body. Manuel lay on the floor looking sightlessly up at the ceiling. She didn't see a mark on him, but she suspected from the odd angle of his head, his neck had been snapped like a twig.

Geoff eased open the front door, then yanked it closed when he saw Hector and Rico, guns drawn, heading for the house.

"Son of a bitch," Geoff growled. He glanced at Sawyer. "Take her out the back door and run like hell. I'll keep these two occupied."

Sawyer grabbed her arm and all but dragged her across the room toward the kitchen. She called out to Geoff, "You stay alive, do you hear me?" Then she followed Sawyer through the kitchen, out the back door, and into the warm, murky night. They hadn't made it more than twenty feet from the house before they heard the sound of repeated gunshots. She hesitated for a split second, wanting to go back and help Geoff.

Sawyer nudged her forward. "He's doing his part. Now you do yours."

With Sawyer at her side, she broke into a run and together they headed for the nearby forest. As they went deeper into the wooded area behind the cottage, she could still hear the gunfire. *Please, God, keep Geoff safe.*

Clouds obscured the stars and the moonlight barely managed to peek through a break in the clouds now and then. She couldn't really see where she was going and was mostly feeling her way; but she kept running. What choice did she have? Low tree branches slapped across her shoulders and thick underbrush scratched her feet and legs. Her leather sandals had not been designed for running wild through the tropical forest. The soles were so thin that she felt every rock she stepped on as they fled.

"I can't see two feet in front of me," she told Sawyer

as she slowed to catch her breath. "I don't suppose you've got a flashlight."

"Got one," he said, then gulped in several deep breaths. "But if one of the guards got away and follows, he'd be able to spot the flashlight and pinpoint our location. We need to start backtracking soon and get to the Jeep Geoff and I stashed about half a mile away from where you were being held. Otherwise, we'll be walking about ten miles to the rendezvous point."

"Are you telling me that we've been going in the wrong direction, that the rendezvous point is west of here and we're going east?"

"The house faced west and in order to get away, we had to go in the opposite direction and go as fast and as far as possible to get you away from your captors."

Lucie doubled over as she continued to take in deep breaths, replenishing her lungs with much-needed oxygen. "So, do you think we've gone far enough?" she asked as she stood straight up and stretched. "Can we start backtracking now?"

"Maybe. Stay quiet and listen."

Silence. And the soft rumble of the sleeping forest. A humid breeze swept over them and a streak of jagged lightning zipped through the distant eastern sky.

"I don't hear any gunfire," he said.

"That's good, right?"

"It could be. My guess is Geoff's got everything under control. Either that or—"

"Don't say it. Don't even think it."

"Geoff's been up against worse odds than two against one." Sawyer glanced at the charcoal, predawn sky just as a rumble of thunder forecast the weather. "It's going to rain and it looks like it's coming in from the west. We'll probably run into it."

"So, we're turning around and going back the way we came," Lucie said.

"We're turning around and heading west," Sawyer agreed, "but we're not going back exactly the way we came."

"I hope you've got a compass."

Sawyer slid his hand into his pants pocket and pulled out a round object. "I don't think Rita forgot anything essential. I've got food and water in my backpack and several rounds of ammo for our weapons."

Lucie just then noticed the small tan burlap pack strapped to Sawyer's back. "Who's Rita?"

"She's Dundee's contact in Ameca. She hid Cara for us until Ty, Geoff and I could get to San Luis. Ty escorted Cara back to the U.S."

"Then Cara's all right? She's safe?"

"As safe as Bain Desmond can keep her. He's the only person, other than Deke Bronson and a few essential Dundee personnel, who knows the truth. Everyone else believes that Lucie Evans is on an extended vacation to recover from her ordeal and that Cara Bedell has been kidnapped."

"Thank God, Cara knew what to do," Lucie said. "I was pretty sure she'd contact Deke and I knew he'd take it from there. What I don't understand is why you're here in Ameca. I figured you'd send Geoff and maybe Ty or—"

"I told you that Ty took Cara back to the U.S."

"Why didn't you escort her home and send Ty with Geoff after me?"

"We need to get moving," Sawyer told her, deliberately avoiding answering her question. "The rendezvous point is a good ten miles west of Morelos and the house where they kept you was several miles out. We've run at least a mile or more, so we're looking at about twelve miles between us and the old coffee plantation where Geoff will meet us. If we're lucky, we'll be able to find the Jeep. If not, we'll be walking all the way."

"Sawyer?"

"Not now, Lucie. Later."

"All I was going to say was let's go. You lead the way."

Facing her, he grabbed her by her upper arms, his fingers biting tightly into her flesh. Taken off guard by his sudden move, she gasped as she stared right at him, barely making out his features in the darkness.

"That was a brave thing you did exchanging identities with Cara. You probably saved her life."

He released her as quickly and abruptly as he'd grabbed her. "Let's head out. If we lose what moonlight we have now, we'll have no choice but to stop until daybreak."

When he cupped her elbow and gently urged her to move, she walked alongside him, damned and determined to keep up with him.

GEOFF FELT THE BULLET as it ripped into his shoulder and exploded. Toppled by the pain, he fell to his knees, but kept his M16 pressed against his chest. He and one of the kidnappers had been exchanging gunfire while the other guy escaped, no doubt going after Sawyer and

Lucie. They'd had him trapped in the house for quite a while, but about fifteen minutes ago, he realized there was only one shooter remaining, so he'd ceased firing and had drawn the guy partially into the open.

He sure as hell couldn't pass out. Not if he wanted to stay alive. He needed to remain alert. Before he did anything else, he had to stop the bleeding. The ever resourceful Rita had included a first-aid kit in both his and Sawyer's makeshift backpacks.

Keep the rifle close, but if you don't take care of your shoulder, you're going to bleed to death and nothing else will matter.

As he tried to remove his pack, agonizing pain radiated through his shoulder and jarred his entire body. He slid the pack down and off, then dragged it around and placed it in front of him. After retrieving the kit, he flipped it open and yanked out the three small gauze pads, a roll of tape and a small tube of antiseptic cream. After ripping open his blood-soaked shirt, he ran his hand over the wound. Blood seeped through his fingers. Damn, he needed something thicker than this gauze to absorb the blood.

Geoff managed to get to his feet and walk into the kitchen, where he found a couple of tattered hand towels hanging from a rusty nail on the back of the door. Using one of the towels, he wiped off as much blood as possible, then smeared the ointment over the wound, cringing when the stuff burned like fire. Then he pressed the gauze over his wound. After folding the towel twice, he laid it over the gauze, held it with one hand and applied pressure while he used the other to bring the tape to his mouth. He cut the tape with his teeth. Once he taped the dressing in place, he went back into the living room.

Since he hadn't heard anything from his opponent in the past few minutes, he wondered if the guy was wounded, dead, or waiting for the right moment to storm the house.

He eased down on his haunches and rummaged inside the first-aid kit until he found a small bottle of acetaminophen. He removed the cap, upended the bottle and downed the contents. He figured it was no more than six tablets. They wouldn't erase the pain, but they might dull it a bit.

Forcing himself into motion, he stood up and went back into the kitchen. He slipped out the back door and made his way cautiously around the side of the house, and came up behind the back of the bullet-ridden van. Despite the lack of light, other than a hint of moonlight, Geoff could see the man lying facedown, his body half-hidden under the vehicle. Geoff lifted his booted foot and kicked the guy. He groaned.

Damn son of a bitch was still alive. Just as he aimed his rifle, the man rolled over and looked up at him. He spoke rapidly in Spanish, begging Geoff not to kill him.

"Please, do not kill me. I will tell you anything you want to know. I will do whatever you tell me to do." He eyed the rifle lying on the ground within his arm's reach, but he made no attempt to grab it.

Geoff kicked the rifle aside.

The man shoved himself up into a sitting position. That's when Geoff noticed the blood staining the lower half of his shirt on the right side. He'd taken a bullet to the gut.

"What's your name?" Geoff asked in Spanish.

"Rico."

"Well, Rico, just what do you know that's worth it to me to keep you alive?"

"I know the name of the man who hired us to kidnap Senorita Bedell."

"Is that all?"

"I will tell you his name. It is Arturo Torres-Rios." Rico coughed several times and spit bloody saliva on the ground.

"We already had that information." Geoff aimed his rifle at Rico. "If that's all—"

"No, no, wait, senor. I know that Arturo was working for someone else. Someone very rich and very powerful hired him to kidnap the senorita. We were to keep her until the ransom was paid, then Arturo was supposed to kill her.

"Any idea who hired your boss?"

Rico shook his head, and then he coughed up more blood. "If you do not kill me…"

"Look, Rico, I'm not going to shoot you again," Geoff told him. "But you have to know that you're as good as dead, so why not leave this world with as clear a conscience as possible. If you know anything else, just tell me."

Rico slumped over, his breathing shallow, his hands trembling. "I heard Arturo talking on his phone." Cough, spit, cough. "He called…the man…Josue." Heaving one final breath, Rico fell over. Passed out or dead?

Geoff checked for a pulse. He was dead.

Poor bastard.

Geoff slung his rifle over his good shoulder and headed out. Too bad there was no cell phone reception this deep in the forest. If there was, he could call Sawyer and warn him that one of the guards got away so he'd better be on the lookout for trouble. There was no way to know if the one kidnapper who had escaped would go after Lucie or simply go into hiding. But the one thing Geoff did know was that if he wanted to live, he needed to make it to the rendezvous point so he could get medical attention as soon as possible. He had managed to doctor his wound and slow the blood flow, but he'd lost a lot of blood. He still had a bullet in his shoulder and infection could set in at any time.

DAISY HOLBROOK woke up crying. She jerked straight up in the middle of her bed and sobbed. Dear Lord, her dream had seemed so real. Even now, awake and trembling with relief, she couldn't quite shake the horrible feeling that something bad had happened to Geoff. In her dream he had been fighting a giant red dragon with nothing but a sword. He was her gallant knight, fierce and brave and strong. She wiped the tears from her face, tossed back the covers and got out of bed. If only she could call Geoff right this minute, hear his voice, know that he was all right. But calling him was not an option.

She wandered out of the bedroom, flipped on the wall switch that turned on the light in her great-room/kitchen combo, and walked into the kitchen. The digital microwave clock read four-fifteen. If it was that late in the morning, there was no use going back to bed and trying to sleep again. Her alarm was set for five forty-five. The coffeemaker was programmed to start brewing at the exact time her alarm went off, so she simply reset the timer so that it would begin the process immediately. While waiting for the coffee, she went over to the windows overlooking the circular drive of the cul-de-sac on which she lived. As much as she liked living in the duplex she had bought three years ago, she wanted a bigger, better house when she got married. The rent she collected on the other duplex went entirely into her savings account, which by now had become a sizable nest egg.

When she got married?

And just when would that be?

When she convinced one very stubborn, confirmed bachelor that they were meant for each other, that's when.

Daisy turned from the view of the moonlit street, the manicured lawns and the vintage streetlights, and glanced at the coffeemaker. Not even half-full. She'd wait. She looked at the corner bookcase in the great room. As if drawn by an invisible cord, she walked straight to the bookcase, reached out and lifted a framed photograph from the top shelf. It was a group photo of her with several Dundee agents. The snapshot had been taken this past summer during a cookout in her backyard. The others in the photo—Lucie, Ty and Whit Falkner— faded away as she concentrated on Geoff's smiling face. He wasn't classically handsome, not her Geoff. He was far too rough-hewn and rugged to be good-looking. With his military short blond hair and his weathered skin, he looked every one of his forty-four years.

She hugged the photo to her bosom, closed her eyes and said a quick prayer. "If Geoff's in trouble, dear Lord, help him. Take care of him and bring him home to me. He may not know it yet, but he's going to be the father of my children. And I promise You that before I bring any children into this world, I'll be a married woman."

She remembered the first day she saw Geoff Monday. It hadn't been love at first sight, not exactly; but it certainly had been attraction at first sight. Some might say lust at first sight. He had grinned at her and called her "love" and her toes had curled. Every time the man stopped by her workstation, she got butterflies in her stomach. And the one time he'd kissed her, skyrockets had gone off. He had laughed about the kiss, passing it off as nothing but a friendly little smack. Yeah, sure. A friendly little smack included his tongue being halfway down her throat. She had been kissed enough in her life to know the difference.

You love me every bit as much as I love you, Geoffrey McDougall Monday. The only thing keeping us from living happily ever after is your damn stubbornness. You think you're too old for me. You think because you've been a mercenary—a killer for hire—that you aren't good enough for a sweet, gentle girl like me. But you should realize that I'm just what you need. You need sweet and gentle. You need a woman who loves you with her whole heart, with every fiber of her being. I don't give a damn that you're fifteen years old than I am.

Daisy looked up at the ceiling, her eyes cast heavenward. "I know something's wrong. That's why I had the dream about the dragon wounding him. Whatever's wrong, look after him. When he comes home, I'm going to ask him to marry me and I will not take no for an answer."

LUCIE AND SAWYER had gone less than two miles when the rain had begun, but they had kept walking, determined to make it to the Jeep. Drenched to the skin and sloshing in mud, they had forged ahead until a flash of lightning hit a nearby tree. That's when they had realized they had no choice but to find some kind of cover and wait out the storm. Unfortunately they hadn't found any caves or even hollow logs, so they'd taken shelter beneath a giant kapok tree towering over a hundred feet above them, the umbrella-shaped top acting as a canopy for the shorter trees on either side of it.

They had stood huddled together for a long time until they realized the storm was worsening and not likely to end any time soon, so they'd eased down onto the wet moss beneath the trees and rested. Lucie wasn't sure exactly how much time passed before the storm ended, but it had seemed like forever. She had tried talking to Sawyer while they waited, but he hadn't been inclined to carry on a conversation, telling her to shut up and sit tight. Finally, wet to the skin, muddy and sleep-deprived, they had headed out of the forest. Thankfully, the moon had been visible after the rain clouds passed.

They had backtracked for miles and now, shortly after dawn, they finally found the Jeep. Their relief at having quick transportation to the rendezvous point was short-lived. After climbing into the Jeep, Sawyer inserted the key into the ignition, but the damn engine wouldn't start.

"What the hell!"

He hopped out of the Jeep and used his flashlight to check under the hood. "I don't see anything out of place."

She wanted to ask him if he'd actually know if anything was missing or out of place, but she didn't. After all, it wasn't as if Sawyer had ever had to work on a vehicle in his life. Of course, he did know his way around expensive sports cars. Maybe there wasn't that much difference under the hood.

He ran the light over the side of the Jeep and then down along the wheels. Suddenly he cursed a blue streak.

"Somebody shot a hole in the gas tank and all the gas drained out on the ground," he told her.

"Who could have—?"

She didn't finish her sentence before gunfire erupted, bullet after bullet hitting the Jeep and barely missing them.

"Get down," Sawyer yelled.

Before he got the words out, she had dived out of the Jeep and rolled under it. Just as she pulled out her handgun, Sawyer slid underneath the vehicle alongside her and propped himself up enough to use his M16.

"I don't think there's more than one," Lucie told him.

"Yeah, I think you're right. It looks like Geoff didn't get both of the other guards."

"Do you think he's—"

"I don't know," Sawyer snapped. "But right now isn't the time to speculate. If we can kill this guy before he kills us, we'll find Geoff later."

CHAPTER TWELVE

GEOFF STOPPED, SAT down on a moss-covered boulder and eased his backpack off his uninjured shoulder. After retrieving a bottle of water, he drank half of it in one long swig; then he wiped his mouth with the back of his hand and closed his eyes. Just for a second. He couldn't waste any more time. Drawing in several deep breaths, he opened his eyes and took in his surroundings. The path Rita had told them about that led from the road to the abandoned plantation was overgrown with knee-high weeds and ankle-deep brush, but enough of the old horse and buggy lane remained to guide him to his destination. The morning sun slithered through the tall trees overgrown with thick vegetation. On the surface, the earth was moist and rich, the smell of rotting wood potent. The lush forest fed on itself, forever in a state of death and rebirth.

As Geoff rose to his feet, he winced as pain shot through his wounded shoulder. He glanced down and noticed fresh blood staining his shirt.

Son of a bitch!

He needed medical help and soon. His only hope was making it to the rendezvous point before passing out.

As he trudged along the path, each step became more

and more difficult. The early morning sun was hot and not even a hint of a breeze stirred the scent of sweet decay that surrounded him. Sweat dotted his forehead and beaded on his upper lip. One of the aftereffects of last night's rainstorm was increased humidity; or at least he hoped that was what was causing him to perspire. If he had a fever that would mean infection had already set in.

Forest creatures scurried about in the distance, the sounds of their chirps and cries and growls mingled into a tropical melody. Ahead, Geoff saw more trees and high grass and thickets of small trees and shrubbery—and the overgrown road seemed to disappear.

As sweat trickled off his forehead and into his eyes, he swiped the moisture away. Damn, it was hot. No, he was hot. He slapped his palm down on first one cheek and then the other. He was burning up with fever.

Have to get to the rendezvous point. Have to make it to the old coffee plantation.

The backpack and rifle he carried seemed to grow heavier with each step he took and his feet felt as if they were made out of lead.

Can't pass out. Have to keep moving. Only chance I've got.

He made his way a good thirty feet before the forest began to spin around and around and his knees buckled. He staggered, doing his best to stay upright. He slid the backpack off his shoulder and tossed it aside.

Lessen the load.

With each listless, sluggish step, he struggled to maintain consciousness and to continue moving forward, regardless of how slow. And if his vision hadn't deceived him and the road actually ran out up ahead, he would somehow find his way.

Suddenly he saw a shack about fifty feet from him, off to his left. It had to be part of the old coffee plantation. All he had to do was go in that direction. One step at a time.

His breathing grew shallow, each breath difficult. His limbs grew weaker and weaker, until he stumbled and dropped to his knees.

He heard a voice saying softly, sweetly, "Geoff... Geoff...come back to me, come home...."

"Daisy?" He looked all around him, his blurred vision seeing only a haze of green in every direction. "Daisy, is that you?"

Damn it, Monday, Daisy's back in Atlanta. She's not here in this damn tropical forest. You're hallucinating. You're hearing voices.

He knew he was going to pass out and there wasn't anything he could do to keep it from happening. As he toppled over, he clutched his M16 tightly and for just a split second in that moment between consciousness and unconsciousness, he saw Daisy smiling down at him and heard her tell him that she loved him.

MORNING SUNLIGHT brightened the sky and warmed the earth. Lucie wasn't sure how long they had been trapped under the Jeep, keeping their attacker at bay. Apparently, he had an unlimited supply of ammunition because he had wasted a lot of it shooting up the Jeep. He had taken cover in a nearby ditch, which acted as a protective barrier, all but making it impossible for them to hit him. He had effectively kept them pinned down, confined to this one position for quite some time.

"He's got enough ammo to wait us out, so we can't just stay here and do nothing," Sawyer whispered. "I want you to swap weapons with me." He held out his M16 for the exchange.

She eyed him questioningly, then handed him her pistol and took the rifle. He shoved the gun under the back waistband of his pants. "I'm crawling out the other side and going into the woods. You keep him busy concentrating on the gunfire coming from here. I'll try to circle around and sneak up on him and take him by surprise."

As Sawyer began scooting away from her, she grabbed his hand. "Be careful. Don't go getting yourself killed."

"I don't intend to."

She waited until he emerged on the other side of the Jeep, still crawling, and then she opened fire on their attacker. Too busy keeping the enemy focused on the firepower under the Jeep, she didn't watch Sawyer as he disappeared into the forest. All she could do was pray that he got away.

After several minutes, she stopped firing and waited. The guy got off another couple of rounds, then he, too, settled back into a waiting position behind his barricade.

And then she saw Sawyer coming out of the woods behind their attacker. He walked with deadly quiet, stealth movement his only hope of a surprise attack. Lucie kept the M16 aimed and ready.

Just as Sawyer slid into the ditch and up behind the man, he lifted his right hand and raised his left arm, bending it at the elbow. Lucie opened fire, drawing the man's attention, but she was careful to aim away from Sawyer.

Reaching around from behind, Sawyer covered the man's mouth and jerked him back, then used his left hand to strike the guy's neck. The man fired his gun repeatedly, most of the bullets peppering the air, until Sawyer took him down to the ground and used a choke hold on him. Struggling to free himself, the guy released his grip on his weapon.

Lucie held her fire.

Her heartbeat thundered in her head. Perspiration dampened her face and trickled between her breasts. She couldn't see what was happening because both Sawyer and the other man were in the ditch.

The sound of a single shot rang out in the morning stillness, echoing through the jungle. Lucie gasped. Holding her breath, she waited, her gaze glued to the ditch.

Less than a minute later, Sawyer stood and crawled up and out of the ditch and onto the road. *Thank You, God!* Lucie scrambled out from under the Jeep, lifted herself to her feet and broke into a run. When she met Sawyer in the road, she skidded to a halt.

"Are you all right?" she asked, looking him over from head to toe.

"Yeah, I'm fine."

She nodded toward the ditch. "Is he dead?"

"Yeah, he's dead."

She glanced at the bullet-riddled Jeep. "I guess we'll be walking."

"You guessed right."

He pulled the recently used pistol from his waistband

and handed it to her. She eyed it for half a second, nodded and then exchanged weapons with him.

"We need to get moving," he told her. "Geoff's probably waiting for us and wondering what's held us up."

SEVERAL HOURS LATER, Lucie and Sawyer reached their destination. The dilapidated plantation house stood on a weed-infested rise, the grass thigh-deep surrounding the two-story structure. The front side of the roof had caved in and the once whitewashed stucco was now a weathered cream. They circled the house, cautious and vigilant, taking no chances that they might be walking into an ambush. As far as they knew, there had been only four guards, but it was possible the guy that Sawyer had killed might have been able to put in a call for reinforcements before they showed up. It was also possible that something had gone wrong on Rita's end and she wasn't waiting for them, ready to whisk them to safety out of the country.

As they made their way toward the back where the remnants of a patio and garden were now barely recognizable, a plump, dark-haired woman in tan pants and shirt, with a rifle slung over her shoulder, emerged from the interior of the house.

"That's Rita," Sawyer told Lucie. He threw up his hand and waved.

"I don't see Geoff."

"He should already be here. Could be he's resting inside."

Rita approached, her black eyes filled with concern. "I was beginning to worry. I thought perhaps you weren't able to rescue Senorita Bedell." Rita sized up

Lucie, taking stock of her five-eleven frame and unruly mass of curly auburn hair.

"I know I must look like a drowned rat," Lucie said. "We got caught in that rainstorm early this morning."

Rita nodded. "You look alive. That's all that matters." She glanced from Lucie to Sawyer. "Senor Monday is not with you?"

"No," Sawyer said. "Then he's not here?"

Rita shook her head. "I have not seen him."

Sawyer cursed under his breath. "He should be here by now."

"You think something happened to him, don't you?" Lucie grabbed Sawyer's arm.

Frowning, he threw off her hand. "He's in trouble. Otherwise, he'd already be here."

"We need to find him," Lucie said. "We can't leave Ameca without him."

Ignoring her completely, Sawyer turned to Rita. "She'll stay here with you. I'm going to find Geoff. If I'm not back in an hour, get her to the chopper and—"

"No," Lucie cried. "I'm not leaving here without you."

He whipped around and glared at her. "You'll do what I tell you to do. This is no time for you to be stubborn. For once in your life…" He didn't finish the sentence. "I'll find Geoff and if we don't leave on the chopper with you, Rita will come back for us."

She eyed Rita. "Is he lying to me?"

"As soon as I put you on the helicopter, I will come back here and wait for them," Rita said. "I promise."

When Sawyer turned to leave, Lucie grabbed his arm again. He glanced over his shoulder. "Be careful."

His gaze narrowed as he gave her a hard look. Without saying a word, he walked away, heading back into the forest again.

Rita came up beside Lucie and patted her on the back. "He is your man, yes?"

A lump of emotion lodged in Lucie's throat, making it impossible for her to speak. In her heart, Sawyer *was* her man. He always had been and always would be.

"It is good to have a man love you so much that he is willing to die for you," Rita told her.

He doesn't love me. He hates me.

But he came with Geoff to rescue me. He didn't send someone else and he could have. If he didn't still care about me, why would he have risked his life to save me?

CARA EASED OPEN the bedroom door and tiptoed into the living room. Every morning since they had been at the cabin, Bain had awakened first and usually had finished showering and shaving by the time she got up. But this morning, he was still asleep on the sofa, which was really too small for a man of his size. If he wasn't such a stubborn jackass, he could be sharing her bed. There was nothing she wanted more than for Bain Desmond to make love with her.

Why had she fallen in love with one of the few men on earth who was bothered by the fact that she was a billionaire? Most men would have loved having a rich wife. But not Bain. If she were simply a successful businesswoman who made more money than he did, that wouldn't bother him. But her kind of wealth scared him.

She crept closer and closer to the sofa, then leaned over and stared at him. He was tall, dark and handsome, but he wasn't a pretty boy like Gray. His features were sharply chiseled, as if cut from stone, his cheekbones high and sharp, his nose hawkish and long, his mouth wide and sensuous. And his broad, bronze chest was matted with thick, dark hair. She longed to touch him, to rake her fingers through that black thicket on his chest, to nuzzle against his darkly tanned neck, to lie in his muscular arms.

Every nerve in her body tingled as arousal spread from her feminine core. She dropped down on her knees beside the sofa. Wondering if he slept in the raw or in his shorts—as a matter of fact, she didn't even know if her wore boxers or briefs—she grasped the edge of the blanket that lay across him midchest and slipped it down ever so gradually. Just as she dragged it below his waist, his right hand shot out and grabbed her wrist. She yelped as if she'd been shot.

"What do you think you're doing?" He opened his eyes and stared at her.

"Checking to see if you wear briefs or boxers," she admitted.

Keeping a tenacious hold on her wrist, he kicked at the blanket until it fell off him and onto the floor. Before she caught more than a glimpse of his brightly colored pajama bottoms, he yanked her down on top of him. The moment she landed against him, he released her wrist and ran his hand down her spine and caressed her butt.

She felt his sex, hard and ready, straining against her mound.

"Bain?"

"It's not going to happen," he told her.

"Why not? You want me. I want you."

"I want you too damn much," he confessed. "It's driving me crazy being cooped up here with you twenty-four-seven."

She snuggled against him. He growled. She kissed him on the mouth. He grabbed her waist and tried to lift her off him, but when she kissed him again, he slid his hands down and cupped her buttocks.

"It would be so good," she said. "You know it would."

He returned the kiss, taking charge. Leaving one hand stroking her butt, he lifted the other to the back of her head and pressed her into the kiss, his tongue lunging deep inside. They devoured each other.

She ached for him, longing for him to take her completely. Whimpering with desire, she urged him to move things to the next level, but just when she thought she finally had him to the point of no return, he halted and shoved her up and off him. Then he brought her with him when he came up off the sofa.

He held her by the shoulders and looked into her eyes. "You don't play fair, sugar."

"Haven't you heard, all's fair in love and war," she said breathlessly.

"It won't work between us," he told her. "God knows I wish it could, but it can't."

She pulled free of his grasp, moved back a few steps and took a deep breath. Then she studied him, from the top of his dark head, down his hairy chest and on to the— My God! He was wearing white pajama bottoms with red and blue firecrackers exploding in sparkling sprays of yellow light all over them.

Cara giggled. "Where on earth did you get those?"

"The same place I bought your lovely gown," he said, sizing her up in the knee-length, lavender cotton gown covered with huge purple flowers. "Some dollar store off the interstate between here and Chattanooga."

She twirled around, giving him an early morning fashion show. "I don't have on any panties."

He huffed loudly. "Yeah, I figured that out when I was patting your butt."

Okay, so she'd lost this battle, but that didn't mean she would lose the war. Sooner or later, she would wear him down and in a vulnerable moment…

No, she didn't want it to happen that way. She wanted more than just a one-night stand and so did he. And that was the problem.

"Do you know how to make pancakes?" she asked.

He lifted a curious brow, as if not quite trusting her. "Yeah, I know how. Why?"

"Do we have the ingredients for pancakes?"

"I bought a box of mix and a bottle of syrup. They're in the cupboard over the sink."

"Would you teach me how to make pancakes this morning?"

"Sure. After we've both showered and gotten dressed."

"Oh, shoot. I was thinking we'd strip off naked and—"

He turned her around and swatted her on the behind. "Go take a shower while I put on a pot of coffee."

When she stopped at the bathroom door, she turned and looked at him. "You know I love you and nothing is ever going to change that fact."

Before he could respond, she hurried into the bathroom and closed the door. She shut her eyes and said a silent prayer.

Please, God, there has to be a way for Bain and me to be together. Nothing is impossible for You. Would it be wrong for me to ask You for a miracle? Just a little miracle. I want to be Mrs. Bain Desmond. I want to spend the rest of my life with that rugged, stubborn, Chattanooga cop out there.

RITA CHECKED her watch and then scanned the area at the back of the plantation house where she and Lucie were waiting.

"How long?" Lucie asked.

"Fifty minutes."

Where was Sawyer? Had he found Geoff? If so, why weren't they back by now? *Please, Lord, don't let Geoff be dead.*

"You know that in ten minutes, we must leave," Rita told her.

Lucie nodded. "I know, but…"

"You will do as Sawyer asked and not give me any trouble, yes?"

"Yes. I'll do what Sawyer told me to do and we'll leave in ten minutes."

The last thing she wanted was to leave without Sawyer and Geoff. But she would follow orders.

She could hear Sawyer's voice inside her head. *This*

is no time for you to be stubborn. For once in your life...

For once in her life, what?

For once in your life do what I tell you to do. For once in your life don't dig in your heels and refuse to see reason. For once in your life don't fight me every inch of the way. For once in your life be reasonable.

The final ten minutes ticked by quickly, far too quickly.

"We need to go," Rita said.

"Please, couldn't we wait just five more minutes?"

Rita frowned. "You promised Sawyer that you would—"

"Oh, God!" Lucie saw two men coming slowly toward them, one halfway carrying the other. "It's them. Sawyer found Geoff."

She and Rita, both armed, ran toward the men. When she was only a few feet away, Lucie realized that Geoff was wounded. Badly wounded. A mix of dark, dried blood and fresh red blood stained his shirt. He was sweating profusely and could barely manage to stand.

"We need to get him to a hospital," Sawyer said. "He's lost a lot of blood and—"

"I'll get my car and bring it back here," Rita said. "We're not far from the helicopter."

While Rita hurried away, Lucie rushed over and helped Sawyer place Geoff on the ground. Kneeling beside Geoff, Sawyer ripped open his bloody shirt and removed the soaked bandage. "We need to stop the bleeding. He can't afford to lose any more blood."

Lucie grabbed the edge of her full skirt, the one she had bought on her shopping spree with Cara, and ripped off the tattered ruffle. She tore it into three pieces and folded each piece into a thick wad, then swiped Geoff's wound with one of the rags. He groaned and mumbled a string of curse words.

Rita brought her car to a screeching halt, opened the door, jumped out and rushed over to them. She carried a half-full bottle of whiskey in her hand.

"Here, use this to sterilize the wound." She handed the bottle to Sawyer.

"I've called ahead and there'll be a doctor waiting when you cross the border. He'll go with you and there will be an ambulance waiting when you reach Barbados. Come. We will take him to the car and put him in the backseat."

Lucie used the other pieces of her torn skirt as a makeshift bandage to cover Geoff's wound; then she and Sawyer lifted him to his feet and soon realized that they would have to carry him. By the time they had him laid out in the back of Rita's car, he was unconscious. Lucie crawled in the rear, lifted Geoff's head and placed it in her lap.

Sawyer slid into the front seat beside Rita, who put the gears into Reverse, backed up and slammed her foot on the gas pedal. The old car took off like a rocket and zoomed around the house and onto the gravel road that would take them to where the helicopter waited.

CHAPTER THIRTEEN

DEKE BRONSON GLANCED from Bedell VP Grayson Perkins to Cara's former stepmother, Patrice Bedell, who had flown into Chattanooga once Gray had phoned to tell her that Cara had been kidnapped. Why the son of a bitch had gone against Deke's orders to keep the kidnapping under wraps, he didn't know. Perkins had told him that since Patrice was family, she had a right to know about her stepdaughter's predicament. Deke suspected that both Gray Perkins and Patrice were licking their lips at the prospect of Cara not making it back alive and their inheriting part of the sizable Bedell fortune. Perkins professed his undying love for Cara, but even she knew that, first and foremost, the man loved himself. Since Cara had repeatedly turned down his marriage proposals, Perkins had to know that he wasn't getting his hands on her money that way. And Deke seriously doubted that Cara had left a considerable amount of money or Bedell stock to either her former brother-in-law of her stepmother. Of course, they probably intended to contest the will. They were a worthless, greedy pair.

Okay, so maybe his judgment of Perkins was a bit

harsh and maybe the guy had some real feelings for Cara, but he figured that his love for money outweighed his love for Cara.

As for Patrice—even Cara had suspected there had been some hanky-panky going on between Patrice and Perkins, possibly even before Cara's sister Audrey had died and while their father had been alive.

"If one word about Ms. Bedell being kidnapped leaks out, I'll hold you personally responsible," Deke said.

"Mr. Bronson, are you forgetting to whom you're speaking?" Perkins tilted his nose haughtily, his expression implying indignation. "I am your superior. I have the authority to fire you."

"No, sir, you do not. Only Ms. Bedell has that authority."

"In her absence—"

"You oversee Bedell, Inc. on a temporary basis, but you do not oversee Bedell Security. I do."

Patrice slinked toward Deke, her talonlike nails sparkling a bright coral that matched her lipstick and the skin-tight slacks and sweater she wore. "So forceful and manly," she purred. "But you should remember that if anything happens to Cara, Gray will be in charge permanently and then he could and probably would fire you."

Squinting until his eyes were half-closed slits, Deke smirked. "I'm sure that Ms. Bedell will be returning, but if the worst were to happen and she didn't, I believe that Mr. Perkins would remain in charge only until the board voted on a new CEO. And if Mr. Perkins were to gain that title, I can assure you that I would resign before he could fire me."

Perkins gasped. Patrice laughed.

"Now, if you'll excuse me," Deke said and turned to leave.

"Wait up," Perkins called to him.

Just as Deke glanced over his shoulder, his phone rang. He retrieved it from the holder attached to his belt and checked the caller ID. "I need to take this call. It's urgent."

"Is it about Cara?" Perkins asked.

"It could be," Deke replied. "It's Sawyer McNamara."

"Be sure to tell him that I should have the twenty-five million ready to wire to the kidnapper's bank account by first thing in the morning."

"Sure," Deke said as he walked out of Perkins's office and took the phone call. "Yeah, Sawyer. Do you have some good news for me?"

"We've got Lucie," Sawyer told him. "She's fine."

Deke grunted. "Good job. Tell Geoff—"

"Listen up. Geoff was shot during the rescue mission. He took a bullet in the shoulder. The Dundee jet landed at Grantley Adams International in Bridge-town, Barbados, an hour ago. Lucie and I are at the Queen Elizabeth Hospital waiting for him to come out of surgery. As far as anyone knows, Lucie is still Cara Bedell. Thank God the resemblance is close enough that no one is questioning us."

"How bad is it for Geoff?"

"Bad enough. He lost a lot of blood, but we had a doctor with us on the plane and he probably saved Geoff's life."

"Have you called Daisy?"

"Not yet. That's next on my agenda," Sawyer said. "I need for you to do two things. One, inform Grayson Perkins that we've rescued Cara and tell him that she'll be back in Chattanooga tomorrow sometime. Then get in touch with Bain and fill him in. Tell him that I'll contact him once the jet lands in Knoxville to get directions to the place where they're staying."

"Will do. And when Geoff comes to…well, just tell him I knew he was too mean and stubborn to let a single bullet kill him."

Sawyer snorted. "Damn right about that."

"Anything else?"

"That's it for now. I'll keep you posted about Geoff."

"Thanks."

Deke returned his phone to the belt clip as he headed back to Cara Bedell's office, where her former brother-in-law had moved in during her absence.

He couldn't wait to tell the cocky bastard that their boss lady was safe and sound and would be back to take charge tomorrow.

"WANT ME TO CALL DAISY?" Lucie asked.

"I thought I'd wait until he comes out of surgery and then call her with some good news," Sawyer said.

Lucie nodded. "She'll want to come down here on the first available flight."

"There's no need for her to do that."

Lucie stared at him as if he had just proclaimed that the world was flat.

"What?" He gave her a puzzled look.

"You do know that Daisy is in love with Geoff, don't you?"

He'd heard rumors around the office, of course, and he'd noticed the way the sensible, efficient Daisy mooned over Geoff. "She has a crush on him."

"Daisy's not a teenager with a crush. She's a grown woman and she's in love. She'll want to be here to personally look after Geoff."

"Doesn't she know that he's too old for her. Geoff's nearly forty-five and Daisy's how old—twenty five?"

Lucie huffed. "She's twenty-nine and age has nothing to do with it. Love isn't reasonable or sensible or logical."

The last thing he wanted to discuss with Lucie Evans was the subject of love. "Okay, okay. You can call her as soon as the surgery is over. Tell her to make arrangements for the first flight out of Atlanta and I'll have a hotel room for her by the time she arrives. And Dundee's will pick up the tab."

He'd let Lucie make the call and deal with whatever lovesick nonsense that would transpire.

"My, my, Mr. McNamara, you do have a heart after all."

He glared at Lucie. "Daisy is a valued employee, as is Geoff. Dundee's takes care of its own."

"Yes, of course. Forgive me for misunderstanding."

"You're good at doing that," he mumbled under his breath.

"What?"

Before he could respond, a nurse called his name. "Mr. McNamara?"

He and Lucie turned and looked at the tall, slender, middle-aged RN.

"I have an update for you on Mr. Monday," she said. "He is doing well. There have been no complications and he should be out of surgery in another hour."

"Thank you," they both said in unison, and then Lucie hugged Sawyer, the action completely spontaneous. And for a split second, he wrapped his arms around her and returned her hug. Then he realized what he was doing and released her.

When their gazes connected, he saw that Lucie was crying. Typical female. And totally in character for Lucie. She'd always been highly emotional.

Lucie wiped the tears from her cheeks. "I think I'll go see if I can find us some coffee."

"Black. No cream or sugar."

"Yes, I remember."

He walked away from her. Remembering was another subject he did not want to discuss with Lucie.

BAIN DESMOND ended his brief conversation with Deke Bronson. He had good news to share with Cara. Lucie Evans had been rescued and was unharmed. Dundee's had saved her from the kidnappers and she would be coming back to the U.S. tomorrow. And tomorrow, his time with Cara would come to an end. She would return to her CEO job, running her father's worldwide conglomerate, and he would return to his job as a Chattanooga police detective. They would go their separate ways once again.

The sooner the better, he told himself. Being stuck with her around the clock, day after day, was getting to him. Hell, *she* was getting to him.

Just how much could a guy take before he gave in to his baser instincts?

It took every ounce of his willpower not to make love to Cara. What had started out a few years ago, when he'd been the lead investigator in her sister's missing-person's case, as a harmless mutual attraction had escalated into something neither of them had bargained for—love. And not just I-want-to-fuck-you love, although that was a major part of the way they felt. No, what he felt for Cara went far deeper than that. If she weren't a billionaire heiress, he'd have already asked her to marry him. But how did a guy live with a woman who could buy and sell half the countries in the world? Yeah, okay, so that was a slight exaggeration, but not much of one.

He couldn't fit into her world of couture clothes, private jets, villas in Italy, ski lodges in Aspen, hobnobbing with royalty, presidents and prime ministers, and giving away more to charity in one week than the average person earned in a year. And she sure as hell couldn't fit into his world of living from paycheck to paycheck, doing his own laundry, cleaning his own apartment, enjoying baseball and football games with his buddies and buying his clothes off the rack.

"Bain, is everything all right?" Cara called to him as she came out on the front porch.

He had gone for one of his many daily treks around the cabin and had been halfway down the gravel drive that led to the winding, one-way road when Sawyer had phoned. Tossing up his hand, he waved at Cara. "Sawyer just called." He walked back up toward the house. "They rescued Lucie. She's fine."

Cara bounded down the steps, ran across the yard to the drive and flew into his arms. "Oh, Bain, I can't tell you how relieved I am." She hugged him. "I'm so happy that Lucie is all right. I've been worried about her, afraid…" She swallowed her tears of joy. "This is wonderful." She kissed Bain, a quick smack right on the mouth, then she kissed his forehead, his cheeks and his chin.

Damn, didn't she know what she was doing to him him? But right this minute, she wasn't thinking about anything except Lucie being free and safe. He reached up, eased her arms from around his neck and took both of her hands into his.

"Sawyer's bringing her back to the U.S. and they're coming here tomorrow so the two of you can exchange places. You can go back to being Cara Bedell and not have to keep on roughing it here with me."

She squeezed his hands. "I like roughing it with you." Looking at him with all that she felt showing in her eyes, she told him, "I wouldn't care where I was as long as I was with you."

"I know you think you mean that, but—"

"I do mean it. If you want me to live in your apartment and learn how to cook and clean and—"

Bain laughed. "I know you'd give it your best shot, but believe me, it would get old fast." He brought her right hand to his lips, kissed it and smiled. "We've had a few days together alone. It's more than I ever thought we'd have. It has to be enough."

Cara yanked her hands out of his and planted them on her hips. "It damn well isn't enough. The entire time we've been here, you've been keeping me at arm's length, avoiding physical contact and running off outside every chance you got. If we had spent these past few days making love, then maybe..." Tears glistened in her eyes. "Damn, I'm not going to cry."

"Cara, sugar, I... What do you want me to say?"

She stared at him, an incredulous expression on her face. "I don't want you to say anything. Nothing! Not a word. Just stay away from me. And when we get back to Chattanooga, if you want to do something for me, then leave Chattanooga, move halfway across the country and never come back." She turned around, stomped across the yard and marched up the porch steps. Then she stormed into the house and slammed the door behind her.

AFTER GEOFF came out of surgery and recovery, the doctor allowed Sawyer and Lucie to see him for a few minutes. He was still groggy from the anesthesia and by the time they left, he had fallen asleep.

"Let's check in to the Hilton, shower, grab a bite to eat and get a few hours of sleep while Geoff's resting," Sawyer said. "You can call Daisy on the taxi ride to the hotel, but when we get there, remember that you're still Cara Bedell."

"I remember. I'm not Lucie Evans until Cara and I change places again tomorrow."

"I'll leave my number at the nurse's station and then we'll go."

Ten minutes later, on their way to the Hilton Barbados in Needham's Point, a fifteen-minute drive to the airport, Lucie placed a call to Daisy on Sawyer's phone.

"Dundee Private Security and Investigation," Daisy answered. "How's it going down there? Have you and Geoff—"

"Daisy, it's me," Lucie said.

"Oh, thank the Lord. Are you all right? Where are you? How are Geoff and Sawyer? When are you coming home?" Daisy rattled off the questions quickly, not stopping until she was out of breath.

"Slow down. I'm fine, just a little battered and bruised, but otherwise all right. Sawyer and I are in Barbados, in Bridgetown." She hesitated, hating to tell Daisy about Geoff. "We…uh…we just left the hospital. Geoff's going to be all right, but he was shot—"

"Shot! How did that happen? No, forget I asked. It doesn't matter. Where was he shot? How serious is it? You tell Sawyer that I'm getting the next flight out of Atlanta. I'll turn things here at the office over to Staci. She'll be able to take over without any trouble."

"Daisy, listen to me. Calm down. Geoff was shot in the shoulder and lost a lot of blood. He's out of surgery and recovery. The doctor assured us that there's no reason to believe he won't be just fine."

Lucie could hear Daisy sobbing and doing her best to do it quietly.

"Hey, it's all right," Lucie said. "Go ahead and cry. Then go home, pack a bag and take the first flight down here. Geoff's at the Queen Elizabeth Hospital in St. Michael Parish. Sawyer and I will be at the Hilton for a few hours and then we'll head back to the hospital. Take a taxi when you get here. Give us a call if you need anything."

"As soon as I brief Staci, I'll make reservations and if I have time, I'll go home and pack a bag. If not, I'll just pick up whatever I need when I get there. When you talk to Geoff again, if he wakes up before I arrive, tell him…" She swallowed her tears. "You tell him he'd better not flirt with any of the nurses."

Lucie laughed. "I'll tell him."

After Lucie finished her call, she handed Sawyer his phone. He looked directly at her.

"How did Daisy take the news?" he asked.

"In typical efficient Daisy fashion, if a bit more flustered than usual. She gave me a message for Geoff."

Sawyer lifted his brows inquisitively.

"She said to tell him not to flirt with any of the nurses."

Sawyer grinned. "That would be like asking him not to breathe."

"Yeah, I know, and I'm pretty sure Daisy knows that, too."

THE HILTON BARBADOS, located on the beach, looked like a typical upscale chain hotel, a high-rise with little to distinguish it from others of a similar design. Sawyer realized that he and Lucie looked like a couple of dirty vagabonds, so when the doorman stared at them questioningly, he didn't blame the fellow.

"I used your name when I booked the suite," Sawyer told her.

"My name? Oh, of course, you told them that the suite was for Cara Bedell."

"I booked a two-bedroom suite so that when Daisy arrives, you and she can share tonight and then tomorrow, we'll turn the suite over to her for however long she stays here, probably until Geoff is released from the hospital and is fit to fly home."

"I'm sure Cara would want Daisy to have a suite and anything else she needs."

Sawyer nodded.

When they entered the large terrace reception area, the atmosphere changed from typical to tropical. There was a splendid view of the turquoise Caribbean from the lobby. Bright colors, dark wood furniture and native artwork graced the lounge.

The clerk at the reception desk widened her eyes as they approached.

"May I help you?" she asked with a hint of uncertainty in her voice.

Lucie marched right up to her, smiled condescendingly and said in a hushed tone, "I'm Cara Bedell. I believe you have a suite booked for me and my companion, Mr. McNamara."

The woman's dark eyes widened even more and her mouth opened on a startled gasp. "Yes, of course, Ms. Bedell. I understand you're traveling incognito. I can assure you that we will respect your privacy. If there is anything you and your guest require, simply let us know."

"A change of clothes," Lucie said. "We were in a bit of an accident and lost our luggage. Perhaps you could send someone out to pick up a few items for us."

"Yes, of course. If you make a list of everything you

require, I'll send someone to pick up the list and we will do our best to fill it."

"Thank you." Lucie sighed. "Now, if you can have someone show us to our suite, I'd appreciate it."

"Of course. Uh...er...we do need a credit card number."

"I'm afraid I lost my purse and everything in it. But if you'll contact my office in the U.S. they'll give you a credit card number and provide any other information you need." Lucie rattled off a series of numbers that Sawyer suspected was Deke Bronson's private office number.

"Certainly, Ms. Bedell."

The clerk called for a bellman and within minutes one appeared. She handed him the keys to their suite and gave him precise instructions.

As they went up in the elevator, Sawyer watched Lucie in his peripheral vision. She kept glancing at him, but neither of them said a word.

The bellman unlocked the door, ushered them inside and waited for Lucie to make out her needed-items list. She didn't bother asking Sawyer what size clothing or shoes he wore and when he offered to provide the information, she told him not to bother.

"Don't you think I know exactly what your sizes are?"

While she spoke to the bellman, he made a quick survey of their luxury accommodations. The parlor, like all the other rooms in the hotel, had an ocean view. The master bedroom had a private balcony and a king-size bed. The adjoining bedroom had two beds.

As soon as the bellman left, Sawyer met Lucie in the center of the parlor. "There's a whirlpool tub in the master bathroom," he told her. "I'll use the shower in the other bedroom."

"I've dreamed about a tub bath," she said. "Is there any bubble bath?"

"I don't know. I didn't look for any. But there could be. There are a couple of robes in the bathroom, so toss one out to me before you start soaking."

When she went into the master bedroom, he followed her, but instead of immediately heading for the bathroom, she walked out on the balcony. Sawyer paused in the doorway. She glanced back at him.

"Thank you for saving my life," she said.

Damn, Lucie, don't do this. Don't go all sweet and female on me. You've been to hell and back and I traveled halfway there to get you.

He didn't want to have to deal with her gratitude. He had done what needed to be done. Nothing more. Nothing less.

Damn, McNamara, you're lying to yourself. If it had been any other woman on earth or any other Dundee agent or former agent, you wouldn't have gone to Ameca with Geoff. You'd have sent another agent in with him, another guy with a military background.

"You're welcome," Sawyer finally managed to say.

She smiled, then came back inside and headed straight for the bathroom.

He heard her let out a long, low whistle and say through the half-open door, "This tub is huge. I can't wait to soak for at least an hour."

"Soak as long as you'd like. I'm going to call room

service and order something for both of us. Any preferences?" he asked.

"I want a thick, juicy steak. Other than that, order whatever you want."

She peeked out of the bathroom. "Here, catch." She tossed him one of the white bathrobes.

He caught it with his right hand. "I'll knock on the door and let you know when the food arrives."

"Yeah, thanks. That would be great." She closed the bathroom door.

He stood there staring at the door for a full minute, then shook off his wayward thoughts and went into the lounge. He picked up the phone, called room service and ordered. The minute he told them he wanted one steak medium and the other medium rare, he cursed himself for remembering the way Lucie liked her steak. Medium.

Hell, he remembered way too much about her, a lot more than the fact she liked her steaks pink and juicy, but not bloody. She liked gourmet coffee, preferably caramel-flavored; cheesecake drizzled with chocolate; baked potatoes, fully loaded; good wine; and her favorite mixed drink was a Cosmopolitan.

Odd how a man remembered those kinds of things.

Sawyer tossed the robe over his shoulder and headed for the other bathroom.

"OUR CLIENT IS very unhappy. He expected you to do the job properly."

Josue had dreaded calling Arturo with the bad news. He had never known Arturo to fail at completing an as-

signment. This was the first time and it was understand-
able that he would be upset.

"I should have been informed that there was a possibility that a rescue team would be sent in. They were
undoubtedly paid mercenaries," Arturo replied, anger in
his voice. "The men I chose to guard the senorita could
not have been overpowered by anything less than a
group of trained soldiers."

"None of that matters now, does it? Our client will
not accept excuses. There will be no ransom money, so
we cannot expect any further payments."

"I do not expect payment unless the job is completed. Tell him if he wishes to hire me to do finish the
job and personally eliminate his problem, I will do so
for half the price we agreed on."

"Very well," Josue said. "I will make him the offer
and contact you with his response."

"Tell him that finishing this for him is a matter of
honor for me."

CHAPTER FOURTEEN

LUCIE SLIPPED INTO the thick terrycloth robe and tied the belt at her waist. A person couldn't imagine how much they would miss the luxury of taking a tub bath until they were deprived of that pleasure.

It felt great to be clean!

After removing the towel wrapped around her wet hair, she used it to rub the moisture from her unruly curls. Then she checked the array of toiletries and found a small bottle of lotion. She uncapped the lid, emptied the entire contents into her hand and lifted one freshly shaved leg up on the commode. Just as she finished lathering one leg and had lifted the other, Sawyer knocked on the bathroom door.

"Our food's here," he said.

"Great. I'm starving."

She quickly covered her other leg and then both arms with the remainder of the lotion before checking herself in the mirror. Scrubbed clean. No makeup. She could see the beginning of laugh lines at the corners of her eyes. Faint lines, but lines never the less. At thirty-six, she should expect a few early signs of aging, shouldn't she? After all, a woman couldn't look like a girl forever.

Sighing, she adjusted the belt on her robe, squared her shoulders and opened the bathroom door. Sawyer stood by the serving table, obviously waiting for her. God, why did he have to look so good? Good enough to eat.

Get that thought out of your mind.

His dark, damp hair touched the collar of the robe he wore. The contrast between his dark complexion and the white robe made him look all the more tanned and fit. Sawyer had always been handsome in a strong, masculine way. Even as a teenager, he had possessed a raw sex appeal that could turn a woman's head. But now, at forty, he epitomized masculine beauty.

Crazy how her heart still beat a little faster just at the sight of him and the way butterflies danced in her stomach. Her physical reaction to him had only grown stronger as the years passed, yet remained so similar to the way she'd felt the first time she saw him. Only then she hadn't known that it was sexual. She had thought it was simply love at first sight.

"Are you going to come over here and sit down or are you going to stand there all day staring at me?" Sawyer glared at her.

Her face burned with an embarrassed flush. What could she say? She could hardly deny his accusation. She had been staring at him. Lusting after him. Some things never changed.

"Something sure smells good," she said, choosing not to react to his comment.

When she approached the cloth-covered serving table, Sawyer pulled out a chair for her. Always the gentleman. She remembered how his good manners had impressed her when she was a teenager. And even now, she found them admirable. So few men were true gentlemen.

"Thank you," she said.

After Sawyer sat down across from her, he lifted the stainless covers from the plates of food. When Lucie eyed the luscious steak on her plate, her mouth watered. She picked up her knife and fork and then surveyed the table, checking out the array of delicious food. A green salad, topped with her favorite French dressing, sat beside the steak. Just to make sure the steak truly had been prepared the way she liked it, she sliced into it and smiled. She speared the piece with her fork, brought it to her mouth and then sighed with contentment.

"Good?" Sawyer asked.

"Heavenly," she replied.

She noticed that the baked potato on her plate was loaded with cheese, chives and crumbled bacon. Had Sawyer actually remembered how she liked her baked potato or had it simply come this way? She glanced at his potato. Plain, only butter, the way he liked it.

Don't get all excited just because he remembered something as insignificant about you as the way you like your baked potato prepared.

He lifted the silver carafe and held it over her cup. "Coffee?" he asked.

"Yes, thank you. They brought me coffee every morning, but it tasted a lot like dirty dishwater."

"It's not flavored," Sawyer told her. "Just plain."

"Plain old coffee is just fine." Not flavored. Just

plain. Not only had he remembered that she took her potato loaded, but that she liked flavored coffee.

He poured their coffee. She lifted her cup, took a sip and smiled.

"Oh, that's good." She released a long, contented sigh.

He gave her a peculiar look, then glanced away and picked up his knife and fork. When he cut into his steak, it oozed a light red liquid. She didn't like her steaks overcooked by any means, but she wasn't sure how anyone ate their meat when it was still bloody.

They ate in relative silence, both of them devouring their food. Occasionally she glanced his way, but he apparently was determined not to look directly at her again.

"I ordered dessert," he said as he poured them both a third cup of coffee.

She eyed the covered dessert dish. Dare she hope he also remembered her favorite?

"I'm stuffed, but you know me, I can always make room for something sweet."

"One of your weaknesses."

"Yes, one of many." *You're my major weakness, Sawyer McNamara, but then you know that, don't you?*

She removed the cover from the dessert plate and almost cried out with joy. Cheesecake drizzled with chocolate sauce. He had remembered.

They looked at each other, their gazes connecting for several seconds before he looked away and reached down to remove the cover from his dessert.

A bowl of fresh fruit: pineapple slices, papaya, kiwi, cantaloupe and mandarin oranges. Ever health-conscious, it was so like Sawyer to prefer fruit over something rich and fattening.

Lucie sliced off a bite of cheesecake and lifted the fork to her mouth. She hadn't realized she had sighed again until she heard Sawyer chuckle. She glanced at him and smiled.

"Hey, I'm enjoying this meal, every single bite. Don't begrudge me this little pleasure. Not after what I've been through these past few days."

"With the kind of healthy appetite you have, I'm surprised you don't weigh three hundred pounds." He grinned. "But you haven't gained a pound since you were twenty."

"Just wait until I hit fifty. I'll be like my grandmother and spread out. But for now, I work at keeping the pounds off. I don't eat like this all the time, you know. And I exercise. I take dance classes. Bet you didn't know that, did you?"

He shook his head. "There's a lot that I don't know about you."

"Yeah. That works both ways. There are things I don't know about you, too."

Neither of them said anything else. They sat there staring at each other, the tension between them palpable. Why didn't he say something? Why didn't she?

A loud knock on the lounge door ended the tension. Each of them sucked in a deep breath. He shoved back his chair and stood.

"That's probably the bellman with the list of items you ordered," Sawyer said as he approached the door.

"I can't wait to put on some clean clothes. I threw my old ones in the garbage."

Sawyer opened the door and three members of the hotel staff entered, each with his arms filled with sacks and garment bags. "Where do you want all this stuff?" he asked Lucie.

"Put everything down on the sofa," she instructed. "We can go through it and sort all of it later."

Just as Lucie was signing the receipt—as Cara Bedell—Sawyer's phone rang. By the time she had shooed the hotel employees out the door, after adding a generous tip to the bill, Sawyer had finished his brief conversation.

"Daisy's in Miami. She has a layover there," Sawyer said. "She'll arrive in Barbados around ten tonight."

"How did she sound?" Lucie asked.

"Optimistic and determined."

"I have a feeling that Geoff Monday is not going to know what hit him when Daisy takes charge. Something tells me that she's coming here to get her man."

"And if he doesn't want to be gotten?"

Lucie grinned. "He doesn't stand a chance against her. She's a woman in love. I'll lay odds that before the end of the year, they'll be engaged. And come next spring, we'll be attending their wedding."

"A long engagement, huh?"

"Daisy's the type who'll want a big fancy wedding. That takes time to plan and execute."

"I can't see Geoff wanting to get married, let alone agreeing to some elaborate wedding."

"He'll do it for Daisy. Because if he loves her, and I

have a feeling that he does, he'll want her to have her heart's desire."

"Still a romantic, I see. I thought you might have outgrown such silliness. In so many ways, you're nothing like the girl I once knew, but in other ways you're exactly like her."

"Like you said, there are a lot of things you don't know about me now."

"Obviously. So, tell me, when you get married, will you want an elaborate wedding, white gown, big church—"

"I'm not ever getting married," she told him. "But hypothetically speaking, if I ever did, I'd want something simple, nothing big and elaborate." She looked directly into his eyes. "So, what about you?"

"What about me?"

"When you get married—?"

He grunted. "Marriage is not in my future plans."

"It was once."

He frowned. "That was a long time ago and it was a mistake. Lucky for Faith and for me that I realized it in time. If we had married, it would have been a disaster."

"Yeah, lucky for both of you." Lucie went over to where the sacks and bags lay on the sofa. "I ordered you khaki pants and a sport coat. They're off the rack, which you're not accustomed to, but they'll do for now." She laid his clothes aside and went through everything until she found her clothes. "I'll get dressed. We probably need to go back to the hospital and check on Geoff."

He picked up his clothes and the shave kit she had ordered. "I want to take time to shave before we go."

"I figured you would. Although I kind of like the roguish look that dark beard stubble gives you."

"I won't shave if you won't comb your hair." Grinning, he glanced at her rioting, unruly curls.

"Go shave. Now!"

They shared a smile. Lucie's heart lodged in her throat. It had been such a long time since they had been civil to each other that she'd forgotten how wonderful it was to be with a noncombative Sawyer.

She broke eye contact and hurried off to the adjoining bedroom. After dropping her armload of items on the bed, she closed the door. Taking a deep, calming breath, she leaned back her head and momentarily closed her eyes.

Faith Edwards.

Even after all these years, the name still had the power to anger Lucie.

Sawyer had met Faith through mutual friends after he sold his interest in the family business to his uncle and became a federal agent. Faith had been the niece of a Virginia senator, Vassar-educated, her family even wealthier than the McNamaras. Sawyer had brought her home for Christmas Lucie's freshman year of college and had surprised everyone with the announcement that they were engaged. The news had broken eighteen-year-old Lucie's heart. But Brenden had been there to pick up the pieces.

By the time Sawyer and Faith called off their June wedding, exactly two months before the big day, Lucie was already dating Brenden.

If only she could go back and undo the decision

she'd made to date Sawyer's brother. She had allowed him to think they might have a future together when she'd known in her heart that she would never love anyone except Sawyer. She had given Brenden false hope and in the end it had destroyed him. Actually, it had destroyed all three of them.

DAISY ARRIVED AT Queen Elizabeth Hospital shortly after midnight. Lucie and Sawyer were in the waiting area, each of them on separate couches. Although she was sitting upright, Lucie had her legs and feet across the sofa and her eyes were closed. Sawyer sat on the sofa directly opposite her and he had his legs stretched out, the heels of his shoes on the floor. When she entered the room, Sawyer glanced her way and the minute he recognized her, he got up and came toward her. She didn't wait for an invitation; she walked straight into his arms. He hugged her and then patted her on the back.

She eased out of his embrace and asked, "How's Geoff?"

"He's doing fine, all things considered. Lucie and I went into the ICU and saw him during the last visitation. He was sound asleep. They're keeping him sedated so he'll rest."

"Do you think there's any chance they'd let me see him now?"

"I doubt it. They seem to be pretty strict around here."

"I'm sure he needs rest more than he needs me standing over him crying," Daisy said. "But I'll be here when he wakes up again." She bit her bottom lip in an effort not to cry.

Lucie, who had apparently been asleep, called to Daisy, "When did you get here?"

"I just arrived."

Lucie got up, walked over to Daisy and they hugged each other while they both cried for a couple of minutes. Sawyer cleared his throat. Daisy and Lucie looked at him and laughed. He shrugged, his expression saying plainly that he would never understand women.

"We were waiting for you to get here before we went back to the hotel," Lucie said. "There's nothing any of us can do for Geoff tonight."

"Y'all go on," Daisy said. "I'm going to stay here."

"That's ridiculous," Sawyer told her. "They won't let you go in to see him until morning. And your being here at the hospital won't help him in any way."

"I'm staying."

"Daisy, be reasonable," Sawyer said.

"Leave her alone." Lucie gave him a hard look. "I'd do the same thing in her shoes. If the man I loved was in there recovering from surgery, I'd want to stay as close to him as possible."

Daisy's smile widened. "I knew you'd understand." She glanced at Sawyer. "If the woman you loved—"

"Don't go there," Sawyer warned her.

"You two go back to the hotel. I'll bed down here. And I promise that after I see Geoff tomorrow, I'll go back to the hotel every night, after the last visitation period."

"I take it you plan to stay here in Barbados until Geoff gets out of the hospital," Sawyer said.

"Yes, I do. I'm not leaving him. That man needs me even if he doesn't know it."

"I won't argue with you," Sawyer said. He looked at Lucie. "Are you going with me or are you staying here?"

"She's going with you," Daisy answered for her.

WHEN THEY ARRIVED back at their suite at the Hilton, Sawyer opened the minibar and removed a beer.

"Want one?" he asked.

She shook her head. "Is their any fruit juice?"

He rummaged through the fridge's contents. "Apple, cranberry and orange."

"Apple."

He set his beer on the coffee table, removed the canned apple juice and undid the lid. "Here." He handed the juice to her, being careful not to let his fingers touch hers. *Was the very thought of touching her that abhorrent to him?*

After nine years, she should be used to the subtle ways he avoided her. She'd certainly grown accustomed to the not-so-subtle ways he had shown his contempt.

Let it go, Lucie, let it go.

She took the bottle, slumped down on the sofa and kicked off her shoes. These sandals were not expensive leather like the ones Cara had bought for her in San Luis, but they were comfortable yellow flip-flops with a big pink flower attached so that it perched on top of her foot. Oddly enough, the sandals sort of matched her yellow cotton slacks and floral pink-and-yellow blouse. Whoever had done the shopping had actually tried their best to coordinate the clothes they'd purchased. Sawyer's khaki pants looked good with the white cotton shirt and navy jacket, all the items lightweight cotton in a casual style.

Sawyer sat in the chair across from her and propped his feet up on the coffee table. "We need to get a few hours of sleep. I plan for us to leave first thing in the morning. It's at least a seven-hour flight from here to Knoxville and there's a two-hour time difference. If we get in the air by eight in the morning, we should be in Tennessee by two. I don't know how long it will take us to get to wherever Bain took Cara. Then we'll need to discuss where we'll go from there. I think it's probably a good idea for you and Cara to show up back in Chattanooga together."

Lucie nodded and then took a sip of the cold apple juice. "You realize, don't you, that this nightmare isn't over?"

"What are you talking about?" He picked up his beer bottle. "Be specific."

Lucie cringed. How many times in the past had he chastised her for not being specific, reminding her that vague details were of little use in an investigation.

"Whoever ordered Cara's kidnapping had no intention of letting her go free when the ransom was paid."

Holding the beer between both hands, Sawyer looked directly at her. "How do you know what they were going to do?"

"I overheard bits and pieces of the guards' conversations. And even though my Spanish isn't all that great, I picked up enough to know that they were taking orders from someone and once the ransom was paid, this person was going to kill Cara."

Sawyer grunted. "Why kill Cara once the twenty-five million was paid?"

"Good question." Lucie emptied half the juice bottle in one long swig. "I have a gut feeling that there was a lot more to Cara's kidnapping than just the ransom money."

"Maybe. Maybe not. After all you saw the men who kidnapped you. It could have been nothing more than not wanting to leave a witness to ID them."

"Yes, I saw the kidnappers," Lucie said, "and yes, maybe I could have identified them, but I don't think that's the reason whoever hired them was going to kill me himself. I think the plan all along included killing Cara."

"If that's true, then she could still be in danger, even back in the States."

"Do you have any idea who might have been behind the kidnapping?"

"We've got a few theories, but nothing concrete," Sawyer told her.

"I heard the kidnappers mention the name Josue, but I'm not sure how he is connected to what happened."

"It's a name we'll check out and see if he's connected to Castillo or President Ortega or Arturo Torres-Rios."

"The first person I'd investigate is Tomas Castillo. He has a lot to lose if Bedell Inc. signs a deal with Delgado Oil and the man knew that was inevitable. Could be he thought if he eliminated Cara, whoever took over for her as CEO would be more inclined to see things his way."

"Castillo is a possibility, but why would he ask for a ransom if he simply wanted her eliminated? He could have hired this guy, Arturo Torres-Rios, to kill her. After all, the man's an assassin. Why go to the trouble of kidnapping her and holding her for ransom?"

"The kidnapping was a smoke screen to take suspicion off Castillo since he would be the obvious suspect," Lucie said. "The twenty-five million was just a bonus."

"Could be. Like you said, he's the obvious suspect."

"But you don't like the obvious, do you?"

"Sometimes things are just what they appear to be, but more often than not, the truth isn't always apparent and you have to dig deeper to find it."

A chill shivered up Lucie's spine. Sawyer was referring to investigating a crime, but his words hit a nerve with her, striking at the very heart of their relationship. The truth between them was buried so deep—six feet under in the grave with Brenden—that it would never see the light of day.

"Whoever wanted Cara dead probably still wants her dead," Sawyer said.

"Cara needs to know all of this before she and I switch places tomorrow. If she's still in danger, if there's a contract out on her life…"

"If there is, we'll deal with it. But if you're suggesting that you two not make the switch and you put yourself in the line of fire and continue pretending to be Cara, forget it. First of all, once back in Chattanooga, you can't pass yourself off as Cara Bedell. Yes, you and she are the same height, both of you are redheads and there is a slight resemblance, but anyone who knows her—"

"We need to consider all the possibilities. But we need more facts before we can formulate a workable plan."

"Damn it, Lucie, you'll be in enough danger if you continue as Cara's personal bodyguard, especially if someone actually has been hired to kill her."

If she didn't know better, she would swear that he cared and was genuinely concerned about her.

Oh, Lucie, the man risked his life to save you. He wouldn't have done that if he didn't care. And that's the problem. That's why he hates himself and hates you even more.

CHAPTER FIFTEEN

SAWYER RAN HIS hand over her naked shoulder, lifted her long, curly hair away from her neck and lowered his mouth to the hollow of her throat. She smelled like flowers and tasted sweet and slightly salty. He had waited a lifetime to touch her this way and he was as nervous as a boy with his first woman.

She pressed her breasts against his chest, the feel of her nipples burrowing into his chest hair exciting him. He was hard and ready and didn't know how long he could prolong the foreplay.

As he slid the tip of his tongue up her throat, over her chin and to her parted lips, she moaned seductively. Finally, as his mouth covered hers, the dam of reserve he had kept in place all these years broke and released the passion he could no longer restrain.

She returned his kiss with equal force, silently telling him that she wanted him as much as he wanted her.

He couldn't get close enough, couldn't taste her enough, couldn't hold her tight enough, couldn't get enough of her.

If he could wait, he would; but he couldn't. He had to have her. Had to take her now!

"I love you," she cried out as he thrust inside her. *"I've always loved you...."*

Sawyer's eyes flew open and he shot straight up in bed, knocking the sheet and comforter down past his waist. His breath came in deep, trembling gulps.

God in heaven, he hadn't had that dream in years.

He flung the covers from his legs, slid from the center of the bed to the edge and stood up. Naked and aroused.

He cursed under his breath, then reached out and picked up the briefs he'd tossed into the chair. He eyed the bedside clock. Four fifty-three.

After going into the bathroom and using the toilet, he put on his briefs. Then he turned on the sink faucet, leaned down and ran cold water over his head.

Don't think about the dream. Think about the reality.

Only one room stood between him and Lucie. All he had to do was walk through the lounge and into her bedroom.

He grabbed a towel off the rack and rubbed the moisture out of his hair. The alarm was set for five-thirty. Breakfast would arrive at six-thirty. They would leave for the airport at seven and the Dundee jet would take off at eight. If everything went as planned, they would arrive at the Knoxville airport around two this afternoon, Eastern Standard Time.

His khaki slacks lay across the arm of the chair and his shirt hung from the back. He grabbed the slacks, slipped into them and walked into the lounge. The room lay in semidarkness. Neither of them had drawn the drapes last night, so the security lighting from outside cast a dim glow over the room. He went through the motions of preparing coffee, all the while pushing thoughts of his erotic dream from his mind. But the harder he tried not to think about it, the stronger the memory became.

With the coffeemaker brewing, he moved quietly across to the closed door of Lucie's room and without giving his actions a second thought, he turned the knob and opened the door. She had left the bathroom light on and the door halfway open so that a shaft of light spread across the carpet and bed. He walked slowly to the edge of the bed where Lucie slept, sprawled on her stomach and lying atop the covers. She was as naked as the day she was born.

His body reacted to the sight of her, his penis growing instantly hard as he stared at her long legs, her firm butt, her slender waist and the curve of one round breast pressed against the comforter.

His hands itched to touch her, to caress her back and buttocks, to flip her over and—

What the hell was he doing? Why was he standing here with a hard-on thinking about making love to Lucie?

It was that damn dream. That's all it was.

You're lying to yourself. You want her now as much as you did nine years ago. But unlike nine years ago, he was not going to give in to his baser instincts.

He took one last look. It was all he could do to make himself turn around and leave the room. When he was almost to the door, he heard her moan. He glanced over his shoulder. She had flipped onto her back, bringing the comforter up and over her.

"Sawyer?"

Caught red-handed!

"Yeah." He kept his back to her and looked away, staring through the open door at the lounge. "I've got coffee on. It should be ready by the time you take a shower."

"What time is it?" she asked.

"About five. I woke early and—"

"Is everything all right?"

"Yeah, everything's fine."

He rushed out of the bedroom and into the lounge. Had she known he was standing beside her bed looking at her? Did she have any idea what the sight of her naked body did to him? Or had he, during the past nine years, done an effective job of convincing her that he hated her and would never want her again?

What did it matter? How she felt or what she thought was not the issue. When she had left Dundee's and gone to work for Bedell, Inc., she had cut the ties that had bound them together in a self-inflicted hell. She had finally set them both free from the past. Or so he had thought; so he had hoped. But the moment he had found out her life was in danger, he'd been forced to admit that he still cared, so much so that he'd risked his life to rescue her instead of doing what he should have done and sent another ex-military agent with Geoff.

Just keep things from heating up, he told himself. *Take a shower, shave and get dressed. Then drink some coffee and later eat breakfast and leave for the airport.*

Once Lucie and Cara reunited and each took her own identity, he'd go back to Atlanta and let Bedell security work with Dundee's to keep both women safe.

He could send as many agents as Cara wanted or needed. And he could stay the hell away from Lucie.

"ARE YOU BY ANY chance Daisy?" The ICU nurse stood in the doorway of the waiting room. "If you are, Mr. Monday has been calling your name."

"Yes, I'm Daisy!" Half-asleep, Daisy jumped up off the sofa and rushed to the doorway where the nurse waited. "Did you say Geoff is asking for me?"

"Actually, he's just coming to, but he keeps mumbling and the one word we're able to make out is the word *daisy*." The young dark-eyed woman smiled. "I finally realized that the word didn't refer to a flower, but to a woman. And since one of the other nurses said there was a young woman in the waiting room, I thought perhaps you were Mr. Monday's Daisy."

He'd been calling her name in his sleep. Daisy felt like jumping for joy. And if not for the fact that Geoff had been shot and now lay recuperating in the ICU, she would be ecstatic.

"Would you like to see him?" the nurse asked.

"Yes, of course I would, but I thought visiting time wasn't until—"

"I'm Ms. Shadwell, Veronica Shadwell," the nurse said. "And you are?"

"Daisy Holbrook. I am…I'm going to marry Mr. Monday."

"Well, in that case, I believe we can make an exception. Mr. Monday will wake soon and it would be good for him to see his Daisy there at his bedside."

Daisy had to stop herself from hugging the nurse. "Thank you." Tears gathered in her eyes. "I love him so much. If anything had happened to him, I don't know…" She swallowed her tears, and then laughed. "I can't wait to see him."

"Come with me."

She followed the woman into the intensive care unit and paused outside Geoff's cubicle while Ms. Shadwell went inside and checked on him.

"Good morning, Mr. Monday."

"Where am I?" Geoff asked groggily.

"You're in Queen Elizabeth Hospital in Bridgetown, Barbados."

"How long have I been here?"

"You were brought in yesterday," she told him. "You had surgery to remove a bullet from your shoulder. We've kept you sedated so that you would rest. When you came out from under the anesthesia, you were quite restless."

"Sorry if I gave you any trouble."

"That's quite all right."

"Where's Sawyer? You know, Mr. McNamara, the guy who brought me here?"

"I'm not sure, I believe he and the lady who was with him have left, but there is someone here who can probably answer your questions, someone who's been waiting all night to see you."

The nurse motioned to Daisy. Suddenly she felt shy and hesitant. What if Geoff didn't want her here? She took several cautious steps into the room and smiled when she saw him lying there looking remarkably healthy for a man who had been shot. Big, tough, badly in need of a shave. And all man. Her man.

He grinned from ear to ear when he saw her. "Daisy? My God, woman, what are you doing here?"

She marched over to his bed. "What do you think I'm doing here? Where else would I be?"

"Where else indeed." He lifted his hand, an IV tube attached to the top, and reached out for her. He frowned with he saw the tube.

She took his hand, laid it gently back at his side and then caressed his grizzly cheek. "I'm here to take care of you and make sure you follow orders."

"My own private duty nurse, huh?"

Daisy glanced at Ms. Shadwell. "When can he be moved out of intensive care?"

"Tomorrow, I expect," Ms. Shadwell replied. "Now, I'll leave you two alone." She glanced from Geoff to Daisy. "I'm afraid I can't give you more than ten minutes, but later, at the regular morning visiting time, you may stay thirty minutes."

"Thank you," Daisy replied and as soon as the nurse left, she leaned over Geoff's bed and kissed him—right on the mouth.

Instead of reacting as if were startled, he kissed her and raised his good arm up to cup the back of her head and hold her there for a second kiss. When he released his tender hold on her, she lifted her head, opened her eyes and stared at him dreamily.

"You have no idea how glad I am to see you," Geoff whispered.

"And you have no idea how glad I am that you didn't

get yourself killed. When Lucie called and told that you'd been shot, my heart stopped. If anything had happened to you…"

He grinned at her. "You can't kill an old warhorse like me. Don't you know that?"

"I know that I couldn't bear to live without you. Damn it, Geoff Monday, I love you. I love you so much it hurts. And I'm sick and tired of holding all this love inside me and pretending that—"

He reached out and clutched her chin between his thumb and fingers. "Look at me, Daisy."

She stared at him, her eyes filled with tears.

"You know what I'm going to say. You know all the arguments I'm going to give you, starting with the fact I'm way too old for you and ending with you deserve someone better than a bruised and battered old warrior who's never done anything in his life to deserve a sweet, gentle and loving woman such as you."

Her tears cascaded down her checks and dripped on his hand that held her chin. "Do I deserve to be happy?" she asked.

"More than anyone I know."

"Do I deserve to be with the man I love?"

He hesitated, then said, "Yes, of course you do, but—"

She grabbed his hand and jerked it away from her chin. Staring at him, her eyes wide, her heart hammering in her ears, she asked the one question that would determine their future. "Geoff Monday, do you or do you not love me?"

"Whether or not I love you isn't important," he told her.

"It's all that's important. Answer me, do you love me?"

"Yes, I love you, but—"

She pressed her right index finger over his lips to silence him. "Hush, now, and rest. We'll work out all the details when you're fully recovered."

He mumbled beneath her finger. She smiled triumphantly and lifted her finger. "What did you say?" she asked.

"I said work out what details?"

"About our engagement and wedding, of course."

"Our what?"

She leaned over, kissed his forehead and patted his cheek. "You rest now and I'll be back at the morning visiting time. Perhaps Ms. Shadwell will allow me to feed you your breakfast."

Daisy headed for the exit.

"Come back here," Geoff called. "We need to get things straightened out."

"Oh, there will be plenty of time for that later." She blew him a kiss and waltzed merrily out of the ICU, all the while Geoff calling her name.

He loved her. He had admitted it. She had him hooked now. All she had to do was reel him in. Slowly but surely.

HE WAS DREAMING. He had to be.

Cara stood over him, smiling down at him. She was beautifully, gloriously naked. How many times in the past few years had this type of dream plagued him? Too many times to count. In reality, they had never done anything more than kiss, but in his dreams they made love often.

His whole body was tense with arousal, his penis erect and ready. He reached up and caressed her smooth, creamy hip. She shivered and sighed. God, this dream seemed so real.

"Cara…" He said her name aloud.

"Make love with me. Please, Bain. I want you so much."

Usually in his dreams, Cara didn't talk to him; she simply went wild in his arms.

He closed his eyes and reopened them quickly. "I'm not dreaming, am I?"

"No, you're not dreaming," she told him. "You're awake. And I'm real."

"You're naked."

"Noticed that, did you?" The corners of her mouth tilted upward.

He shoved back the blanket and nearly knocked Cara down as he rose to his feet. Standing her ground, she didn't move an inch.

"Go put on some clothes," he told her, his voice gruffer than he'd intended.

"And if I don't?"

"Cara, don't do this."

"Do what?" She draped her arms around his neck, leaned into him and rubbed his nose with hers.

He grabbed her shoulders and shoved her an arm's length away from him. "Damn it, sugar, do you know what the sight of you like that is doing to me?"

Without a moment's hesitation, she glanced down at

the crotch of his exploding-firecrackers pajamas, grinned, and then slid the palm of her hand up and down his erection.

Bain groaned, the sound rumbling from deep in his chest.

"If I promise not to ask for anything more than just today, would that make any difference?" she asked.

He grabbed her hand and yanked it away from his crotch. Holding her by the wrist, he glared into her hazel-blue eyes. "Do you think if we make love, either of us can walk away and pretend it never happened?"

"No." She swayed toward him. "But I don't want to pretend it never happened. I want to remember it for as long as I live. If all I can ever have is one day with you, even one hour, I'll take it."

"And if I agree, what then? After today comes to an end and Sawyer and Lucie arrive and we make the exchange, you'll go back to Chattanooga and return to your life as head of Bedell, Inc. and I'll be back on the job as a detective. Then what happens? We don't have a future together. We both know that."

She nodded. Tears gathered in her eyes.

"Oh, sugar, don't cry." As tears slipped from her eyes, he brushed them away with his fingertips.

"We never have to see each other again," she told him. "I'll never come to Hair of the Dog again. And we hardly travel in the same social circles. If I have to, I'll move Bedell headquarters out of Chattanooga or you could leave and get a job in Knoxville or Nashville or Memphis."

God, he was tempted. He had wanted her for such a long time. He had fought the good fight, hadn't he?

He'd been noble and done the honorable thing. But here she was offering herself to him with no strings attached. She wanted him and he wanted her. Hell, she loved him as much as he loved her. If love wasn't involved, it would make this whole damn situation easier.

Bain yanked on her wrist and walked around the sofa, dragging her with him. She skidded to a halt.

"What—?" she asked.

"I'm not making love to you on that couch." He nodded at the sofa where he'd been sleeping every night. "I want to do this right. In a bed."

"Oh…oh, Bain, do you mean it? Are you serious?"

He pulled her along with him into the bedroom, then shucked off his pajama bottoms and kicked them aside. She stared at him, her gaze traveling over him from head to toe and then up again, pausing on his straining sex.

She reached for him. He took a step back and held up both hands.

"Wait a minute. Don't take this the wrong way and think about why I've got them, but…" He gulped. "I've got some condoms in my shave kit."

"You do?" Cara giggled.

"What's so funny?"

"You are. Do you think I believe you've been living like a monk since the first time we met? I know there have been other women in your life these past few years. I just don't want to hear details about any of them."

"There haven't been that many," he assured her. "And no one in quite a while." He looked her right in the eye. "If I tell you that it was just sex with them—"

"Just shut up and go get those damn condoms. Don't you think you've kept me waiting long enough."

Chuckling, he lifted his hand and saluted her. "Yes, ma'am."

CARA RUSHED OVER to the bed and hurriedly straightened it, turning the covers down to the foot and smoothing the bottom sheet. Morning sunlight filtered through the wooden slats in the shutters, creating just enough light for a romantic glow. Not quite candlelight, but it would do.

How did she look?

Naked. That's how you look.

Stripping off her gown and walking into the living room to wake Bain and proposition him had been a spur-of-the-moment decision. In her heart, she had known that it was now or never. Once they went their separate ways later this evening, the odds of them ever reconnecting were slim to none. In the past couple of years, she had done everything in her power to convince Bain that they could make their relationship work, but he had rejected every compromise she had suggested. Choosing between never being with him, never knowing what it would be like to be his lover and accepting only one day with him, she'd made her choice.

Now wasn't the time to worry about how she looked. Her body was far from perfect and she was certainly no raving beauty. Her hips were too broad, her breasts wouldn't fill a C-cup by any stretch of the imagination and her entire body was covered in freckles.

What if the sight of her turned him off?

Get real. The man practically devoured you with his eyes and he's got a hard-on solid as a rock. He wants you. Damn it, Cara, he loves you, too.

"You're not in bed," he said as he emerged from the bathroom, the condom sheathing his erection.

Cara stared at his penis.

Oh, mercy, my me! He was quite impressive. From his shiny black hair, his handsome face, his broad and hair-roughened chest, to his slim hips, protruding penis and long, hairy legs.

"You're staring," he said, humor in his voice.

"You bet I am. I'm memorizing how you look, so in the future when I have to resort to using my vibrator—"

Bain attacked her, tumbling her backward and onto the bed. He came down over her, laughing, his dark eyes bright with desire. She could feel his naked body against hers. He was big and hard and aroused. She lifted her arms up and around his neck.

"How many condoms did you find?" she asked.

"Three."

"Oh, that may not be enough."

"Hey, woman, I'm not a teenager, you know. Three times may be my limit." He pressed his face between her breasts and nuzzled her, then lifted his head. "Besides, there are other things we can do." He sighed. "There are a lot of other things I want to do to you."

"Is that right? Care to tell me about them?"

"Nope. I'd rather show you."

"I like the sound of that."

He straddled her hips, and then ran his gaze over her, slowly, as if just looking at her gave him pleasure.

"You're beautiful," he said.

"I am not. My hips are too wide, my breasts are too small and I'm covered in freckles. You're the beautiful one."

"Your breasts and hips are perfect. And I adore your freckles. I intend to kiss every one of them."

He lifted her arms up to rest on either side of her head and held them down against the pillow.

"Promise not to touch me until I tell you to."

"I promise," she said breathlessly.

Using his index finger, Bain skimmed over her throat, between her breasts and down to her navel. She sucked in her breath. He slipped the tip of his finger into her navel, and then removed it to travel south, all the way to the red curls between her thighs. With a gentle touch, he parted her legs and ran his finger over her mound, across her damp lips and paused at her core. When he rubbed her there, she shivered, excitement rippling through her entire body.

He continued down her leg, going all the way to her foot, and then, moving to the other foot and leg, he slid his finger upward, going over the same territory on his way back up to her throat.

"Your nipples are tight, like pink pebbles." He flicked one nipple with his thumb.

Cara whimpered. He did the same with the other. She reached out and grabbed the spindles on the headboard. Using his thumb and forefinger, he tormented her nipples until she was writhing beneath him.

"When can I touch you?" she asked.

"Not yet. Wait. But I want you tell me what you want right now."

"I want your mouth," she told him. "I want your mouth on mine. I want it on my breasts. I want it all over my body."

He lowered his lips to hers and kissed her. She bucked up against him, her mound pressing against his sex. He slid his tongue inside her mouth and her tongue met his for a mating dance. When they were breathless, he lifted his mouth from hers and licked a soft, light path from her chin downward, pausing between her breasts. While his hand caressed one breast, his lips covered the areole of the other and sucked greedily. She moved against him, lifting up, rubbing, silently pleading.

"When can I touch you?" she asked, her voice a trembling gasp.

"Not yet, sugar. Not quite yet."

He eased his tongue down her body, over her belly, in and out of her navel, across from hipbone to hipbone, then he bypassed her mound, much to her regret, and licked across her left thigh, down over her knee and onto her calf. He lifted her foot and kissed each of her toes and then moved to the right foot and repeated the process. When he reached her upper thigh, he parted her legs and ran his hand across each inner thigh. His tongue followed the path of his hands.

And then suddenly his head was between her legs, his breath hot against her mound, his tongue licking her intimately. Cara went stiff as tension tightened her body painfully. He sucked and licked and delved his tongue inside. She squirmed and whimpered and begged him for more.

Just as she was on the verge of climaxing, she lifted her hands up into the air and brought them down on his head. She clutched his head, urging him to finish and end the torment as she threaded her fingers through his hair.

He accelerated the tempo and added just the right amount of pressure to send her over the edge. As her orgasm rocketed through her, she cried out, bucked halfway into a sitting position and grabbed his shoulders. He didn't let up until he had forced her into complete fulfillment and she lay there sated and spent.

When he lifted himself up and over her, she reached for him languidly, her whole body damp with perspiration and limp with pleasure. She slipped her hand between them and stroked him, gradually guiding him until the tip of his penis touched her wet feminine lips. He reached under her, lifted her hips and lunged into her, deep and hard, not holding back, stopping only after he was buried to the hilt. She wrapped her legs around him as he pumped into her.

Nothing she had ever experienced could compare to this. Making love with Bain, giving and taking, sharing an intimacy that neither of them had shared with anyone else, was all she had ever wanted, and more.

He tensed and she knew he was ready and unable to wait. He paused, but she would have none of it and urged him on. He came with a groan and a shouting grunt, his big body shaking with release. Cara climaxed for a second time only moments later.

After a few minutes sprawled out on top of her, he

slid off and onto the bed. He pulled her into his arms and kissed her temple.

"I love you," he said.

"And I love you."

CHAPTER SIXTEEN

PATRICE WAS AN amusing bed partner, but a bit too demanding for Gray's taste. However, he intended to keep the lady happy for as long as he needed her. Her Bedell, Inc. stock was worth quite a bit to him. He had hoped to buy her out, but that wasn't going to happen anytime in the foreseeable future unless he somehow got his hands on quite a bit of money. His net assets were sizable, due to his inheriting stocks, bonds, a penthouse and some cash from his late wife, the dead but never forgotten Audrey. He had once loved that bitch, but in the end he had hated her. She had all but emasculated him with her indifference and her sordid affairs. Long before she had been accidentally shot and killed, she had rendered him impotent. At least with her. And she hadn't cared that he had turned to other women, countless others whose names and faces he couldn't even remember.

Except for Patrice, Audrey and Cara's stepmother, who was half her former husband's age, the other women had been either high-priced call girls or women he had picked up in a bar and with whom he had seldom exchanged more than first names.

After Audrey's death, Gray had moved in on Cara, perhaps too quickly. He had known that she'd once had a schoolgirl crush on him and thought seducing her would be easy. She had held him off, although he'd known she was tempted, until that brute of a cop had caught Cara's eye. Gray supposed that if you liked your men big, brutish and broodingly handsome, Bain Desmond could be irresistible. Apparently he was to Cara.

Gray had spent the past several years doing a balancing act trying to keep Patrice appeased and at the same time trying to woo Cara. Keeping Patrice happy hadn't taken much effort because she'd been living abroad since shortly after Edward Bedell's will had been read and she'd found out that the bulk of the Bedell fortune had gone to Cara. He visited Patrice a couple of times a year, called her ever so often, and made no objections to her string of young lovers. Cara was a different matter. She had turned down his marriage proposal so many times that, for a while, he had stopped asking her. When it had become apparent that Lt. Desmond wasn't interested in being Mr. Cara Bedell, Gray had thought he might have a chance with Cara. He'd been wrong.

When Cara had been kidnapped, he had anticipated the worst. If Cara's abductors had killed her, the board of directors would no doubt have turned to him for leadership and voted him in as the new CEO. But Dundee's had rescued her. She would be coming home and taking over again. If only Cara would marry him, he would be the happiest man on earth. But was it worth trying again to persuade her how deeply he loved her? Once she was back in Chattanooga, he'd test the waters. Cara had loved him once, hadn't she? Perhaps she could love him again.

Patrice turned over in bed and reached out, searching for him. When she realized the other half of the bed was empty, she opened her eyes and scanned the room. He smiled at her when their gazes met.

"You're up awfully early," she said. "Come back to be, darling."

She slipped the covers down enough to reveal her large, firm breasts, a product of top-notch implants. Her breasts had been enlarged and lifted; her tummy had been tucked; her butt had been lifted; and her nose had been shortened. Her hair was dyed a light, shimmering blond and hung to her shoulders in a stylish blunt cut. Patrice was an attractive woman, one any man would enjoy fucking. But even as lusty as his appetite was for sex, the lady had worn him out and he was in no shape for more of the same. She liked being on top, figuratively and literally, demanded oral sex and told him what to do from the beginning of foreplay until she climaxed. And he had to pretend to like her aggressive attitude.

As his mind went into high gear trying to think of a suitable reason why he wasn't coming back to bed for more of the same, the telephone rang.

"Don't answer it," she whined.

"I have to. It could be important. I could be something about Cara."

Patrice grunted. There had never been any love lost between Patrice and her younger stepdaughter.

Gray lifted the receiver from the crystal phone base on the nightstand. "Grayson Perkins speaking."

"Mr. Perkins, this is Deke Bronson. We've got some good news. Ms. Bedell just telephoned and she should arrive home on the Dundee jet sometime tonight. She asked that I let you know that she would be going straight home and she would see you tomorrow. She will call you in the morning."

"Thank you, Deke." Despite his dislike for Bedell's new head of security, Gray forced himself to be polite. After all, Cara and Deke's wife, Lexie, were close friends. "We've certainly received a miracle, haven't we? I can hardly wait to see her."

Gray hung up the receiver and turned to Patrice. "Cara will be home tonight."

"Are you happy about that or not?" Patrice asked. "I can't tell by the expression on your face and the way you're acting."

"What a thing to say. Of course I'm happy that Cara is coming home, that she is safe. My God, she could have been killed."

Patrice got out of bed, stark naked, and slinked over to him. She draped her arms around his neck. "Has she taken you into her confidence about her will? Are you one of the beneficiaries?"

"I believe I am, yes, but—"

"She isn't married and has no children, so who other than you would inherit?"

"I doubt seriously that she would leave Bedell, Inc. to me," Gray said. "If we were husband and wife…but she refuses to marry me. Considering how deeply involved she has become in charity work these past few years, I wouldn't doubt that she's arranged for a huge portion of Bedell profits to be divided among her favorite charities, Helping Hands International being the primary one."

"We could, of course, contest any will." Patrice smiled. "I *am* Edward Bedell's widow and you're Audrey's widower. We were cheated out of so much that was rightfully ours. Edward and Cara weren't all that close. She certainly wasn't his favorite child. I assumed that after his precious Audrey was gone, he would at least split everything fifty/fifty, between Cara and me."

Gray pulled her arms from around his neck. "You're talking as if Cara is dead. She's not. She's alive and well and on her way home."

"You sound almost disappointed." Patrice laughed.

Gray glared at her.

"Oh, Grayson, precious, don't look at me that way. Erase that little look of hurt from your gorgeous face." She laughed again. "You didn't by any chance have something to do with our dear Cara's abduction, did you?"

Gray gasped. "Most certainly not." He glowered at Patrice. Suddenly she wasn't all that pretty and appealing. "But perhaps you did. Is that why you're pointing the finger at me? Did you hire someone to kidnap Cara?"

"If I had, I would have hired someone who wouldn't have bungled the job and right now, instead of being on her way home, Cara would be dead."

LUCIE GLANCED AT Sawyer. He sat across from her in one of the plush leather chairs aboard the Dundee jet. He was immersed in working a crossword puzzle, paying no attention to her whatsoever. The last time he had spoken to her was shortly after they boarded the jet. They had called the hospital from the airport and talked to Daisy, getting a firsthand update on Geoff's condition. For the past four hours, she had glanced through half a dozen magazines, listened to a music CD and watched a few minutes of a boring movie. She had snacked on fruit, cheese and crackers and drank two glasses of wine.

She rose from her seat and walked around inside the large, deluxe cabin, doing her best to make Sawyer look at her. He didn't.

"Damn it, look at me," she shouted. "I'm not invisible, you know. Act like you can see me."

He glanced away from his puzzle and looked up at her. "What's wrong with you? Why are you screaming at me?"

"We've been cooped up together on this plane for four hours and you haven't so much as said 'boo' to me."

"Boo." He returned his attention to the puzzle.

Lucie groaned.

She had thought that after the past thirty-six hours they had spent together, Sawyer wouldn't revert to the way he'd treated her for so many years, as if he hated being near her. But his present attitude certainly dashed any hopes she'd had of their being able to, at the very least, be cordial to each other.

"Damn it, don't do this," she told him. "I know you don't hate me, so stop acting like you do."

He neither replied to her comment nor looked at her.

"If you hated me, you wouldn't have risked your life to rescue me," she said. "And if you hated me, you wouldn't have stood over my bed this morning looking at me while you thought I was asleep."

"All right." He looked up at her. "You want me to tell you that I don't hate you, then listen because I'm saying this only once—I don't hate you." He glanced down at his crossword puzzle and ignored her again.

She walked over and stood directly in front of him. "Is that all you have to say?"

"What else is there to say?" He penciled an answer in one of the boxes of his puzzle.

"Why did you come into my room this morning?"

"To wake you. I was up and had put on coffee. I thought you might want an early start."

He was lying and they both knew it. He had been slipping out of her room when she called to him and stopped him in his tracks.

She leaned over him, bracing herself by grabbing the arms of his chair, and brought her face up to his, eye-to-eye, nose-to-nose, only inches separating them.

"You still care, don't you?" She felt his warm breath on her lips. "You still want me just as much as I want you."

His eyes narrowed and darkened. His nostrils flared. His breathing quickened. "Do not do this to us," he told her.

"Do what?"

"Torment us."

He reached up, slid his hand beneath her hair and grasped the back of her neck. She trembled, every nerve in her body alert and tingling.

"Damn you," he growled just before he took her mouth, ravaging it savagely.

Lucie tumbled into his lap and returned the kiss with equal intensity. She didn't think, didn't consider the consequences; she simply responded and savored the moment. His hands went to her waist, then down over her hips and caressed her roughly. She gave herself over to pleasure unlike any she had known since the last time she and Sawyer had kissed.

Suddenly, he ended the kiss, shoved her away from him, almost pushing her into the floor. He caught her as he rose to his feet and for half a second, they stared at each other. Then he released her and walked over to the minibar, pulled out a bottle of whiskey and poured himself half a glass. She stood there and watched him, feeling his rejection with every fiber of her being.

Oh, God, he did still want her. The kiss had told her all she needed to know. The passion between them was as powerful as it had ever been, perhaps even more so since they had denied it for nine years.

But just because he had admitted that he didn't hate her, it didn't mean he loved her. But he cared. He cared enough to risk his own life to save her.

Shivering as hope took root in her heart, she told herself not to expect too much too soon.

She walked over to the minibar. "Mind if I have a sip of that?"

He glared at her, tossed back a hefty swing, coughed several times and then downed the remainder. When he poured the glass a third of the way full, he handed it to her. His fingers grazed hers. She felt the instant jolt of electricity and was certain he had, too.

"Thank you," she said.

He eyed her questioningly. "For what?"

"For not lying to me and for not lying to yourself."

His lips twitched. "Oh, that. I thought maybe you were thanking me for the kiss."

"The kiss, too." She smiled.

"It's not going to happen again."

"Not ever?"

"Lucie…Lucie… You just don't know when to give up, do you? You push and push. You drive me crazy. If you had just left me the hell alone, I wouldn't have retaliated over and over again for the past nine years. Whatever I did, I did to defend myself against you."

"I know." She lifted the glass to her lips and took a sip. The liquor burned as it went down, making her gasp and cough. "God, I'd forgotten how strong straight whiskey is."

"Once you're back at work with Bedell Security and I'm home in Atlanta, we can both move on with our lives," he told her. "You had made a good first step when you left Dundee's. We both need to get back to where we were before all this happened."

"Before you risked your life to save me." Lucie held out the glass of whiskey.

He grabbed the glass and set it on the minibar. "What I did and why I did it has no bearing on our future. Going our separate ways is our only hope. We're bad for each other. We bring out the worst in—"

"It doesn't have to be that way."

"Yes, it does. We can't change the past. We can't go back and undo what we did to Brenden. If not for us, my brother would be alive today."

"No one regrets what happened to Brenden more than I do. And for a long time afterward, I thought maybe I deserved your hatred and contempt. But I didn't. Not then and not now. What we did wasn't wrong."

"How can you say that? I have to live with the truth every day of my life—my actions killed my brother as surely as if I'd taken a gun and shot him." He looked right at her. "We killed Brenden."

"No, we didn't. Brenden killed himself."

Sawyer lifted the glass of whiskey and slung it across the room. The liquor splattered in every direction when the glass hit the wall and shattered into pieces. And in that moment of fury, Sawyer broke Lucie's heart all over again.

She turned and walked away. He left her alone in the main cabin and went into the cockpit to speak to the pilot. When he didn't return, she eased down on the sofa, turned toward the back and hugged herself as she curled into a ball.

Sawyer didn't hate her. He hated himself. He still cared about her. But he couldn't forgive himself for what had happened to his brother. His guilt over Brenden's death stood between them now as it had nine years ago. That much hadn't changed and probably never would.

WHEN THE PHONE RANG, the caller's identity had not been a surprise. He had known it would be only a matter of time. Did this mean that Cara Bedell was dead? Or had she been persuaded to do what was in her best interest so that she could live?

"Hello."

"We need to talk. There is a problem."

"What kind of problem?"

"All is not lost, I promise you. Unfortunately, Cara has been rescued."

"How is that possible? I believed you had hired competent people to—"

"I hired someone who was supposed to be the best, but his people came up against a superior force," the caller said. "He has offered to complete the job himself for half the original price."

"And you have agreed?"

"Not yet. Cara will be back in the United States tonight, but it will take her days, perhaps even weeks, to fully recover from such a horrible ordeal. She will be advised not to make any business decisions for the time being. Once things are back to normal and she feels safe, that will be the time to strike."

"This time, make sure the job is done right. Unless she can be persuaded to see things our way, then she has to die."

"Yes, of course, I agree."

CARA CRIED OUT when she climaxed. As her body shuddered with release, she melted into Bain, who lay beneath her. He caressed her bare buttocks, allowing her to gradually come down from the sensual high. Once her breathing returned to normal, he flipped her over onto her back and straddled her, then wasted no time seeking his own fulfillment.

This would be their last time. He was wearing his

third and final condom. And within an hour, Sawyer and Lucie would arrive at the cabin. But for now, his whole world centered on the woman lying beneath him. Cara. The woman he loved. The woman who could never truly be his.

He came with a vengeance, hard and fast, his ears ringing, his head exploding. God, it was good with Cara. So damn good.

Sated and perspiring, he eased off her and onto his back. She cuddled against him. He slid his arm under her and drew her close.

They had been making love all day and had left the bed only to eat a few bites, use the bathroom and freshen up between sessions. He'd been on top; she'd been on top; they had done it from the side of the bed. He had explored every inch of her body and she had explored his. They had shared kisses, caresses and gentle bites, as well as oral sex. Since they both knew that this would be their only day together, they had tried to pack a lot of loving into a few brief hours. But Bain realized that if he made love to Cara every day for the rest of their lives, he would never get enough of her. She had become as important to him as the air he breathed. But all too soon, they would go their separate ways, she back to Bedell, Inc. and the old family estate on Lookout Mountain, and he back to the C.P.D. and his modest apartment.

"Tell me again," Cara said as she kissed his shoulder.

He turned his head toward her and smiled. "I love you."

"I wish I could record your saying that so I could play it back and listen to it every day." She sighed. "But I'll be able to hear it in my mind."

"Sooner or later, you'll have to let it go and so will I. We have to move on and stay apart. It won't be easy, but—"

She tapped her index finger over his lips. "Hush. Please. We have a little more time. I want to spend it right here in your arms. For just a few more minutes, there is no tomorrow."

"Sawyer and Lucie will be here soon. They're not more than an hour away. We should shower and dress and be ready when they arrive."

"I don't want this day to end. I want it to go on forever."

He leaned over and kissed her. "Yeah, that would be nice, wouldn't it, if we could stop time."

"Bain?"

He looked into her eyes. "Yeah?"

"Is there anything I can do, any way I can persuade you to—"

"Don't do this to me, sugar." He sat up in bed.

She sat up and when he turned his back to her, intending to get out of bed, she laid her hand between his shoulder blades. "I want to renegotiate terms."

He glanced over his shoulder. "You do, do you?"

"Let's not see each other for a month. Then let's meet and talk and—"

"Six weeks."

"What?"

"We won't see each other for six weeks. Then we'll go out for dinner and talk."

"Can we talk about our having an affair?"

Bain chuckled. "No affair. In six weeks, we will have cooled off and be able to think rationally. I figure that we'll be able to end things once and for all by then."

"Oh, I see. All right, we have a date in six weeks." She leaned over and kissed his back.

He shuddered, then pulled away from her and practically ran to the bathroom.

Fifty-four minutes later, Bain opened the front door and greeted Sawyer and Lucie. Cara rushed toward Lucie, grabbed her and hugged her. The two women cried and laughed and talked nonstop while Sawyer and Bain stood back and watched them.

"Let's talk a short walk," Sawyer said to Bain.

Bain nodded.

"Ladies, if you two will excuse us." Sawyer looked at Lucie. "You need to explain the situation to Cara so she can make some decisions."

"Yes, I'll tell her everything."

Bain opened the front door and he and Sawyer walked out onto the porch. The night air was crisp and cool and held a hint of autumn.

"Is Lucie all right?" Bain asked.

"She'll be fine."

"What is she telling Cara?"

Sawyer looked up at the starry sky. "She overheard bits and pieces of some things her kidnappers talked about. It seems even if the ransom had been paid, Cara Bedell was supposed to die."

"My God! Does that mean she's still in danger?"

Sawyer shrugged. "It's possible."

"And you have no idea who was behind the kidnapping plot?"

"Nothing concrete, but Dundee's will continue to investigate and we'll work with Bedell security to keep Cara safe."

"I can extend my leave of absence and stay with Cara," Bain said.

"Lucie intends to continue as Cara's bodyguard."

"Sounds like we've got a couple of stubborn women on our hands. Lucie wants to continue as Cara's bodyguard and I figure Cara will refuse to go home and hide away. She'll be back at work tomorrow unless I miss my guess."

"Deke can tighten security at Bedell, Inc. headquarters and at the Bedell Estate," Sawyer said. "And Lucie can stay with Cara twenty-four-seven. In the meantime, Dundee's will work around the clock to try to find out who hired Arturo Rios-Torres to kidnap and kill Cara."

"You know the guy's name?"

"Yeah. He's an assassin. Finding him won't be easy and even if we eliminate him, that won't solve the problem. Whoever hired him can simply hire someone else. This nightmare won't be over until we discover the identity of the person behind the kidnapping and murder plot."

CHAPTER SEVENTEEN

"THEN YOU THINK I'm still in danger?" Cara looked straight into Lucie's eyes and the two women shared a moment of complete truth and honesty. They were now bound together in an ancient way that only those who had shared a similar experience could understand. Lucie had saved Cara's life by risking her own and although she had simply been doing her job as a bodyguard, that fact did not lessen the debt Cara owned her. In some cultures, if you save someone's life, it becomes your duty to always look after that person. The one thing Lucie knew for certain was that she would continue doing her best to keep Cara safe.

"I think that whoever was behind your kidnapping didn't get what they wanted," Lucie said.

"It's terrifying to believe that someone actually wants me dead."

"Dundee's and Bedell security will work together to keep you safe, but the first order of business will be to try to figure out who wants you dead and why. Do you have any idea who that person might be?"

"No, I can't think of anyone," Cara said. "When we believed the kidnapping had been solely about the twenty-five-million-dollar ransom, it made sense. After all, it stands to reason that anyone in my position could be the target of kidnappers. But this new information—that the plan had been to kill me even if the ransom had been paid—changes everything, doesn't it?"

"I'm afraid it does. The ransom money could have been nothing more than a smokescreen to mask the person's identity. It's possible the money wasn't the primary reason for your kidnapping. Does anyone who would profit from your death come to mind?"

"You're thinking about the oil deal that Bedell, Inc. will make with either Delgado or Castillo, aren't you?"

"Tomas Castillo wants Bedell, Inc. to sign with his company and when he couldn't seduce you into the deal, maybe he figured if you were out of the way, the Bedell board might be more inclined to choose him over Felipe Delgado."

"Castillo is a possibility. He's certainly ruthless enough to order my death."

The front door opened. They both turned to see Bain and Sawyer enter the cabin.

"You two plotting strategy without us?" Sawyer asked.

"Not really," Lucie replied. "We were just discussing who would profit most from Cara's death."

"We decided that Tomas Castillo should head the list," Cara said. "I told him the day Lucie was kidnapped that I was definitely leaning toward signing a deal with Delgado Oil. A man such as Castillo, who is accustomed to always getting what he wants, would have no qualms about ordering my kidnapping and murder."

"I agree," Sawyer said. "But I don't think we should narrow our investigation to only Castillo." He looked directly at Cara. "Who else would gain a great deal if you were dead?"

Cara eyed him curiously. "Are you asking me who will inherit Bedell, Inc. and all my holdings?"

"Yes, that is exactly what I'm asking," Sawyer told her.

Cara slumped down on the sofa. "My will is complicated." She glanced up at Bain. "The board of directors would choose my successor as CEO of the company, of course. But as far as Bedell, Inc. itself, my stock in the company, which is sixty-five percent, would be divided among several charities, Helping Hands receiving the most shares, and a few people who don't even know they're my beneficiaries will receive sizable chunks of stock. The way Daddy had things set up, Patrice would inherit cash and stocks, and the same holds true for Gray. I can't change the provisions he made even if I wanted to."

"So, Grayson Perkins and Patrice Bedell both stand to gain financially from your death," Sawyer said.

Cara nodded.

"Are you certain that the other beneficiaries don't know anything about their inheritance?" Sawyer asked.

"I'm positive."

"That narrows the possible suspects, doesn't it?" Lucie said. "Castillo, Gray Perkins and Patrice Bedell."

"If we're only going to look at this from one viewpoint, that the motive is greed, then those three are definitely the major suspects," Sawyer said. "But what if greed isn't the motive?"

Cara and Lucie looked straight at Sawyer.

"He's right," Bain said. "We're overlooking hatred and revenge."

Cara's eyes widened in shock. "I never considered—"

"Edward Bedell made a lot of enemies over the years," Bain reminded her. "It's possible that someone hated him enough to transfer that hatred over to you. Killing you would be a secondhand revenge, but it would still be revenge."

"Do you know of anyone who had a grudge against your father?" Lucie asked. "Someone who possibly threatened him?"

"I have no idea. My father and I were never close. He didn't share things with me. But it's possible some of the older board members might know. Leland Chastain went to school with my father, first at Baylor when they were boys, and later at Vanderbilt. He might know. And Margaret Vaughn and her husband were friends from the time Daddy was married to Audrey's mother. Miss Kate or Mr. Alfred might know of someone."

"I'm sure you'll want Bedell security to be in charge of bodyguard duties," Sawyer said. "But you'll need Dundee's to head up the investigation. I can have several of my best people on the job first thing tomorrow. I simply need your okay."

"Yes, of course. Do whatever you think is necessary," Cara told him. "Work with Deke. I'll give him permission to cooperate fully with Dundee's." She turned to Lucie. "Do you want some time off before going back to work or are you ready to resume your duties as my personal bodyguard?"

"I'm ready whenever you are," Lucie said. "As far as I'm concerned, the minute we get back to Chattanooga, I'm on the job, twenty-four-seven."

Smiling, Cara stood and held out her hand. "Then we have a deal."

She and Lucie shook on it, and then she turned to Sawyer. "If I need to sign a contract, fax the papers to Deke tomorrow."

Sawyer nodded. "I don't want to rush you, but the Dundee jet is waiting in Knoxville and—"

"Yes, of course. Time to go home." Cara glanced at Bain.

"I'll close up the cabin before I leave," Bain said. "Y'all go on ahead. I'll be driving back to Chattanooga tonight."

Cara glanced from Lucie to Sawyer. "Would you two mind giving me a few minutes alone with Bain before we go?"

"No, of course not." Lucie grabbed Sawyer's arm. "We'll wait outside for you."

Sawyer glared at her, but didn't say anything as she all but dragged him to the door and out onto the porch.

CARA WALKED OVER to Bain. They stood there gazing at each other.

"We have a date in six weeks," she reminded him. "Don't forget."

"I won't." He reached out and took her hands in his. "I'm going to talk to Deke every day, you know, and check on you."

"You are?"

"Even with Lucie watching your back, I'm going to worry about you."

Cara wished he would pull her into his arms and kiss her. "We both already know that Lucie will protect me with her life. She's proven that she's willing to die for me."

"She's not the only one."

"I know. I—"

He grabbed her and kissed her.

She clung to him, never wanting to leave his arms. But the kiss ended all too quickly and Bain held her at arm's length.

"I'll call you in six weeks," she said.

He nodded.

"I love you."

He released her, cleared his throat and said, "I love you, too, sugar."

Cara turned, hurried to the door and walked outside, leaving her heart behind with Bain Desmond.

AT ELEVEN-FIFTEEN that night, Sawyer and Bain met with Deke Bronson in his office at Bedell, Inc. headquarters in downtown Chattanooga. After Sawyer had escorted Lucie and Cara to the Bedell estate, he had telephoned Deke and then Bain, requesting the urgent nighttime meeting.

"Dundee's will need full cooperation from both Bedell security and the Chattanooga police department," Sawyer explained. "I prefer that the three of us coordinate our efforts from the very beginning."

Deke and Bain agreed.

"I suggest that your people beef up security at the office and at home and provide backup for Lucie around the clock," Sawyer told Deke, then turned to Bain. "If the C.P.D. can offer assistance in any way, I assume you'll make sure we receive the department's full cooperation."

"Absolutely," Bain said. "Even without my limited influence in the department, the chief is no dummy. He knows exactly who Cara Bedell is and what Bedell, Inc. means to Chattanooga."

"Dundee's will begin an in-depth investigation, both here in Chattanooga and in Ameca," Sawyer said. "We aren't limiting our investigation only to Castillo, Patrice Bedell and Gray Perkins. I'll have several agents working on a different angle and they'll start by interviewing Mr. Chastain and Mr. and Mrs. Vaughn. If Edward Bedell had enemies who hated him enough to seek revenge by killing his daughter, we need to know."

"Cara's not going to play it safe," Bain said. "She'll be down here in her office tomorrow, putting herself at risk on the drive to and from her home. And there are dozens of people in and out of this building every day, not including the employees." He looked at Deke. "Even with Lucie at her side every minute, someone could still get to her. If I had my way…" He shook his head. "Neither of you have to say it. I know that all we can do is the best we can do."

"I'll speak to Cara and Lucie in the morning," Deke said. "I'll suggest that we make Cara's office off-limits to everyone except her private secretary and Bedell vice presidents."

"She needs a different office, too," Bain suggested. "That wall of windows—"

"I'll suggest she move into an office with fewer windows," Deke said. "Or even into one of the smaller interior offices."

"I'll be in charge of the entire operation from Dundee headquarters in Atlanta," Sawyer said. "I'll send Ty Garrett and a couple of agents to Ameca and I'm going to pull Whit Falkner in off another case to head things up here in Chattanooga."

"I'll arrange for daily conference calls with the two of you," Deke told them. "I'm aware of the fact that this is no ordinary case for either of you."

Bain and Sawyer exchanged questioning glances, then both of them stared at Deke, who shrugged. "Hey, there's no need for secrets among friends and associates, right?"

Neither Bain nor Sawyer replied.

"Bain has a very personal interest in Cara Bedell's welfare," Deke said as he looked at Sawyer. "Just like you have a personal interest in wanting to keep Lucie safe."

"Son of a bitch," Bain mumbled under his breath. "I thought I was picking up on some odd vibes between you two."

"Lucie is a former Dundee agent," Sawyer said, as if that explained his concern for her.

"Yeah, sure." Bain grinned. "I got it. I'm not a guy who needs to know another man's personal business. But we're all in agreement that our first priority is to keep Cara and Lucie safe while we find the person behind Cara's kidnapping."

"Agreed," Deke said.

Sawyer nodded. "Agreed."

IF SHE HADN'T BEEN bone-weary, Lucie would have been just as impressed with the sight of the antebellum Bedell mansion tonight as she had been the first time she saw it. But nothing would impress her right now more than a good soft bed and about ten hours of uninterrupted sleep.

When Sawyer had walked them into the house, the butler, a distinguished middle-aged man named Aldridge, had met them, but Cara had quickly dismissed him.

"Please, go to bed. I can show Ms. Evans to her room," Cara had told him.

Once Sawyer had left, without a backward glance, and nothing more than a "take care" remark to Lucie, she and Cara had taken the elevator upstairs.

Lucie requested a room near Cara's. "Even though this place is probably as safe as Fort Knox, considering the security Deke has in place, I'd still prefer to be close by and not in a different wing of the house."

Cara showed Lucie to the room across the hall from hers, a large suite, with a private bath, dressing room and sitting area. "This was Patrice's room," Cara said. "When she moved out, I redecorated, not just her room, but Audrey's old room and my old room, too. The rooms I use now were once my father's."

"I'm afraid I'll need to borrow a nightgown or a pair of pajamas. I don't have any clothes with me," Lucie explained.

"Anything of mine is yours. Come in my room and choose whatever you'd like. I'm at least one size larger than you, but with pajamas or a gown, I don't think it matters. Tomorrow, we'll order you a whole new wardrobe."

"That's not necessary."

"In the morning, write down your sizes and I'll have my secretary arrange for a personal shopper to pick up whatever you need."

"Treatment like that will spoil me."

"You deserve to be spoiled. I owe you my life."

"Cara—Ms. Bedell—it was my job to protect you."

"Please, it's Cara. Now, come into my room and pick out something to sleep in. And if you can find something suitable for work tomorrow—" She glanced at Lucie's feet. "What size shoe do you wear?"

"A nine," Lucie replied. "Nine medium."

Cara smiled. "My size exactly, so you can raid my shoe closet and take whatever you like."

"For work, I prefer comfortable flats and usually slacks, shirt and blazer." Lucie grimaced. "Damn."

"What's wrong?"

"Nothing serious. I just don't have a gun and shoulder holster, but I'm sure Deke will provide me with what I need in the morning."

"I'm sure he will." Cara grabbed Lucie's hand. "Come choose something to wear tonight and whatever you'll need for tomorrow. And feel free to sleep as late as you'd like. As you said, I'm quite safe here in my own home. In the morning, I promise not to leave the house until you're with me. I'm not planning to go into the office until around eleven."

Half an hour later, Lucie washed her face with some type of expensive liquid cleanser, brushed her teeth with a borrowed toothbrush, combed her hair with a silver comb and put on a pair of gold silk pajamas. The pj's were only slightly baggy and had probably cost somewhere between a week and a month's salary for her.

The bathroom was large and airy, the style clean and simple, with pale grayish-white walls, a decorative tile floor and white curtains on the single window. The biscuit sink boasted a brushed nickel faucet. A ladder-back wooden chair, finished in a blue-gray satin color, rested against the wall and the seat held a stack of pristine white towels and washcloths.

The dressing room contained two huge side-by-side closets, deep and wide and empty, except for numerous rows of padded hangers. The elaborate dressing table was made of glass and intricately carved white wrought iron.

Lucie paused to take in the luxury of her surroundings. She couldn't imagine living this way. For people like Cara, who had been born to wealth and privilege, it probably seemed like nothing. But for Lucie, who had once shared a small two-bedroom house with her grandmother not much larger than this bedroom suite, these accommodations were exquisite. The richest people Lucie had known when she was growing up had been the McNamaras, but they had been only millionaires where Cara Bedell was worth billions.

The bed was a black iron four-poster without a canopy. She flipped back the heavy white goose down comforter and found white cotton sheets, probably no less than 800 thread count Egyptian cotton, beneath. Four pillows, decked in embroidered white cases, rested against the slatted headboard. The walls were a light gray, the same color as the tufted velvet chaise at the foot of the bed. A carpet in shades of gold, green and gray covered the center of the room, leaving the aged hardwood showing around the corners.

After turning off the glass-and-metal bedside lamp, Lucie snuggled into the bed, pulling the covers up to her waist. She lay there and stared up at the ceiling.

She supposed that by now Sawyer was winging his way to Atlanta on the Dundee jet. Although it was possible that their paths would cross again during the course of the Cara Bedell case, she had to accept the fact that there really was no hope for them. She could cherish the knowledge that he still cared about her, that he still wanted her, that he had risked his life to save her, but what good did it do her? He refused to accept the truth about Brenden's death and as long as he continued to blame himself—and her—for what had happened to his brother, they could never be together.

In the beginning, she had felt as guilty as Sawyer had, but eventually, she came to realize that the only thing she had been guilty of was being in love with Sawyer and not Brenden.

Lucie tossed and turned, trying to relax, doing her best to stop thinking about the time she had spent with Sawyer in Ameca, in Barbados and on the Dundee jet. But she couldn't forget the way he had kissed her. Even now, hours later, she could almost feel his lips on hers.

You're an idiot, Lucie Evans.

Are you going to spend the rest of your life waiting for a man who will never allow himself to love you?

You aren't getting any younger, you know. If you want a home and a family, time's a wasting. Out there somewhere, there has to be man who can make you forget about Sawyer.

Yeah, sure. When pigs fly.

Lucie groaned. She pulled the covers higher, all the way up to her ears.

Go to sleep. Get some rest. Tomorrow, you'll need to be at your best. You'll be back on the job guarding Cara Bedell.

CARA LAY WITH her back propped against a stack of pillows braced against the headboard of her bed. Her body ached from the hours of passionate lovemaking that she and Bain had shared. Making love with him had been all she had dreamed it would be. Actually, the reality had been even better than the fantasy.

But now, she felt so alone. Poor little rich girl once again. She had everything money could buy. Too bad Bain Desmond wasn't for sale.

Don't give up. You're closer to getting what you want than you've ever been. You and Bain are now lovers. He's not going to forget about how good it was between the two of you, no more than you will be able to forget. He'll think about you, dream about you, want you, just as you will him.

They had a date in six weeks. Just forty-two days. All she had to do was stay alive until then.

BAIN DESMOND unlocked the door to his apartment, went inside, locked the door and headed for the bedroom. After stripping off his clothes, down to his briefs, and placing his wallet, change and keys on the dresser and his phone on the nightstand, he went into the bathroom. He took a piss, washed his hands, brushed his teeth and tossed his briefs into the laundry hamper inside the linen closet.

He was home, back in Chattanooga, and tonight he'd sleep in his own bed instead of that damn uncomfortable sofa at the cabin. But he would be sleeping alone.

Don't think about how you spent the day today. Don't think about Cara.

Yeah, sure.

Not in a million years would he ever forget one detail of his hours with Cara. He had fought against his own needs for the past couple of years, knowing damn well that once he'd had her, it would be all the more difficult to walk away from her. But he had to do it. For her sake as well as his.

If for one minute, he thought they could make a go of marriage, he'd have her in front of a preacher so quick it would make her head spin. But the thought of Cara trying to fit into his run-of-the-mill middle-class life was ludicrous. But not any more so than him trying to fit into her high-brow, richer-than-God lifestyle.

They had met under the worst of circumstances—her sister's disappearance. He had watched her deal with her sister's murder, and shortly after that her father's suicide, and had admired her strength and courage. He had seen the way Grayson Perkins had leaned on her, demanding her attention as if he had every right to claim her. Even then, before he'd admitted to himself that he was in love with her, he had known she was far too good for a leech like Perkins.

She was too good for him, too, but that didn't stop him from wanting her. Day and night. And he would for the rest of his life.

Fate sure as hell had a cruel sense of humor.

CHAPTER EIGHTEEN

CARA'S RETURN TO Bedell, Inc. was met with no fanfare whatsoever and for several reasons. First of all, no one other than Grayson Perkins and Deke Bronson knew about the kidnapping and only Deke knew the truth— that Lucie and not Cara had been abducted. Also, the fewer people who knew the reason why the security around Bedell's CEO and chief stockholder had been tightened, the better. Jason Little's body had been discreetly claimed by friends of Rita Herrera from the San Luis morgue and returned to the U.S. His family and friends had been told that he had risked his life to save Cara Bedell, and Bedell, Inc. had paid for the funeral and arranged a sizable monthly pension for his wife. Deke had issued a memo that due to a bomb threat, security would be increased to the maximum extend and remain at critical alert until he felt the Bedell Building and its occupants were no longer in danger.

As instructed, Cara and Lucie had come directly to his office upon their arrival at eleven o'clock. His secretary had brought in coffee for Cara while he discussed security plans with Lucie.

He handed her a pistol and a shoulder holster. "It's

a SIG P226. It's the weapon I prefer for bodyguard duty because of its high magazine capacity and its great accuracy."

Lucie removed her loose-fitting silk jacket, strapped on the shoulder holster, and picked up the SIG. She inspected the weapon, slid it into the leather sheath, and slipped on her jacket.

Deke nodded to his desk. "If you want a backup, I've got a Seecamp .32 for you. Or if you prefer there's a Downsizer WSP single-shot derringer. Take your pick or take both."

"Thanks." She picked up the Seecamp .32 auto and the small folding knife lying beside it. She slid the gun into her jacket pocket and the knife into the pocket of her slacks, which Deke had noticed were also slightly baggy.

"I've beefed up security," he told Lucie. "No one gets in or out without clearance, which means only employees and invited guests. All deliveries will be made to the front door, inspected, and brought into the building by employees."

Lucie nodded. "I think it was a good idea to move Cara into an interior office. The bomb threat excuse should work for a while to keep everyone around here from asking questions."

"I've already instructed Cara's secretary, whom, by the way, she chose herself and promoted to the position when she took over as CEO, to have everything set up in the new office space."

"And the secretary is Ginger something-or-other, right?"

"Ginger Allen," Cara said as she rose from a chair

across the room and walked over to where Deke and Lucie stood by his desk. "And her assistant is Lisa Burton. They're both blondes, so if you confuse them at first, just remember that Lisa is the one who wears glasses."

"Got it." Lucie glanced from Deke to Cara. "We need to come up with another reason, other than the bomb, that I'm sticking to you like glue when in the past you didn't normally have twenty-four-seven protection. The bomb story will work for a few days, a week at most."

"We can always tell the truth or at least part of the truth," Cara suggested. "Just say that there's been a threat on my life."

Deke grinned. "We'll use the bomb threat for a few weeks, then switch over to a death threat from an unknown source. If we're lucky, Dundee's will come up with something soon and life can return to normal for all of us."

"Until that time, I plan to go on with business as usual," Cara said. "I have phone calls to make, people to see, arrangements to be made and a board meeting next week."

"It would make things easier for me if you'd provide me with a daily itinerary and if possible let me know well in advance of any trips or social engagements. Even if you're going out for lunch, we'll want to secure the location the best we can."

Cara sighed. "I'm not going to enjoy working and living this way, but I'll do whatever is necessary. I'll have lunch in every day for the next few weeks, except when it's necessary for me to have a business lunch. I can cancel a few social engagements on my calendar for the remainder of September and early October. But there are two events that I'll have to attend."

"And those are?" Deke asked.

"One is a bachelorette charity auction. I'm one of the prizes."

Deke groaned. Lucie frowned.

"When is this charity auction?" Deke asked.

"In six weeks. And before you say I need to withdraw, I can't. Last year a date with me brought in fifty thousand dollars."

"We'll have to rig the auction this year," Lucie said. "We'll simply arrange to have someone we know outbid everyone else. Maybe your brother-in-law could do it or one of the Dundee agents or even Lieutenant Desmond."

Cara smiled. "I think Lieutenant Desmond would be the perfect choice, but I'll leave it you two to arrange it. Of course, I'll pick up the tab."

"What's the other social engagement you can't decline?" Deke asked.

"I plan to ask Senor and Senorita Delgado to come to Chattanooga for us to sign the papers for Bedell Inc.'s deal with Delgado Oil and it will be expected for me to host a dinner party for them."

Deke grumbled quietly to himself. "Is that absolutely necessary?"

"I'll limit the guest list to Bedell board members and vice presidents and a handful of close friends, including you and Lexie." She glanced at Lucie. "You know I discussed this with Suelita Delgado when we stayed with them. They'll be expecting it and I do not want to disappoint them. This deal with Delgado Oil is far too important to both Bedell, Inc., and to Ameca."

The outer door of Deke's office flew open and Grayson Perkins came storming in, followed by Patrice Bedell right on his heels.

"Cara, darling!" Gray rushed to Cara, threw his arms around her and hugged her passionately. Then he kissed her on both cheeks and grabbed her hands. "My God, it is so good to see you home and safe." He looked her over from head to toe. "Those beasts didn't hurt you, did they? I imagined the most horrible things."

Cara jerked free from Gray's tenacious hold and glared back and forth from him to her stepmother. "What are you doing here?"

"Gray called me the minute you were kidnapped," Patrice said, a self-satisfied smile curving her lips.

Cara confronted Gray. "Why on earth would you call her and tell her what had happened?"

"Darling, don't be upset with me," Gray said, a hurt expression on his much-too-handsome face. "After all, Patrice is family. I thought she had a right to know that her stepdaughter's life was in danger."

Cara groaned. "Let's finish this conversation in my office. I'm sure Deke has better things to do than listen to a family squabble." She glanced at Deke. "I'll have my afternoon itinerary to you by noon." She checked her watch. "Make that twelve-thirty since it's eleven-forty now. And I will not be going out for lunch. Lucie and I will order in."

AFTER TALKING TO the chief, Bain had left police head-quarters at eleven forty-five. His leave of absence was over, but he wouldn't be back on the force officially until Monday, which gave him today and the weekend free. After grabbing a quick bite at the Hair of the Dog, his favorite restaurant/pub in Chattanooga, he drove past the Bedell Building.

Wonder how Cara is today?

It wouldn't be easy for her knowing her life was still in danger. It sure as hell wasn't easy for him. He wanted to be the one to protect her, but that wasn't possible. Lucie was a damn good bodyguard and she had already proved she was willing to sacrifice her life to save Cara. What more could he ask?

He had awakened this morning with a hard-on, every thought in his head about Cara. Memories of their time together yesterday both comforted and tormented him. Nothing had ever been sweeter. He had known it would be like that between them, all hot, raw passion and yet lovingly tender.

She was expecting that six weeks of abstinence would weaken his resolve. Six weeks without seeing her, even from a distance. Six weeks without touching her, holding her, making love to her.

Maybe she was right. They'd been apart less than twenty-four hours and already he was going nuts without her.

You'll be okay if you can make it through the weekend. Monday, you'll be back at work. You'll stay busy. It'll be easier then.

He had three days to fill between now and then. He

could call up someone he'd dated in the past and ask her out. Yeah, sure, he'd be great company for any woman when all he could think about was Cara.

He headed his Corvette out of downtown Chattanooga. He'd go by his apartment, pack his duffel bag and drive over to Murfreesboro, where his sister and her family lived. He'd call on his way there and let Mary Ann know he was coming for a visit. A few days with his boisterous nieces and nephews would take his mind off his troubles. In a time of need, a guy could always count on family and they would definitely provide him with a diversion.

What if Cara needed him? He'd be only a phone call away and could be back in Chattanooga in less than two hours.

But she wouldn't call him. She had an entire security force at her command and a top-notch personal bodyguard with her around the clock. It was past time he got used to the idea of living the rest of his life without Cara Bedell.

DAISY WAITED PATIENTLY outside the private room. Geoff had just been moved out of ICU because he was doing so well. The doctor had said that if he continued to improve at such a quick rate, it was possible he'd be dismissed from the hospital by Monday. She would call Sawyer this evening and give him an update. She was sure he'd send the Dundee jet to Barbados to transport Geoff home to Atlanta. And when she said home, she meant her house. There was no way she would allow him to go back to that tiny studio apartment where he lived.

The orderlies came out of the room. One smiled at her as he passed and the other stopped to talk to her. "If you need anything, Miss Holbrook, just let us know."

"Thank you so much."

"Daisy!" Geoff called loudly.

"He's missing you already," the orderly said.

"I'd better see what he wants."

She hurried into the room and halted when she saw Geoff sitting up in bed, clean-shaven and grinning at her.

"You weren't flirting with those orderlies, were you?" He winked at her.

"Jealous?"

"Why would I be jealous? Considering how handsome I look now that I've had a shave and a bath and am wearing a clean gown, you couldn't possibly want anyone else." He pinched the hospital-issued gown a couple of inches off his chest. "Stylish, isn't it?"

"You look lovely."

They both laughed.

"Come here, Dimples." He patted the edge of his bed.

Daisy's heart skipped a beat. It had been quite a while since he'd called her Dimples, a pet name he'd given her not long after he'd come to work at Dundee's. For some reason, he had stopped calling her that and she'd wondered why.

She walked over, eased down on the edge of the bed and looked right at him. "May I ask you a question?"

"What do you want to know? Ask me anything, love. After all, if you're determined to make an honest man of me, you have a right to know all my deep, dark secrets."

"Hmm…" She tapped her chin contemplatively. "I'll get around to asking about those later." She laid her hand in the center of his chest. "Why did you stop calling me Dimples?"

His smile vanished. "Noticed that, did you?"

"Yes, I noticed. You'd called me Dimples for several years and then suddenly you stopped. Why?"

"It was pointed out to me, by our mutual well-meaning friends, that you had a crush on me and that by my giving you a pet name, I encouraged your feelings for me and gave you false hopes."

She went rigid as a stone statue. Geoff reached up and covered her hand with his, pressing it against his chest.

"I've tried to discourage you because I truly believed it was in your best interest," he told her. "I have given you every argument against our being a couple and you've overruled every one of them. If, in a few years, you find you've made a mistake—"

She leaned over and kissed him, then lifted her head and smiled. "The only mistake would be for us not to be together for the rest of our lives."

"You'll probably be a young widow," he told her. "Considering women live longer than men and I've got a fifteen-year head start on you."

"I plan to take very good care of you, Mr. Monday. I expect you'll live to be at least a hundred and by then our age difference won't matter, will it? You'll be a hundred and I'll be eight-five." She kissed him again, a quick, energetic peck. "Besides, our children will keep you young."

Geoff gasped, then strangled and coughed a few times. "Our children?"

"Uh-huh. I'd like two or three. And I'm fine with them being all girls or all boys or a mix. What about you?"

"I've never thought about being a father," Geoff admitted. "But then again, I've never thought about getting married, either."

"Well, you'd better start thinking about both. And I'm warning you that I expect a big, fancy wedding, with half a dozen bridesmaids or matrons, a huge wedding cake and a honeymoon in paradise."

"Just when did you start planning all of this?"

"Hmm…not long after I first met you. I just didn't realize then how long it would take me to persuade you to admit that you loved me."

"I tend to be stubborn," he said. "It's the Scots in me. I told you that I'm half Scots, didn't I?"

"I can be pretty stubborn myself and determined and pigheaded and bossy. Do you mind that I'm bossy?"

"It's part of your charm." As she leaned over him, her face close to his, he patted her on the butt.

She gasped, then giggled.

"I think I'll like having my very own Ms. Efficiency," Geoff told her.

She sat upright, grabbed his hand that was still on her rear end, brought it up to her waist and looked him in the eye. "I think you should know that I'm not a virgin."

Geoff chuckled. "Neither am I."

She swatted him playfully on his good arm. "I was twenty and a junior in college the first time. I thought I was in love, but it turned out to be infatuation. And I was—"

He kissed her to silence her. When she stared at him wide-eyed and wondering, he said, "I don't want to know anything about any other man and I'm certainly not telling you about other women. We'll do this right or not at all. We're both starting off with a clean slate. As long as there's no one else now or in the future, the past doesn't matter."

"No, the past doesn't matter, because we're going to have such a wonderful future."

Sawyer replaced the receiver on the phone base in his office after his conversation with Sam Dundee. Although Sawyer maintained contacts in the FBI, Sam had contacts with various other agencies, including the CIA. He needed all the help he could get to find Arturo Torres-Rios. It was possible that whoever had hired the man to kidnap Cara Bedell and kill her would use Torres-Rios to finish the job. If Dundee's had a physical description of the man and/or knew his whereabouts and could track his movements, they would know if he entered the U.S. More than likely, if he came after Cara, he would probably use fake ID, including a forged passport, to get into the country. After all, the man traveled internationally in his profession as an assassin. His list of aliases was probably lengthy.

Of course, it was possible that the person behind the kidnap and murder plot would hire someone else. Until they could find that person, Cara wouldn't be safe. Nor would Lucie.

Sawyer had tried not to include Lucie in the equation, but like it or not, she was not only a part of it, but was also what mattered most to him. If when she had left Dundee's, it could have been a clean, permanent break, he might have been able to forget her. But fate had a way of playing jokes on a man.

Why, God, why hadn't he sent someone else with Geoff Monday to rescue Lucie? Why had he been so damned and determined to go to Ameca personally to find her?

Because you still care about her, you stupid son of a bitch!

How many times had he thought about her today? Almost constantly.

What kept replaying over and over in his mind? That damn kiss on the Dundee jet.

What did he want to do right this minute? Call Lucie, just to hear her voice.

But he wouldn't telephone Lucie. Not today or tomorrow. Not next week or next month. Not even next year.

He had to call Deke Bronson to let him know that Whit Falkner would be in Chattanooga tomorrow to head up the Dundee investigation and that Ty Garrett was on his way to San Luis at this very moment. He'd get an update on how Cara's first day back at Bedell, Inc. had gone, and maybe Deke wouldn't mention Lucie.

CHAPTER NINETEEN

THE PAST THREE weeks had been uneventful, which had made Lucie's job of protecting Cara relatively easy, but not simple. She had to remain alert and ready to act on a moment's notice and not fall into a rut of complacency. Perhaps whoever had originally ordered Cara's kidnapping and murder had changed his—or her—mind. But they could also simply be biding their time, giving Cara and those protecting her a false sense of safety.

In the past twenty-one days, she and Cara had become friends. It seemed that despite the difference in their social and economic backgrounds, they had more in common than they could have imagined. They had both been tall, gangly, self-conscious teenagers who had hated their red hair. They had both grown up for the most part without mothers. And where Lucie's father had died, Cara's had been distant and unloving. They liked the same music, the same movies and the same books. And they laughed at the same jokes. Even their political views were similar. Cara was a liberal conservative and Lucie was a conservative liberal. But the one factor that had cemented their bond even deeper than

Lucie risking her life to save Cara was the fact they were both in love with men who kept rejecting them.

The only other person with whom Lucie had discussed her obsession with Sawyer was Daisy, who also had dealt with unrequited love. But it seemed that Daisy just might get her happily ever after.

"I proposed to Geoff and he accepted," Daisy had said, barely able to contain her happiness when she had phoned Lucie while Geoff had still been in the hospital in Barbados. "But we're not rushing things. He knows I want a spring or summer wedding, something huge and fancy. Of course, you have to be my maid of honor."

"I'd love to be your maid of honor. Thank you."

"There's so much to do when we get back to Atlanta. Geoff will stay with me until he's completely recovered. Sawyer's already agreed to give me as much time off from work as I need. And Geoff wants me to choose my engagement ring instead of him picking it out. The crazy man told me he had a nice little nest egg put away so he wanted me to buy something outrageously expensive." Daisy had continued talking without even taking a breath. "Once we're officially engaged, Sawyer plans to host an engagement party for us. Isn't that sweet of him and we both know Sawyer isn't known for being sweet. Naturally, I want you to be there. Will that be horribly difficult for you, seeing Sawyer again?"

"No, of course not. I'll certainly be there with bells on. If this situation with Cara isn't resolved by then, I'm sure Deke can stand in for me for twenty-four hours so I can be at your party."

Daisy had phoned every day while she was in

Barbados; and since their return to Atlanta, she had called every other day with updates on Geoff's progress. Both of them had returned to work this past Monday, but Geoff wouldn't be taking another assignment out of the office for another month. The engagement ring—a two-karat diamond—had been purchased and the engagement party was in the works.

"We're thinking sometime right after Thanksgiving," Daisy had said. "That gives us a little over a month. Surely, things will be settled with Ms. Bedell's case by then."

"I certainly hope so."

Lucie loved seeing her friend so deliriously happy, but she had to admit that a part of her was envious. How must it feel to know that you were going to marry the love of your life.

Stop moping around. Be happy for Daisy.

I am. It's just that I wish…

No time for wishing or hoping. Not now. Not tonight. You have a dinner party to attend.

Felipe and Suelita Delgado had arrived in Chattanooga two days ago and planned to spend three weeks in the United States. Cara was hosting an intimate dinner party tonight for the Delgados here at the Bedell estate. Security had been taken up another notch at the front gates and not only would Deke Bronson be here this evening, but Dundee Agent Whit Falkner would also be in attendance.

The Delgados planned to stay in Chattanooga over the weekend, then they were flying to New York to take in a Broadway show and to shop. On their way back to Chattanooga the following week, they would stop by to visit friends in Kentucky for several days. Everything was set for Bedell, Inc. and Delgado Oil to go into partnership, with the board of directors' approval only a formality. The papers would be signed and an official announcement made to the press before Felipe and Suelita returned to Ameca.

Lucie studied herself in the mirror. She had tried to talk Cara out of buying her this outrageously expensive dress, but Cara had insisted.

"The gown was made for you. My God, Lucie, look at yourself. You're gorgeous," Cara had said.

Was she gorgeous? She smiled. Maybe. She had never worn a dress that cost a month's salary. The dark cinnamon silk draped her curves, touching them lovingly without clinging. The straight skirt hit her midcalf; the bodice fit her like a glove; the neckline draped just low enough to give a glimpse of her décolletage; and the tiny spaghetti straps crisscrossed in the back of the gown, which dipped to an inch below her shoulder blades.

If Sawyer could see me now.

Stop it! Sawyer is out of your life. Permanently.

A loud rap on her bedroom door and Cara calling her name jerked Lucie from her unwanted thoughts.

"Come in," Lucie said.

Cara entered looking every inch the wealthy sophisticate in her knee-length black dress adorned with a row of tiny glittering crystals just below the bustline. She also wore a one-inch-wide diamond choker around her neck and teardrop diamonds dangled from her ears.

"I have something for you." She held a black velvet

box in her hand. "And before you say no, I'm not giving them to you. I'm loaning them to you for the evening."

"Cara, I'm your bodyguard, your employee," Lucie reminded her. "You're treating me as if I were one of your guests."

"You're more than my bodyguard. You're my friend. And with all the Bedell security guards on duty and the Dundee agents in attendance, I don't think you'll need to worry about work tonight." She flipped open the box to reveal a slender gold necklace with a single dazzling topaz, surrounded by diamonds, set in the center. A pair of small diamond-circled topaz earrings lay nestled alongside the necklace.

"No, no, I couldn't possible wear these."

"Sit," Cara ordered. "You're putting them on and wearing them tonight and that's an order, Ms. Evans."

Lucie sat on the vanity stool. Cara placed the open velvet box in front of her, and when Lucie put the necklace around her neck, Cara fastened the clasp.

"I need to check with Aldridge and make sure everything is going smoothly with the caterers," Cara said. "I'm afraid Deke's people have put the poor caterers through quite an ordeal."

"If you'll wait—"

"I don't need you with me every minute," Cara said. "Besides, Whit Falkner arrived about ten minutes ago. If it will put your mind at ease, I'll keep him at my side."

"Yes, that will make me feel a lot better."

"The guests won't be arriving for another thirty minutes, so take all the time you need." Cara gave Lucie's shoulders a pat before she hurried off.

Lucie slipped on the earrings and looked at herself again. Amazing. She *was* gorgeous.

She laughed.

Tonight she would not think about Sawyer McNamara again.

TOMAS CASTILLO placed the long distance call, determined to persuade his coconspirator to act quickly before it was too late. They each had their own reasons for wanting Cara Bedell dead. For Tomas to achieve his goal, the woman had to be killed before she signed a deal with Delgado Oil, which was slated to take place sometime in the next few weeks.

"Senor Castillo, what can I do for you?"

"You can give the order to eliminate our problem," Tomas said. "Make the call, give the order and do it immediately."

"We have time. It is possible that Cara can be persuaded not to sign the deal with Delgado."

"You are insane. Delgado and his wife are there at the Bedell estate tonight, are they not? Senorita Bedell is hosting a dinner party for them and introducing them to the board of directors. The deal between Bedell, Inc. and Delgado Oil is a foregone conclusion, yes? I want you to act now or I will be forced to—"

"Don't threaten me. And do not threaten Cara Bedell. I'll decide if and when she is to die. I've rethought the situation and decided that it might not be in my best interest to eliminate Cara."

Tomas cursed in his native language, then said, "The ransom money was never paid, but my offer to give you ten million dollars is still good. All you have to do is find a way to make sure that Bedell, Inc. signs with Castillo, Inc. instead of Delgado Oil. If that means contacting your hired killer and instructing him to go into action, then so be it."

"Ten million is a very tempting offer, one to which I will give due consideration."

EIGHT OF THE TEN board members had arrived. Cocktails and hors d'oeuvres were being served. Music and laughter filled the foyer and front parlors. Deke Bronson and his beautiful blond wife, Lexie, mixed and mingled with the guests, as did Grayson Perkins and Patrice Bedell. Lucie knew that Cara had not wanted to invite Patrice, but Grayson had pointed out that the board members knew she was in town and would expect to see her. Cara stayed close to Suelita and Felipe, making sure they were properly introduced to everyone. Lucie had made the rounds and Cara had introduced her as my friend Lucie Evans, not as her employee.

"Who says the rich are just like the rest of us?" Whit Falkner looked up at the huge crystal chandelier hanging from the thirty-foot foyer ceiling.

Lucie smiled at Whit. He was a good-looking guy with a wide, toothy grin that seemed both friendly and flirtatious at the same time. Just to look at him—all six-two, a hundred and ninety-five pounds of sleek muscle—you'd never suspect he wasn't in perfect physical condition. And he certainly wouldn't want anyone to know the truth about his war injuries. As an army ranger, he had been severely injured in a bomb explosion. The left side of his face had undergone reconstructive surgery, which was not discernable to anyone who hadn't known him before. The only reason she knew that he was legally blind in his left eye and completely deaf in his left ear was because he had told her.

On the first assignment they had shared last year, he'd been up front with her, explaining in brief detail what he thought she had a right to know about him.

"Just in case no one has told you, you look like a million bucks tonight, Ms. Evans." Whit looked her over, his smile widening. "Are those rocks around your neck and dangling from your ears real?"

"One hundred percent real. Cara—Ms. Bedell— loaned them to me for the evening."

"You two are getting quite chummy, aren't you?"

"I like her. She's nothing like people think she is. She's a genuinely nice person."

"Yeah, that's what everybody says, including all the Bedell, Inc. board members and all the office staff, too. But for every person who likes Cara, there are that many who hated her old man. Seems Edward Bedell wasn't as well liked as his daughter."

"But you haven't discovered that anyone made threats against Mr. Bedell, have you?"

Whit shook his head. "A lot of people didn't like Edward Bedell, but most people at least respected him. We haven't been able to unearth any personal enemies who might be a threat to Ms. Bedell. And most of her father's enemies are dead, retired, or no longer in business."

"What's the latest news from Ty?" Lucie asked.

"Nothing new really. Still no sign of Rios-Torres in

Ameca. Ty thinks the guy may have already left the country."

"What about Tomas Castillo?"

"He's being kept under surveillance, but so far the guy hasn't done anything even remotely suspicious."

"I'm afraid we're being lulled into a false sense of security," Lucie said. "I keep expecting the axe to fall and I have to admit that I almost wish it would. This waiting and wondering and not knowing is nerve-racking."

A waiter paused with a tray of champagne flutes.

"No, thanks," Whit said.

Lucie lifted a glass from the tray. "Might as well enjoy myself since Cara made it perfectly clear that I am not on guard duty tonight."

"Eat, drink and be merry."

Lucie shuddered. "Why did 'for tomorrow ye shall die' just pop into my head?"

Whit chuckled. "Relax, Red. Everybody's safe for tonight," he told her in typical cocky male fashion. "There are more security agents here tonight than there are guests."

In her peripheral vision, Lucie noticed Aldridge greet a late arrival at the front door where the butler had been stationed for the past hour. For half a second, her heart stopped, then when it started again, it raced wildly.

"What's wrong?" Whit asked. "You look as if you've seen a ghost."

"Not a ghost," Lucie replied. "Just your boss."

Whit turned and looked at Sawyer McNamara decked out in a simple black tux, looking elegantly debonair and breathtakingly handsome.

"Yeah, didn't I tell you that he was driving in from Atlanta for this shindig?"

"No, you didn't. Why is he here?"

"Ms. Bedell invited him."

"Why?"

"You really are out of the loop, aren't you? It seems Senor Delgado hired Dundee's to provide private security for him and his wife while they're in the States."

"I thought Bedell, Inc. was providing security for them."

"Only until the Delgados leave Chattanooga. That's when Dundee's will take over. Case Warren and a new agent, Kayla Fuller, will accompany them to New York."

Whit's voice hummed in Lucie's ears. She heard what he was saying, but her heartbeat drummed so loudly in her head that it almost deafened her. Sawyer approached them. She took a deep breath and steeled her nerves. This wasn't supposed to happen. They had said their goodbyes—twice now—but here he was again, back in her life.

"Good evening." Sawyer glanced from Whit to Lucie. His gaze traveled over her from head to toe and back up to her face.

"Not on duty this evening?" Sawyer asked.

Before she could manage to form even a one-word response, Whit said, "Our Lucie's a guest tonight, that's why she looks like a cover model. I told her she looked like a million bucks."

"Two million," Sawyer said, his gaze locked on Lucie's face.

Whit looked at Sawyer and then at Lucie. He cleared his throat. "Well, guess I'd better earn my salary and check in with the other agents to make sure all is as it should be."

"I'll see you later," Sawyer told him as Whit winked at Lucie and walked away. "You looked surprised to see me here this evening."

"I was. I am. I didn't know you would be here."

"Cara didn't mention it to you?"

"No, she didn't. But then she's been busy entertaining the Delgados since they arrived."

"My appearance here tonight is a command performance, more or less," Sawyer explained. "Senor Delgado insisted. Otherwise, I wouldn't be here."

"I didn't think I'd see you again."

"If it could have been avoided—"

"Oh, yes, I understand."

"If you'll excuse me, I should let our hostess know that I'm here."

"Of course."

The moment Sawyer walked away, Lucie released a deep breath, feeling as if she might faint. She swallowed hard, doing her best to keep her emotions under control.

Why, God? Why do this to me now?

CARA KNEW THAT Gray had been trying to get her alone all evening and until a few minutes ago she had managed to outmaneuver him. But he had finally caught her coming out of the powder room. She glanced in every direction, searching for any sign of another human being. Unfortunately, there was no one in sight.

"Cara, darling," he sighed as he clasped her hands to his chest. "Alone at last."

"I can't leave my guests for long." When she tugged on her hands to free herself, Gray held on all the tighter.

"But surely you can spare me a few moments. I feel as if you've been deliberately avoiding being alone with me and not just this evening, but ever since your safe return from Ameca."

"Don't be silly, Gray. I've been busy since I returned. And it's necessary for my safety that Lucie stays with me all the time."

"But not tonight, and yet you've—"

"We're alone now, aren't we? Is there something we need to talk about?" Glancing over Gray's shoulder, she saw Whit Falkner. She smiled at him. It took all her will-power not to motion to him to come and rescue her.

"If you're referring to business, then no," Gray said. "I've done my best to persuade you to think twice about signing with Delgado Oil, as have several board members. But since you seem to have a majority backing, I have no choice but to concede to your wishes." He brought her left hand to his lips and kissed it. "What I wish to speak to you about is personal."

Oh, shit! Not again.

"Gray, please—"

Taking her by surprise, he kissed her.

Startled, she jumped back, but he held on to her hand.

She noticed Whit move toward them, a concerned expression on his face. She looked right at him and shook her head. He halted immediately, but stayed nearby.

"You know how deeply I love you," Gray said. "I'm not asking that you commit to me tonight, but if you can give me even a kernel of hope. Please, darling, tell me that there is hope for me, for us."

Cara heaved a deep sigh. Why wouldn't he give up? Why did he keep putting both of them through this torture?

"Gray, you're family and you always will be." She squeezed his trembling hand. "I love you as an old and dear friend and value you as a Bedell vice president. But I don't love you the way you want me to."

"But you do love me, don't you?"

Did she? There had been a time when she'd thought she was madly in love with him. But what she'd felt for Gray had been little more than a young girl's fanciful crush on her sister's boyfriend.

"I love you as a dear friend and as my former brother-in-law," Cara told him. "But I'm not in love with you."

"It's that policeman, isn't it?"

"Yes. I won't lie to you. You know that I'm in love with Bain."

"But he'll never marry you, darling, and even if he would, he could never fit into our world."

Cara jerked her hand away. "I don't want to hurt you, Gray, but please do not ever again ask me to marry you. The answer will always be no. Even if Bain Desmond didn't exist, I would never marry you."

Tears pooled in Gray's dark eyes. He laid his hand over his heart. "He's not good enough for you, Cara. I wish you could see that." As tears trickled down his cheeks, he turned and walked away.

Cara sighed, glanced at Whit, squared her shoulders and offered him a weak smile. He came toward her.

"Is everything all right, Ms. Bedell?"

"Yes, Whit, thank you."

She had the overwhelming urge to talk to Bain. If she called him, would he answer his phone? She hadn't promised not to call him, had she? It had been three weeks since she'd heard the sound of his voice. Even if she got his voice mail…

Damn it, Cara, call the man. The worst that can happen is that he won't answer.

MATEO GOMEZ, aka Arturo Torres-Rios, checked into the motel, paying in cash for two nights. He had arrived in Miami earlier this evening. After renting a car, he had gone straight from the airport to a local bar that had been recommended to him by a friend. In a back room at the bar, he had purchased several weapons, including an AK-47.

The motel room was adequate, but far from luxurious. When working, luxury was unnecessary and unwise. His best defense was blending in with the crowd, by doing and saying nothing that would draw attention to him.

He had been ordered to come to the United States and wait for further instruction. "Apparently the person who hired you to kidnap and kill Senorita Bedell is undecided about whether or not to reissue the order to kill her," Josue had told him.

Naturally, he would do whatever his employer wanted him to do. After all, he had a half million of their money in his bank account. It was a matter of honor to him that he earn that money. He took full responsibility for what had happened with Senorita Bedell. If all four of his men hadn't been killed, they would be dead now. The one thing he didn't tolerate was failure—in himself or others.

CHAPTER TWENTY

LUCIE DID HER best to steer clear of Sawyer the rest of the evening, but during dinner she had found it impossible. He had been seated directly across from her. Whether or not Cara was responsible for the seating arrangement, Lucie didn't know, but if she was, she'd done it with the best intentions. It was agony and ecstasy seeing Sawyer again, being close enough to reach out and touch him and yet not daring to do more than glance his way when he wasn't looking. Dinner had been a seven-course affair and seemed endless. Lucie knew the food was excellent although she hadn't enjoyed a bite. Everything had tasted like cardboard to her and she had forced down the few morsels she'd eaten.

Shortly after dinner, Gray and Patrice left. Together. Their early exit would have normally piqued Lucie's curiosity, but not tonight. As the evening wore on and, one by one and couple by couple, the guests left, Lucie wondered why Sawyer seemed to be lingering.

Certainly not because of me.

By midnight, all the guests had left except Sawyer, who was in the study with Felipe Delgado, leaving Lucie, Cara and Suelita alone in the living room.

"I hope you do not mind, but I believe I will go up to bed now," Suelita said. "The evening was lovely and I so enjoyed meeting your friends and business associates, but I am rather tired."

When she stood, Cara stood, too, and gave Suelita an affectionate hug. "If there's anything you need, please contact Aldridge and let him know."

"I cannot imagine anything else we will need. You have thought of everything, my dear."

Once Suelita left them alone, Cara sat down on the sofa with Lucie. "I should have told you that Sawyer would be here tonight, but I thought it might be a nice surprise. But it wasn't, was it?"

"He still can't stand to be in the same room with me."

"Oh, Lucie, surely you're wrong. I see the way he looks at you."

"He may want me, but he hates himself for feeling that way."

"I invited him to stay the night," Cara said.

"You did what?"

"When I invited him to tonight's dinner party, I told him that Felipe insisted. Just a little white lie." Cara measured half an inch with her thumb and forefinger. "And I invited him to stay the night instead of making the long drive back to Atlanta or staying at a hotel."

"I'm sure he turned down the offer. I can't imagine—"

"He accepted. He's staying the night. And I had Aldridge put Sawyer's bag in the room next to yours."

"Oh, Cara, you didn't!"

"I'm never going to stop trying to persuade Bain

that we're meant to be together for the rest of our lives. If you love Sawyer as much as I love Bain, you'll do whatever is necessary to—"

"Bain doesn't blame you for his brother's death. You don't have a wall of guilt standing between the two of you."

"You're right, all we have between us is money. My money. Billions of dollars make a pretty impregnable wall."

"I'm sorry. I didn't mean to belittle your situation with Bain. And I know you mean well, but—"

"I had tried to persuade Bain to become my lover for quite some time, but he managed to resist every advance I made. But while we were hidden away in the cabin, the two of us alone together, I finally managed to seduce him. That's why we have a date in three weeks. I'm counting on him missing the sex so much, he'll beg me to marry him."

Lucie smiled. "I hope you're right about you and Bain. But just putting Sawyer and me under the same roof isn't going to change anything. We were alone together in Barbados and he managed to keep his hands off me."

She hadn't told anyone, not even Daisy, about the kiss she and Sawyer had shared on the Dundee jet.

"Want some advice?" Cara asked.

"Why do I think you're going to give it to me whether or not I want it?"

"Do what I did—strip off naked and refuse to take no for an answer."

Lucie laughed. "Did you really do that?"

"Desperate times call for desperate measures."

"I appreciate the advice and the gesture, having Sawyer placed in the room next to mine, but I'm afraid what worked for you, won't work for me." Lucie rose to her feet. "I think I'll follow Suelita and go up to bed, unless you need me to—"

"Go...go. Everyone has gone home and the house is locked and the guards are in place outside. I'm perfectly safe without you. Feel free to sleep as late as you'd like tomorrow. I promise not to leave the house."

THE INCESSANT RINGING woke Bain from a sound sleep. Groggily, he reached across the bed and felt around on the nightstand to find his phone. He flopped over onto his back, held the phone in front of him and looked at the lighted face to check the caller ID. When he recognized the name and number, he sat up in bed and answered the phone.

"Cara, are you all right?" His heartbeat accelerated.

"I'm fine except for missing you."

Bain grunted. "Sugar, you're calling me at—" he glanced at the lighted digital beside clock "—twelve thirty."

"I woke you, didn't I?"

"It's okay. I'm off work tomorrow." He propped a couple of pillows against the headboard and leaned back against them. "How did the dinner party for the Delgados go?"

"How did you know about the dinner party?"

"Deke and I keep in touch on a daily basis and Deke keeps in touch with Sawyer every day."

"Oh, I see."

"It's been three weeks and you've managed not to call," Bain said. "So, why tonight?"

"Gray asked me to marry him again."

"Good God, you didn't say yes, did you?"

"It would serve you right if I did."

"Cara?"

"No, of course I didn't say yes. Even if I weren't madly in love with you, I'd never marry Gray."

"Good girl. You had me worried there for half a second."

"But if you don't marry me… I want children, Bain, and I want them the old-fashioned way."

"You're still young. You've got plenty of time."

"I didn't say I was going to rush into marrying just anybody. But I won't wait for you forever, you know."

"I don't expect you to." Did he really think she would never marry, never have children, simply because she loved him? The thought of her with any other man tightened his gut painfully. He was in a no-win situation with Cara. Without her, he was miserable, but if he married her, how long could it possibly last?

"I love you," she whispered.

"Ah, sugar, don't you know calling me only makes it worse for both of us."

"You're a stubborn jackass, Bain Desmond!"

"Cara?"

Silence.

"Cara?"

"I won't call you again for three more weeks, but don't you dare forget that we have a date then. And between now and then, think about how good it was for us. Think about me lying here in my bed, naked, and wanting you so much."

"Ah, sugar…"

He knew she'd hung up. He groaned. Just the thought of her naked and aroused had given him a hard-on.

AFTER SAWYER said good-night to Felipe Delgado, Aldridge showed him upstairs to his room. The Bedell mansion was huge and the Delgados were in the opposite wing from where Sawyer was staying. He wondered which room was Cara's and which room was Lucie's. He had halfway expected Lucie to be waiting up for him, after his talk with Felipe, but Aldridge had told them that the ladies had retired for the evening.

You're an idiot for being disappointed.

He should be glad that Lucie had done her best to avoid him all evening. Hell, she had barely looked at him. But she had looked at Whit Falkner. She'd smiled at Whit, laughed with him and even flirted with the guy.

But had she done all that to make him jealous?

No, he didn't think so. Maybe she really liked Whit.

Why did that thought bother him so damn much? It shouldn't. It wasn't as if he believed Lucie had been celibate for the past nine years, no more than he had. But he had never met any of her boyfriends and didn't know anything about them.

When Cara had invited him to tonight's dinner party in honor of the Delgados, he had declined. But she had insisted, convincing him that Felipe had personally requested that she invite him.

"He'll be terribly disappointed if you don't come," Cara had said. "And he really won't understand why you declined the invitation."

Reluctantly, he had accepted, but he'd thought for sure Cara would tell Lucie that he would be there. Apparently, from the surprised look on her face when he first arrived, she'd had no idea he would be among the guests. And he certainly hadn't thought that seeing her again would affect him the way it had. But good God, she'd looked incredibly beautiful in that silk dress, the exact rusty red color of her auburn hair. And she had smelled like exotic flowers. He recognized the perfume. She had never changed her fragrance, not since he had given her the first small and outrageously expensive bottle on her seventeenth birthday.

Upon entering his room, Sawyer found that his bed had been turned down, his garment bag had been hung in the closet and his shave kit had been placed on the bathroom vanity. After undressing, he hung his tux and shirt in the closet, and then brushed and flossed his teeth. He should be tired and sleepy, having driven in from Atlanta, staying up past one and sharing a brandy with Felipe. But instead he was wide-awake and restless.

Do not think about Lucie Evans.

Yes, she was somewhere nearby, asleep in one of the many bedrooms here at the Bedell mansion. But it wouldn't matter if she was in the room next to his. She was off-limits. He had made a promise to Brenden on the day of his funeral, a promise that had cost him more than he could have realized at the time.

Had giving up Lucie atoned for his sins?

I'm sorry, Brenden. God, I'm so sorry. I had no right to take what wasn't mine. Lucie was your girl, the love of your life.

Sawyer stretched out on the bed, reached down and pulled up the sheet and lightweight blanket to midchest, and then closed his eyes. Images of Lucie flashed through his mind. Smiling, laughing and flirting—with Whit Falkner! Her brown eyes shimmered vibrantly as she held out her hands to him, beckoning him to come to her. The silk dress, the color of her hair, flowed around her like copper liquid, caressing her body lovingly as he longed to do. But she walked past him and straight into Whit's open arms.

No, don't go to him. Come to me. I want you. I've always wanted you.

Sawyer's eyes flew open. He stared up at the dark ceiling and looked at the shadows created by the moonlight filtering through the transparent sheers hanging between the heavy silk drapes at the windows.

Every muscle in his body was tense, every nerve acutely alert, and his sex was hard. He lifted his hand and rubbed the back of his neck, trying to ease the tension

Stop thinking about Lucie. Yeah, sure, easier said than done.

He had spent the past nine years trying to erase her from his mind, trying to forget the night they had made love.

No, damn it, no. It had been sex, not love.

Sawyer flung back the covers, got up and walked over to the floor-to-ceiling windows that overlooked the enclosed courtyard. For a couple of months after

Brenden's funeral, he hadn't been able to sleep. He had existed on whiskey, catnaps and guilt. He had resigned from the bureau, retreated into his misery and fought his need for Lucie. She had come to him time and time again, trying to talk to him, offering him comfort, and he had rejected her over and over, blaming her for Brenden's death. Finally, he had left his apartment and rented a motel room just to get away from her.

Four months after Brenden's funeral, when Sam Dundee had offered him a job with his private security and investigation agency in Atlanta, Sawyer had jumped at the opportunity to start all over again. He'd had no idea that Lucie would follow him and that the then CEO of Dundee's, Ellen Denby, would hire Lucie as an agent. He should have resigned then and there, the very day Lucie had signed on; but he had refused to admit her presence bothered him in any way. He had done everything to prove to himself and to Lucie that she meant nothing to him. And when Ellen had retired and Sam offered him the job as CEO, he had thought he could use his position to persuade Lucie to resign. He had given her every shit assignment that came along, some that Dundee's shouldn't have handled and wouldn't have except he knew how humiliating they would be for Lucie. But the more he dished out, the more she took. She grumbled and griped and threw hissy fits on a regular basis, but she refused to resign.

When she had finally said enough was enough and left Dundee's to go to work for Bedell, Inc., he had foolishly believed that he had won their nine-year war. But now he knew that until he found a way to purge Lucie from his heart and mind, he would never be free of her and the war raging inside him would continue.

As he lifted back the sheer panel and stared out the window, he caught a glimpse in his peripheral vision of something moving. He blinked, did a double take, and realized that there was a balcony outside his room and someone was standing out there at one thirty on a chilly October morning. He glanced down at the windows in front of him and discovered that of the three windows overlooking the balcony and the courtyard below, the middle one was actually a door. Only after he searched and found the brass handle on the door did he remember that he was naked. He released the handle and peered through the glass panes.

The woman on the balcony stood there in the moonlight, her long, curly red hair glistening like polished copper, her Amazonian body wrapped in a quilted comforter.

Lucie!

Had Cara Bedell deliberately put him in the room next to Lucie's or had Lucie instructed Aldridge to put Sawyer's belongings in the room beside hers?

What difference did it make? It wasn't as if he intended to go into her room or allow her to come into his.

But what the hell was she doing outside at this time of night? The temperature was probably in the mid-forties, not freezing, but hardly warm enough to enjoy being outside for very long.

As he watched her, he realized she had no idea that she wasn't completely alone and unobserved.

Stop looking at her. Turn around and go back to bed. Forget you saw her.

He released the sheer panel, allowing it to fall back in place and cover the single French door. He turned around and, instead of going back to bed, walked straight into the large closet. After feeling around in the dark, he found his tuxedo pants, jerked them off the hook and slipped into them.

Don't do it. Don't open the door and walk out onto the balcony.

The moment he opened the door, the cold night air hit his naked chest. He shivered, but didn't let the cool breeze deter him from going outside.

Lucie stood a good eight feet away, halfway turned away from him, but he could see her quite well in the moonlight. Her shoulders quivered. She swiped her fingertips across her cheeks.

She was crying.

He heard her soft, quiet sobs.

His mind demanded that he retreat while he could, warning him that if he went to her, he would regret it. But his body refused to listen. And his heart. He wanted to hold her, comfort her and dry her tears.

When he took several tentative steps toward her, she whirled around as if instinctively realizing she was no longer alone. Their gazes met and locked, neither able to look away. She stood frozen to the spot, while he walked slowly toward her.

"Sawyer?" Her voice was a mere whisper. She stared at him as if unable to believe her eyes.

"What are you doing out here at this time of night?"

"I couldn't sleep," she replied. "So, you *are* in the room next to mine?"

He nodded. "Was that your doing?"

She shook her head. "No, believe me, it wasn't. Cara was playing Cupid."

"You should go back inside before you get chilled."

"What are you doing out here?" She raked her gaze over his bare chest. "You don't even have on a shirt."

"I saw someone on the balcony and wondered if something was wrong? It's the middle of the night and it's damn cold out here."

"Why were you still awake?"

"I couldn't sleep, either," he admitted.

"You shouldn't have come here for the dinner party. We said our goodbyes three weeks ago and I thought—" The words caught in her throat as fresh tears gathered in her eyes.

"We were both at the dinner party for business reasons," he told her. "I was there in a professional capacity. Considering Dundee's is working for Cara Bedell and her guest, Senor Delgado—"

"Apparently my leaving Dundee's and putting a hundred miles between us wasn't enough to keep us apart." Tears streamed down her cheeks as she clutched the comforter tightly where it crisscrossed over her chest. "After we know that Cara is safe from whoever was behind the plot to kidnap and kill her, I'll leave Bedell, Inc. and find another job farther away. Maybe I should go to California or even Alaska."

"Maybe you should. But for now, you need to go back inside and try to get some sleep."

"Why did you come out here on the balcony when you saw me?" She glared at him. "Why didn't you just stay inside your room and leave me the hell alone?" There was a distinct tremor in her voice.

"I told you that I saw someone out here and wondered—"

"You had to know who it was." She shook her head from side to side, bouncing her long, thick curls. "My hair is a dead giveaway."

"Yes, I knew it was you." He sucked in a deep breath. "I was concerned when I realized you were crying."

She gritted her teeth. "Crying over you. Again." She looked at him, anger in her eyes as tears dampened her face and trickled over her lips and chin. "You've punished me for nine years for a crime I didn't commit. Isn't that long enough?"

"I'm not having this conversation," he said and turned to go back inside.

Lucie pounced with the speed of a jaguar claiming its prey. She swooped down on him. Her hands reached out and grabbed his shoulders from behind, her nails biting into the bronzed flesh and hard muscle. "Don't you walk away from me, damn it. Be a man and face me. Face the truth!"

In turning around, he knocked her hands off his shoulders and inadvertently shoved her backward. When he saw that she had lost her balance, he reached out and grasped her around the waist, realizing too late that the comforter lay at her feet and she was completely naked. His gaze skimmed over her body.

His chest ached with each breath he took. His

erection strained against the fly of his pants. His hold on her waist tightened as he pulled her to him and he lifted his gaze from her breasts to her face. She stared at him, her eyes wide and glistening with tears.

He was as powerless to stop the inevitable as he was to stop the earth from revolving around the sun. God knew that he did not want to want her. But he did. Everything male within him wanted all that was female within her. He wanted her with a hunger that defied reason, with a passion that overruled common sense, and with a need that he could no longer deny.

Lucie tensed the moment her breasts touched his chest. They stared at each other. Neither of them said a word. Sawyer cupped the back of her head and pressed her head up and forward until their lips met. He took her mouth in a kiss that shattered the last fragments of his self-control. Without even a millisecond of hesitation, Lucie returned the kiss, opening her mouth as she slid her arms up and around his neck.

While they kissed, he caressed her back and hips and buttocks, bringing her body as close to his as was humanly possible. When they were both breathless, he slid his arms under her, lifted her and carried her from the balcony and into her room. In his rush to take her to bed, he left the door ajar, allowing the cool morning air to seep into the room.

He laid her down on the bed, then hurriedly yanked off his pants and came down over her. She held open her arms for him, her gaze never leaving his face. He looked at her and saw his own desire reflected in her eyes.

When he hesitated, she reached between them and caressed his penis. He grunted. She stroked him. He groaned. She circled him and pumped gently.

He grabbed her hand to still it. Then as she guided him into her, he lifted her hips and plunged hard and deep.

Lucie cried out with pleasure and wrapped her legs around him. He thrust deeper and harder with each frantic lunge, wanting her, needing her, taking her.

He came quickly, his climax so powerful that he thought he was dying. While he still shuddered with release, Lucie came completely unraveled as her orgasm hit.

HOURS LATER, before daybreak, they made love again. This time Sawyer explored every inch of her body, savoring the taste and smell of her, just as she did with him. They didn't exchange any words and Lucie understood that if either of them spoke, it would instantly shatter the dreamlike atmosphere that cocooned them in a world where no one and nothing existed except the two of them. No past. No future. Only these moments out of time.

She didn't think about what they were doing or what the aftereffects might be and she knew he was doing the same. They didn't think; they simply acted on the impulses they had denied for such a long time.

After their second loving, Lucie fell asleep, sated and secure in Sawyer's arms. She was where she had always wanted to be—with the man she loved.

When Lucie woke again, sunlight flooded her bedroom and the hum of a leaf blower wafted through the open balcony door. She sighed deeply and smiled.

As she turned over in bed, she opened her eyes, ready to say good morning to Sawyer, but found she was alone. Easing up and out of bed, she grabbed her robe off a nearby chair. After putting it on, she walked through the open door and out onto the balcony. The door to Sawyer's room was closed. She tried the handle and the door swung open.

His bed had been neatly made and the room was empty. Deciding he had probably already gone downstairs for breakfast, she turned to go back to her room.

One of the daily domestics came out of the bathroom carrying a handful of dirty towels.

"Good morning, Ms. Evans," the woman said.

Lucie remembered the plump, middle-aged brunette's name. "Good morning, Abby. Have you seen Mr. McNamara this morning? Has he already gone downstairs for breakfast?"

"No, ma'am. Mr. McNamara left over an hour ago. I believe he went back to Atlanta. He gave Aldridge a message for Ms. Bedell."

"Oh, I see. You don't happen to know if he left a message for me, do you."

"No, ma'am, I don't know. But you can ask Aldridge."

"Yes, I'll do that. Thank you."

Lucie backed out of the room and when she reached the balcony, she turned and fled to her bedroom. She barely managed to close the door, before she cried out in pain.

Damn him. Damn him for running away again.

Oh, Sawyer, don't you know that we belong together. We always did. We always will.

CHAPTER TWENTY-ONE

DAISY PUT THE call through on Sawyer's private, secure phone line and when the distinct ring alerted him, he picked up the receiver and identified himself.

"Sawyer McNamara."

"It's Sam. I've just received a message from my one of my contacts whose people have been searching for Arturo Torres-Rios."

"Good news, I hope."

"Good and bad. He was spotted in Miami three days ago and was followed north to Orlando and on to Tallahassee. They lost him somewhere near Birmingham, Alabama."

"He's on his way to Chattanooga," Sawyer said.

"It's only a matter of time before they pick up his trail again."

"Tomorrow evening is the charity auction that Cara Bedell is taking part in. Deke has done everything he can to persuade her to withdraw as a one of the bachelorette prizes and simply make a donation."

"Without any luck I presume."

"The lady is stubborn."

"All of them are, aren't they," Sam said.

"All I've ever known." Sawyer cleared his throat. "I've

sent six extra Dundee agents to Chattanooga to help Deke and his security force secure the ballroom for tomorrow night. Unfortunately, the auction is open to the public, anyone who can buy a five-hundred-dollar ticket."

"You aren't going yourself?"

"No, I don't see any need. Whit Falkner can handle things for Dundee's and we both know security agents don't come any better than Deke Bronson."

"I agree. When I receive an update on Torres-Rios, I'll get in touch immediately. Let Whit and Deke know he's on his way to Chattanooga."

"It would've helped us if we'd had a physical description of the man."

"It seems the man is an expert at hiding his identity, so that probably means he never deals directly with any of his clients. He has a go-between, someone who brokers all his jobs. Rita Herrera has a lead on a lawyer named Josue Soto in San Luis who just might be this go-between. They're looking into his business affairs and bank accounts. If we can nail him, we'll be one step closer to Torres-Rios."

"If our guy shows up at the charity auction, y'all should be able to capture him. I wish there was another way of leading him into a trap, one that didn't involve using Cara as bait." And Lucie, who would, if necessary, shield Cara with her own body.

After his conversation with Sam, Sawyer placed a call first to Whit Falkner and then to Deke Bronson, filling them in on the latest information.

"I'll let Lucie know," Whit had said. "She'll be Ms.

Bedell's first line of defense, so she needs to be aware that there's a definite possibility that an attempt will be made going to, at, or coming back from the auction."

Sawyer had spent the past few weeks trying his level best not to think about Lucie Evans and the hours he had spent in her bed.

But how did a man forget Lucie?

He had left her that Saturday morning three weeks ago while she was still asleep. Every instinct he possessed had urged him to wake her and make love to her again. His conscience told him to explain why he couldn't stay, why what had happened between them had been a mistake. But he knew he couldn't face her, so he had let his absence act as an explanation. Apparently she had gotten his message loud and clear. She hadn't called him.

The crazy thing was he didn't know if he was relieved that she hadn't tried to get in touch with him or if he was disappointed.

WHEN LUCIE AND CARA arrived at the ballroom, they entered quickly through a back door of the hotel. Whit Falkner and two Bedell security guards accompanied them straight to Cara's dressing room and both guards stayed at the door.

Providing security for an event such as this was a complex matter. Bedell security and Dundee's had sent in an advance team to check out the ballroom and surrounding areas within the hotel, including all entrances and exits. Whit coordinated the liaison with the hotel management, the Chattanooga P.D. and the two security forces. All the guards in the ballroom were armed. Dundee's had two guards inside, along with two from the Chattanooga P.D., and four from Bedell, Inc. The regular police officers were in charge of traffic duties, which included valet parking. Deke's personnel handled the fixed-post security at all entry and exit points.

Except for Lucie, all members of the combined Dundee and Bedell security forces wore color-coordinated ID badges that showed the wearer's photo and name. The local police officers wore their uniforms.

"If we need to get Cara out of the ballroom immediately, our evacuation plan should take no more than five minutes," Whit had told Lucie. "Take her straight through the kitchen and to the service elevator, then go to the basement parking garage where a car will be waiting."

"You really think this guy is going to show up tonight?" Lucie had asked.

"Yeah. Maybe. Probably. Deke agrees. Since this event is open to anyone with the price of a ticket, all our assassin needs is five hundred dollars and he's in. But it could work in our favor and a turn out to be our best chance to catch him."

This was far from Lucie's first assignment, but in the past, the principal had never become a close friend and few assignments had lasted as long as this one had. Most jobs were routine and relatively safe. She'd never been shot, not as a Dundee agent nor as an FBI agent. And only once during her years with the bureau had she been forced to shoot an assailant.

"Lucie," Cara called from where she sat in front of the mirror. "I think I'm going to throw up again."

"Take a few sips of the ginger ale Whit brought you," Lucie told her. "It's probably just nerves. I'd be sick as a dog if I knew men were going to be bidding on me." *And if I knew some hired assassin was on his way here to kill me.*

"You're probably right, it's just nerves. If it were a stomach virus, I'd be a lot sicker and it wouldn't come and go the way it's been doing for the past couple of days."

"It's not too late to change your mind, you know. Just say the word and we'll leave immediately. They can announce that you were taken ill."

Cara sucked in a deep breath and then released it slowly and repeated the process several times. "I think I'll be fine."

"You know there's every chance there will be an attempt on your life tonight," Lucie reminded her.

"If not tonight, then tomorrow or the next day or the next. I'd rather go ahead and give him the opportunity tonight while I'm surrounded by so much security. Both Deke and Whit have told me that there's a good chance they'll catch him."

"Yeah, but it's what might happen between him making his move and our guards taking him down that concerns me."

"I know what you're thinking," Cara said. "You don't need to remind me that this man is a hired assassin and the person who hired him has to be found and stopped before I'll be safe again."

Lucie went up behind Cara and clamped her hands down over Cara's bare shoulders. She gave her a reassuring squeeze.

"Lieutenant Desmond is here," Lucie said.

Cara whipped around and looked up at her. "Is he? I had hoped…" Cara swallowed. "We have a date tomorrow evening, you know, so I wasn't sure if he'd show up tonight."

"Where else would he be? He's aware of what's more than likely going to happen tonight. Even knowing this place is swarming with security, he had to be here."

Cara scooted back the vanity stool and stood. "How do I look?"

"Like ten million dollars," Lucie told her.

Cara laughed. "I'm not talking about the diamonds and sapphires I'm wearing or this Cavalli gown."

"Oh, well then, you look like about five million."

Lucie inspected Cara. The dark blue, exotic-print evening gown fit Cara's statuesque body to perfection. Strapless, with a train that boasted an underlay of navy tulle, the dress made Cara's hazel eyes appear a deep blue, almost the exact color of the sapphire and diamond earrings she wore and the matching bracelet that completed her jewelry selection.

"Do you want something to eat?" Lucie asked. "I can send for a sandwich or a salad, if you'd like. You have about half an hour before you go on stage."

"No, I couldn't eat a bite."

"You barely touched your lunch today. You must be hungry by now."

"Actually, I'm not, which is definitely not normal for me." As she paced back and forth in the small dressing room, Cara glanced at Lucie. "If you're hungry—"

"I ate a big lunch. I'm fine."

"I wish you had let me buy you another evening gown for tonight." Cara studied Lucie in her simple black floor-length gown, topped with a short-sleeve jacket. The dress was not a designer creation. It wasn't even an expensive off-the-rack evening gown. It was a dress provided for female Bedell security guards to wear when they were on duty at formal affairs. It was nice enough so that she easily fit in with the guests, and the hip-length jacket allowed her to hide the shoulder holster she wore.

"I'm wearing the pearl earrings." Lucie turned her head from side to side, showing Cara the white South Sea pearls that Cara had loaned her to wear tonight.

"When this is all over, I'm going to miss having you with me all the time." Cara smiled. "I like having a friend to share things with."

"You have Lexie Bronson. I thought you two were good friends."

"We are, but Lexie has her hands full with little Emma. And she hasn't told many people, but she and Deke are expecting again." Cara sighed. "She has what I want—a husband who worships the ground she walks on…and children."

"Who doesn't want that?"

"Well, I'm not giving up and neither should you."

Lucie couldn't make herself reply because she didn't agree with Cara. She had given up. Finally. If Sawyer could make love to her the way he had and leave her without a backward glance, then there was no hope for them. He had walked out on her while she slept. Hadn't left a note. Hadn't phoned her.

WHEN SHE STOOD off stage, waiting for her name to be called, Cara glanced out into the audience. She caught a glimpse of Bain standing to the right of the stage, next to the wall, his gaze traveling over the room as if he were searching for someone. Dozens of tables had been arranged throughout the ballroom, enough to accommodate up to four hundred people.

As she scanned the room, able to clearly see the first few rows of seats that partially circled the stage, she saw Gray sitting front and center. Patrice sat at his table and beside her was a man Cara recognized immediately—Tomas Castillo. My God! What was he doing here and why was he sitting with Patrice and Gray? If Gray thought that by bringing Tomas here, the two of them could persuade her not to sign a deal with Delgado Oil, then he was sadly mistaken.

"Lucie…" Cara motioned to her friend. "Look out there. Do you see who's at the same table as Gray and Patrice?"

"I'll be damned," Lucie said. "He actually showed up."

"Did you know he'd be here?"

"I didn't say anything because you were already nervous enough as it was," Lucie said. "Dundee's has been tracking Senor Castillo for quite some time and as soon as he left Ameca for the U.S., Deke has been kept informed of his movements. He arrived in Chattanooga this afternoon and guess who met him at the airport?"

"Who?" Lucie held her breath.

"Your step-mommy-dearest."

"Patrice?"

"Uh-huh. Interesting, don't you think?"

"You're not implying that Patrice and Tomas Castillo are working together and hired an assassin to kill me?" Cara said, keeping her voice low so that only Lucie could hear her.

"I don't know." Lucie shrugged. "It's a possibility, but it could be he's here simply at Gray and Patrice's invitation to plead his case to the board of directors and try to stop you from signing the deal with Delgado Oil."

"Oh, my. Do you think Felipe and Suelita have seen Tomas? If they have, what must they be thinking?"

"They're probably thinking that Senor Castillo is trying to pull a fast one."

"Oh, crap, I'm up next." She grabbed Lucie's hands. "I can't tell you how nauseated I am. What if I throw up while I'm on stage?"

Lucie squeezed her hands. "Take some deep breaths, then go out there and strut your stuff. Remember, you're doing this for charity. And you are not going to throw up."

Cara breathed deeply. The announcer recited a brief bio that praised her to high heaven, then he called out her name.

"You're surrounded by security," Lucie reminded her. "And I'll be right here, not more than fifteen feet away."

With her head held high, Cara glided out onto the stage.

BAIN STOOD BY and watched while dozens of men bid on a date with his woman. Even knowing in advance that tonight's results were rigged and Whit Falkner had been authorized to bid as high as necessary to win Cara for the rest of the evening and supposedly for a subsequent date, Bain still felt a twinge of jealousy. Yes, it was all for a good cause, the money earned tonight going to charity, but Cara was putting her life at risk. On stage alone, she was a perfect target. If anything happened to her...

They had a date tomorrow night, one he intended to keep. He had thought that he was strong enough to save himself and Cara from making a huge mistake by making a commitment. He had tried to tell her that once they made love, he would never be able to walk away from her for good, that once or twice or a dozen times would never be enough for him. For either of them.

He loved that woman. Loved her with everything in him. The very thought of marrying a woman worth billions scared the hell out of him, but living the rest of his life without her sweet love scared him even more.

Mary Ann had helped him pick out an engagement ring. A one-karat square-cut that had cost him an arm and a leg. He knew Cara had rings worth ten times as much, but he had a gut feeling that she wouldn't give a damn about the size of the diamond he gave her.

He didn't know how, but they would find a way to make marriage work for them. He'd hate living in the Bedell mansion and having hot and cold running servants. He'd despise being ribbed on a daily basis by his buddies at the station and down at the Hair of the Dog pub. And he figured it would be only a matter of time before someone referred to him as Mr. Bedell.

Sawyer contacted Deke Bronson to alert him that Arturo Torres-Rios, using the alias Mateo Gomez, had been tracked directly to Chattanooga.

"They're seventy-five percent certain that it's Torres-Rios. He managed to give them the slip a couple of times, but a guy fitting the description of the man identified by a night clerk at the motel in Miami was seen entering the hotel there where the charity auction is being held. He's somewhere among the guests, but the Feds are holding back because they don't want to panic him and him start shooting into the crowd."

Deke alerted Bain to the latest development and the two of them contacted their people via the wireless communication devices they all wore. Slowly, carefully, the security agents in the ballroom began milling about in as subtle a way as possible, searching for an Amecan male, five-ten, approximately a hundred and sixty-five pounds, wearing a long, black evening coat over his tux.

The bidding on Cara Bedell had reached forty-five thousand, with only two bidders remaining—Whit Falkner and Grayson Perkins.

Deke contacted one of the female Dundee agents and gave her a message to deliver to Whit. Once she approached Whit and whispered in his ear, he made his next bid.

"A hundred thousand for a date with Ms. Bedell," Whit shouted.

A round of applause shook the rafters.

The emcee, who was also the auctioneer, made a big hoopla over the bid, calling for someone—as he looked directly at Grayson Perkins—to offer a hundred and five thousand. Perkins shook his head.

"Congratulations, sir," he told Whit. "You are the lucky winner."

As the emcee brought Whit up on stage for the purpose of claiming his prize, Lucie Evans made her way from the wings and walked around the back edge of the stage. Suddenly, to the astonishment of almost everyone present, Lucie pulled her weapon from her shoulder holster as she ran toward Cara.

As if he were seeing everything in slow motion, Deke's gaze moved from Lucie to Cara just as the room suddenly went dark, only the candlelight on each table illuminating the room. Half a second later, gunfire erupted and people started screaming.

CHAPTER TWENTY-TWO

COMPLETE PANDEMONIUM ensued, with some people screaming and trying to escape the ballroom in the dark while others hid under tables and trembled with fear. After Lucie saw a man who fit the description she'd been given of Arturo Torres-Rios standing in the back of the ballroom, she had watched him as he made his way near one of the side exits. The moment a reflection of something metallic glimmered beneath his evening coat, she had drawn her weapon and moved onto the stage.

When the first shot was fired, Whit Falkner shoved Cara to the floor, but before he could cover her body protectively with his, he took a hit in the lower gut, slumped forward and toppled off the stage. As his body fell across the table nearest the stage, the people sitting there screamed in horror.

Lucie dove onto the floor where Cara lay, facedown, just as another shot rang out, followed by another and then another. A bullet ripped through her hip. She barely managed to transform the yelp of pain into a deep grunt as she draped herself across Cara.

"Are you okay?" Lucie asked.

No response.

Damn! "Cara, answer me."

Silence.

Lucie looked out into the ballroom, into the frenzy of movement, and spotted Deke Bronson running out the side exit, past the guard who had been shot and lay crumpled in a heap at the door. Then she saw Bain Desmond, gun drawn, coming toward the stage.

Suddenly the lights came back on as quickly and unexpectedly as they had gone off. Bain jumped up on the stage, rushed over to them and squatted down. He grasped Lucie's arm.

"I can't get Cara to respond," Lucie told him, her voice as unsteady as her nerves. "Help me off her. I took a bullet in the hip."

"We've got ambulances coming," Bain told her as he rolled her over onto her back. "Just stay put. The shooter escaped, but he won't get far."

Lucie rested on her uninjured side and watched while Bain spoke to Cara, calling her name; but she lay there unmoving and silent. He inspected her, starting at her head and moving down the front of her body. With the utmost care, he turned her over slowly.

"I don't see any sign of a bullet wound," Bain said. "Cara, sugar, wake up." He patted her cheek softly. He glanced at Lucie. "How bad is it?

"Hurts like hell and I'm bleeding like a stuck hog," she told him. "But the bullet didn't hit an artery, thank God." She slid her hand over her hip and felt the damp, sticky blood seeping from the gunshot wound. "I don't think I'm dying, but what about Whit?"

"I don't know," Bain said. "Don't worry about him right now. Worry about yourself. Help is on the way."

Bain shoved back Cara's hair, where it had fallen across the side of her face, and uttered a couple of distinct curse words.

"What is it?" Lucie asked.

"She's got a knot on the side of her head the size of a goose egg."

"She must have hit the floor pretty hard. It's probably only a mild concussion."

Lucie didn't know how long they actually waited, but despite her excessive blood loss and her deteriorating mental state, she was aware of the fact that Bain had taken a look at her injury. He had used his jacket as a bandage to absorb the blood as he applied gentle pressure to the wound. He had stayed with them, keeping watch over Cara and her until the medics arrived. And one of the Bedell security guards had checked on Whit, told them that he was still alive, and had remained with him while they'd waited.

They were taken on stretchers to two different ambulances and just as they started to close the ambulance door, Deke Bronson hopped into the back with her.

She stared up at him when he leaned over her. "Whit?" she asked.

"He's still alive," Deke said. "You two saved Cara's life."

"She's unconscious. Probably a concussion, right?"

"Probably." He took her hand and squeezed it. "We got him. Torres-Rios. Or should I say the Feds got him."

"Did they take him alive?" Lucie asked.

"Unfortunately, no." Deke shook his head. "We needed him to give us the name of the person who hired him."

"Cara's still in danger. She'll have to have around-the-clock protection at the hospital."

"You just worry about yourself, Ms. Evans, and let me worry about everything else."

She tried to smile, but whatever the medics had injected into her IV drip was taking effect quickly. "Call Daisy. Tell her…I'm…okay."

"Sawyer's probably already called her. I got in touch with him as soon as the Feds took out Torres-Rios and the police secured the hotel."

"Sawyer?"

"He's on his way here from Atlanta." Deke squeezed her hand again as she drifted off into a drug-induced sleep.

CARA OPENED HER EYES. At first, she didn't know where she was or what had happened. Her head hurt. It felt as if someone had hit her with a sledgehammer.

"Hey, sugar. It's about time you opened those beautiful eyes."

She stared up at Bain Desmond's smiling face. "Bain?"

"The one and only."

"What happened? Where am I?" She glanced around the room. "Am I in the hospital?"

"You've got a nasty bump on your head," he told her. "The doctor said it's a concussion. Do you remember coming to for a few minutes and answering the doctor's questions?"

"No, I don't think…maybe. Did the doctor look like Al Pacino?"

Bain chuckled. "Yeah, there's a slight resemblance."

"He asked me my name and what year it was and my address and phone number." She lifted her hand and discovered that Bain held it securely in his. "I don't remember seeing you."

"They made me leave the room," he said. "You'd conked out again by the time they let me see you. I've been worried sick waiting for you to wake up. The doctor was concerned because they couldn't keep you awake, which is not a good thing for someone with a concussion. You had everyone worried, sugar."

"Am I going to be all right?"

"Yes, ma'am, you are, now that you're awake. Their biggest concern was that you couldn't seem to remain conscious. They did a CAT scan and there are no fractures and no internal bleeding, but you're going to need a lot of rest."

"Oh, God, Bain, what about Lucie and Whit!" She squeezed his hand tightly and tried to sit up.

He pressed her gently back down into the bed and kept his hand resting in the center of her chest. "Stay calm, sugar, stay calm."

"I remember. The ballroom. The gunfire." She wished she hadn't remembered. "Whit? He was shot. He fell off the stage."

"Whit's in surgery."

"Was anyone else hurt? What about Lucie?"

"Lucie took a bullet in the hip," Bain told her. "She's in surgery right now, too."

Tears gathered in her eyes. Suddenly she felt horribly

sick at her stomach. She tried to sit up again, but Bain held her down.

"I'm going to be sick."

He grabbed the small, kidney-shaped, plastic bowl on the bedside table, laid it in her lap and then slipped his arm behind her back and helped her into a sitting position. She grabbed the bowl, heaved once and vomited. When Bain tried to take the bowl from her, she clutched it tightly and shook her head. Before she could say anything, she threw up again.

She released her tight grip on the bowl and allowed Bain to take it. When he went into the bathroom, she laid her head back against the pillow. After dumping the contents of the bowl into the water, Bain flushed the commode, rinsed out the bowl and set it in the sink. Then he came back to her with a damp washcloth in his hand. First he rubbed the cool cloth over her face and then wiped the corners of her mouth.

"I need to tell the nurse about this," Bain said. "It's probably nothing, something caused by the head trauma, but—"

"I don't think it's from the blow to my head. I was sick before the charity auction. Lucie thought it was a case of nerves, but maybe it's some weird stomach virus."

"Could be, but the nurse needs to know. Just to be on the safe side."

"Don't leave me."

"I won't be gone long, a few minutes at most."

"Check on Lucie and Whit while you're at the nurse's station."

"Will do."

When he opened the door, she saw two uniformed guards, one a policeman and the other a Bedell security guard. "Bain?"

He paused and looked back at her. "Yeah, sugar?"

"Was anyone else hurt?"

"Only the guy who shot Lucie and Whit."

"The hired assassin?"

"He's dead." Bain nodded at the two uniformed men. "The guards are here for your safety. No one comes in here, not even a nurse, without my say-so."

When he left, she closed her eyes and sighed. Whoever had hired the assassin was still out there and he or she still wanted Cara Bedell dead. Would he find another professional killer to do the job or would he come after her himself?

SAWYER PACED the floor in the waiting room. What the hell was taking so long? She'd been in surgery for hours. If only he could have gotten here sooner. He had left home the minute Deke had contacted him. He'd thought about taking the jet, but considering the time to and from airports, he had figured he could drive and get here quicker than flying.

Daisy and Geoff entered the waiting area, each carrying cups of coffee. Deke Bronson met them, took one of the cups from Geoff and the two men sat down together in side-by-side chairs. Daisy came over to Sawyer and held out a cup.

"Take this and drink it," she told him.

He looked at her, saw the determination in her eyes and accepted the coffee she offered. "Thanks."

"Come sit down for a few minutes." She laid her hand on his arm.

He tensed. "This is taking too long. Something's wrong."

She squeezed his arm. "Nothing's wrong. Surgery takes time."

"I should have been there tonight. I knew the risk she was taking. I knew what might happen."

"Whit was there and so was Deke and dozens of guards," Daisy said. "If they couldn't prevent what happened, what makes you think you could have?"

He stared at Daisy as her words sank in, reminding him of just how illogical his thought processes became when he allowed emotion to overrule common sense. "I know. I know." He looked directly at Daisy. "Whit might not make it."

"He'll make it. We'll double up on our prayers."

Sawyer nodded. It had been a long time since he'd prayed. The last time had been the day of Brenden's funeral. He had sworn an oath to his dead brother and then prayed for God to give him the strength to keep the promise he had made. If he prayed for Lucie and for Whit, would God hear his prayers?

Lucie couldn't die!

He had to see her, hold her, talk to her.

Just as he lifted the capped coffee cup to his lips, he noticed that Deke and Geoff were deep in conversation. Both had serious expressions on their faces. "What's up with them?" Sawyer asked.

"Plotting strategy," Daisy said. "Arturo Torres-Rios is dead, so he can't reveal the name of the person who hired him, but on our way here, a call came through from Ty in Ameca. Josue Soto is going to be picked up by some of Rita Herrera's friends tomorrow and questioned about his association with Torres-Rios."

"If Soto can give us a name…" Sawyer's grip on the insulated cup tightened enough to pop the lid. "I want the son of a bitch now more than ever." The cup lid fell off and onto the floor.

"There is a chance that even if Soto worked with Torres-Rios, he might not know the person's name who paid to have Cara killed," Daisy reminded Sawyer as she reached down and picked up the cup lid. "And if he does, he may not be willing to offer the information without persuasion."

"By God, if I got my hands on him, I'd persuade him."

"Why don't you go over there and talk to Geoff and Deke. Help them come up with some new ideas."

"It won't work, you know," Sawyer said.

She gave him an I-don't-know-what-you-mean look.

"Nothing is going to take my mind off Lucie."

"When she comes out of this, and she will pull through, you'll have the opportunity to make things right with her."

"I doubt she'll want to hear anything I have to say."

"Are all men dense, or just you and Geoff?" Daisy asked him.

He glared at her.

"Lucie's in love with you. She'll listen to you as long as you're saying what she needs to hear."

"Lucie's not in love with me," he said quietly. "She's got love and sex all mixed up."

"No, I think maybe you, Mr. McNamara, are the one who's all mixed up. I don't know exactly what happened between the two of you when your brother died or why you blame Lucie, but I know for a fact that she's been in love with you since she was a teenager."

Sawyer shook his head. He couldn't deal with this, not right now. Lucie might have had a schoolgirl crush on him, but she hadn't been in love with him. She had loved Brenden, dated Brenden, been Brenden's girl. Until the night he had allowed himself to forget that Lucie belonged to his brother.

"Mr. McNamara?" a male voice called from the doorway.

Sawyer snapped his head around and looked at the man in green scrubs standing just outside the waiting room. He set the untouched coffee on a nearby table and rushed toward the doctor. Daisy followed him as Deke and Geoff rose from the sofa.

"I'm Sawyer McNamara."

"I'm Dr. Collins. Are you a member of Ms. Evans's family?"

"Yes, he is," Daisy replied before he could respond. "He's her fiancé."

The doctor nodded. Sawyer didn't contradict Daisy.

"Ms. Evans came through surgery without any complications. She lost a great deal of blood. We were able to remove the bullet. It hit her hipbone, which probably saved her life. The hipbone will have to be replaced, but not until she has recovered from this surgery."

"Then she's all right. She's going to be fine?" Sawyer asked.

"She should be," the doctor replied. "But as with any surgery, the first twenty-four hours are critical."

"When can I see her?' Sawyer asked.

"She's being moved to the intensive care unit. Check with them in about an hour. You should be able to go in and see her for a few minutes. I'll leave orders to allow you five minutes with her."

"Thank you."

When the doctor turned to leave, Sawyer called to him. "A friend and employee, Whit Falkner, is in surgery, too. You wouldn't happen to know—"

"Dr. Lamar has a patient in surgery and that's possibly your friend. I'm sure Dr. Lamar will come out and speak to y'all soon."

Daisy hugged Sawyer.

"Stay here," Sawyer said. "I'm going to the ICU to check with them and make sure I get to see Lucie. When you hear something about Whit, one of you come and get me, please." Sawyer glanced from Deke to Geoff. "After I see Lucie, I want to hear what sort of plan you two have come up with."

"THEY'RE NOT LETTING anyone in to see Cara," Grayson Perkins told his companions who had waited for him in the hospital lobby.

"Is she all right?" Patrice asked.

"I have no idea," Gray said. "They have two guards at her door, one policeman and someone from Bedell security, and both are following Bain Desmond's orders not to let anyone go into her room. Even the hospital staff has to get his okay before they can go in."

"Who does he think he is?" Patrice pursed her lips in a pout. "We're her family. We have every right to know what's going on and if she's going to live or die."

Tomas Castillo, who had his arm draped around Patrice's waist, patted her hip. "Do not worry yourself so, my dear Patrice. I am sure if she dies, you will be informed. We must assume that she is still alive, otherwise why would guards have been posted at her door?"

"I did manage to gain some information," Gray told them.

Tomas and Patrice focused directly on him.

"What happened is all over the news. It's on the local TV stations. I paused by a patient's room when I heard the newscast and when I looked into the room at his television, they announced that four people had been seriously injured during the shooting and one was dead."

"Who was the fourth person?" Tomas asked.

"There was Cara and the two guards," Patrice said. "I have no idea who the fourth was. Unless—" She gasped. "Do you suppose they killed the shooter?" She glanced at Tomas. "I certainly hope so."

He lifted his arm up around her shoulders. "Yes, as do I. It is much preferable for this man to be killed than captured, is it not, Senor Perkins?"

Gray turned pale. "I'm sure the police wanted to question him. I imagine they think he could have told them the name of the person who hired him."

"I have heard that men such as he usually do not exchange names with clients," Tomas said. "And they often have a go-between, someone who knows both of their identities. If I were the guilty party, it is that person I would pray is never caught and questioned."

In his peripheral vision, Gray glimpsed Senor and Senora Delgado being escorted by two Bedell guards as they emerged from one of the nearby elevators. He walked away from his companions and approached the couple as they exited the elevator.

"Have you been upstairs to see Cara?" Gray asked, wondering if they had been allowed entrance to her private room.

"No, Senor Perkins, we were not allowed to see Senorita Bedell," Felipe Delgado said, his voice terse.

"Did anyone tell you how she is? I couldn't get a word out of any of the nurses."

"We were told she is resting and cannot be disturbed," Suelita Delgado said as her gaze wandered across the lobby to where Tomas Castillo stood with his arm around Patrice's shoulders. "You have allied yourself with a very bad man, Senor Perkins."

"Suelita!" her husband warned her in a rough whisper.

"Senor Castillo is Mrs. Bedell's guest, not mine," Gray assured them.

"Come, we must be going." Felipe grasped his wife's elbow. "We will return tomorrow and perhaps be able to see Cara then."

The Delgados dismissed Gray as if he were an errand boy. Let them treat him with contempt. Their opinion was unimportant to him. Nothing mattered at this precise moment except finding out how badly hurt Cara was and knowing if she would live or die.

"YOU HAVE FIVE MINUTES," the nurse told Sawyer as he entered Lucie's ICU cubicle. "She's sedated, so don't try to rouse her."

Sawyer nodded. He walked over to the side of the bed and looked down at Lucie, her red hair like glowing flames against the pristine white pillowcase. She lay there so quiet and still that if he didn't see the gentle rise and fall of her chest, he would think she was dead.

"You're going to be all right," he told her, keeping his voice soft and low.

She was so pale, and despite her size and height, she looked delicate and fragile.

He grinned. "You've never been fragile and delicate have you, Lucie. Not you. You're a fighter, a pit bull, a stubborn, hardheaded…"

He ran his fingertips over her arm, careful not to touch the tubes and wires connecting her to the IV and monitors.

"When you get better, we're going to talk. That's what you've wanted all these years, for the two of us to talk about Brenden. It won't be easy for either of us. I need for you to know that I don't blame you. I haven't in a long time."

He leaned down and kissed her forehead. "Rest well, Lucie Locket. I'll be right outside, waiting for you to wake up."

CHAPTER TWENTY-THREE

"Do you think I can go in to see Lucie this morning?" Cara asked.

"If the doctor says you're up to it," Bain told her as he handed her a mirror to check the job he'd done brushing her hair. "The first visitation isn't until eight thirty and I think Sawyer has dibs on that time."

"But Deke told you that she's doing okay, right? She came through surgery fine and she's going to fully recover."

Bain hadn't told her that Lucie would have to have a second surgery to replace her damaged hipbone. There was no need to worry her right now. Once she was released from the hospital and at home, he would explain the situation in detail.

"Yes, she's going to be fine," he said. "Keeping her in intensive care is standard procedure after that type of surgery."

"And what about Whit?"

"I told you that he's alive, that he survived the surgery."

"But what haven't you told me?"

Bain grasped her shoulders gently. "Whit Falkner is in a drug-induced coma. It's touch-and-go, but there's every reason to be optimistic. Sawyer told me that Whit has survived a lot worse."

"I feel so responsible," Cara said. "Both Whit and Lucie were seriously wounded protecting me."

"That was their job."

"I know, but…" She took a deep breath. "Okay, I'll stop this guilt trip I'm on."

"Good girl."

She offered him a halfhearted smile. "I can't believe I'm hungry. Not after my being so sick last night. But I am starving to death. Any chance breakfast is on its way?"

Bain grinned. "I'll go find out. And if it's not, I send somebody to get you some breakfast from the closest fast-food place."

"I want orange juice, too. A big glass."

He paused at the door, winked at her and then left.

CARA HIT THE BUTTON to raise the head of her bed a little higher, then held up the hand mirror and looked at herself. Early this morning, Bain had helped her into the bathroom and stayed with her while she took a shower and washed her hair, which was still damp. Right now, she was scrubbed clean and looked as plain as an old shoe. She was nearly thirty and yet without makeup, she still had that cute-kid look so common among freckled redheads. Yeah, like Bozo the Clown.

She laughed.

As she lifted her hair back and inspected the oval bruise on the side of her forehead, between her temple and her cheekbone, Bain came back into the room carrying a tray.

"Breakfast is served." He wheeled the adjustable stand with one hand and held the breakfast tray with the other. He pushed the stand into place in front of her and set the tray down on the tabletop.

Cara eyed the orange juice—two small cartons. Before she could reach either one, Bain opened each and poured the contents into a glass. She took the glass from him and downed half the juice, then sighed and wiped her mouth.

He whipped the cover off the plate to reveal bacon, eggs, grits and a biscuit.

She picked up her fork.

"Want your coffee?" he asked.

She shook her head. "Actually, I don't. And that's odd since I love coffee, but for some reason, the thought of coffee…yuck."

He removed the paper cover from the mug and picked it up. "May I?"

"Help yourself."

He took a sip of coffee and made a face.

"That bad, huh?"

"It's not bad, but I've had better."

Fifteen minutes later, Cara had managed to clean her plate and was surprised to realize she was still hungry. She was just about to ask Bain if he could get her some more orange juice when someone knocked on the door. Bain went to the door, opened it a fraction and then spoke to the person before opening the door wide enough for him to enter. He was in his mid-thirties, with a receding hairline and a slight paunch visible beneath his open white coat.

"Good morning, Ms. Bedell. I'm Dr. Sanderson.

How are you feeling?" He glanced at the swollen bruise on her head, and then looked down at her empty breakfast plate. "Apparently your concussion didn't affect your appetite."

"I feel quite well, thank you. I don't even have a headache. And concussions must make a person hungry. I seem to be ravenous this morning."

"I don't believe that's the result of your concussion."

"Really, then what—?"

"Bear with me a few minutes while I examine you, then we'll discuss the results of your blood work."

"My blood work?" She glanced from the doctor to Bain, who shrugged and looked as puzzled as she felt.

Several minutes later, with his routine exam completed, Dr. Sanderson, pulled up a chair by her bed and sat. He looked over at Bain, who stood on the other side of the bed, hovering protectively.

"Are you by any chance Mr. Bedell?" the doctor asked.

"He's not Mr. Bedell," Cara said hurriedly. "He is Lieutenant Bain Desmond, a detective with the Chattanooga Police Department. He and I are...we're friends and—"

"We're engaged," Bain said. "I'm Ms. Bedell's fiancé."

Dr. Sanderson smiled. "I see. Then I assume that whatever I have to say to you, I can say in front of your fiancé. Is that correct?"

Cara hadn't quite recovered from Bain declaring that they were engaged. Rendered speechless by his proclamation, she merely nodded.

"Ms. Bedell, you're pregnant," Dr. Sanderson said.

"What?" Cara and Bain spoke simultaneously.

LUCIE FELT AS IF a Mack truck had run over her hip, but she realized that she would be in far worse agony if they weren't injecting some type of pain medication into her IV drip. She vaguely remembered that not long ago a woman with a soft voice and a kind smile had given her a sponge bath and brushed her hair very gently. Apparently, she had drifted off to sleep shortly after that and only now woke to the hum of voices outside her cubicle. She lifted her head from the pillow and tried to look outside to see who was talking.

A nurse entered, walked over to the bed and smiled at Lucie. "Good morning, Ms. Evans. How are you feeling? Is there anything I can do for you, anything you need?"

"A new hip," Lucie said. "This one hurts like hell."

"All in good time," the nurse told her. "Dr. Collins will be in to see you later this morning and explain everything and answer any questions you might have."

"Am I going to live?" Lucie asked, only halfway joking.

"I'm not a fortune teller," the nurse replied, "nor am I a doctor, but I believe I'm relatively safe is saying that yes, you're going to live."

"I assume Dr. Collins is the surgeon who removed the bullet from my hip."

"Yes, that's right." The nurse glanced toward the open doorway. "You have someone waiting to see you. He came in last night for a few minutes, but you weren't awake. And I believe he's been here all night." She motioned to the person waiting outside.

Lucie held her breath and then released it when

Sawyer walked in. Even lying flat on her back, hooked up to an IV and feeling like death warmed over, her stupid heart did a happy dance at the sight of him.

"Visitation is for thirty minutes," the nurse said as she walked past Sawyer on her way out.

Sawyer nodded to the nurse. He paused several feet away from the bed and looked at Lucie.

"Hi there," he said.

"Hi there, yourself."

He took several tentative steps forward and then stopped. "Daisy and Geoff are here. I won't stay long. I know they want to see you."

"When did you get here?"

"Last night."

"How is Cara? Is she—?"

"She'll be fine. She has a concussion."

"Whit?"

Sawyer frowned. "Not so good. He's down the hall from you, but he's in pretty bad shape. He's in a drug-induced coma for the time being, but the doctor told me that if he makes it through the next forty-eight hours, he has a good chance of making a full recovery."

"What about the shooter?"

"The Feds got him."

"Alive?"

Sawyer shook his head.

"So we still have no idea who hired him."

"That's not your concern right now." Sawyer came over and stood at the edge of the bed. "The only thing you need to worry about is getting well."

"How bad is my hip messed up?"

"Not too bad."

She studied his expression. "You're not a very good liar."

"The bullet shattered your hipbone. Once you recover from this first surgery, you'll need a second one. They'll have to go in and do a hip replacement."

Lucie heaved a deep sigh. Pain radiated from her hip. She groaned.

"Are you hurting? I can get the nurse and she can give you—"

Lucie reached up and grabbed his hand. "I think they're giving me as high a dosage as they can." She glanced at the IV tube.

He held her hand and looked directly into her eyes. "Is there anything I can do for you?"

"Are you just making conversation or do you mean that?"

"I mean it, but now isn't the time to get into any soul-searching discussions."

She tried to smile. "I wasn't going to ask for that. Not yet."

He gave her hand a tender squeeze.

"Would you sit with me?" she asked.

He glanced around and she realized that there was no chair in her cubicle.

"Sit on the bed." When he gave her a skeptical look, she said, "Please."

"I don't want to hurt you. I'm afraid if I sit down, I'll jostle you."

"I'll be okay."

He eased down on the edge of the bed, taking his

time and being extra careful. Once he was seated, she pulled her hand from his, reached up and ran her fingertips over his stubble-rough jaw.

"You haven't shaved this morning." She slid the back of her thumb over his lips. "The nurse said you'd been here all night."

He grabbed her hand, brought it down to the center of his chest and held it there. "Where else would I be?"

When he looked at her, an odd expression on his face, she wondered if she was imagining things. If she didn't know better, she would swear that he was in agonizing pain, far more pain than she was in.

"Sawyer?"

He brought her hand to his mouth, turned it over and kissed the center of her palm. "Hmm…?" Still holding her hand, he eased it back down to her side.

"If it's too difficult for you to do this, to stay here with me, I'll understand. I know you hate—"

He leaned over and kissed her, then lifted his head. "Just shut up, will you, Lucie Locket. The only thing that's difficult for me is seeing you like this and knowing how close you came to dying."

"Oh." Stunned by what he'd said, she couldn't control the joy bubbling up inside her. He had called her Lucie Locket. That told her all she needed to know. For now.

BAIN DROPPED DOWN on one knee beside Cara's hospital bed. "This isn't exactly the way I'd planned to do this. It's not the ideal place, but here goes."

"What are you doing?" Cara looked down at him while he dug into his jacket pocket and pulled out a small square box.

"Cara Bedell, I love you. I love you more than anything on God's green earth. I know that making marriage work for us won't be easy, but—" He swallowed hard. "Will you marry me?"

He flipped open the box lid to reveal a diamond solitaire nestled in black velvet.

"When did you—? How long have you—? You didn't just rush out and buy that. You spent the night here with me and you haven't left my side."

"I bought it nearly a week ago," he admitted. "I know it's nothing to compare to a lot of your other rings, but it's what I could afford." He chuckled. "Actually, it's more than I could afford." He removed the ring from its velvet cushion. "Well, say something. Is it yes or no?"

Cara smiled. Tears glistened in her eyes. She held out her left hand. "Yes. Yes…yes!"

Bain stood, clasped her hand and slipped the ring on her finger. She reached up and threw her arms around his neck. He collapsed into her, but quickly caught his weight by placing his hands on either side of her hips. And then he kissed her.

She clung to him, fully participating in the kiss. Finally he lifted his head and grinned at her.

"We're going to have a baby," he said.

"And it's all your fault," she told him teasingly. "One of those condoms must have been defective."

Bain's grin widened. "You're right. I take full responsibility for getting you pregnant." He looked straight up.

"Me and the Man upstairs. Apparently He figured I needed a little nudge in the right direction."

"When were you going to propose to me?" she asked.

"On our date tonight. But this sure isn't how I'd planned anything. I had reservations for a fancy dinner, with music and flowers, the whole nine yards. And I thought we'd wind up back at my place and make love all night."

She snuggled against him. "I'm ready to leave now."

"The doctor might dismiss you this afternoon, but you're not going anywhere except home and straight to bed."

She laughed. "I don't care if it's your bed or mine, as long as we're in it together."

"There will be no hanky-panky until you're fully recovered."

She kissed his neck. He shuddered. "I'm feeling just fine. Actually, I'm feeling better than fine."

"Don't forget that you're pregnant. You have to be extra careful now."

"I will be. But you know I think it's true what they say about pregnant women."

"Okay, I give—what do they say about pregnant women?"

"That they get awfully horny."

Bain placed his open palms on either side of her still flat belly as if sound proofing her stomach. "Watch your language. You don't want to corrupt my little girl, do you?"

"Your little girl, huh? What makes you think it's not my little boy?"

"Boy or girl doesn't matter, does it?"

"Not to me."

"I had thought you might want a June wedding, but I don't believe we'd better wait that long." He patted her stomach. "All things considered."

"You'd hate a big affair, wouldn't you, something with all the trimmings?"

"Yeah, I probably would, but if it's what you want—"

"You're what I want, Bain Desmond. If I have you, I don't need anything else." She laid her hand over his where it rested on her belly. "You and our baby."

SAWYER MET WITH Deke and Geoff in the chapel. He realized it was an odd choice, but it was the one place available to them in the hospital where they could speak privately.

"I just heard from Ty Garrett," Geoff said. "They haven't been able to track down Josue Soto. It seems he's unavailable. His secretary says he's away on vacation with his family and is supposedly due back in Ameca in a couple of days. It's possible he's somehow found out that we're on to him and he doesn't want to be questioned. Ty has been assured that it's only a matter of time until Soto is found."

"I realize that our best bet to gain any information is to get it from Soto," Deke said. "But we have no way of knowing if whoever hired Torres-Rios has a backup plan. Another assassin could be on his way to Chattanooga right now. Or the person who hired Torres-Rios may decide to take matters into his own hands."

"We have the three major suspects here in Chattanooga right now." Sawyer listed the three. "Tomas Castillo, Patrice Bedell and Grayson Perkins."

"If we only knew which one," Geoff said.

"Or knew for sure that it actually is one of them."

"My gut tells me that it is," Deke said. "And it's possible they're all three in it together or possibly just two of them. We know Castillo's reputation. He's a ruthless SOB. Patrice Bedell and Gray Perkins are both greedy and unscrupulous."

"If Soto did leave the country and doesn't return to Ameca, we could go after him no matter where he is," Geoff suggested. "But it might take weeks, even months to find him."

"He's good to us only if he can give us information on the person who contacted him to hire Torres-Rios," Sawyer said. "It is possible that no names were exchanged, only money wired to an account number. If that's the case, he can't give us a name, but he could tell us if the person he spoke to, the person who hired him, was Amecan or not, and if the person was male or female."

"The longer we wait, the more dangerous it could be for Cara," Deke told them. "Besides, there's more than one way to skin a cat." When Sawyer and Geoff stared at him, he continued, "Instead of waiting for info from Soto, we have an alternative, but my plan would require Cara's cooperation. Since she's been here at the hospital, no information about her condition has been released and she's had no visitors other than Bain Desmond, so it would be possible to announce that she was seriously injured and will be moved to a private facility to recuperate."

"And security at this private facility would be a bit more lax than here at the hospital, right?" Sawyer thought he knew where Deke was going with this. "What you're suggesting is using Cara as bait to trap her would-be killer."

"We'd be playing a waiting game," Deke admitted. "It would be hell on Cara's nerves and there's always a chance that something could go wrong, but she'd never actually be alone."

"Let's wait a day or two and see if Soto turns up and can give us the information we need," Sawyer said. "But a backup plan isn't a bad idea. We'll need to discuss this with Cara and point out the risk she'll be taking."

"Bain Desmond is not going to like the plan," Deke said. "I know I wouldn't if Lexie was putting herself in harm's way."

"I suggest we check on Cara this morning and see if she's up to discussing strategy." Sawyer glanced from Deke to Geoff. "The sooner this nightmare ends for her, the better."

THE MINUTE SAWYER, Deke and Geoff entered her room, Bain took a protective stand at Cara's bedside. They both realized that something had happened, possibly something really bad; otherwise, why would all three men pay her a visit together?

She looked up at Bain, who smiled at her, but when he turned to their guests, his smile vanished.

"You're looking well," Deke said to Cara. "Lexie is eager to see you. She sends her love."

"Tell her I'll call her soon." Cara glanced at Sawyer. "How is Lucie?"

"All things considered, she's doing okay. I saw her at eight thirty. When I see her again at twelve thirty, I'll come back by and give you an update."

Bain focused on Deke. "We all know this isn't just a friendly little visit, so why don't you cut to the chase and tell us what's going on."

Deke nodded and then settled his gaze on Cara. "First, I need to know if you're feeling up to discussing the situation and working with us to make plans to—"

"I'm fine," Cara interrupted. "I'll probably get to go home today."

Her three visitors exchanged peculiar glances.

"Gentleman, it's my life that's in danger. Please, don't hold anything back. And whatever plans y'all are working on, I need to be informed."

"Yes, ma'am." Deke stated in simple, no-nonsense terms exactly what the situation was—Cara was still in grave danger—and then he went on to explain his plan to trap her would-be killer.

"Absolutely not!" Bain said.

Cara reached out and grabbed his hand. "Don't lose your temper. They don't know about my condition."

"What condition?" Sawyer asked.

"Well, you see, if it were just my life on the line, I'd be perfectly willing to agree to act as bait in your trap, but I'm not willing to risk my child's life."

"Your child?" Deke's eyes widened in surprise.

"You're pregnant?" Sawyer looked from her to Bain.

Bain squeezed her hand. "That's right. We're going to have a baby."

"So you see why I can't—"

"Yes, of course," Deke agreed. "But you do realize that until we find the person who hired Torres-Rios to kill you, you'll be in danger. You and your baby."

CHAPTER TWENTY-FOUR

"No way," Sawyer said. "No way in hell!"

"I knew you'd react this way," Lucie told him. "But will you please calm down and listen to me."

"You're not doing this. I won't let you."

"Sawyer McNamara, when has that tactic ever worked with me? Telling me that you won't allow me to do something is a surefire way to make me do it."

He paced back and forth in Lucie's small private hospital room, mumbling obscenities to himself. Stopping abruptly, he glared her. "Who told you about this plan? If I had thought you'd find out—"

"Daisy told me," Lucie admitted. "And don't you dare holler at her the way you're hollering at me. She thought she was simply bringing me up-to-date on the case. Believe me, if she thought—"

"I'm not hollering at you." Sawyer lowered his voice as he walked over to her bedside and looked right at her. "Do I need to remind you that you're less than thirty-six hours out of surgery? You can't walk. And you're facing another surgery in a few weeks."

"I know. So, what difference does it make if I spend the next week or so here in this hospital or at a private facility? You can have the place crawling with Dundee agents and you can let me keep a gun under my pillow. But if there's even a slight chance this will work, you have to let me do it."

"The risk is too high. What if something goes wrong? Have you ever thought about that?"

"Cara is not going to be safe until we stop the person who wants to kill her. And it's not just Cara we'll be saving, but her baby, too. Don't you think she and Bain have a right to look forward to a long and happy life together? Think about what insurmountable odds they've had to overcome to be together."

Sawyer looked away, took in a deep breath and said, "What about you, your life, your future?"

She lifted her hand and reached for him, barely managing to graze his arm with her fingertips. He glanced down at her hand. She wiggled her fingers. He took her hand in his and sat on the edge of her bed.

"If you think I have a death wish, you're wrong. If you think I'm sacrificing myself, I'm not. I have no intention of dying. You and I still have to settle things between us, you know."

"Now's not the time for that." He held her hand tightly. "Not until after your next surgery and you're on the mend."

"I guess I can wait a while longer. I've been waiting for nine years."

"I'm sorry about that. I'm sorry about so many things."

"So am I."

He leaned down to kiss her, but before their lips touched, the door opened and a startled gasp interrupted them.

"Oops, sorry," Cara said. "We can leave and come back later."

"No need for that." Sawyer rose from the side of the bed and stood up to face Lucie's guests.

Bain brought Cara into the room in her wheelchair.

"I came in here to tell you that you don't have to do this," Cara said to Lucie. "You'll be risking your life for me again. I can't ask you to do something so dangerous."

"If you weren't pregnant, you'd do it," Lucie said. "Besides, I'm the logical choice to impersonate you."

Bain glanced at Sawyer. "Are you on board with this now?"

"No, not really," Sawyer replied. "But Lucie is damned determined."

Cara looked at Lucie. "Are you sure?"

"I'm sure," Lucie said.

"We've got everything set for tomorrow morning." Bain's gaze traveled from one person to another and settled on Sawyer. "Daisy has the wigs and makeup and the clothes for each of them. At nine o'clock, Lucie, disguised as Cara, will be taken out the E.R. entrance and put into an ambulance. I'll be with her every step of the way, her devoted fiancé. She'll be taken to Riverside Rehabilitation Center. Everything on that end has been arranged. I'll stay there for a couple of hours, then leave and go downtown to headquarters where I'll pick up a rental car. Then we'll move on to Step Two."

"Tomorrow afternoon, I'll leave the hospital, disguised as Lucie," Cara said. "No one other than certain hospital staff know the extent of her injuries or mine, so it's unlikely that the press or anyone else will question Lucie Evans leaving the hospital in a wheelchair. As far as people in general know, Sawyer will be taking Lucie back to Atlanta with him to recuperate."

"I'll meet y'all at the designated spot on I-75 and take Cara off your hands," Bain told Sawyer. "I've already contacted my sister in Murfreesboro and she's expecting us tonight."

"No one will question Bedell security guards or Dundee agents being at the rehab center." Lucie looked at Sawyer. "And no one will wonder why Sawyer McNamara is visiting Cara Bedell. You just can't visit all that often and you can't stay for hours when you do visit."

"I see you three already have this all worked out, don't you?" Sawyer glowered at Lucie.

"With any luck our guy—or gal—will make a move very soon," Lucie said. "After all, the press release that Dundee's will put out this afternoon should prompt him into action."

"I haven't authorized that press release yet," Sawyer told them.

"But you will. Just as you'll do your part in pulling off this little charade." Lucie reached up and clasped Sawyer's hand. "You'll do what has to be done."

"Yeah, sure." He pulled his hand from hers, walked past Cara and paused when he reached Bain. "I'll take care of your woman," he whispered. "And you'll take care of mine."

The two men looked each other squarely in the eye. Bain nodded. Sawyer walked out of the room.

LUCIE WATCHED the ten o'clock news in her suite at the Riverside Rehabilitation Center. Her private duty nurse was actually a new Dundee agent, Kayla Fuller, one of the two agents who had accompanied Felipe and Suelita Delgado on their recent trip to New York. Kayla stayed in the sitting room, just beyond the open bedroom door. A Bedell security guard was on duty in the hall.

"This just in," the announcer said. "CEO of Dundee Private Security and Investigation, Sawyer McNamara—" they flashed a photo of Sawyer on the screen "—has announced that Cara Bedell—" her photo flashed across the screen "—the target of a recent attack by a professional assassin, has been moved from Memorial Hospital to a private location to ensure her safety. Despite her close call with death, Ms. Bedell will be signing an agreement between Bedell, Inc. and Delgado Oil while she is recuperating."

Lucie held her breath and waited. "Come on, come on. Please don't tell me you're not going to report juicy gossip."

"Also from an undisclosed source close to Ms. Bedell comes some interesting personal news. Ms. Bedell will soon be announcing her engagement. The future groom's identity is unknown at this point, but it's been widely reported that a change in Ms. Bedell's will take place while her lawyers are present on the day she signs the deal with Delgado Oil."

"Yes!" Lucie shouted. "Now, we'll get some action."

Kayla peeped in on Lucie. "Are you all right?"

"I'm fine."

"If you need anything, just let me know."

"Sawyer said that my phone line would be secure. Do you know if it is?"

"It is. You can place outside calls directly, but any incoming calls will go through the rehab center first and be screened by us before they're connected to your phone."

"Thanks. And would you mind closing the door?"

"Sure thing."

Why hadn't Sawyer called her?

Suddenly her phone rang. Her heart skipped a beat.

She grabbed the receiver and tried not to sound disappointed when she realized it was Bain calling her from Murfreesboro to let her know that he and Cara were settling in at his sister's.

"They've got an in-law suite in the basement for when Keith's parents visit," Bain said. "We're as snug as two bugs in a rug. Cara's already asleep. She's pretty exhausted after all our play acting this afternoon. I'll be back in Chattanooga in a couple of days to pay you a visit. In the meantime, expect flowers from me every day."

Lucie laughed. "You're too thoughtful."

"It was Sawyer's idea. The flowers will be from him, but they'll have my name on them. Just part of the subterfuge."

After their brief conversation, Lucie leaned back against the pillows and closed her eyes. *Call me, Sawyer, please call me.*

She opened her eyes, eased herself over on her good side, and stared at the phone. *Ring, damn it, ring.*

She knew that Sawyer couldn't hover around the rehab center without creating suspicion. After all, she was supposed to be Cara Bedell, not Lucie Evans. But he could at least call, couldn't he?

Stop looking at the phone. What's that old saying about a watched pot never boils? Go to sleep. Get some rest. You're supposed to be recovering, you know. If you can't sleep, you can always ask for a sedative. It's not likely anyone is going to try to kill you tonight.

TOMAS CASTILLO flipped off the television and turned to his companion. "It would seem that neither of us will get what we want. Our plans to eliminate our problem have not worked out as we had hoped."

"Mr. Soto assured me that he knew the perfect person for the job. It's hardly my fault that the hired assassin he lined up to do the job not only failed miserably, but got himself killed, too."

"If they discover Soto's identity, he will no doubt sing like bird, yes? He will give your name to the authorities."

"Do you think I was foolish enough to use my real name?"

Tomas smiled. "Then there is no way they can trace the money you paid Soto back to you?"

"I believe I covered my tracks quite nicely."

"Too bad there isn't a way we can get to Cara while she is recuperating."

"Yes, it is too bad. But no doubt, she's surrounded by guards. Besides, we have no idea where she is."

"You are a member of her family, are you not? Surely, someone at the hospital would tell you where Cara was taken."

"And if we learn where she is, what then? Hire

another killer? I certainly couldn't do it. The thought of actually murdering her myself… No! I couldn't."

"Is the ten million I offered you not a great enough incentive?"

"If the kidnapping hadn't been screwed up, I'd have your ten million and the twenty-five million ransom."

"The ten million is still yours, if—"

"I told you that I can't kill her myself. I simply can't."

Tomas shrugged. The man was a brute! "It's just as well you feel that way. I doubt anyone could get to her, kill her and escape. Besides, unless she is killed before she signs the deal with Delgado, whether she lives or dies means nothing to me. On the other hand, if she changes her will, what will that mean for you?"

"I have no idea if I'm even mentioned in her will. I doubt it. But I believe since I am, as you pointed out, a member of the family, I am entitled to large part of the Bedell fortune. If necessary, I would contest the will."

"And if she leaves everything to this secret fiancé of hers?"

"His identity is no secret. And it would be just like Cara to leave that stupid policeman her entire fortune."

LUCIE'S PHONE RANG at ten fifty-seven. She didn't realize she had dozed off until the ringing roused her. She reached out and yanked the receiver off the base, wincing when pain sliced through her hip. Her last round of pain meds was wearing off and it was at least an hour or more before she could get another shot.

She put the receiver to her ear. "Hello."

"Did I wake you?" Sawyer asked. "You sound—"

"I'm fine now that you've called."

"Sorry that it's so late, but I've been on the phone with Ty. They've got Soto, but so far he's not talking."

"He will though, won't he?"

"Sooner or later, he'll tell them all he knows," Sawyer said. "Let's just hope he knows enough to actually help us."

"And if he doesn't know who made arrangements with him to hire Torres-Rios?"

"Then we'll hope that Deke and Geoff's plan to use you as bait works. Our next step in the plan is to leak the information about the name of Cara Bedell's rehab center."

"A lot of good that will do. A person would have to be stupid to try to kill me while I'm being guarded so well. But if you take away my guard, they'll smell a trap."

"We'll give it a week, then—"

"A week? That's not very long."

"The charade won't hold together much longer than that," Sawyer told her.

"And if no one tries to kill me?"

"Then Cara will resume her identity and return home. Between Bedell security and Dundee's, we should be able to keep her safe."

"But for how long? Without knowing who hired the assassin—"

"Enough, Lucie! We'll give this thing a week. You'll have done all you can to help Cara. But then you're coming back to Atlanta and staying at a rehab center here until you can have your second surgery. It's going to take time for you to get back up to speed and I intend to see that you take good care of yourself."

"Is that right?"

"That's right."

"And when will we have our soul-searching talk?"

"After your hip replacement."

Lucie sighed.

"Go back to sleep," he said. "I'll call you tomorrow."

"Sawyer?"

"Yes?"

"Tell me."

"Tell you what?"

"Tell me that you don't hate me."

"I don't hate you."

"Tell me that you still care about me."

"Lucie…damn! I still care about you."

"Okay. Call me tomorrow." She put the phone on the base, turned over on her back and closed her eyes.

He never told you that he loved you. Not even the night you made love. He's always cared about you, ever since you were a kid, but that doesn't mean he ever loved you. It certainly doesn't mean he loves you now.

"I NEED YOUR HELP," Gray told Patrice as they lay side by side in bed late that night. "I have to find a way to see Cara. If she truly is engaged to Lieutenant Desmond and marries that man, she will be lost to me forever. I can't bear the thought of it."

"And how do you think you can stop her?" Patrice tapped her fingers across Gray's naked chest.

"I don't know, but if I could see her, talk to her, plead

my case one more time. But I have no idea where she's been taken. You'd think she would at least have someone call me to tell me where she is."

"Poor darling." She draped her arm across his chest and snuggled against him. "If she marries that handsome policeman, you'll never get your hands on all her beautiful money, will you?"

Gray shoved Patrice away from him, sat up in bed and glared down at her. "He can't possibly make her happy and I believe I could. I'm a part of her world. He isn't. I'm a refined gentleman. He isn't."

Patrice eased up, pressed her naked breasts against his chest and hugged him. "Don't fret, my precious. We'll find out where Cara is and I promise I'll help you. We'll both be much happier, not to mention richer, if she marries you."

Gray shoved Patrice flat on her back and straddled her. "Help me stop Cara from marrying Bain Desmond and I'll give you anything you want."

CHAPTER TWENTY-FIVE

LUCIE'S SUITE—or rather Cara Bedell's suite—at the Riverside Rehabilitation Center was beginning to look like a florist shop. Or maybe like a funeral parlor. Ever since three days ago when "someone" had leaked the info about where she was recuperating, flowers and gifts had been arriving nonstop. The first day something had been delivered every hour, and then every other hour the second day. Today, she had received only five new bouquets and two gifts. Everyone from the governor to the mayor had shown their concern for Cara Bedell.

This was Lucie's fifth day at the center, one week from the day she'd been shot at the charity auction, and so far everything had been disappointingly peaceful. On Monday, Cara would assume own her identity and Sawyer would take Lucie to Atlanta.

Whoever wanted Cara dead would be free to try again.

And on Monday Cara would sign a deal with Delgado Oil.

Apparently, Tomas Castillo was still in Chattanooga, presumably a guest of Patrice Bedell, although they were not sharing a hotel suite. Did Castillo's continued presence in the area mean that he thought there was still a chance of stealing the merger with Bedell, Inc. from Delgado Oil?

Sawyer called every night and they talked, but only for a few minutes. And Bain Desmond had visited her every day for the past three days. He had returned to his apartment and reluctantly left Cara with his sister. Of course, Dundee agents kept watch on the house around the clock. Bedell security continued to stand guard at the door to Lucie's suite and Kayla rotated twelve-hours shifts with Dundee Agent Case Warren, who posed as a male nurse. Naturally, all the actual nursing duties were handled by members of the center's staff, but those allowed into her room were limited in number to employees okayed by Dundee's after a background check. These people wore ID badges, even those in the house-cleaning staff and the nurse's aides.

Thankfully, along with the beautiful peach roses— her favorite—that had arrived each day with a card signed, *I love you, Bain*, Sawyer had sent her a supply of paperback novels. If not for reading, she would have been bored to tears. It had been years since she'd had the luxury of watching daytime television and somehow couldn't get interested in anything after the morning news and weather. Except there was one favorite soap opera that she had watched with her grandmother as a child and she still recorded it on a regular basis.

Why hadn't Sawyer visited her? No one would have thought it strange that Sawyer McNamara was concerned about Cara Bedell, after all they were business associates. Maybe he didn't want to see her. Maybe…

Enough of this, Lucie Evans. You're creating problems where there are none. Sawyer hasn't made any promises. She needed to be satisfied with his friendship, at least for the time being.

The door to her bedroom opened. Kayla rose from her chair, where she'd been sitting quietly reading one of Lucie's paperbacks.

"Lunchtime, Ms. Bedell," a woman's voice called from the sitting room of the suite. "May I bring in your tray?"

"Just a moment," Kayla replied as she opened the door between the two rooms and walked into the other room to check the woman's ID.

Lucie heard the two women talking although she couldn't make out what they were saying through the closed door.

The door opened again and the nurse's aide entered pushing a cart. She parked the cart, closed the door behind her and lifted the tray. Lucie didn't pay much attention to the woman until she stopped halfway to the bed, tray in hand, and gasped.

"You're not Cara!" the woman said.

Lucie looked directly at the nurse's aide and the bottom dropped out of her stomach. Wearing a Riverside Rehabilitation Center uniform and a black wig, Patrice Bedell stared at Lucie.

"And you're not a nurse's aide," Lucie said.

"Damn, we went to all this trouble for nothing." Patrice placed the lunch tray down on the bedside table. "Gray, we wasted our money bribing three people so I could get this uniform and ID badge so we could get in here to see Cara. You might as well come on out."

"Where is Mr. Perkins?" Lucie asked as she leaned back against the pillows and casually slipped her hand under the bottom one.

"Oh, he's scrunched up under the food cart. We draped a tablecloth over it to hide him."

Lucie's fingers touched the gun hidden under her pillow.

Grayson Perkins flipped back the tablecloth, crawled out from where he'd been hiding under the serving cart and stood up straight.

"Well, this is disappointing," he said. "It seems they've pulled a fast one on us, Patrice."

A loud rapping on the door told Lucie that Patrice had locked the door and Kayla was shut out on the other side. Lucie inched her fingertips toward the gun under her pillow until she managed to get a secure hold on it.

"Would y'all mind telling me just what's going on?" Lucie asked.

"It's quite simple, Ms. Evans." Gray frowned. "I needed to see Cara, to convince her not to marry that Neanderthal policeman and Patrice agreed to help me sneak in here to see her."

"Oh." Lucie breathed a sigh of relief. Was that what this was all about?

"I don't suppose you'd tell me where Cara is." Gray approached the bed.

Lucie tightened her hold on the gun. "Sorry. I can't do that."

"I see. Well, nothing ventured… If you talk to Cara, please tell her that I need to speak to her, that I love her, that…" Gray hung his head in a melodramatic fashion and sighed as if his heart was broken.

Suddenly the closed and locked door flew open. Gray and Patrice swung around to face the rescue team. Lucie remained as she was, with the gun securely in her hand under the pillow. Kayla marched into the room, the Bedell security guard directly behind her. Lucie felt a sudden rush of relief, but then she saw Bain Desmond and two uniformed police officers.

Just what the hell was going on?

Bain walked directly toward Gray. "See if he has a weapon."

One police officer held Gray's hands behind his back while the other officer checked him from head to toe.

"He's clean."

"Then cuff him," Bain said.

"What do you think you're doing?" Gray demanded. "I admit that Patrice and I used a rather unorthodox method to get in here to see Cara—" He grunted when the burly officer jerked his hands behind his back and cuffed him. "Would you please be careful. I happen to be wearing a designer suit."

"Is this necessary?" Patrice asked. "After all, the poor darling was dying to see Cara and we simply did what we had to do to sneak him in here to see her. Of course, we had no idea that we'd find Ms. Evans instead."

"Call my lawyer," Gray said.

"Please, can't we settle this without your arresting him?" Patrice asked.

"I'm afraid not," Bain said. "Grayson Perkins, you're

under arrest for the kidnapping and attempted murder of Lucie Evans and the attempted murder of Cara Bedell." He looked at the officer who had cuffed Gray. "Read him his rights and then get him out of my sight."

Patrice stood there, her mouth agape and her eyes wide with shock. When they removed a protesting Gray Perkins from the room, she slumped down in the nearest chair.

"Would somebody tell me what the hell just happened?" Lucie looked at Bain. "Did he come here to kill me—I mean kill Cara?"

"I don't think so," Bain said as he approached the bed. "I think he really did come here hoping to try one final time to persuade Cara to marry him and not me." He looked over his shoulder at Kayla. "Would you show Mrs. Bedell out, please, and have someone drive her back to her hotel."

"I'm confused," Patrice said. "Was Gray really behind the plot to kill Cara? I joked with him about it, but I never thought that he... My God! I actually thought it was Tomas. I guess I owe him an apology."

"I'd hold off on that apology if I were you," Sawyer McNamara said as he walked into the room. "Senor Castillo is being detained at police headquarters. We have every reason to believe that he and Grayson Perkins were partners and I'm sure that once each is offered a deal to testify against the other, one of them will break and confess everything."

"It'll be Gray," Patrice said. "He'd give up his own mother to save his beautiful neck."

"Let's clear the room," Bain shouted and herded everyone out the door.

Sawyer came over to Lucie, sat down on the edge of the bed and slid his hand under the pillow. She released her tenacious hold on the gun. He brought the gun out and laid it on the bedside table. "I don't think you'll need this."

"What just happened?" she asked.

"Josue Soto did a lot of talking," Sawyer said. "He gave up everything he knew, including the alias that Perkins used when he contacted Soto to arrange for Torres-Rios to handle Cara's kidnapping and murder."

"If he used an alias, then how—?"

"Soto is a very cautious, very careful man. While those who contact him know who he is and how to reach him, most wish to remain anonymous. But as a precaution to use as blackmail should a client ever threaten to expose him, Senor Soto used certain safeguards, such as recording his phone conversations. We have Grayson Perkins, on tape, arranging with Josue Soto to hire an assassin. Actually we have Perkins on tape several times—every conversation he ever had with Soto."

"And Tomas Castillo?" Lucie asked.

"We're playing a hunch," Sawyer confessed. "We don't have anything on him, but Bain and I agree that he's involved, up to his eyeballs. We figure Perkins will hand him to us on a silver platter if he thinks he can make a deal."

"Then this is really over?" Lucie looked at him and smiled. "Cara's safe now? She can come home and marry Bain and live happily ever after?"

"Well, she can come home and get married, but I can't promise you that they'll live happily ever after."

"Sawyer McNamara, you're such a pessimist. Why shouldn't they live happily ever after? They love each other and they're going to have a baby. What more could anyone want?"

"Sometimes love isn't enough," he said. "We both know that, don't we, Lucie?"

Her heart caught in her throat. "Yes…I guess we do."

CHAPTER TWENTY-SIX

CARA AND BAIN married on New Year's Day. The wedding was a small, immediate, family-and-friends-only affair held at the Bedell estate and no expense had been spared. Cara wore an empire-waist, floor-length cream-white gown of silk overlaid with delicate lace. She carried a bouquet of white lilies and roses. Lucie, who was recovering quite well from her hip replacement surgery, was her maid of honor and Lexie Bronson was her matron of honor. They both wore satin gowns in rich jewel tones, Lexie in deep ruby-red and Lucie in a dark emerald-green. All three dresses had been flown in from Paris, each created by Cara's favorite European designer. Deke was Bain's best man; Sawyer escorted Cara down the aisle; and Bain's niece and nephew acted as flower girl and ring bearer.

The reception following the elegant wedding lasted well into the night, long after the bride and groom had left for the first stage of their month-long honeymoon.

"We're going back to the cabin in Gatlinburg for our wedding night," Cara had confided in Lucie. "Then we're off to London and Paris and on to Italy, to the Bedell villa. I thought about trying to ease Bain into my lifestyle gradually, but I decided it might be best just to throw him into the deep waters first thing. He'll either sink or swim, as will our marriage." Cara had laughed as she patted her round tummy. "But I have a feeling he'll eventually swim, even if at first it might be a struggle. He's told me that he'll do anything for me and his little girl, even be Mr. Cara Bedell, if necessary."

Lucie and Sawyer had left the Bedell mansion shortly after the bride and groom zoomed off in Bain's vintage Corvette. Instead of driving home to Atlanta as Geoff and Daisy had done, Sawyer took her to the Reid House in downtown Chattanooga, where he had booked a suite for them and where they had left their overnight bags this morning.

Her heart beat at an alarming rate on the elevator ride up to the suite. She smiled at Sawyer. He returned her smile. He'd been doing that a lot lately—smiling. For the past couple of months, he had been caring and attentive, checking on her every day, if not in person, then by phone. He had been at her side through her second surgery and the recuperation process. But every time she had mentioned that soul-searching talk he had promised her, he had put her off.

"When the time is right," he'd kept saying.

Although his attitude toward her had softened and he had admitted that he did care about her, he hadn't said anything about love. And other than a few affectionate kisses, he hadn't touched her. Of course, for a while, she had been in no condition for lovemaking.

"Tired?" Sawyer asked as they emerged from the elevator.

"Not really. I'm on a glorious wedding-day high. It's so wonderful to see Cara and Bain together, married and expecting their first child."

He led her down the hall and to the door of their suite. As he inserted the keycard into the slot, he said, "I thought tonight might be a good time for us to lay our cards on the table and finally have that soul-searching talk. But if you'd rather not end such a perfect day with—"

She grabbed his arm just as the door swung open. "I've been waiting nine years for this talk. I'm more than ready."

He gave her a look that told her how much he dreaded what was to come, a rehashing of events that had led to Brenden's death.

"It's a two-bedroom suite," he said as they entered the lounge area.

"Yes, of course." Was that his way of telling her that he didn't expect the evening to end with the two of them sharing a bed?

"It's late, but I believe they have twenty-four-hour room service, if you'd like something to eat or drink."

"I'm good. I ate way too much at the reception and I actually drank three glasses of that heavenly champagne."

Sawyer closed and locked the door, then walked into the lounge behind Lucie and laid the keycard on the dining table. She sat on the sofa and kicked off her heels that had been dyed to match her green satin dress. He removed his tuxedo jacket and hung it across the back of one of the chairs.

She looked up at him. "So, who goes first?"

He sat in a chair across from her, the coffee table between them. "I think I should."

"All right." Her stomach muscles tightened and every nerve in her body went on high alert. *Please, God, please, don't let me screw this up. Help me say what's in my heart and help Sawyer understand.*

"What happened to Brenden was my fault," Sawyer said, with absolutely no emotion showing on his stoic face. When she started to reply, he held up his hand. "No, don't try to take the blame. I've spent years blaming you for something that was far more my fault than yours. It was easier blaming you than admitting the truth, that my actions drove my brother to suicide."

Lucie leaned forward, desperately wanting to reach out, pull Sawyer into her arms and comfort him. Instead, she looked at him and said nothing, waiting for him to continue.

"I knew you were Brenden's girl and had been for years. I knew you loved him and that he had proposed to you." Sawyer rose to his feet and walked away from her. "But that night…God, Lucie, if only we could go back and… I'd give my soul if I could bring him back."

Lucie got up and walked over to where Sawyer stood by the windows overlooking downtown. She longed to wrap her arms around him and lay her head on his back and tell him how wrong he was about everything.

"I've never wanted anyone the way I wanted you that night," he admitted. "You and Brenden had had another one of your tiffs—you two were always breaking things off and then getting back together. But that night you came to me because you knew what had happened the day before, you knew I'd killed a man in the line of duty and was pretty torn up about it. You came to me just to offer me your sympathy as a friend and I took everything you offered and more."

Standing directly behind him, she laid her hand on his back. He tensed instantly. "You didn't take anything that I didn't want to give," she said softly, doing her best not to cry.

When he didn't respond, didn't turn to her, but stood there stiff as a poker, she removed her hand from his back. He released a labored sigh.

"I'll never forget the look on Brenden's face that morning when he walked in on us and found us in bed together." An agonized groan rose from deep inside Sawyer. "And I'll never forget what he said."

"You've always wanted her, haven't you? And now you've got her. You've taken the only thing in the world that matters to me. Lucie was mine, damn you, she was mine!"

Lucie remembered every word, just as Sawyer did. Neither of them would ever be able to forget Brenden's heartbroken tirade.

"He was wrong, you know," Lucie said, doing her best not to cry. "I wasn't his. I'd never been his except in his own mind."

Sawyer turned and looked at her then, his eyes searching her face for the truth. "How can you say that? You two loved each other. You were going to get married."

"No, that's not true. Brenden asked me to marry him and I turned him down. I told him no, but he thought that eventually I'd change my mind."

"You told him no?"

"Yes, I told him no every time he proposed. And

yes, I loved him, but not that way, not the way a woman loves a man she wants to marry. And yes, Brenden and I dated on and off for years and that was my fault. I shouldn't have dated him, but he was there and he was attentive and—" she took a deep breath "—and you wouldn't give me the time of day and I wasn't interested in anyone else."

"You were my brother's girlfriend," Sawyer reminded her.

"I was never Brenden's girlfriend."

"You were lovers. He told me that you were."

"Then he lied," Lucie said. "I never had sex with Brenden."

Sawyer stared at her in disbelief. "I don't understand. You followed him when you got out of college. You joined the bureau just because he had and—"

"He joined the bureau to be like his big brother because he knew how much I admired you. And I joined the bureau because I was following you, not Brenden. You're the man that I loved, the one I wanted. It was always you, Sawyer, only you."

He staggered as if the truth of her words had wounded him. He stared at her, his expression hardening into a skeptical frown.

"Did Brenden know?" Sawyer asked. "Did he know how you felt about me?"

"He would have had to have been as blind as you were not to have known. Damn it, yes, Sawyer, he knew, but he kept telling me that you didn't love me, that you'd never love me as anything except a kid sister. He told me about all the women in your life, about how you enjoyed playing the field, about how you bragged about your conquests."

Sawyer grabbed her shoulders, his big hands clutching her painfully. "Brenden told me about the first time you two made love. He said it was the greatest moment of his life. He told me you were fantastic in bed."

Emotion lodged in Lucie's throat, threatening to choke her. She swallowed hard. "He lied to you. We did not make love, not ever. My first time was with you. I thought you knew. I thought…" The tears she had tried so valiantly to repress broke free, pooled in her eyes and overflowed onto her cheeks.

He loosened his hold on her shoulders and gently eased his hand down her arms. "That night, I was out of my mind wanting you, needing you, loving you the way I had wanted to for such a long time. I took you over and over again. God, Lucie, if I'd known it was your first time—"

"It was everything I'd ever dreamed it would be."

He slipped one arm around her waist and lifted the other, wiping the tears from her face with his fingertips. "Brenden knew how I felt about you and he lied to me again and again."

"How—how did you feel about me?"

"I was in love with you," he told her. "I think maybe I'd been in love with you since the first day I saw you, but finding out you were only thirteen had scared the hell out of me. And then over the years while I was doing my best to keep my hands off you, you became Brenden's girl." Sawyer shook his head. "No, I thought you were Brenden's girl, but you weren't, were you? You were never in love with Brenden."

"Never. It was you, always you, only you."

Sawyer pulled her into his arms and kissed her, tenderly, sweetly; then he held her as she rested her head on his shoulder and wept.

"Poor Brenden," Sawyer said.

"Yes, poor Brenden."

Neither of them said more. Each knew what the other was thinking. Brenden had loved selfishly, claiming Lucie for his own when he had known she loved Sawyer and that Sawyer returned her love.

No one had been to blame for Brenden's death except Brenden. He had chosen to take his own life rather than accept the truth.

Lucie wasn't sure how long Sawyer held her while she cried or when exactly he had lifted her in his arms and carried her into the bedroom, but as he began undressing her, she came to life.

Their loving was slow and tender and Sawyer took her as if it were her first time.

"I love you, Lucie Locket. Can you ever forgive me for wasting all these years when we could have been together?"

"I think we need to forgive each other and put the past behind us."

"I promise that I'll make it up to you. I'll find a way—"

She tapped her index finger on his lips as she crawled over and on top of him. "I know a way you can make me happy right now."

"Is that right?" He skimmed his hand over her butt.

"Make love with me again."

"It would be my pleasure."

EPILOGUE

THE GUESTS HAD arrived by boat on Sam and Jeannie Dundee's private island, Le Bijou Bleu. The tropical paradise was the scene of a very special event this balmy Saturday in late June. Mother Nature had provided a clear blue sky, a soft southerly breeze and temperatures in the high seventies. The wedding of Daisy Dee Holbrook and Geoffrey MacDougall Monday, held on Sam and Jeannie's front lawn, with the waters of the gulf as the background, was a grand and elegant affair, truly every little girl's dream wedding.

The reception was held under several enormous white tents where champagne flowed from crystal fountains and music wafted in the air, coming from the band on the portable stage. A bride and groom; seven bridesmaids and one matron of honor, each dressed in springtime pale pink gowns; seven groomsmen; one best man; a ring bearer; and a flower girl made up the wedding party. Three hundred guests had witnessed Daisy and Geoff exchange vows.

This wedding day and the wedding itself were as perfect for Daisy as Cara's had been for her. Despite the elegant splendor of both weddings and as perfect as both days had been, neither could compare to the day Lucie had become Mrs. Sawyer McNamara.

She had gotten pregnant on Cara's wedding night, back in January. But even before she'd known she was pregnant, they had flown to Mississippi on the Dundee jet in late January, along with a small group of their closest friends, and exchanged their vows in the small church in their hometown. The church that was only a stone's throw from the grassy knoll where she'd seen Sawyer for the first time and where they had shared their first kiss when she was seventeen.

As a teenager, she had dreamed of marrying Sawyer, of them exchanging their vows in that church.

Her grandmother had walked her down the aisle. Daisy and Cara had been her matrons of honor. Sam Dundee had been Sawyer's best man. The small, intimate reception for their fifty guests had been held at Sawyer's ancestral home and all memories of Brenden had been good ones, memories from the days when they had been teenagers. And Lucie knew in her heart that the Brenden she remembered and had loved would wish them well.

Sawyer looked across the table at Lucie and smiled. He, too, was no doubt remembering their own wedding day. He stood and held out his hand to her. She rose from her seat, placed her hand in his, and he led her onto the dance floor and into his arms. She tossed back her head and laughed. She had never been happier in her life.

Deke and Lexie had turned their daughter and son over to the nanny that Cara and Bain had brought with them to look after three-week old little Miss Katherine Desmond, named in honor of Bain's mother and affectionately called Katie. Bain was still a C.P.D. detective and Cara continued as CEO of Bedell, Inc. Their marriage had its up and downs like any marriage, but they had discovered that they could weather any storm as long as they were together.

Lucie glanced around at all the happy couples, which included numerous former Dundee agents as well as Sam and Jeannie. Sam looked at his wife with such genuine adoration that no one could ever doubt his love and devotion to her. Their daughter, Samantha, was now twelve and quite a beauty. She was already as tall as her mother and willowy slender, with blond hair that hung in soft waves to her waist. MJ, their ten-year-old son, had his mother's coloring, but he, too, like his sister, had inherited Sam's height. Jeannie's adopted father and the beloved caretaker of the island, Manton, a giant of a man with bronze skin and a bald head, had played the piano for the wedding. "Jeannie's Song," which he had written for her and played at her wedding to Sam years ago.

As Sawyer waltzed Lucie around the dance floor, he lowered his head and whispered, "You're the most beautiful woman here."

She gazed into his eyes and smiled. "And you, my wonderful husband are the most handsome man here."

"With such gorgeous parents, our son should be strikingly handsome." Sawyer slipped one hand between them and caressed her slightly protruding belly.

After years of loneliness and praying for what seemed like a hopeless dream, Lucie had finally received her miracle. Sawyer loved her as much as she loved him and he had told her repeatedly, "I intend to spend the rest of my life doing everything in my power to make you happy." And she knew he would. Sawyer McNamara was a man of his word.

DANGER, LIES AND A RUTHLESS KILLER

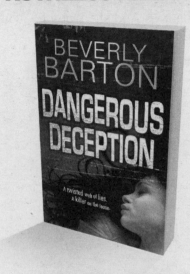

After being hired by wealthy Edward Bedell to find his missing daughter, Audrey, private investigator Domingo Shea determinedly tracks her down and returns her to her father.

Except the woman he has found turns out to be Lausanne Riley – a phoney employed to impersonate Audrey Bedell.

It becomes clear that Domingo has been drawn into a web of deceit. He has limited time to make sense of all the lies before the net snaps shut. And *the clock is ticking...*

MIRA

Sometimes love is stronger than death...

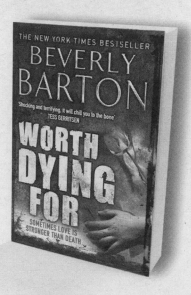

For Agent Dante Moran, finding Tessa Westbrook's missing daughter becomes personal when he sees the teenager's resemblance to his murdered girlfriend.

Tessa needs to know who told her daughter the terrifying story of her conception. And it soon becomes clear to Dante that the truth is dangerous—but is it worth dying for?

www.mirabooks.co.uk

MIRA